AND GOD IS THEIR PEACE

Other Works by
Rebekah Tyne McKamie

The Trees of Eden

The Snow Fence: Renewed Edition

The Foolish Things

To My Beloved Richie

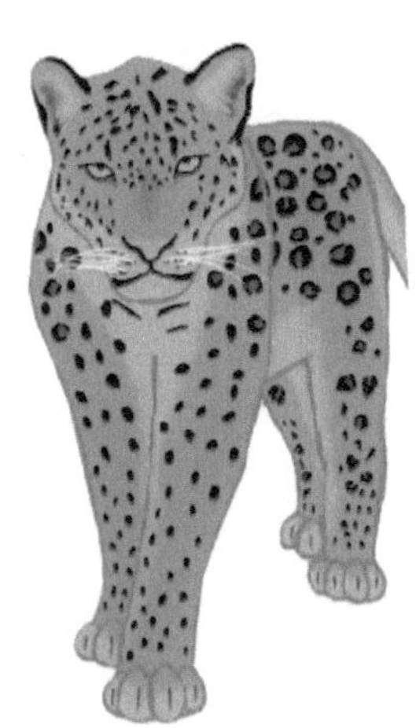

AND GOD IS THEIR PEACE

REBEKAH TYNE MCKAMIE

Nampa, ID

Len & Tyne Books
Nampa, ID

ISBN (paperback): 978-1-7348040-8-9
ISBN (eBook): 978-1-7348040-9-6

Library of Congress Control Number: 2026908848

Printed in the United States of America.

Crafted by Humans

The work you are about to read was carefully written over thousands of hours using the power of an inspired human mind and eventually the assistance of other humans.

NO artificial intelligence (AI) was used in the writing, editing, or design of this book. The author disables all AI tools and even most non-AI editing features attached to her word-processor because she finds the colorful lines under the words to be distracting. If any program or person flags this work as having used AI, that program or person is mistaken. (I just like em dashes, okay?)

No permission will be granted to use this book, or any of its elements, to train AI.

CONTENT ADVISORY

Here, you are a bright light among bright lights. . .But my people are broken, Debbie. There, you could be a light in the darkness. What is your light for if not to put on a lampstand and light the way in a dark place?
—*Capac,* And God is their Peace *by Rebekah Tyne McKamie (The book you are holding)*

This is the darkest book I have ever written. It is still Christian Fiction, more accurately Theological Fiction, and the storytelling vehicle is Romance, or perhaps Romantic Suspense. I take my inspiration and themes from the Word of God. So. . .darkness happens.

I have learned that it makes much more sense to turn on the light in a dark room than to be a beacon in a room that is already flooded with light. Darkness flees from light. That's the whole point in letting our light shine (Matthew 5:16). Jesus came into a world so dark that His Light was incomprehensible (John 1:5).

So if you ask me if I write "clean" books, my answer will always be ***no***, even if I can always use the "no or low spice" label, and even if they *are* clean by most definitions most of the time. Why? Well, I (barely) survived purity culture, so I refuse to sit on a holy high horse and condemn literature with dark themes and *gasp* that beautiful *thing* that God Himself created and uses as the mechanism for creating new life. I might stray from official or unofficial definitions of "clean," because my standard is God's standard. Dark themes sometimes require an unhealthy depiction of something God created good, so I will show you the healthy, godly version too. Yes, even if I have to "crack the door" a little. How else do we battle darkness but with light?

However, because you have picked up a book that is likely labeled as "Christian Fiction," it is prudent for me to include this advisory:

This book contains mature and dark themes that may not be appropriate for some audiences.

Before you call it unclean and move on, just remember that the same advisory could be applied to the Bible, though I would recommend the Bible to everyone.

The ultimate goal of my books is to glorify our Holy God and to lead you to a deeper understanding of who He is. Therefore, I do not shy away from keeping Christ the center. I do not merely *hope* you will see Jesus in something that is actually just "clean." I am not ashamed of the gospel of Jesus Christ (Romans 1:16). Thus, no matter how dark it seems in those scary moments, I will always turn on the Light and let it flee.

__For RJ and Bekah__
(The Fall 2024 version)

Hold on. God is faithful.

He is going to teach you to count the miles.

Open rebuke is better
Than love carefully concealed.

Proverbs 27:5

ONE

The jungle is never peaceful. But the quiet of snow can be oppressive.

"Don't make me lose you to that Godforsaken jungle too," was my grandpa's plea. "And my *girls*? John, no."

"God hasn't forsaken the jungle, Dad. I have to go." My dad was in pursuit of a world of a million voices. "*We* have to go."

The last time I saw snow, I watched a snowflake land on my baby sister's nose. I was only three, but I remember we watched her eyes cross there, fixed on the resting place of that flake until it melted against that cold-kissed ruby. My parents' laughter should have echoed, but the snowfall kept our joy a secret—our world a private shaken globe. Without that laughter, and with closed eyes, I could hear each frozen flake softly coming home to rest with her billion fallen fathers.

"Peaceful." Mom looked up into Dad's eyes, I think. His protective embrace half hers, half my sister's. Or maybe I just remember it that way because the sight is so familiar to me now. I only have the word in my memory because at age three, I wondered what "peaceful" meant. I was spinning in circles, catching flakes on my tongue, but staying close enough to hear the crunch of Dad's boots when he shifted his weight.

That night was the last time I saw snow. Peaceful and oppressive. For my parents, it was too quiet.

When I was just three years old, Mom and Dad uprooted us from grandparents, Wyoming, and snow. From there, they grafted us in to a once-abandoned mission in the deep, humid rainforest dotted with thick, practically impassable jungle. The mission was a day in a Jeep down a forgotten road from the nearest form of modern civilization. There, my parents protected us from far more than cold that would bite a baby's nose. We needed protection from the million voices—the million dangers—of the jungle.

The jungle is never peaceful. Lizards scaled the walls, monkeys taunted and stole, and we lived in fear of a jaguar's eyes.

The four of us slept in a little shack that my great-grandfather built as an afterthought for the mission, and it took time to acclimate to the creatures screaming through the night. My mother told me that God's creation was singing me a lullaby, so I learned to love those million voices.

Each room of my childhood home was in a different building. Because the primary danger was hungry animals, it wasn't safe to eat where we slept. A wastewater trench had to be dug and maintained, so the bathhouse was in yet another building. Our "living room" was divided. I have early memories of card games with my sister on the bed we shared and of wild family game nights in the chapel building.

Mom and Dad were early risers, and I would often awaken in the morning and they'd be arriving at our bedroom shack to take us to breakfast in the kitchen. Yet sometimes, they were night owls, sending us to bed then disappearing until long after I was asleep.

My mind as a three-to-five-year-old knew them only as my gentle, loving parents. My hindsight embarrassingly realizes they were also young lovers. Mom started feeling sick, and when she told Dad, he seemed far too pleased for his wife feeling so sick. My brother Andrew was born in Mom's requested clinic shortly after Dad finished building it. Andrew cried almost constantly after he was born. Mom and Dad started putting us to bed behind a thin wood partition in the shack, then falling asleep themselves and barely waking in time to feed us breakfast.

Mom was so tired in those days, and my parents debated whether we should have undertaken this adventure in the jungle. But as Andrew got to be a couple months old, they fell into a routine. In the early years, Lydia and I spent our mornings homeschooling with our mother and our afternoons repairing the mission's buildings with our father. Repairing it for what, we did not understand.

"To minister to the natives," Dad would say. We had never met anyone but us. Andrew was a jungle native, in my eyes, and Lydia didn't even remember snow. I started to believe my grandfather's claims that Dad was insane.

Around the time Andrew started walking, Mom and Dad had a conversation over lunch that I only remember because it confused me at the time.

"One more?" Dad asked it after a doting smile at his three greatest treasures enjoying a meager feast.

Mom didn't hesitate before her answer. "No. Absolutely not. The risk? The food insecurity? No. Just love the ones we have."

"I do. I will. All twelve you give me."

Mom's laugh echoed out, another voice among millions. "No, John. Three is plenty."

"Eight?"

"John!"

Lydia and I giggled when Dad made a silly face. Mom threw a peanut at him. He winked an eye at her. Conversation over.

In the weeks that followed, they went back to their early mornings or late nights a few times a week. I was only seven, but the pattern seemed familiar.

Lo and behold, Mom started feeling sick again.

Seven is when my memory starts to get less foggy. At seven, your mind can retain the names of the lizards that escaped from the cage you built from sticks. And certainly, today my palms can recall the way Daniel's feet felt when he pressed them through Mom's velvet skin at her stomach. Lydia and Andrew had simply appeared in my life without my understanding. But I had the privilege of loving my youngest brother for months before I ever saw his face. Mom circled her due date on a calendar, and I crossed out each day until then.

Mom would later tell me that my enthusiasm kept her going. That pregnancy was difficult for her, leaving Dad to do the building and me to do the teaching and much of the food prep while she lay in bed most of the day. She had put herself on bed rest after a bleeding scare early on. Dad held her to it.

Two weeks before Mom's circled due date, I awakened to Dad's gentle shake, as was routine. I wearily put on my clothes and headed to the animal shed under Dad's careful watch as he headed to the chapel restoration.

At seven, I recall being frustrated with my hands for not coaxing the milk from the goat as easily as Mom could. My bread was never as fluffy as Mom's because I lacked the strength to knead it well. The slices of pomegranate and melon were not so uniform. Still, in time, I was adept at serving bread, fruit, and milk. I rang the bell outside the kitchen, and my family began our thrice daily gathering for modest meals.

Mom waddled over first, Andrew's hand in hers. The safety of separate food took precedence over her self-imposed bed rest order. She entered the kitchen with warm gratitude, but looked around.

"Oh, Lydia must have gone with Dad."

"She was sleeping," I corrected.

Mom shrugged and assumed my curious sister had followed our father without my knowledge. It wouldn't have been the first time. Dad finally arrived, his head turning here and neck craning there when he entered the kitchen.

"Is Lydia asleep?"

"No, she wasn't there. I assumed she was with you or Debbie."

"No." Dad shrugged at the mystery only a few seconds before he realized that the mystery was really a tale of horror.

Lydia was missing.

When a five-year-old girl goes missing in the modern world, the dangers are many. There are human predators and zooming cars, and numerous other dangers. But those are modern dangers with modern safeguards. We were a modern family transplanted into a wilderness. Those million voices signaled a million dangers, and even if we had a phone, it would not have connected to a 911 operator. Mom could barely walk, and Andrew wasn't even two years old.

Lydia was a tiny thing—a perfect treat for a hungry snake or jaguar. The nearest village of natives, to which my great-grandparents used to minister, had not even made contact in the years we'd been there. Other natives were said to be violent. There was no way to track Lydia. There was no way to find her. All was lost, even then. My dearest companion was the victim of a jungle my parents had committed themselves to rescue.

I think it was the weight of a mother's dropping heart that made her water break just then.

"No. . .No, no, no," Dad said of the puddle that appeared at Mom's feet.

Baby four, Mom had warned me, might come fast. The powerful contraction that ensued confirmed her hunch.

"There are fourteen days left," I told them. "The baby won't come today."

"Debbie, take care of your brother." Dad's command was confusing. He was already lifting Mom up to carry her to the clinic.

"What about Lydia?"

That question destroyed my parents. They were faced with a choice no parent should ever have to make. Mom needed Dad for a smooth delivery. We only had each other. They had to choose Daniel, whose name wasn't even Daniel yet, over their lost little girl. They couldn't even look for her. Mom's cries of agony as Dad rushed her away likely had little to do with the pangs of childbirth.

Once a year, we had to make the journey to Wyoming to remain United States citizens. My parents would stock up on seeds, clothes, and nonperishable foods. I had picked out the set of overalls Andrew was wearing that day. Dad had laughed at the idea of being able to catch and redirect the energetic little boy with just a grasp of his clothing.

My eyes went first to those overalls and second to the tattered old curtain my great-grandmother had likely installed in the kitchen. I tore a long strand, tying one end to the back of my brother's denim overalls and the other to the clunky table leg. I set his breakfast on the floor in front of him, and he giggled, then folded his hands.

"Oh! Jesus, thank You for this meal. Help me find my sister and help Mom not hurt so much with the baby. Amen."

"Maymen!" Andrew declared, then dug in.

I quickly packed some more food in a backpack we used for picnic lunches usually accomplished only twenty feet from the kitchen, still in the safety of the clearing.

"Be good, Andrew. Stay here." I tested the integrity of his makeshift leash, then set out.

Mom was screaming out in pain, and that was good. That way, I didn't have to. I felt small because I *was* small, the jungle stretching up a hundred feet over my head to form a canopy everywhere except the football-field-sized clearing my great-grandfather commissioned decades before. I gave our camp a quick once-over. No Lydia. The next bet was hundreds of miles of rainforest with deep, dark jungle in every direction, interrupted only by a vast river half a mile away.

She knew not to go to the river because she watched it take her handmade doll away last year. There were still a thousand trajectories. A hundred fates. A million voices and a billion dangers.

"I don't know which way to go. God, which way did Lydia go?" I shed a tear. I needed my sister safe.

When I wiped the silly childish leaking from my cheek, I looked straight ahead. A few butterflies were flirting in circles, and I smiled. Lydia loved butterflies because of a lullaby our grandpa taught us back in Wyoming. She always begged me to sing that song, and thrilled at the sight of a butterfly. She would have gone no other direction.

I called her name as I went, standing for a time at the edge of the clearing.

"Lydia! Come back! It's breakfast time!"

I was not to go into the jungle alone. We only went at all if Dad and a Jeepful of supplies and guns were with us. We'd only seen the river once. The well was at the mission. Everything we needed was here at this mission. One of the lambs bleated to my right. Lydia had named her "Lambie."

Lydia. Lydia was alone, and my parents couldn't lose her to the jungle they loved. My first foot entered with fear. But I followed the butterflies with confidence that couldn't have fit in my little body. I knew *I* was not alone.

I called her name, walking slowly for about fifteen minutes before I heard the bleating of another lamb. No. It was the desperation of a little child.

"Mommy!" Her voice was raspy by then. "Daddy! Debbie!"

I tried not to panic as I followed those cries. I nearly fell down into a grave-deep pit within twenty yards. I carefully looked down inside, where her two desperate sapphires were frantically searching above. Lydia was disgusting, her black hair patched with brown. She likely tumbled down into the pit on the far side, a steep incline.

"Debbie!" she screamed, and a thousand birds responded with their cries.

"I found you!" I began to sob, but I had to keep my head.

I carefully crawled backward into the pit, meeting my sister right where her foolishness had planted her. We held onto each other for ten minutes, our relieved tears mingling with jungle mud.

"Butterfly song?" she rasped as her tears calmed.

I had never been happier to sing the silly little song about a butterfly with fire on its wings. That song gave us both renewed strength. Still, it took us an hour to climb back out.

Our stomachs were growling when we reached the top. We walked closer to the clearing, where we could see our buildings, then sat and shared breakfast. Half the jar of goat milk was used to rinse our hands of mud. The other half was sacrificially shared between us, knowing a greater reward lay just beyond the trees. Our bellies full, we journeyed on.

In the bathhouse, I combed Lydia's thin black hair after a shower, frustrated I couldn't braid it like Mom did. I scolded her there for her foolishness, safe enough from the jungle pit for cleanliness and lessons.

Dad met us outside, respecting the "women" label on the door, but likely having heard everything. He had Andrew in his arms and greeted his clean, fed daughters with generous sobs, rivers of tears, and forests of kisses.

"I thought—" But that's all he ever said about what he thought.

I told him the story in direct seven-year-old terms. He sighed and looked between us, telling us a different tale.

"Would you like to meet your baby brother?"

Mom's relief when we stepped into the clinic, compounded by flooding hormones, nearly made her pass out and drop the baby from her arms.

Dad retold the story to Mom. In the end, I heard him murmur to his love, "Marla, I don't even want to think of all the things God protected them from. I've seen jaguars that direction."

"It's an absolute miracle." Her whisper was weary. "Let's not have more children than we have eyes between us, John?"

"I can agree to that." He somehow grabbed up all four babies and his wife into one bedside embrace. There, he whispered,

"Daniel. Let's never forget the day God saved my girls alive from danger. We'll call him Daniel."

"That's my favorite story!" Lydia cried. "Daniel and the lions! Daniel was so brave. Will my brother be brave and fight lions?"

Dad released that first embrace, then took my shoulders into his hands, looking into my eyes with the origin of the sapphires that had looked up from the pit and crossed to behold a snowflake.

"Well, Daniel didn't fight the lions, Lydia. God shut their mouths." He squeezed my shoulders. "Still, Daniel was brave, alright. Brave enough to obey God against all logic. Brave enough to be among lions for as long as it took."

Lydia was then preoccupied by our baby brother, saying his name as many times as possible. Dad came in close and spoke only to me.

"Do you know what indebted means?"

"No. But debt means you owe money or something, right?"

"Yeah, but indebted doesn't necessarily mean money. It means you owe someone something. And sometimes you'll never repay it, but Deborah Joy Davies, I am deeply *indebted* to you. And I hope you remember to call up that debt one day. But chances are, you'll just keep running up my tab. You are already twice the man I'll ever be."

"I'm a girl and I'm seven."

"Yeah." Dad laughed across his thick red beard. I didn't understand then. "Don't rub it in."

Two

Together, my parents could fix anything or anyone, no matter the ailment or state of disrepair. By the time I was nine, our mission resembled something like a summer camp in the States. Mom had a fully functioning, fully stocked clinic. The six of us were ready for anything, but us kids were mostly convinced nothing would ever happen.

God had told my parents differently, practically handing Dad blueprints like He had for Noah. They needed a clinic for now, and we maintained the other buildings as well. Lydia insisted we were just camping out for no reason.

Dad kept a wall of maps in his tiny portioned "office" in the chapel and took monthly treks into the jungle to search for the "people," he called them. His grandfather never did find this specific tribe or village or whatever they were. However, they made contact, and my great-grandparents ministered to them at the mission before it lay fallow for seven years. There were rumors that my great-grandmother and namesake had begun translating a Bible into their language. It was her life's work, but we had never seen a verse of it.

Grandpa still doesn't forgive his parents for spending his first forty years at this mission then dying here for him to mourn at primitively marked graves dug by savages. He was born here, then left as soon as he could. His son, my dad, got back as soon as his life would allow.

When I was nine, six years after we had arrived, we were having a picnic.

I had a picture book out. We read about snow and a mitten and creatures who had crawled inside for warmth. When I noticed little Daniel comparing the illustrated white ground to the lush jungle grasses, pawing at one with his hands and the other with his confusion, I realized the story was falling on deaf ears.

Mom winked at me, then giggled before teaching, "Before you boys were born, we used to live where it would get so cold we needed to cover our hands with mittens. It was so cold, the rain would sometimes freeze and fall like feathers. We called it snow. It would freeze and gather into—" midway through that sentence I watched fear flow into all the flecks of her lovely brown eyes. She was looking behind us, and all of us quickly turned.

There were three brown men and a teenaged boy standing in my great-grandfather's clearing. The trees had grown still those five decades since, a canopy around us. We were safe. It was the perfect location until those half naked men stared down us six strangers. One of them carried a wooden staff, and the others carried machete-like weapons and a culture frozen in time a thousand years before.

My mother feared them. My father stood and approached them. God allowed the teen to be injured—a terrible laceration on his arm he had covered with leaves. He was bleeding through.

"Hello." Dad's rugged red beard and gentle tone somehow set them at ease. But those machetes made us all nervous. Us kids were all frozen. "My name is John Davies. You're injured. We can help you. Marla?"

Mom's name snapped her back into her nurse training. She was transported back to the year she spent in the chaos of an emergency room. She ran into the clinic for her trauma kit.

"John Davies," said the teenager. The others nodded, recognition in their faces. When Mom returned, my father had coaxed the young man into offering his injured arm.

"This could be infected. We have medicine that could help you." They didn't understand much of it, of course. But interestingly, some of their language was English. My great-grandparents had caused English to be part of their tradition.

"Medicine," the oldest of the men remarked, lighting up.

But when Mom reached out to touch the young man's outstretched arm, both the young man and oldest man protested and the one of the other men began to draw a machete. Panic was about to ensue, but I was analyzing. I could see that the older man was the teen's father. The resemblance and his care for his son were unmistakable. Both that man and the teenager wore more garments than the other two men. They all had some type of gathered cloth garment around their loins as well as a skirt-like garment. The teenager and his father wore a long open vest of the same material, a red thread sewn about the edges. The man who had drawn the blade had coverings on his feet, perhaps of animal hide.

Lydia jolted me from my thoughts when she screamed and grabbed up Daniel, likely ready to run to our established panic room beneath the clinic. Still, to me, they didn't seem hostile. The oldest man was even tapping that threatening blade to lower it. He began gesturing at Dad, then putting a hand out at Mom to stop her. Dad tried to understand.

"We won't give you medicine if you don't want us to." Dad had his hands outstretched in in surrender, having instinctively stepped in front of Mom to protect her.

"Medicine," the older man said, then touched his son's arm. He gestured a hand at Dad. "Medicine."

"Dad, I think he wants *you* to do it," I inferred.

Dad looked at me, as if I was the one requesting it. "But I'm not the nurse. Mom is the nurse."

"I know, but they obviously don't want Mom to touch him." I shrugged.

Mom tried again. "Can I. . .look?" She pointed at her eyes and then his arm. "And John Davies touch?" She gestured to Dad, then touched her own arm.

They talked among themselves, but it seemed somehow like they understood. The older man looked at Mom, then put his own hands behind his back in a demonstrative fashion. Mom did the same.

"I won't touch. I just have to look. John Davies does not know medicine," she explained again.

Mom examined, giving Dad instructions. Mom was surprised when Dad removed the leaves.

"There's no infection." She looked to my dad. "John, I think there must be a natural antiseptic in these leaves."

"I think we should give him the penicillin, Marla. They need to trust us."

"But it isn't infected, John. It could cause him problems in the future if we give it to him. We can just stitch it. I'll talk you through it."

"Marla." Just her name, and that was enough. Mom talked Dad through how to administer the medicine from a syringe.

"You'll need to stabilize it to stitch it. A second set of hands," Mom sighed, then looked to the men. "Can our daughter touch him?"

And they all looked at me, examining my messy ponytails and probably the flatness of my chest at the time. With all the endearment of a father, the oldest man smiled, and we learned that a nod meant yes, just as it did for us. Apparently, a child was safe to touch one of them.

"Good. Debbie, help me out. Marla, tell me what to do." I assisted my dad, holding the young man's glistening brown forearm steady as Dad stitched. Dad attempted communication as he worked. I always imagined they'd be savages, hollering and cutting us down. Instead, they stood up tall, despite their shorter stocky stature. And they were calm, making as much of an effort as Dad at communicating.

The teen barely flinched at the needle and the stitches. He fixed his eyes into a curious scrunch on my blond curls. I don't resemble my mother in the least. Mom's mother was from Mexico, and her dad had dark hair. They were both gone by the time I was born, having been older when *she* was born. Mom was olive-skinned and black-haired. I was like Dad—practically translucent-skinned and blond-haired with only brown eyes as the proof that Mom and I were kin. I assumed that's what the young man was noticing.

As Dad worked and conversed, something strange happened. It was the first of many such instances, but I didn't quite understand what was happening.

Suddenly, a word the men had been repeating became something else. To be clear, it became English.

"Sheep." Followed by, "Two sheep. Four vines."

I blinked, looking over and examining the men. The two without the vests were carrying long green vines wrapped around their shoulders. The vines were the thick kind Dad always wished he could access, but they were too high in the trees. He said they'd be excellent in construction.

Mom gasped quickly, powerless to correct me with her own hands, "Debs, keep it still."

"Sorry." I refocused on the task in my hands.

But again, I heard, "Sheep. Two sheep. Four vines."

"I don't understand. I'm sorry." Dad was so remorseful and preoccupied with the stitches.

I spoke up, trying to stay focused on the boy's arm. "Dad, I think he said, 'Two sheep. Four vines.' "

"How did you—" But Dad didn't examine the gift horse too closely. "You want to trade two of our sheep for four of your vines?"

The boy stirred, rattling off something quickly. His father responded with scolding. The boy gestured to his injured arm with the other. The man gestured to his garment. The boy gestured to his. After all that, I released the giggle of the young girl I was then.

"What, Debs?" Dad was intrigued. "What are they saying?"

"Um. . ." I looked around again, first to Mom's stern face that begged me to keep the boy's arm still, then to my nearby siblings, then back to the arm as I spoke. "So, I think this boy doesn't want to make the trade because he got hurt getting those vines. But it looks like they want the sheep for the wool for their clothes. But the boy says they don't need it because they already have clothes."

"How are you doing that, Debbie?" Dad was astounded.

"They are speaking English, Dad." I laughed. Dad wasn't laughing. He did not respond at all yet, still focused on finishing up the stitches and bandaging them. When the task was done, the older man spoke again.

"Pair. For lambs." The words were clearer this time.

"They want a ram and a ewe so they can have babies." I understood I needed to continue to translate.

Dad gave Lydia the order, telling her specific sheep to grab. They were some of our best sheep. He was giving them our best. While Lydia ran off to complete the chore, the man looked to the man on his left, who had vines on his shoulder.

"Belen. Four vines for the sheep."

The response was reverent, though reluctant, obedience. This man, Belen, though not much older than the injured one, was not his son; he seemed like a servant or even a subject. That man obeyed, handing Dad four vines.

We sent the men away with our best pair of sheep and a few more provisions. As soon as they were gone, Dad took me aside as though I was in trouble.

"Debbie, they weren't speaking English."

"Yeah, they were, Dad. I mean, sort of. They had to be. I understood them." I blinked.

"Tongues. Just like Grandma Deb." Dad smiled. "I guess I should have seen that coming."

"What is tongues?"

"Well, at Babel back in Genesis, God confused our languages and the gift of tongues sort of breaches that barrier. If and when God allows, of course. For some people it is intermittent, but for your great-grandma, it was mainly a gift for learning and interpreting languages. Your grandpa says she started translating a Bible, I think for these people. They seemed to recognize my name."

"Where is the Bible?"

"No idea. I've looked everywhere, and so did Grandma and Grandpa when they came to bury *Great*-Grandma and Grandpa. Only they'd already been buried. . .That's not my point, Debs. You have a gift. That's my point."

I answered like a nine-year-old as I wiped a smear of the young man's blood onto my jeans. "Oh. Okay."

Though it has happened periodically ever since, I believe that was the first midnight I recall my father awakening with an unsettling gasp that set us all to a renewed fear of the jungle's voices. The words that followed were indeed chilling, but not because of a rogue monkey or a jaguar in the camp. They were something far more sobering.

The gasp was always so deep with horror that I have always wondered what nightmare could demand it.

"John?" Mom would groggily wonder.

"We're running out of time. We have to reach them, Marla."

"God won't forget them, John. Trust Him to do the work and remain diligent in your part of it."

"We've barely made contact. I don't even know where to find them."

"Lead with love, John Davies. Love is powerful, and that is all God asks of us. Build this mission with me. Love the children we were given. *Love* is the mission and the battle you've been given. Try to do anything else and you'll never succeed."

"We have to go and make disciples. They have to. . ." He would become delirious with fatigue, and his voice would soften and fade. "We're running out of time."

"Shh. . .rest now, my love. We have battles to fight in the morning." Then Mom would sing that lovely, dancing melody my sister loved so well,

> *"The perfect butterfly with the fire on its wings*
> *A beacon for the caterpillar's change*
> *The wings will burn the trees but if the caterpillar knows*
> *He'll be caught up in the wings and fly away."*

Mom is a good wife; a good woman. I see God's faithfulness for sending her to Dad and both of them to this jungle and to these people we'd barely met. Until that first night we made contact, though, I'd miscalculated who or what we were battling—or if there was a battle at all.

Time. We were battling time. How does a person—bound up in minutes and hours and seasons and wait—even battle so terrible an enemy? We had all we needed to serve, because the God we served was bigger than even time. But perhaps it was time that reminded us each day that the battle wasn't ours at all. One cannot battle time. According to Mom, our only job is to stitch wounds and raise children between the seconds and seasons.

THREE

The following winter, which is from June until September in this part of the world, the first baby arrived. The mission was up and running, and the locals began to trust us for periodic trades. Dad pardoned the locals when they'd steal sheep, always saying that they didn't know better. We saw them every few weeks for six months or so. Then we didn't see them at all. But things changed that first winter. It was June, and I awakened to what I thought was a monkey. We'd learned to fear monkeys, and I alerted my parents.

"It's alright, Debbie. You're safe," Mom assured me, but her ears perked. She was a mother of four. She knew a baby's cry, even against the jungle's lullaby.

Dad followed Mom out into the cool jungle night, a loaded shotgun in his hand and a watchful eye on the deep darkness. The baby was wrapped in some rough, beautiful sort of cloth and tucked in the shelter of our porch.

"My goodness. Everything is still attached. Her cord and placenta. . .she's less than an hour old, John."

"And they just abandoned her?" My father resented his father, who resented his father. But never would any of them for generations imagine abandoning their own children.

"Debbie," Mom said. I was the only child awake. "Run into the kitchen and warm up some of the goat milk. I'll be there in a moment to find the bottles."

"I remember where they are," I told her. I had warmed hundreds of bottles when Daniel stopped breastfeeding.

As I arose to head to the kitchen, Mom made another demand, "And put this in the burn pile. It's filthy."

She handed me the baby's blanket, wrapping her instead in a towel and modestly opening up her nightgown, holding the baby against her skin. I pawed at the piece of fabric as I walked to the other building where our kitchen was. The fabric was white, sullied only by the newborn baby's blood. Even at ten, I smiled when I realized what it was.

It was wool, carefully cleaned and spun and woven into this small blanket. Wool came from sheep. The sheep came from us. Dad had always muttered about hoping the locals enjoyed their mutton. But wherever these sheep were in their hidden dwelling out in the jungle, they were living and cared for. I tucked the fabric into my pocket and went about my errand.

Mom named the baby Genesis. We could all sense that she was the beginning of some new call. No one ever came to claim her, so Mom cared for her as her own. She was brown, and we were not. That was the only difference. We taught Genny to walk and talk and worship Jesus, and Dad was delighted to have been given another child.

The following year, there were two babies, placenta attached. They came within one week of each other, dropped on the stoop at night. Mom sent for another nurse from the States, because we had less hands than children. Our sponsoring church found us a fifty-year-old midwife who could also cook. Jane was a longtime widow with two sons. Jackson was a twenty-five-year-old who had just graduated with a teaching degree, and Jeremiah was a twelve-year-old Jane confessed was the result of short-lived sin during a lonely widow's life.

Dad, guided by the Holy Spirit, prepared for their arrival by constructing an additional building that would serve as both a schoolhouse and home. He built it much bigger than it needed to be. We only needed one room—the nursery—to begin with, but the plan was for the children to have space to grow, learn, and play together in a structured environment, no matter how many of them came. He built it close to the kitchen, on the other end of the mission from our house. That way, he could use the walls between them to create the covered dining area he had always talked about. One room of the schoolhouse was the living quarters for Jane, Jackson, and Jeremiah Cooper, who were the primary caregivers and teachers through every stage. They were with us from that time on, faithfully serving. Each winter, we would keep watches throughout the night, receiving anywhere from one to six newborn babies per year. The locals no longer came to us for trades, but they abandoned their children to us with faithful consistency.

My parents didn't mind. Jane and her boys didn't mind. Us kids were glad for the company and the exciting school lessons Jackson taught us and the children. Mostly, we were grateful. If their culture was so hopelessly pagan to abandon their own children to strangers, at least those children would know Jesus.

Our mission finally had a purpose. The children spoke, read, and wrote English astoundingly early. They were properly dressed and ate well. They knew their Bibles and times tables and were given strict schedules and chores to accomplish. When I was young, before Genesis arrived, I missed the quiet of snow. But as the years crept on, I realized that following God's purposes is far more joyous than mere quiet.

When I was fifteen, the purpose expanded again. Our oldest children, though still tender and young, began experiencing the lasting trauma of abandonment. Genesis realized when a baby arrived that she was not one of us. She was abandoned like them— left on a porch. She refused to even sleep in our shack then. She stayed with her kin in the schoolhouse. Dad asked, and we were sent a psychologist to help them cope. We called her Dr. Tara. I will mention her only briefly, because her methods and attitude were barbaric, though that is what she called the children.

"They need a place to be kept from the others when they have tantrums," she demanded of my father.

So Dad, as Dad does, built such a place. Dr. Tara called it the time-out hut, but it was a prison, complete with shackles, chains, and two barred cells for the disobedient. The time-out hut was isolated from the school house, and on the edge of the mission near our family hut.

"Are they animals?" Mom asked Dad when he was constructing it to Dr. Tara's specifications.

"Before they obey, they act it. Tara is right; this will keep them from running for their village and getting killed," Dad replied.

It was true. It would have been easy to lose a rebellious, hurting child to the wild of the jungle or the chill of the night.

Dr. Tara was with us for a year. When the children would act out, they'd be sent to her. She did not attempt empathy or reason. She would chain them in the hut until they calmed, which usually took about an hour. One night, however, Genesis missed dinner, screaming in anguish and chained in that hut.

Dr. Tara seemed indifferent as she sipped her evening tea while Mom and Jane did dishes. Genesis had been screaming horrible things for two hours by then. For the next fifteen minutes, she began screaming "Marla!" which she had called Mom since the abandonment issues arose. But that morphed, quickly, into a desperate, "Mommy!".

Mom dried her hands and left to tend to her child.

"Marla, if you go to that barbarian now, she will never learn her place."

Mom looked at Dad, but pointed at Dr. Tara, saying what her heart had been screaming for a year, "John, I want this barbarian gone by the end of the week."

Mom, followed by Dad, followed by me and Lydia and the boys, wrapped Genny up and we all cried with her.

"I am so *angry* that you got left here." Mom sobbed. "But I love you, so I am *thankful* you got left here." She repeated, "I am angry *and* thankful. Genny, it is okay for you to be both too."

After Dr. Tara left, the children were allowed to hurt, and we loved them through all of it with God's grace.

Dad built more beds for the schoolhouse as the mission grew, and we brought in a few other staff members to assist Jane. Genny was about six when she told us she loved us, but she wanted to remain in the schoolhouse with her brown siblings.

"I am the same as them, Mommy. I want to live with them."

"I love you, Genny. You are the same as my own children to me."

"Do you love the others?"

Mom assured Genny that yes, every child was loved. But Genny knew she was special. She knew she was set apart. It wasn't just that she was the oldest or that she was the only baby we raised without other staff; Genny seemed to have a different sort of spirit in her. Mom tried not to let on.

"I am the same as them. And I am the same as you. Let me be *both*."

From then on, only us Davies children lived in the shack with Mom and Dad. But though the others were encouraged to call Mom "Miss Marla," Genny made it a point to call her Mommy.

When I was seventeen, we had twenty-three children of varying ages in the schoolhouse. Volunteers from our home church would come down once a year to help us with Vacation Bible School programs to give the children further enrichment. They loved the "experience" of sleeping on the floor of the chapel, but seemed oblivious to how much we loved our life there. That year, the locals got wind, and when we thought they were leaving us children to participate in the program, we eventually understood that they were giving us older children too, up to about age five—abandoning them to us. Our number of children doubled in one day.

They were brown, but that was not the only difference between "our" orphans and these children. In subsequent months and years, we were tasked with teaching them English and removing their pagan garb and behaviors and gods. We would cycle volunteers every six months to keep up with the needs of the mission.

It would be fulfilling. When the children would accept Christ, we would all travel down to the river the following Sunday and baptize them. When Christ was all they knew, it was beautiful. When they had come from barbarian ways into a saving knowledge of Jesus Christ, it meant exponentially more.

We eventually baptized them into the family of God and American customs and rules. We saved them in many ways.

I don't mean to jar you away from this backstory. But I need you to understand that it sickens me now to think like that. That I, Deborah Davies, could have been so ignorant to think there was any way someone could be saved but by Jesus. But I was seventeen, and thought we were carrying out a greater work than even my great-grandfather had. He was at that mission forty years, but never considered the people group to be reached for Christ. They could barely communicate with them from what I understood then. Our work was greater and was beginning to require my dad's nonprofit organization that he founded to help keep us funded. That is all I understood.

The day the older children arrived with Capac, my understanding broadened. He brought about two dozen children under about age five, making sure that Jackson was playing outside with the others to accept them. It was as though he knew our routine, that additional volunteers would be there, and planned it accordingly. Or maybe God did.

Capac was a man in his mid-twenties then. I think. I've never known his actual age, but he believes he is likely just "a few winters" older than me. I believe it is close to ten winters, but as I said, I have no proof or concern for that.

That day, the brown, stocky young man stood at the edge of the trees watching the group of children we'd accepted. He was too old to be one of them, and though he seemed to care for all of them, he didn't seem to be a father to any of them. He wore that wool they all arrived in. White cloth around his waist, girding his loins and a skirt sort of garment relenting at his knees. But his was different. He also had a sleeveless cloak that hit him at mid-calf. Through each, there was a single stripe of red at the hem. I'd never seen the cloak on the children. I'd never seen any color, except once, but it was foggy by then. I fought for the memory as Dad approached this young man.

"I'm John. Are these children staying with us?"

"John Davies." He understood enough. That's all we figured at the time. He tapped his own chest. "Capac."

"Hello, Capac. The children—" Dad gestured to the kids. Such an odd contrast in his Wyoming jeans, boots, and flannel that June winter. "Stay?" He flowed his hands up and down once. "Or go?" He gestured to the trees.

"Stay!" Capac was insistent. His eyes widened with desperate fervor.

"And you. Capac. Stay? Or go?"

"Stay." Many moments fog over time, but this one is perfect in my memories. I see it now as clearly as then the way Capac took the wooden walking stick in his hand and planted it in the soft ground before him. He clasped his hands atop it and spread wide his stance, his eyes stayed on the dozens of children as they played an American three-legged race game. Natives tied to locals. Different. The same.

Dad only sort of understood. See, while Capac meant for the children to stay permanently, the version of "stay" had a temporary connotation for him. I'd heard it. He wanted to be sure the children would be alright, like a parent dropping off a child at summer camp. But Dad thought they'd finally sent an adult representative to help with the children permanently. And thus he treated Capac.

"Okay, you can stay. But we have a uniform. See?"

Dad gestured first to his own shirt, then to me, dressed in scrubs as I logged the names of the new children, working hard to figure out the spellings of the foreign tongue and their probably poor pronunciations of their own names. We'd realized the versatility of scrubs early on, and everyone—volunteers, children, staff—wore green scrubs. Adults could wear jeans on the bottom, or skirts in the hot months, and sturdy shoes of our choice. But we wore scrubs on top. My grandparents ran the nonprofit from the States and had hundreds of sets a year sent with volunteers, embroidered with the logo.

Southern Hemisphere Genesis.

Genny loved to see her name everywhere like that.

"No." Capac didn't love it quite so much. He touched his own garments, clinging to them. Unwilling to trade them for a set of scrubs, despite all previous trades.

"Then you must go," Dad said.

It was my first quarrel of thousands with my father. Why couldn't Capac wear his own garments? He wanted to watch over the children. He knew the jungle. We could have used his eyes and expertise, even for a day. But for the sake of what my father called "modesty," he refused.

I don't remember exactly how or why it happened. But they ended up dragging that young man into the time-out hut. Capac was about five foot five, but mostly muscle, so it took every male volunteer to get him chained in that hut.

Capac screamed in his native tongue, chained in that hut for six hours before he quieted.

That night, after everyone else managed to fall asleep, I heard a light whimpering out on the front porch. Accustomed now to a need to attend to such things, I went out to find that it was my youngest brother of wild blond curls and tender heart. The boy was sitting with his knees against his chest, weeping quietly against the jungle's lullaby.

"Daniel?" I was gentle, but still it startled him.

"Did I wake you up?" he whispered.

"No. I couldn't sleep." I sat with him, barely able to make out those blue eyes.

"Yeah. I just don't understand why Dad did what he did. And I trust him, Debbie, I just don't understand. That man is innocent." He tried not to rise above a whisper. "Do *you* understand?"

"No," I admitted in a whisper. "But Mom and Dad have kept us alive out here all these years, Daniel. All your life. That is no easy task. We are commanded to honor our parents, and with them, it isn't so hard."

Daniel, always obedient, even though usually abounding with energetic joy, nodded his head. Agreeing. Understanding. All the exuberance that was turning him into quite an athlete at this tender age was quiet in him that night. Perhaps newly quiet, as when Genesis had learned her origins.

He breathed in a shaking breath before responding with, "Dad is the best man in the world, Debbie. But it's like he's not. . .following his maps, I guess. Nothing he has taught me matches that he did to that man."

"Even the best man in the world can get a little lost, Daniel."

"But how does he find his way? Will Mom help him? What is he going to do to that man?"

"Daniel, you're trying to carry something that is too heavy for you. You need to trust that God will help Dad know what to do. What God does and who He uses. That's up to Him. Not you."

"I know. I'm just a kid or whatever. It's what Andrew always says."

"Daniel, no kid is ever *just* a kid. Even Jesus was a kid once." I smiled. "I think your heart is acting much older right now."

Daniel looked up at me then, examining my eyes and tilting his head.

"Well, you *are* older, Debbie. Dad always listens to you."

"Does he?" I laughed once.

"Yeah." The ten-year-old in him finally re-emerged, and mischief spread across his face. "But. . .you don't always listen to *him*. You listen to God. Lydia always says that's why she's alive."

I brought Daniel back into the safety of home, but couldn't shake what he had said. I wasn't always obedient. Was that true? If so, what was Daniel asking me to do?

Each day, they offered Capac a set of men's scrubs to replace his increasingly soiled garments. Each day, it renewed his fervor. He ate our food out of necessity, but refused to learn enough English to explain his side of things. And he wouldn't change his garments.

To Dad he was an animal, despite the children simply being precious children. So there sat Capac for days, chained like an animal. He was filthy, refusing to bathe when taken out twice daily to use the bathroom in the bathhouse. Bathing would have meant relinquishing his clothes, and he seemed to know how they would handle that.

I watched Capac those days as he walked, dejected yet obstinate, from that hut to the men's room. I listened to his screams. The same few words over and over. I knew it then. I understood our disgusting flaw, yet no one else seemed to notice.

Maybe they were lost, but they were not the only ones. We had been found by Jesus, civilization, and a strange draw to conflating the two. A grave bitterness took root that night. A righteous bitterness. I wondered, if Dad planned to teach this man to be civilized using a method we *knew* to be barbaric, how exactly did he plan to teach him about Jesus? With hate? Disrespect? Humiliation? Maybe that's what he was doing.

Daniel was right. Dad was lost. We were running out of time, and Dad had lost sight of the upward call, the Great Commission, and maybe more. Over a stupid set of scrubs.

With every cry, my heart awakened. My mind alighted. My spirit steadied. My focus obsessed over the babies we'd rescued. Their too-soft skin and helpless cries. I was seventeen when God called me. Those children, His children, became mine. I whispered into the dark amid a million voices and a man's desperate cries,

"Here I am, Lord. Send me."

Four

"Tell me your angle, John," Mom asked Dad early one morning as we dressed for the day.

"My angle?" He was standoffish.

Capac was fifty yards away, sobbing into the early hours in his prison. He was repeating those same few words we didn't understand. Lydia was behind me, brushing my blond hair, just curly enough to wisp against the humidity at my brow, no matter how tight my French braid.

"He is upsetting everyone," Mom gritted into her teeth. "Why is he chained in there?"

"The children can't focus on their lessons with his screaming." My sister Lydia had found her niche working alongside Jackson and Jeremiah in the schoolhouse. Jackson was more of an administrator by then. Two other teachers had joined our staff. Jeremiah was the most gifted, especially in math, like Lydia. At fifteen, Lydia was Jeremiah's teaching assistant.

Andrew and Daniel, still finishing up school themselves, agreed with Lydia in so many words. *Is he an animal? I don't like this, Dad.*

We all quieted when Capac wailed again, *"Res-ga-tei!"* In that same tribal tongue.

I had a dictionary before me, looking for some root of some word to explain his predicament, even though the Spirit was telling me that's not how I'd done it before. Regardless, I missed my dad's direct address the first time. I know because of the fervency of his second.

"Debbie, I'm talking to you."

"Sorry. Yes, Dad?"

"How are the little ones coping?"

"They were upset at first, but they are alright now. He's become just another voice in the jungle to them."

My place, though I wasn't convinced it was my niche, was with the infants and toddlers and Miss Jane. Jane and I kept babies filled with goat milk and sang nursery rhymes day after day. But my favorite times were when they were down for their naps and I could sit under my tree. There was one tree my great-grandpa had not cleared because he had built his own house, now our house, into it. That tree was my favorite place. There, I'd spread-out God's Word with commentaries and dictionaries. I was a student, if not a passionate lover, of the Word of God. At Dad's urging, I had taught myself Greek to better understand the New Testament between rocking babies to sleep and chit-chatting with the ever-cheerful Miss Jane.

"What do you have there, Debbie?" Mom asked of my dictionary that morning.

"Mom, you know she doesn't feel like a whole person if she doesn't have a book or a baby or *both* in her hands," Daniel teased before slipping out the door with a wink to meet his morning chores. Milking. I did that and so much more at seven and he was ten. But I digress.

"No, I'm just trying to figure out what *resgatei* means. I assume he wants out, so maybe he is asking us to release him? Res. . .respite? Restitution? Revenge, maybe? He's no doubt angry," I mumbled, flipping pages.

"I have some perfectly good Christian romance you can read, Debbie," Lydia teased, handing me my brush upon completion of my braid.

She teased because when I had outgrown children's books and not quite grown up enough for Mom's Christian fiction, I would sit and read the dictionary. I loved the way the change of just a letter could make such a difference. My love of language was second only to God's Word, in which I also found a wealth of linguistic pleasures.

"I'm fine, thank you. And thank you. For doing my hair again." I set my book aside, switching places with my sister and completing her braid for her. She had perfect, dark, silky hair. It was straight in any weather, like my mom's. They were both so beautiful.

"You're so awkward, Debbie," Andrew this time, who was also headed out the door.

"It's about time we trim this." Mom's attention was on Dad, who was working on his morning goodbye. He was grasping her by the waist and losing himself in her eyes as she flitted with his blond curls.

"Will you, for once, not nitpick me when I'm trying to kiss you?" She submitted with a giggle to his request. Lydia made a twisted face of feigned disgust just for me.

"So, what's your plan? You never said," Mom redirected the encounter.

"I'll go in and speak with him today. I think he understood some of what I was saying yesterday. He needs the Lord if he's going to be broken."

Dad's words resonated with me throughout the morning as I fed infants and laughed with little black-haired tots. Broken. Why did Capac need to be broken? If he was whole, he need not be broken. If broken, why break him further? Broken things need mending, not breaking. Dad should have known that—he could fix anything. Why break Capac?

When I sat beneath my tree to read during our midday quiet time, my vision caught something across the clearing near the trees. I rose to meet it.

Capac's staff was there, planted.

"*Stay*," he'd said. I removed the walking stick with effort. It was well formed, by skilled hand with a knife, it looked like. Not a splinter or crack, despite its apparent age. The oils from his hands had smoothed out a portion near the top. "*Stay,*" I remembered again.

He wasn't after revenge. He wasn't after release. He was a free man. Free to wear his garments and live unchained. He was a strong, young man. He could no doubt brave the jungle alone, but he adamantly chose to stay with the children. Why?

Just then, a group of the children ran outside to play. The new ones were apprehensive, of course. But Jackson believed they would assimilate better if mixed with a group of the ones raised with us. They all looked the same in their cotton scrubs. The new children had been washed and groomed, and one of the others welcomed them happily.

Soon, the group of four-year-olds were playing wildly, and one of them dangled upside down from a wooden beam on the play equipment my dad had built. Promptly, he fell. Jackson, who was watching that group, caught him before he hit the ground.

Jackson's deep brown face was welcoming to the children scared of the differences. In his native tongue, the little one yelled some exclamation of thanks. It included that word.

Resgatei.

I'll never forget the physical twinge in my heart as I heard it. It was as though the Spirit was guiding me. Their language was unique, but had elements and roots of many languages I recognized from across the globe. I insist, even now, that it wasn't my mind that learned the language. The urgency was too deep for that, the time too short. God injected that language directly into my spirit.

I've read stories of how people everywhere have often decided that gift of tongues is some new gibberish language that couples well with flopping on the floor in the disorderly chaos of some church services. It isn't. I know, because though it is the least of the gifts, it is one of mine. I understand language spiritually. To God's glory, of course. There had only been a glimmer that was barely a memory by then. But everything from this point required this gifting.

I stood there for a long time that day, the staff in my hands, and the buds of a new language in my heart. As I finally walked to our shack, I heard a baby crying.

That's right. I was late! Miss Jane was probably wondering where I was. I returned to Jane, stopping at the shack to hide the stick beneath my mattress for later. After an excruciating day of suppressing what I knew to be my call, I left the babies to the night crew, scarfing down my supper in the dining hall before curling up with a dictionary to confirm what my spirit knew.

I didn't hear Mom enter the house. She sighed as she sat on my bed, wiping a careless crumb from my cheek.

"You're a mess, my sweet Deborah." She looked sad.

"What's wrong?"

"Oh, your dad is just discouraged. He spoke with that young man today. Capac? Tried to get him to communicate, but he won't. There's no helping him."

Later, when Dad came into the house, I addressed him directly. Everyone else was asleep, as usual. He was our pastor and leader. He wore dozens of hats and his late nights were rarely for rendezvous with his love anymore.

"How are you communicating with him?"

"We're not. He's now refusing to speak at all."

"*Resgatei* means rescue, or probably rescuer. Sometimes he uses past tense forms, so I don't think he's calling out for help. Their language has elements of—"

"Debbie. Even if I believed that their language had elements of anything but savagery, I can't today. I'm tired."

He didn't mean it. I have to defend him. He didn't think they were all savages. He and Mom slept behind a thin wooden partition, so if he woke up at night from a nightmare, I could hear it. It was a familiar sound I tried to call to mind then.

An unsettling gasp, then, *"We're running out of time."*

My parents were given a heart for the unreached in measures I have yet to explain. It's important you don't doubt that. I tried not to as my weary dad stood before me calling those people he loved savages. It was always difficult to hear.

"Well, if you can't talk to him, can *I*?" I heard myself say it before I translated it. I spoke with a fifty-six-year-old woman most days. I conversed with babies who could not respond. But I heard myself volunteering to speak with someone who was statistically sure not to acknowledge me.

"You want to speak with him?"

"Yes. I think we've misunderstood him completely and from what he's been saying—"

"I'm not sending you into that hut. It's rancid. He's disgusting."

"So was Genny. Her cord was attached and everything. They always are. You've used that in messages at church on Sundays. We are dirty when we arrive."

"Yes, but we remove the cords. We clean up the babies, just like God cleans our hearts. This young man won't allow us to remove his disgusting garments. He won't even listen to our language."

"Then learn his."

"That isn't how it works. My grandmother tried that. He needs to be willing to—"

"You don't know what he's willing to do. Jackson says some of the new children are very bright and already learning some English. Let me get one of them, and maybe they can help me translate."

"And risk a precious soul we have already impacted for Christ? Lydia says all of the new children seem enthralled by this young man. He has the power to lead them astray—"

"But he led them *here* instead," I interrupted. Insisted. "Obviously, he is willing for us to teach them things, Dad. Be reasonable."

But Dad softened little. "Debs, I don't want you talking to him."

"Do you think I'll be ruined? God's Word is in my veins, Dad. He's not going to change that with any stench or perceived savagery."

"No, but you are my precious jewel. And I wouldn't dare have you tainted by his immodesty. Go to bed. It's late. No more about this."

All my life, God had me in reference books. When I'm studying a book, especially the Bible, I get obsessed. The whole world disappears and I can't rest until I solve the mystery of a word, a passage, a translation. This time, it wasn't a book. It was a young man. Books are just words, however complex. A person, even in a given moment, is infinitely more complex than any word on any page. My obsession, or maybe the call, grew with that complexity. His walking stick was a lump beneath my mattress to remind me not to rest.

It was five in the morning when I rose from bed, removed the walking stick from under my mattress, and walked the fifty yards to where he was chained. The call to do so was greater than my father's instruction. It was barely my own legs that carried me. Approaching the door, I heard the scrape of his chain against the dirt floor.

He was awake. My heart thundered, forcing warmth to my face and a pulse to my lips. But just as when I heard myself volunteer to speak to him, I watched as my hand opened the door. It was barely me. A single Edison bulb was all that could illuminate the hut, and I wasn't supposed to use it. Still, I pulled the chain that triggered the quiet hum and golden swell of the filament.

He'd been talked up like a wild monkey. A snake. A jaguar. But when the light revealed him, I saw a man sitting cross-legged in the dirt, refusing sleep. A thin layer of black hair covered his sweaty skin. He had straight, black, shoulder-length hair. It was the first time I'd seen him up close.

"Hi. Uh, good morning," I began. "I'm Debbie."

The young man smiled. "Debbie." He placed a hand on his chest. "Capac."

"Your name is a palindrome. That's cool. Same backward as forward."

He didn't understand me, even if he spoke my language. But he stared at me, waiting for me to state my business. I pulled his stick from behind my back and placed it in front of the bars between us.

"I have your—"

"*Matteh!*" He lit up like that Edison bulb.

"Yeah, your. . .*matteh.*" I sat in front of the bars.

He didn't look savage. He looked civil, and I could see the intelligence in his eyes as when I conversed with the learned Jackson. His people have strong, broad features, and one may even note some resemblance to a Neanderthal, with perhaps direct ancestry. But I assure you, that is no insult. The secular belief about Neanderthals is not supported by evidence. They may have preceded what we consider to be the modern human, but they are not a subspecies. If anything, *we* are the subspecies. They are stronger, with a much larger brain cavity. We have since degraded, growing weaker and duller with each generation in the modern world.

While Capac's people still did not measure up to those ancients who built Arks and conquered giants, I have often observed, and therefore wondered if their very structure allows for a greater capacity for every discipline and emotion, both perceived and expressed. So what I saw in Capac's eyes that day was not merely humanity, but quite possibly brilliance. He was more welcoming than wary of my presence, his body language palpably soft and relaxed. His eyes were so black that I could not distinguish pupil from iris. But their kindness was conclusive; foundational to his disposition. There was nothing savage about him.

He muttered something with a nod. He was thanking me for bringing the *matteh*. I repeated the word in a question.

"*Gago*?"

"No." He smiled, gestured to me. "*Obri*."

"*Obri*." I nodded. *You're welcome.*

He was pleased, and mindlessly scratched at the shackle on his ankle as he smiled.

Without even thinking about it, I got the key from the hook on the wall to unlatch the shackle through the bars.

"Don't run, okay? I'll get in trouble." I laughed at that. I trusted him not to run. The notion seemed ludicrous.

He chuckled too, calmly twisting his filthy leg aside in preparation for it to be liberated. When I reached through, though, he jumped back and said, "No." He took the keys from me like some slimy thing, then adeptly freed his own leg from the shackle.

"You can't touch me. Why do I remember. . ." I fought for that memory. It wasn't recent for me like it is for you. There had been a change from child to young woman, with all the fading memories that accompany it. I didn't remember what I didn't remember.

Capac again chuckled.

"How much of what I'm saying do you understand?"

"*Tudo*."

"Everything?" How did I know what that meant? "How did you learn English?"

"Debbie," he said. Laughed low. I didn't quite get that joke, but moved on.

"If you understand, that's good. You can help me. I want to understand you and learn your language. Dad won't let me bring in a child to help interpret."

He seemed confused. "Debbie *lamad?*"

"Yeah, I want to learn. So please speak in your language. I can understand some of it."

He began speaking some slow gentle words as if between friends. It sounded like a question.

"I'm sorry, can you repeat that, please?"

"No. You understand." He insisted, in the space between the languages where I'd once found understanding. God granted it again.

"I sort of understand, yes. I can't explain it. I'm good with language. But it's better if you talk slower."

He conceded and repeated those gentle words. *"Do you remember me?"* The tone alone gave me a clue; it was just like an adult might say to a child that met them before their long-term memory started recording.

I had been effectively speaking to his ankle and decided to look up into his nearly black eyes again. His black hair and scant curly beard framed his brown, dirty-with-sweat-and-cage face. Admittedly, he had a nice face. But I didn't know it.

Without warning, he reached his left forearm out of the cage all the way to the elbow. I startled back against the wall outside the cage, unsure what he'd do. I was within reach of that arm. He could have easily grabbed me and subdued me in shackles for his escape. My reaction made both of us smile. I felt foolish, but he seemed to understand. We were strangers. Trust needed to be earned.

Slowly, so that I did not startle again, he bent his elbow so that his forearm was against the outside of the bars. He wanted me to look at it. There was a six-inch, previously stitched gash on that arm, and for a moment I shrugged, drawing a blank.

"You understand. I remember," he insisted.

It returned to me, that first encounter with his people eight years before. My mother coached my father as he stitched the wound of a teenaged boy. I gasped.

"You came with your father and traded with us. I held up your arm while Dad stitched it."

He nodded eagerly, which I was glad meant the same in both cultures. But that nod quickly turned to deep sadness. I didn't need words for that language.

"Your father is gone now."

He nodded again.

"I'm sorry."

He cast his eyes to the floor as he pulled his arm back into the cage. His father's death wasn't a subject he was interested in discussing further. *"You came to ask me something."*

"I came to listen to you. I want you to try to explain *resgatei* to me."

He immediately lit up, passionately angry. I listened as he gestured wildly, repeating words until I could sort of understand. When I did, my heart set aflame again. I sat again with him, watching every gesture and flicker in his eyes. This transpired for a while as I gained a solid understanding. The knowledge was sickening.

"Did you tell all this to my father?"

He nodded. *"He does not listen."*

"He didn't understand, Capac. If you had kept explaining it, he might have understood."

"A man must listen to understand."

He said that like a proverb. It seemed to rhyme and everything, and I wondered if it was a saying among his people. And before I could react, quiet desperation saturated his eyes.

"Debbie, he will listen to you."

I nodded, and since the message was urgent, I didn't waste time. I immediately clamored to my feet and hit the door. I stood outside that hut, translating everything in my mind to convey to my parents. My spirit knew it, not my head. It only took a moment, and I ran into the house just as they were getting out of bed with the sun.

"Mom! Dad!" I yelled.

"Where were you, Debbie?"

"Please don't worry about that. You have to listen to me. Right now."

"We're listening." Lydia yawned. "How could we not?"

"Okay. . ." I confirmed I had their eyes, even though I could see Dad was angry. "Capac rescued the children. He brought them here."

"We know that, Debs." Dad was irritated.

"No, Dad. Always. He has *always* brought the children. He was the boy you stitched that time. And he's the one who brought us Genny. From what I gathered, the women give birth in the jungle and Capac brings the babies here. He didn't say what they were being rescued from. The older ones are the same, though. He used the same words. Dad, Capac spends his winters, three months, between his village and ours. Because the women will give birth there and he brings us the babies."

"So he facilitates this abandonment?"

"I don't think it's quite like that, Dad. More importantly, there are three women out there who relied on him to care for them. One of them. . .there's something special about one of them. I couldn't figure it out, but he said she'll still be there. He thinks the others likely went back to the village to give birth. Apparently, that's bad."

"Of course, it is. They know we'll take in their babies and give them a comfortable, meaningful life. I don't blame them for doing it and it changes nothing. Did he say why he refuses to bathe or change his clothing?"

"Not yet. I barely understood what I'm telling you. He only speaks his language, even though he understands English." I shrugged, not quite understanding that part of it.

"I suspected that." Dad crossed his arms. "He's a stubborn one."

"We need to go find that woman, Dad. I know you aren't happy with this young man and with the natives. But this woman needs us."

Dad was finally reasonable. "Did he tell you where to find her?"

"He says she's in a shelter that is hidden and he wants to lead us there." I nodded fervently.

"He'll run the second he is unshackled," Andrew surmised.

"He's been unshackled for a half hour while we spoke. He isn't an animal, however we've been treating him," I mumbled. "He will lead us to her. He cares deeply for her."

"I bet he does." Lydia snorted laughter. "What if these babies he brings are his?"

"They certainly can't *all* be his, right? Does that matter, though? Please, we need to find her."

We all went to the time-out hut, abandoning our normal morning routines. Capac was standing at the bars, waiting patiently for our return. My father arrived first and addressed our prisoner gruffly.

"If she has been out there a week and is still alive, she can certainly wait ten more minutes for you to bathe and change your clothes."

"John," Mom whispered.

"If you care for this young woman, you will not allow a couple of dirty old rags stop you from helping us find her," my dad insisted.

Capac, about six inches shorter than my dad, looked up into his eyes and smiled before emitting a string of pearls from his mouth that seemed more foreign than his own tongue.

"Did you name Debbie for your grandmother?"

All of us took a physical step back. He'd been howling in something far from English for a week. But his English was perfect, though spoken through a thick accent. I wondered if I was hearing things or if the barrier had shifted again.

"Was that in English?" I asked. I'd been fooled before.

"Yes." My father's reply was sheepish. He suddenly felt less powerful, intimidated by the filthy young man. "And yes, Debbie is named after my grandmother who spent forty years of her life at this mission."

"Then you named her well. Deborah Davies was very good. She taught us to make clothes, and she taught the men in my family to speak English. It is tradition. I do not like this tradition."

"But you speak it so well," Mom said. "Do all the people speak it?"

We all stepped forward again, warily, listening to Capac as one might a storyteller or preacher. He spoke slowly, but that seemed to be more for our benefit. For clarity. We were all in awe, witnessing what seemed a miracle.

"No," Capac continued, "English is only learned and passed to what your grandmother Debbie called royalty. My father taught me, but he died two seasons ago. I am the only one of us to speak English, perhaps forever. Debbie and John helped my people. You, John, have his same name and heart. Only not his wisdom."

"Royalty?" Dad ignored any insults.

"Yes," Capac responded. "My 'dirty rags' are the royal clothes for five generations. They are blessed by a holy man and can only be washed by holy hands. If I remove them, I remove my royalty for a time. You would have them burned, no? You burn the children's clothing and blankets. Their mothers made these things for their babies, and you burn them."

"Dad, he's their king." Daniel, young but wise, understood completely. "You locked up a king."

"We burn them to be sure no foreign diseases are trans—" Mom began, but I rescued her from her own callousness.

"I have kept the blankets for every baby that has arrived. And a bit of the clothes from the older children." A confession about the contents of a chest in the nursery room that Jane and I meticulously kept. "When we name them, I pin their name and birthdate to it. Jane keeps them safe, and keeps a record. They all seem a little different, so if any parent were to ever return, maybe—"

"Deborah," Mom whispered, fearing my father's soft-spoken wrath.

"It's all they have to identify them," I defended when my father turned to look at me. His spirit always seeking God's best until recently, he didn't scold me.

"Holy hands? I am the holy man here. If I wash your clothes myself, will that be acceptable?"

"John Davies is holy to us." Then Capac shook his head regretfully. "But we have herbs to make them clean. The river is not clean alone."

"We have detergent." Flirtatious Lydia shrugged.

"And John, you've never washed the laundry," Mom whispered to him.

Capac heard, then looked to me. "Debbie. You know how to wash?"

"Yeah, I help with laundry sometimes."

"Your hair is not what it was before."

It was true; I'd removed my sad braid with my fingers at some point, probably as I was thinking and walking home to get my parents. I just wasn't sure how that was relevant. He seemed confused.

"I had a braid in it before. I took it out."

His perplexed eyes turned into a surprisingly invasive question.

"Have you opened to a man?"

"Um. . ." I imagine I was bright red, and he told me so later when I explained the awkwardly crass terminology.

"I think he means—" Lydia began, but Mom shushed her.

"I know what he means, Lydia," I snapped, then answered. "No, I haven't. Opened. Or whatever."

"Not married?" he clarified.

"No." I chuckled once. What an absurd thought. I was seventeen at the time.

"You are the unopened daughter of a holy man. You are holy." He'd said it the way I remembered Dad telling me I had a gift. Like he was complimenting a child.

"Uh, okay? So, I can wash your clothes? Yeah, I'll do that."

Dad began delegating. "Excellent. Let's get you to the bathhouse and into some clean clothes. Debbie, I'll make sure you get his clothes when he's changed. Lydia, get to the schoolhouse. Marla, Andrew, go out to the jungle with Capac. Get Jackson, Jeremiah, and the shotgun. Daniel, chores."

"I do not like your language. I will now speak only with Debbie to teach her mine."

It was a quick ultimatum, and I've rarely heard him speak so much English at once since that brief moment to vindicate him. To confirm, no matter what Dad tried, Capac responded only in that foreign tongue that only I understood. From here on, if I document Capac's words in English, it is only for your benefit unless I mention otherwise. Know that he objected to such documentation, but I eventually convinced him that this story was too important to be lost in translation.

I gagged from the stench as I washed his clothes but refused to get help from the staff member assigned to such duties. Holy hands. I didn't know or understand exactly what that meant, but I wanted to honor it. How could he possibly respect us or be open to a witness of Christ if we didn't honor simple wishes? I used our mildest detergent. Then I used our strongest to get out the week of urine, dirt, and sweat stains. He was a civilized young man by his standards. He was royalty. Royalty didn't soil his garments. We did that to him.

When I was done, I set them to drying, proud of my work as they swayed, white as snow with one red stripe, in the cool winter breeze. It was clear that these garments were old—five generations. I wondered what sort of dye could make that red stripe last so long or the seams hold against washing and wear.

They were blessed by a holy man and washed by holy hands alone. What did that mean, and why? I was flattered to be considered holy enough to have washed a royal garment. Moreso, I was overcome with guilt. I wasn't holy. Only Jesus's blood was holy. Any holiness in me was not due to my un-marriedness. It was Christ alone. When our housekeeper left the area, I lifted my hands against the breeze, letting the time-softened wool flow over and around my hands. I closed my eyes.

"Father in Heaven, bless these garments. Bless Capac for Your purposes. Help Him to find You. Seek Him out, guide his leadership, and infect his people with Your truth. I don't know what holiness blessed him before, but Lord, turn these people now to You in Jesus' name. Amen."

I had prayed similar prayers over newborn infants and crying toddlers. I'd prayed over blankets and schoolbooks and playgrounds as I'd seen my father do all my life. But this one felt different. This one seemed to flow from me through my spirit like the night before when I'd volunteered to speak with Capac. King Capac.

FIVE

That evening, as I was passing off our youngest children to the night crew, Jane and I got word that the young woman had arrived from the jungle. We were weary from the day, but joined my mom in the clinic to tend to her.

"*Roi,*" murmured the gorgeous young woman atop the clinic's bed. "*El Roi.*"

I fought hard to understand what that meant, but it eluded me. It rested on the tip of my understanding like a déjà vu.

"She has a fever," Mom said as Jane placed washed hands on the young woman's enormous belly. I almost didn't recognize the other presence in the room as Capac. He was clean and in scrubs.

By then, I'd folded his dry garments and placed them in our home for safekeeping.

"Would you like your clothes?" I asked him, though he seemed more concerned with the young woman. She looked like she was Lydia's age; so very, very young to be so pregnant.

Still stubbornly himself and no North American, he gestured to a picture of my father on the wall. "*Rei.*" He shook his head.

I understood. King. My father was the king here. Capac had relinquished his royalty, submitting to the rule of my dad in his kingdom. Capac always held great respect for my dad and all we had done for his people, despite believing him to be unwise.

Jane did a quick exam and addressed Capac. "She isn't quite ready to give birth, but she's very sick. Debbie, you two needn't be here. Go get some dinner."

"Would you like me to bring some for all of you?"

"Please. I suspect she hasn't eaten properly in days." Mom nodded.

Capac took a seat right outside the clinic on the wood steps I'd watched my father construct when I was a child.

"Would you like me to bring you some food?"

Weary from his journey into the jungle and back, he didn't refuse the offering. I returned with Lydia, who had already eaten, and five trays of food for the rest of us. After delivering food to the three women in the clinic, Lydia had some chores to do. I was left on the steps eating with Capac alone. When we finished, I began to try to solve the many mysteries.

"What is her name? The woman in the clinic."

"Sandani." In his accent, that lovely name rolled out like daybreak across his tongue. He loved this young woman. He'd said that name thousands of times.

"Is the baby yours?" Awkwardly, I asked.

He laughed, which was universal. Then he shook his head and gestured to where Lydia had walked, using his word for "sister."

"Oh!" I laughed too, then panicked. "So then, there's a father. Does Sandani have a husband or partner back at your village? He would be welcome here too."

He shook his head with a tinge of anger. No. The baby's father would not be welcome. I inquired no further.

After a long pause, as he stared out into the growing darkness of the jungle and tapped his *matteh* staff on the steps a few times. He spoke a few words that my spirit understood clearly and retained forever.

"Debbie, my people are broken."

Capac took to a tense silence. I took the opportunity to speak, because the Spirit would have it no other way.

"I got to name the second baby. I called him Moses. He's six now. Very stubborn. But he's special to me. Like Moses was special to his people."

"Moses?"

"Yes. Moses wrote the first part of the Bible, and the account of his life is beautiful. It began when his people were ordered to be killed. All the little boys were to be executed when they were born. But Moses's mother sent him down the river in a basket to save his life. He floated right up to the palace and was raised as royalty. His mother still got to nurse him. My parents think these children were abandoned here. But you have always left the babies on the porch where you knew they would be found, Capac. So, I knew they were not being abandoned. They were being rescued like Moses. Moses eventually grew up and rescued his people from slavery. God used him for wonderful miracles. He had a staff like you do."

"*Resgatei*," Capac whispered, then looked into my eyes. "You understand."

But "understand" isn't exactly what he meant because English is lacking there. He was saying something closer to me having listened with my heart. I didn't have a response for that, and I didn't need one, because Capac asked me point blank about my God. His language used the same word, but lowercase. His gods sat in a holy place in his village. He asked the name of my God.

"The Alpha and Omega. The Beginning and the End. My God is from everlasting to everlasting. He created all things. And when He created people who defied Him, he didn't destroy them all. He saved them again and again despite their sin. Finally, He sent His own Son to die for us to save us from our sins. From our brokenness."

"Does He have other names?"

"Many, across all time and cultures and people. There is one God, but He is infinite. Too infinite to have only one name. His Son's name is Jesus Christ. Emmanuel, because God dwelt with us in human form."

"Sandani's fever is strong. She was speaking of El Roi. Is that a name of your God?"

The meaning of the name suddenly became clear. The clouds parted and the sun echoed in. "The God who sees. Yes. That is also Him. What did Sandani say?"

"I did not leave them alone. I left my servant, and told him to take the women back if I did not return in three days after bringing the children. I knew he would do this, but I knew that Sandani would insist on waiting for me. My servant did no wrong. I told him to leave her there in our safe place with food for three more days. But she was alone for *four* days. The fever began and her food and water supplies ran out. Just when she was sure she and her child would die, a Man named El Roi arrived with good water. Your mother says it was the fever. But how then was Sandani cared for?"

An eerie tremble settled in my shoulders but Capac seemed unconcerned about God manifesting and ministering to his sister. "Something similar happened in the Bible when He used that name."

"When we arrived and Sandani was alive, I heard your father say that God is good. We do not say this. We say, 'the gods require.' Tell me more about your good God who sees."

I told him all I could. Capac had a few questions. But mostly, he couldn't believe that anyone would be willing to come to his little village and save them from brokenness. It took some time, and we ended up moving to the former time-out hut where we could light a fire and talk until morning; no chains this time.

I spoke to him in a language he hated as the Living God wooed him at his heart. He knew of Jesus already from stories passed by my great-grandparents. They were mere rumors and legends then, even though my great-grandparents had only been in Heaven twenty years.

I read to him from the Bible and he came to understand that yes, Jesus could and already had healed his broken people. They need only know Him. By sunrise, Capac had accepted Jesus as his personal Savior. He had fallen in love.

And when the sun was bright, he stood and said, "Now you will tell Sandani of Jesus?"

"With great joy." I had learned that much in his language already. Great joy was all he had been speaking of for hours. When I told Sandani, she told me she had already met Him, but accepted Christ all the same.

In the season that followed, Capac's sister fought a battle against a fever and cough in the final weeks of her pregnancy.

"She's so sick," I whispered one afternoon as I conversed with Capac on the steps.

He nodded solemnly. "We die of this."

I didn't quite understand, and rejected his pessimism. "We have a lot of medicine, Capac. She could easily live."

He smiled to humor me. "Sandani is very strong and stubborn. She will fight enough for her child to live. Then she will go to God, and that gives her peace."

Capac begged me daily to tell him more about Jesus. I begged him to help me learn his language. He began refusing my English after about a week. We conversed then completely in his language.

"You have a gift for language," he told me that week in his language.

"My dad says the same thing." Then I'd say, "Teach me animals."

"I will teach animals if you teach the shepherds at the birth of Jesus."

"I have taught you that one already."

"Teach it again."

We discussed and studied the Bible, and he soaked in all he could, asking me to retell biblical accounts until he could recite them. His memory was impeccable, so I was sure to give him accurate, detailed accounts to memorize. This was all during the care of young infants in the nursery. He was a worthy substitute for Jane, who was spending most of her time with Sandani. His rough hands gently rocked and soothed the babies he'd brought the prior winter.

One day, that sparked a question. "You care for the children, and I held your arm when I was a child. But you would not let my mother stitch you, and I could not take off your shackle. I do not understand."

"It is tradition." That was my first understanding. But then I retranslated that to, "it is law. The royal bloodline must be pure, without question. I touch no woman but the queen all my life."

"Your wife."

"Yes. And my mother until her death. She was also queen. And my sisters who are my blood."

"But touching alone does not change a bloodline or create a child, Capac." They were not an ignorant people, but it is difficult to know what a man knows. His response was patient.

"Many generations ago, a young woman who was a friend to the young king had a child inside her. She claimed that she had made an heir with the king in secret. She wished to be made queen. They had played together and embraced for all to see, so though he knew he had never made a child with her, he could not prove it. But the bloodline is sacred, and so there could be no question. This made my people create new laws and keep them strictly. If a king touches only the queen, and the queen touches only the king, there can be no other claims."

"I see. What happened to the woman?"

He smiled, but it was a half-smile, for me. His eyes read sorrow. "That is not for innocent ears, young Debbie Davies."

Though he left much for me to wonder about, I didn't often ask such things anymore. But I wondered much, even then. I wondered why he would have such a rule even as a teenager, but judging by the age of his pregnant sister, he was probably married even then. I wondered if their culture made it normal for a husband to spend months away from his family. I wondered how many of these children really were his own. Probably none, I surmised. His child from a pure bloodline would be an heir. No one abandons an heir. And how could they even know if Capac had touched a woman besides his wife? How could they know if his wife touched only him? What was the consequence if they did know? But all these wonderings and surmisings were done in the quiet of my mind, and I left the matter alone except to warn the other women to respect his law and avoid touching Capac.

Whether his or not, these babies were each *as* his own, and he recounted bringing each of the children from the labor room of the jungle to the porch. He was grateful when my father had built a box to safely collect them the third year.

But Capac always stopped short of explaining why he was so willing to abandon these, his own people, to strangers. Instead, he would take to apologizing for having stolen sheep in our early years.

They used them for wool, as jaguars had taken theirs. My great-grandparents had given them the first few pair of sheep, and they assumed they were welcome to take ours as replacement after the initial trade for vines.

Capac, hoping to heal his village, said he would like to not bring us anymore babies. He had come this time to see that they were all safe and cared for, but saw that we were nearing capacity and did not want his people to be a burden.

"You are not a burden. You are our God-given work," I told him in his language. I told him about the nonprofit that funded us. The churches that prayed. He felt unworthy of the charity and was overwhelmed to tears. I felt unworthy of this call to hold these babies.

One evening before Capac was leaving dinner to sleep on the floor of the clinic, and I was headed to my house, we both heard a peculiar sound in the nearby stables. Upon arrival, we saw that one of our goats had just given birth. It was that time, but I fretted a little in my heart. One of the kids was stillborn, and the other was small. I saw immediately that her mother was rejecting her.

It wasn't a problem in other times. We'd simply store the milk and bottle feed it to the kid. Tonight, however, we heard another cry of labor. We rushed to the clinic to find that Sandani was laboring, but still so weak.

I can't bear to remember, so I'll spare you the details. But Sandani gave her last breaths that night bringing her child into the world. I watched Capac mourn her. He wailed openly, then sat with her for hours, and I stayed nearby in case I was needed. Mom and Jane mourned quietly together as they tended to the newborn orphan.

"Debbie, we need milk."

"One of them gave birth tonight, but she is rejecting her kid. If we use her milk—" But the end of that sentence was silly. The life of a baby, the image of God, was of far more worth than one sick baby goat.

When I returned with a bottle for the young child, Capac had changed clothes. He was not adorning the garb of a guest at a mission. He was, again, a king.

"Capac. . ." It broke me. I knew what was happening.

From the base of his staff, he took a knife that I never knew to be there, and he cut a piece of cloth from the bottom of his royal tunic. He handed it to me in view of my mother and Jane.

He told me he had to get his sister buried in their village, twenty miles away. But the cloth was for the baby. To document him as I had for the others.

"Is this holy?" I asked.

He nodded. "Raise him as royalty. With holy hands. And pray for my people."

Capac gestured for me to take the child from Jane, which I did. He then bade his nephew goodbye with a single sob and a gentle touch of the child's angelic brown face. He quickly picked up his sister's body and disappeared into the night.

I was too stunned to know what to do, but Jane called me out from my shock.

"I'll give him to the night crew."

"No." I realized we had not been speaking English. "I. . .this one is mine. I need to raise him." I set the holy cloth near the child's face and whispered into his ear. "Roy. His name is Roy." Then in his people's language: "You are royalty, little one. And El Roi, the God who sees, saw fit to save your life."

"This isn't your responsibility, Debbie," my mother argued quietly.

"Roy. I'll get his birth certificate in order." But Jane was wiser "Should I take his blanket or—"

"No, we're going to use it."

The next morning, I carried my adopted son to the stables where Daniel was milking. Miraculously, the new kid was up and about, having been revived by her mother's milk from the source.

"Thank you, Lord, for preserving the lives that You did," I whispered. "And be with Capac and his family as they mourn the life we lost. Help him to reach them for You."

Six

Naturally, my father was resistant to his seventeen-year-old daughter raising a child as her own when so many other orphans came and were raised by our little village. But Roy was the last child that ever came to the mission, so he was indeed special. Dad was also resistant when I only spoke to Roy in his native language and spent hours of my day learning it from the four- and five-year olds that Capac had brought with him. Dad hated it most when what we called Capacsi spread to the English speakers as easily as English to the natives.

"They have a right to retain who they are," I told my father as I fed Roy one evening.

"They are pagans."

"They can retain their tongue and know Jesus. Capac did."

That's when my father banned all talk of Capac from the mission. He told me my infatuation with the young man was unhealthy, despite my insistence that I had only been an unworthy teacher. I was raising Roy out of love for his people, not an infatuation. Dad didn't like it. Still, with a heart of flesh guided by Spirit, Dad allowed me to raise Roy.

I had been instructed to raise him as royalty with holy hands. Therefore, I traded duties and became a housekeeper so that I could devote my maternal instincts to Roy alone. I set him apart from the others, even having Jane circumcise him as a covenant between me and God. Early on, he helped me in the kitchen and with the laundry. Attached to me in a sling when an infant. At my feet when he could crawl. When he started to walk, I tethered him to me with a cloth at his waist and mine. Roy was rambunctious, but obedient. Whatever he may have been, however, I learned how deeply love could take root and how lofty it could grow. I learned more about my heavenly Father when I was tossed into motherhood so young—His patience, mostly. I learned how much I lacked.

Two winters passed without word from the village, and we assumed that was permanent. Roy was our youngest child, and the oldest were getting older. My siblings grew and changed. Lydia grew a bit taller and far more beautiful. She was seventeen when she coupled that beauty with wiles, and it became a problem.

My parents seemed oblivious, but I knew something was wrong the morning she finished braiding my hair and then said,

"Don't worry about braiding mine. I think I'll leave it down today."

It was just after Christmas, and the hottest part of the summer. Lydia's hair was waist-length and thick. Leaving it down was an impractical choice.

She walked out the door to the bathhouse, letting those locks flow.

"Ma!" Roy declared, kissing my lips. And thus, I ignored any suspicions that day.

That night, though, I noticed that Lydia arrived home from dinner half an hour later than everyone else. When Mom and Dad did that together, I recalled, it turned into Andrew and Daniel. But I tried not to equate the two. Lydia was, after all, alone when she arrived at our shack. Dad did that all the time after working late. This continued for Lydia, and she always excused it as a greater workload of grading student schoolwork. No one questioned her. No one ever questioned Lydia. She was too captivating. They only ever questioned their awkward daughter who had taken in a native orphan at seventeen.

At dinner one evening, Jeremiah, twenty then, told a joke as he often did. Lydia laughed louder than all of us. I translated that easier than Capacsi, but since no one else did, I kept it to myself.

Roy and I would rest midday beneath the tree where I'd spent years reading and studying. He would nap next to me or just inside the house the tree embraced. Everyone else would spend that time on the other end of the campus fellowshipping with the staff or napping in bunks. I felt in recent years that God had used my introversion to prepare me for Roy. I preferred the quiet and solitude to rejuvenate me.

It was odd to hear whispers inside the house at that time of the day. I walked around from the side, where my tree was, to the porch, but stopped just short of opening the door. I peeked inside the open window, the linen curtains blowing against the breeze. And in one instant, one frame, I saw all I needed to see: A chaotic mingling of Lydia's long dark hair and Jeremiah's deep brown skin.

I turned away in shock and shame. By the time I returned to the solace of my tree, however, my opinions had rotted into anger.

Lydia was just seventeen years old. True, Jeremiah was only three years older than her, and they'd known each other half their childhood. But that didn't make this circumstance, this lewd sinfulness, acceptable.

I prayed about it for a few days, during which I feigned ignorance when Lydia would lie about her whereabouts. I was finally led to a terrifying decision to be confrontational. I didn't go to Lydia, because I knew she'd just lie to me. I had reason to approach Jeremiah anyway, and begged God to accompany me. I met him in his classroom after he'd dismissed the youngest students for the day.

"Hi, Jeremiah. Do you have a minute?" I tugged on the cloth at my waist and Roy turned and followed, toy truck in hand.

"For you, Debbie? Always." Jeremiah was flirtatious, and many people thought he was soon going to pursue me, nineteen then.

I didn't have many prospects this deep in the jungle, but my parents held out hope that some staff member would eventually look my way. They did sometimes, but since I was attached to a toddler, they always looked away. It was only the rejection that hurt, not the lack of a prospect. I had only ever wanted to get married someday so that I could have children, but I didn't like the idea of taking my focus from God to find some strange passion inside myself and let a man woo me. How shallow when Jesus could woo me with a word.

I was thankful to have acquired Roy sans romantic distraction. Seemed cleaner. Simpler.

Jeremiah, on the other hand, was flirtatious at twelve, wooing even his own mother when the need arose. Lydia was the same, adding a bit of romance into everything and batting her eyes or modulating her voice to win the hearts of any and everyone. Such charms seemed artificial, and sensuality followed. Why so many allowed such things to lead them even astray from God was well beyond my understanding. That is why I was already praying about possible celibacy.

I began my conversation with Jeremiah with the secondary reason for my presence. "I was hoping to get Roy started in some math soon. I already know what to do for language. Reading and writing. But I don't know where to begin for math before he's old enough to come learn from you here."

"He's barely two, Debbie. Take it easy. Let him be little. I'm sure the things you naturally do with him are enough," he both demeaned and encouraged. Winked. Charm tried my patience, indeed.

"Okay. I thought so, I just—" I sighed. Then my unspoken business came flowing from my mouth without warning. "How long have you been intimate with my sister, Jeremiah?"

"Wow. Tactful, Debbie." He crossed his arms defensively.

"I don't see how tact is going to help me breech this subject with you."

"We've been in love for years. The only reason you didn't notice is because you've been looking after Roy and he's all that matters to you. Lydia feels like she lost you to him. And she's not wrong if you honestly didn't notice."

"She's seventeen! How many years?" I refused to be blamed for this.

"We started talking about it around the time Roy was born. She's my assistant. We spend a lot of time together," he admitted freely. "I knew the age gap was iffy then. She wasn't technically of a consenting age, so it was only feelings and conversations. It was only recently that things got out of hand. Not that it's your business."

"How is it not my business?" I demanded with even tone.

"Because a romantic relationship is between *two* people. You're not exactly invited, Debbie."

"Things don't just get out of hand, Jeremiah. People *choose* to become intimate. You are both followers of Christ. You are capable of resisting temptation. This behavior is completely unchaste."

"We *know* that, Debbie. I can't expect you to understand the dichotomy, as you haven't been in love." He sighed, softening. He was convicted. "We want to get married. I planned to talk to your father about it soon."

"Good, because if you don't, I will. Dad is smart. He'll figure it out on his own. Hopefully not how I did."

"How *did* you?"

The sickening image flashed in my mind again.

"You don't want to know." I winced. "What do you have in common with a seventeen-year-old girl? In the States you'd be mostly through college by now."

"We're not in the States." He shrugged. "We both finished high school years ago, but college isn't exactly a prospect here. Lydia is the other person in the world who thinks it is insane that their parents dragged them to the middle of the jungle as a child without access to a computer. I was into software design before we came here. I could code anything, even at ten. I've had to teach Lydia on that ancient computer in the office. It's barely even connected to the generator, let alone the internet."

"Please don't tell me you actually think that's an excuse for your actions with her."

He laughed. Softened even more. "I *love* her, Debbie. She's the most incredible human being I've ever met. We've been talking about getting married for years. Yeah, we fell into sexual sin one day last month when it was raining out of season, and the power went out. That doesn't mean I love her or respect her any less. It means I'm broken and need a Savior."

"And my father's blessing and a wedding."

"That too. So, don't tell him, okay? Let me do it." He rolled his eyes, then winked as he moved behind his desk to get back to whatever he'd been doing. "Thanks for prepping me, though. I needed this. My mom slapped me when I told her and Jack, so that was deterring me from telling your dad."

"Soon?" I demanded.

"Today, if I can get a minute alone with him. He's a busy man."

"Lydia can get a minute alone with him simply by walking into his office." I tried to encourage him. "He spoils her. He'll give her this. You just have to ask."

Jeremiah, I saw, hadn't needed to be confronted and scolded. He was a good man. He just needed to be edified. He looked at Roy playing on the floor of the room with his truck, and saw it. My father was letting me raise this little boy. Maybe he'd also let Lydia marry a too-old-for-her man that had already defiled her.

I was beneath my tree in the heat of the day when Jeremiah entered Dad's office across the campus the next day. Lydia and Mom paced outside the door and Jane, too scared to be too near, was sitting with me.

"How does a man who has never met his father turn out just like him?" she fretted.

"You've told me his father was married to another woman."

"He was charming. Jeremiah looks just like him. I'm sorry for the target he chose."

"I'm not happy about when or how, Jane. But he loves her."

When Jeremiah emerged an hour later, he lifted Lydia off the ground into his arms and they buried their faces in the embrace. Jane and I sighed relief, and she rose to greet them.

Dad came from his office and walked straight to me, taking Jane's former seat next to me under the tree.

He began promptly. "You went to *Jeremiah*? Not Lydia or Mom or me?"

"Going to you wouldn't have been fair. I wanted to give them a chance to make it right. Lydia had already been lying about it. I figured she was the problem here."

"Why did you figure that?"

"You're kidding, right?" I looked at my dad, who seemed genuinely interested in my justification. "Dad, Jeremiah respects you. That doesn't bar him from falling in love with her, of course. But he would have known how forbidden it was to actually *touch* her. He told me they'd had some kind of relationship for years, but that it became physical only recently. I bet it took her months to convince him."

"Even if that is the case, he gave in and that makes him equally culpable. He took the blame. That's admirable if what you suspect is true."

"Were you hard on him?"

Dad nodded. "He's a staff member now and we have rules. I don't disallow platonic romances and less-than-platonic marriages, of course, but I don't like anyone here to be living in a state of sin. And Lydia is seventeen. He shouldn't be sleeping with a seventeen-year-old. He's like a son or a nephew to me, so yes. I gave him an even harsher punishment than I would other staff."

"What's the punishment?"

"I'm making him teach sex-ed to the young men when we come to it in the curriculum. And every year. Forever." Dad snorted laughter and I joined him. Dad hated teaching it to all of us, and was always finding ways to get out of it when Mom would tell him it was time.

"That's the only punishment?"

"No. I'm also giving him wild-child Lydia for the rest of his life. I told him she comes with a no return policy."

We continued our snorted laughter. Dad loved Lydia, don't misunderstand. It's just that she was nothing like him. Dad and I always had a special bond. There were many times that my stubborn father was also my best friend.

"I'm not mad, just so you know. This all reminds me of Mom and I. I never got to meet Mom's father, but I would have had a lot of explaining to do." Dad laughed to himself. Maybe *at* himself.

"This just all seems so messy, you know? I don't mean any offense, but romantic love makes people stupid. You and Mom are so smart and capable. Same with Lydia and Jeremiah. Same with Jane. God has these purposes for you, and you just toss it all aside and get distracted over what? Someone gives you butterflies, and you just go insane? I don't get it."

Dad laughed as a response. "You're not wrong."

"I'm serious, Dad. I'm not doing this. I have Roy, so I get to be a mom. I don't want all this pain and mess. I want to focus on God."

"Celibacy? That's not easy, Debs. But I think you could do it if you're called to it," he said, looking out at Mom, Jane, and Lydia, who were laughing and hugging. Jeremiah, a few feet from that, was getting ridiculed by his brother and my brothers.

"It actually seems *much* easier. Cleaner. I've been praying about it, and God is starting to give me peace."

"Hmm."

Dad only uttered that syllable in that tone when he was about to teach. He presented it gently, settling in beside me. He combed his fingers back through the same curls that grew on my own head, and a memory came to mind of Mom kissing him and telling him he needed a haircut. So what he said next almost didn't seem like truth. "Did you know that when I was eighteen, I also thought celibacy was God's plan for me?"

I laughed, again considering how my parents had copied their combined DNA four times and loved each other disgustingly well. I gave him a look, which was my only necessary response.

He rolled his eyes and confessed, "Also when I was eighteen, I met this hot nurse and married her twice in the same summer. First wedding was in a chapel with Elvis so we could share an apartment after my living situation fell through. Second was before God, because my parents insisted. You happened *between* weddings." He laughed.

"Dad! Stop! I don't want to hear about the end of your celibacy aspirations," I begged, turning red against his laughter.

"That's the thing, Debbie. God does what He does with each of us, so we need to be careful with aspirations. I thought marriage would be a distraction that would turn the whole world rose-colored. But it isn't. It's colored like God's will and this jungle and four babies and lots of other babies and purposes and people. Love is powerful. When I realized celibacy was not for me, it wasn't because I'd have missed out on sleeping with a hot nurse. I'd have missed out on. Well. *You.*"

"I have Roy and I'm a virgin," I said without variation in my tone, trying to correct him.

"Good for you. I have four kids, one of *them* has a kid, and soon I'll have a son-in-law too." He lowered his voice for maximum trauma. "Also, I *do* have that hot nurse. Celibacy is not a thing I miss."

"Ew, Dad."

Travel to the States had become impossible for me. The legal issues of a passport for a mere common-law adoption left Roy bound to his native land. But Lydia and Mom traveled, returning with a lovely white gown while Jackson, Jeremiah, Dad and my brothers spent the week constructing a new room onto our house.

The wedding was attended by an army of people in green scrubs. I was bitter until I saw her in white, and the smiles on the children's faces. It was a joyous day of feasting and dancing. God worked happiness and contentment into my heart that evening when Roy claimed my sister's empty bed as his own.

The next morning, I looked in the mirror, sitting cross-legged, brushing through my hair behind the thin veil that signified my bedroom in the little hut. It occurred to me that I had never braided my own hair. The sadness nearly overtook me until I heard a knock at the door.

It was Lydia, giggling at the same. The new bride entered her childhood dwelling, still in a nightgown, and sat on her knees behind me to braid my hair.

"We can't do this forever," I reminded her.

"Sure we can," she allowed. When we heard our brothers and parents exit, she stated truer business. "I'm sorry, Debbie."

"No, I'm sorry if I neglected you. Jeremiah told me that—"

"Jeremiah gets protective. It's very sweet, but he doesn't always get it right. You didn't neglect me. You just didn't notice that I was in love. I reminded Jeremiah you often don't notice things because a book or a baby is distracting you. With Roy and those books, it's both. But that's who you are."

She wasn't wrong. I continued to listen.

"Thank you for confronting him. We were very scared and didn't know what to do. Debbie to the rescue, as always. I guess this pit wasn't too deep either."

I hadn't thought about rescue in years until that morning. That day, I caught myself thinking about Capac. I wondered how his renewed rescue of his people was going, and what the first one really looked like. Increasingly over the next month, I considered him, prayed for him and his people. I'd learned enough of his language in the time I knew him to teach his nephew. I missed his friendship. I rarely opened up to anyone like I had to him. But I was content without him as well.

Jane, Mom, Lydia and I spent most evenings in the kitchen doing the dishes from dinner. It wasn't a chore. It was a chance to catch up. We all missed Lydia, because she was excused from chores for two weeks. Halfway through her honeymoon reprieve, the kitchen door burst open, and Lydia crept in, sitting on the floor among us. She was hidden there behind the sturdy island.

"Hey, Little Lydi." Mom giggled at her quiet fetal position.

"Shhh," Lydia whispered. "Jeremiah is coming back from the bathhouse any minute. If he comes looking for me, you haven't seen me."

Mom and Jane giggled before Jane asked, "Honeymoon over that quick, huh?"

"No, I just need two minutes of *peace*, you know? Where my body is like. . .mine."

I rolled my eyes at her overshare, wishing I wasn't present and knowing that Mom was about to give advice that absolutely didn't apply to me.

"Lydi?"

"Yes?" She rolled her eyes, knowing a lecture was coming. Still seventeen, despite the change in her last name.

"Whose body did you say that was?"

"Ugh! I know I'm married, Mom, but—"

"And he's not hurting you or ignoring your opinion, is he?"

"No, no! Of course not. I'm just tired," Lydia admitted.

"Then he's keeping his promises. Keep yours?"

Lydia sighed as if she'd heard that before. I know some counseling went on at some point that I obviously wasn't privy to. But I did know that my sister could get quite moody and selfish in those days. She wanted full command of her time and space, and even Jeremiah was an obstacle when she'd get into a mood.

"And you can tell him you're tired, Lydia," Jane added. "The man does *love* you."

"I love him too." Lydia sighed, standing up when we could see Jeremiah approaching the door to retrieve her.

"Peace." Mom laughed low at the joke she'd made that word into. "You're adorable, Mrs. Cooper."

One morning three weeks later, Lydia didn't come to braid hair with me, and instinct told me exactly why when Jeremiah was rushing his mother to their front door. Mom and I both saw and followed.

Lydia was whimpering in her bed, and Jane was checking vitals. Mom joined in, stroking her daughter's hair.

"Is she okay?" Jeremiah was frantic.

"I'd say they *both* are." Jane winked.

"Get some fluids in her and bring her to the clinic a bit later." Mom's advice. "And we'll confirm, but this looks just how I did."

"Mmm-hmm," Jane both confirmed and teased. "Probably seven or eight weeks. That's when morning sickness tends to start."

That caused Jeremiah to nearly have a heart attack, which looked like a quick check for my dad and a hand smoothed across his always bald head.

He cleared his throat. "The wedding was only a month ago. . ."

Both mothers laughed. Then in a move that broke my heart, Mom looked at Jane. "We're going to be grandmothers. Won't this be fun?"

I wanted to stay and congratulate my sister and braid her hair. But I heard Roy whimper through the wall and rescue me.

My mom's gaze snapped to mine as I was backing out the door in devastation. It was confirmed, then. Roy wasn't her grandchild. Not really.

I held him tighter that day. I watched him closer and spoke with him more. He and I were doomed to carry the eternal sense of not being accepted when we'd not sinned. We were stuck here, but "here" was all there was. Stuck misunderstood and almost. I knew I needed to relinquish my bitterness. But that day, it hurt, and I let it.

As I was hanging laundry before lunch, I felt a presence near me.

"Does he know any English at all?" It was Jackson, who was trying not to startle me from speaking with Roy.

"He does. I just want to immerse him with both." I asked, "Did you need something, Jackson?"

"Yes." He was direct. We always got along. "I need an English teacher. I know you aren't great in math, and my brother is going to need a new assistant for a while. Apparently, he is not to be trusted with young women, so I'm going to help him out." He laughed. Lydia and Jeremiah's relationship had been an eye roll for Jackson and me. I always saw Jackson as an uncle and the rest of us as cousins. That change had jarred us both.

"So you want me to take your place in English?"

"Just for a little while. You can keep Roy with you or with my mom. Either is fine. But I don't have anyone else I trust with English, especially as a second language."

"I don't know—"

"Take the chance, Debbie. I've wanted you in this role for a while. You have a gift. I've been begging your dad to let me have you since I saw the way you talked to that Capac guy a couple years ago. While we're all grateful for clean clothes, you shouldn't be hanging laundry when you have a gift like that."

"I'm just. . .teaching is not my favorite thing," I confessed.

"Well, I need you. Can you make it work?"

"Of course."

He thanked me, then hesitated before leaving. "He's your son, Debbie. As much as this baby coming is Lydia and Jeremiah's. Don't let them convince you otherwise. Parenthood is defined by love, not lineage."

"Thank you, Jackson. I needed that." I tried not to let it, but a tear escaped.

Jackson sighed at that tear. "You also need to hear that you're doing a good job. I hope these orphans use you as their standard for the kind of mothers they'll be. I'm glad they'll get a closer view of it for a while."

SEVEN

I'm sure you guessed it before I did. I fell in love with teaching. I taught bilingually with Roy tied to my waist, and their understanding grew exponentially in the four months I had them. You've also probably guessed that God is patient with me. He uses my life as a training program for the next task He has for me. He knows I will follow His lead, but He always prepares me before He does. At that point, however, it was unclear to me whether I was living the life I'd been trained for, or whether even this was preparation for something much bigger.

Halfway through Lydia's pregnancy, I moved from teaching to serving as Jackson's assistant. I enjoyed tutoring even more than teaching. For the first half of the pregnancy, I had spent mornings in her little room of the house braiding her hair through the awful morning sickness and for a month after it ended. I was there when the first kick occurred, and we were all enthralled by it.

Lydia returned to the classroom and Jackson returned to his. At meals, whenever that baby would move, the children would run and put their hands on Lydia's belly. Jeremiah's chest would always puff out in pride and even Dad would smile endearment for his coming grandchild. Again in those days, I thought about Capac and the night he mourned his sister and bade his nephew goodbye. I had to hold Roy tight. I had to love him more.

We were nearing Roy's third birthday, the time of year when the past would have brought us babies. It was a normal morning of tutoring in the back of Jackson's class, and I was walking from the dining hall to my tree after lunch. The cloth between my son and I was becoming a cumbersome precaution, but I held to it still. There were pits and dangers in that jungle. No one else was looking out for him. I was headed for respite under my tree. But when I arrived at the tree with my son and my books that day, my seat was already occupied.

By a king.

"Do you still understand me, Debbie?"

He said it in his language, and Roy was on alert, beginning to speak short phrases in the same language. Capac's eyes snapped to the little boy, and tears came even before the embrace. He took Roy up into his arms, which drew Capac close to me with the cloth. He was taller than I remembered, and nearly three years older than however old he'd been before. His increased muscle mass and full beard suggested established manhood now.

"I named him Roy. You told me to raise him, so—" I explained in his language as he untied the cloth at Roy's waist, setting him free to wander and be admired.

"I knew you would not disappoint me."

After a reunion, which looked like Capac simply watching in enthralled joy as his nephew played for half an hour, he began the conversation.

"You are angry with me for staying away."

"No." Anger had never entered my mind. "I do wonder why you returned."

"I found a book," he said. "It was buried in our holy place. My holy men had hidden it from me. I am losing my patience with them. I have tried to teach them about Jesus, but they have not listened. They are still broken."

"What was in the book?"

"I think it is your Bible. God's Word. But it is in my language, they said. Your great-grandmother dedicated her life to translating the Bible from English to our language. She delivered it to us just before her death. My holy men say it teaches our traditions too."

I laughed. "My family always wondered. We knew she was translating it, but never got to see a finished product. She got sick and we assumed it was lost."

"Only—"

"Only?"

"We do not read. We only speak. Our holy men insist that reading and writing make the mind lazy for remembering tradition."

"Many great philosophers believed the same. But men misuse it. If a person cannot read or write, they cannot confirm truth and a teacher has no accountability."

"I agree. I know that if I read this book, the stories of Moses and Jacob and Jesus will be here as you told me. I know this is God's Holy Word. I do not know if my people's broken traditions are here. I cannot imagine they are."

"I should tell you the story of Josiah. He found a book—"

"No." Capac smiled, removing a tattered old typewritten manuscript from the sack at his side. "Teach me to *read* it, Debbie."

I took the piece of family history from rough hands I was careful not to graze and read my own name.

Translated by Deborah Davies. My great-grandmother. I flipped through a page or two and saw that it was a phonetic translation, which made sense for an oral language. I said the first words to myself in Capacsi,

"In the beginning, God created the heavens and the earth," then clutched the papers to my chest.

"It says that?!" Capac lit up. "*You* said that. You told me the truth! Debbie, I must learn to read the Book to my people. I need to heal them. I need to see that God sees our ways as sin."

"It will take some time. I have never taught an adult to read before."

"Then I will learn as a child, the way you told me Jesus asks." He added, with sadness, "I will stay until the winter is done. I always go away for winter. I cannot bear to stay. I am a coward."

"Why did you not visit if you were not at your village?" I kept my conversation light, not wondering at his sadness.

"I am a coward," he reiterated. "This place makes me mourn my sister."

"I understand."

"Is your family well?"

"Yes, my sister has a baby on the way and my brothers are getting tall like my dad. Mom is as lovely as ever."

"Baby on. . ."

The colloquialism didn't translate. "She's. . ." I patted my belly. "Baby. Pregnant. She um. . .do you have a word for (in English) married?"

"Married," he said in English, which was also his word. "John Davies taught married."

"Oh. . ."

"Before him, we chose one love for a lifetime, but he taught us to have a ceremony and make a promise. I do not know any different. My people love the tradition. But your sister married who? You have no heirs but her brothers."

"No, she married Jeremiah. You met him when you were here. He grew up here like we did. We don't have 'heirs,' but Jeremiah loves her."

He didn't quite grasp something about that but seemed happy to hear my family was well.

"Will you come see them? We can find a bed for you."

"I will stay in the jungle. I am only just inside. I have shelter. But I will come see your family."

Dad's first reaction, to no one's surprise, was rage. It was soft-spoken still, but he was angry.

"Did you honestly come back here after three years and expect some kind of warm welcome? You left my teenager to raise a child alone. What did you say to her to get her to do that?"

Capac, I could see, had to take a moment to translate. His English was rusty.

"Not alone." Capac refused English, looking to me, and holding Roy at his hip. "I told you to raise him like royalty, in the king's house."

"I do. Roy is with me in the house. Dad plays with him and teaches him the Bible."

"What are you saying?" Dad insisted.

"He left him with me knowing I wouldn't be alone. He wanted to be sure you had some part in teaching him," I explained.

Capac handed me Roy, then removed his outer garment, folding it over his arm. He smiled at Dad, who frowned.

"And now you are exposing your whole chest?"

"Dad, no." I kept my tone level, and my actions slight. "That garment is his royalty, remember? He is willingly laying it aside since you are in charge here. That was a sign of great respect."

"Oh." Dad was conceding, but his tone was still harsh.

"Capac is here because he found this." I had the Bible in my other hand and gave it to my father, whose reaction was more emotional than mine.

"Grandma's translation." His anger vanished.

"From what I gather, his holy men are teaching some barbaric things that they claim are in this Bible. Capac didn't know it existed until recently, and the holy men knew exactly what it was but were hiding it from him. They don't read, though, as a culture. Capac needs me to teach him to read this so that he can minister to his people."

"No," was Dad's first response.

"Dad! Isn't that why we are here, to minister to them and teach them to worship God alone as a culture? Please allow me to teach him."

"Jackson can teach him." The anger was gone, but Dad didn't trust Capac. At least not with me.

Jackson was with us, and spoke up. "Not like *she* can. She speaks both languages. She taught fifteen kids to read and write in the last four months that I couldn't reach before. John, she's the woman for the job."

"Can I at least make a copy of this Bible? It could also benefit us here."

Capac nodded, then mumbled to me. "I knew you would have a medicine that could copy it."

"Machine. Not medicine," I corrected his Capacsi in English.

"Same," he said in English, with a smile.

"So, medicine is like. . .something that seems magical?"

He tilted his hand side to side. Sort of. As glad as he was to have an opportunity to learn to read and write, I was gladder still to grow a better understanding of his language.

He gestured to my mother and Jane.

"Medicine."

"Yeah, they're nurses."

Then he gestured to the Bible. "Medicine." He gestured between me and Roy. "Medicine."

"They have fewer words than we do." I taught my family. "Some words mean what would be a category of words in our language. From there, they use inflection and modifiers to specify what they mean. 'Medicine' is English, so it has to be something they learned from our people."

Then he nodded to me with gratitude, "Medicine."

"Oh!" I understood, "So it's not necessarily magical or supernatural. It's something, um. . .helpful? Is that right?"

Capac conceded, though I could see it wasn't an exact translation. We were all laughing when he snickered at our ignorance. Even my father remembered his appreciation for Capac's wit.

"So, the Bible is just medicine?" Dad accosted one last time.

Capac shook his head fervently. I interceded.

"I think he just means the Book. The physical Book is helpful, and. . .healing? Can enhance or fix something that's broken?"

Capac nodded. I was closer to the translation.

"Will you wear the scrubs while you're here?" Dad asked it timidly.

Capac nodded cordially. Not broken, just humbly submissive. The Holy Spirit at work.

Dad caught Capac's eye. "To be clear, Debbie is your *teacher*. Not your *medicine*. Those are different words, right?"

"Dad—" I started, but Capac put up a hand.

Looking at Dad, Capac addressed me in his language. "He protects you. There is no harm in this, Debbie."

Then in English, Capac announced the compromise with an English word, "Friend?"

"I don't know. How many words do they have for friend, Debbie?"

"That was English, Dad. He knows what a friend is. His people consider us friends. That's all I know," I tried.

During supper, Capac sat with me and my family. He was always watching and learning, and I tried to see what he saw. I have never been observant, and wondered if I could learn to analyze the world like Capac. I watched what he watched.

We watched Jane wipe a crumb off Jackson's lip, to his annoyance. We watched Daniel throwing sunflower seeds onto Andrew's plate and observed Andrew request him to stop by reaching across the table and flicking Daniel's nose.

We saw Lydia's flirtatious smile gently spread across her face when Jeremiah put his lips close to her ear and his hand gently swept her hair behind that shoulder. They whispered and giggled. I watched that longer than Capac did. His eyes seemed more patient with the other couple at the table, trying to discuss his presence without him knowing. Dad's hand was rested around Mom's waist, and they were mumbling words here and there into each other's faces, but the rest was just facial expressions. Once or twice, Dad would raise an eyebrow of frustration and Mom would snort a laugh.

It startled me when Capac began speaking to me. He'd turned his head to speak through the echo of the room.

"We have three words for 'friend.' Not all words are 'fewer' and 'categories.' English is fewer sometimes," he said.

"I'm still learning. I'm sorry." I took the correction. "What are the three words? I only know one."

The one I knew, and the connotation he'd used earlier with my father, was the kind of friend that is someone to be trusted. That is what his people called our people. The other two words, he told me between bites of papaya, were different. One translates into English best as "dear friend" or perhaps "confidant." He said they had an intensifier they could add at the end of that word as many times as needed for the closeness of the friends. Sort of like a child saying someone is their "best-est-est" friend.

The third friend, which translates simply as "heartholder," Capac explained by merely shaking his head and then nodding in my sister's direction around the time Jeremiah was kissing her neck.

Dad cleared his throat at that, and Jeremiah apologized. Mom corrected Dad in a whisper. Capac used that word again to describe my parents, but with a smile that time. Dad caught that word, and the look Capac was giving him.

"What does that mean?" Dad asked him.

"Um, he's telling me about all the versions of the word 'friend,'" I explained, then taught. "He used the same word for both you two and those two."

Capac mumbled to me. "Heartholders choose one another for life. When young, the love is strong and makes people dizzy and silly. In time, the love grows deeper and stronger. Heartholders share a home and children and their whole lives."

"So marriage?" I asked.

Capac shook his head. "Heartholders marry, yes. Almost always. But they only make the marriage promise after rituals and before there can be children." Capac sighed as one does when a happiness is forever married to grief. Mom sighs that way when she talks about her parents. Such dichotomy only exists in a fallen world, and only with life experience and suffering and loss. As I have said, I do not know Capac's age, and neither does he. He *looked* twenty-five or so. That sigh added many winters to my perception.

"Marriage?" That word was in English, and Dad caught it.

"Well, I guess like a romantic relationship," I clarified. "And they usually get married."

Capac, knowing I'd translate, told me the word for family while gesturing to Jane and Jackson, then my little brothers, then between my parents and me, then he and Roy, who had been on Capac's lap enjoying his supper.

"That's family," I told Dad.

Dad then looked Capac square in the eye, then shifted his eyes to me, then back to Capac, raising his eyebrow.

Capac was annoyed at the unspoken question.

"I think he's asking—"

"I know." Capac was gruff, but he remained respectful. He used a conglomeration of sounds that took me a minute to understand, but him no time to come up with. He gestured to me for translation.

"So, he used the word for teacher with the modifier that means little and then the word for friend, like trusted person, but with the word they use for outsider, like us. So he just said I am his 'little-teacher-outsider-friend.' " Then beyond the translation, I read, "He told me earlier he appreciates that you are protective of me, which means he's safe for me to be around. Why do you keep questioning that?"

"Put yourself in my shoes, Capac."

"Dad, that's a colloquialism. He isn't going to understand that when he's never worn a pair of shoes in his life."

"Alright. Tell me why I should trust you, Capac." Dad shrugged.

Capac's answer silenced the room. He grabbed that manuscript from the bench between us and slammed it onto the table.

"You trust only God," he said in English. "Your God is my God is Debbie's God. Trust only Him."

"I have no issue trusting God, Capac. And I know you trust Him too. But Debbie is just a kid, like you said. You called her little. She's a *smart* kid, but—"

"So, you think I can't teach him?" Maybe it was me that was the problem.

"I *know* you can. Jackson is right, the way you teach language and the way you tell a Bible story are unparalleled. That's not the concern."

"What's the concern?" I tried to keep from smiling at the sudden flattery.

This time when Dad observed and analyzed the black orbs that were observing his blue ones, the gaze was stayed.

"I'll let you know." Dad sighed, not straying from that intense staring contest. Something was bothering him. "Teach him in here?"

It was the dining hall, which was always "empty" other than mealtimes. In reality, it was just a pavilion that connected the schoolhouse and kitchen. Since it was near the other buildings, it was often used as a pathway between them. Staff and lines of children were constantly walking through, moving between activities and classrooms. I'm sure Dad would have preferred to house Capac in the time-out hut and have bars between us while I taught him, but since Capac had only proven himself to be tame, wise, and honorable, Dad allowed the slight compromise.

EIGHT

I spent afternoons in an empty dining hall teaching a twenty or thirty something man to read and write, mainly as it concerned the Bible. It frustrated him, not being able to fit all his vast intellect into the lines of a page or display it in his fumbled, childlike reading of words. He was dedicated, though. When he emerged from the jungle each morning, he always had an English dictionary open in his hands. A thinker will think. In the first two months he spent with us, he showed that thinking in his untiring love of learning.

That man and that Bible also taught me the lovely intricacies of the language I'd only partially known, and mostly only in spirit. It was a refining intensity that took me from raw talent, much like an amateur painter, and crafted it into a science. My love affair with God's Word was renewed when I learned it in yet another language. As Capac did copy work, I would often relish the Psalms anew. Capac once caught a goofy smile on my face and teased,

"Better than English, yes?" He smirked, still focused on forming letters into Bible verses.

"I like them both," I confessed. "This Bible is written with our English alphabet. The same sounds, the same voices for both. But so different. I just love language."

"But at Babel, sin made language confused." He had read that himself recently.

"Humans were confused by language differences, but *God* was not confused. He created them all, and I see Him in all of them." I smiled, reading another line in another Psalm before rambling on about my favorite subject. This annoyed everyone I knew except Capac. "They do not know where language came from. Science cannot explain why humans can speak and animals cannot. We had a psychologist here for a year that called your people barbarians, which is what people used to call each other when their language seemed unintelligible or animalistic. But I knew you could not be. Your language is too beautiful. You can only use language if you were created in the image of God." I nodded, running fingers over typewritten words and then some cursive notes in the margin. "Great-Grandma Debbie saw that beauty in your people too."

" 'Little teacher.' " Capac snickered, then still copying words, he shared, "My people called Deborah Davies teacher-outsider-friend. You are little only because you are like her, but young. Your mind is not little. We learned very much from John and Deborah Davies."

"Do you remember them?"

Capac nodded solemnly. "I was small, but I remember coming here to your mission and Deborah Davies taught my mother to make clothes. I remember when they got sick and my father buried them like holy men."

"I never knew them." I shrugged, calculating. My great-grandparents died four years before I was born. I wondered how many winters I could add to Capac's age before it became impossible. I knew then his people aged differently.

"You are very much like them, even if you did not know them." He completed his copy work and looked up at me. "Thank you for helping me to continue the work God started with them."

"It is an honor, Capac."

Capac was there when we celebrated my twentieth birthday and Roy's third. It was an odd tradition for Capac, who didn't see the point in birthdays. He was especially confused when the slice of sugary cake at lunch made Roy too restless to nap. Normally, Capac would follow me to my house and stand outside while I put Roy down. That day, Roy was wired, fussy, and impossible.

"Let me try," he called into the window.

I handed Roy to him, and Roy wrapped up around his uncle, sputtering trembled sobs into Capac's shoulder as children do to destroy the heart.

"Oh, Roy. . ." Capac sighed, and asked, "Does he always sleep in your house? Where does he feel calm and safe?"

I led Capac out to my tree, where he sat against it, Roy against him, and rumbled out a low tune that seemed to have the same light, dancing melodic structure as a lullaby I knew well. The words were difficult to discern. Capac sang it twice, running his fingertips across Roy's back. Then, he looked at me with a smirk before singing it in English too. That time, to my delight, I was able to sing it with him.

"The perfect butterfly with the fire on its wings
A beacon for the caterpillar's change
The wings will burn the trees but if the caterpillar knows
He'll be caught up in the wings and fly away."

We shared a quiet giggle after that time when Roy's eyes closed and his limbs went limp. I spoke low to keep Roy asleep.

"How do you know that song? And in two languages?" I knew it was not easy to translate a song on the fly.

Capac smiled. "Your great-grandmother taught us this song. All the children know it, and she taught me the English too when I was very small." He nodded and gripped Roy to describe the age he was.

"My parents sing that song!" I exclaimed, though whispering. "It is a warning about God's wrath, and a promise of His grace."

"The gospel, hidden in a song." Capac nodded. "When you told me about Jesus, I knew this song was about Him. The people do not know who the butterfly is, but still they teach their children this song."

"Haven't you been telling the people about Jesus?"

"I am not the gifted teacher that your great-grandmother was. But I try with my whole heart."

"Well, let's give you more tools." I rose to my feet. "I will go get the things for reading."

I told my dad the predicament while I gathered materials, and he allowed the change for that day for the sake of a sleeping child. It was just as public, in reality. I could see the entire mission from that tree. Dad found exactly nine excuses to walk by, then got his Bible and sat on our porch just out of sight, when he'd normally study in his office.

Another day we spent at the tree for the same reason, Lydia and Jeremiah ran laughing from their hut in kisses, and didn't even notice us there or Dad sitting on the bench. Capac shuddered as they walked away, and asked, "How can they share their dinner like that?"

"What do you mean?"

"Their mouths. Together. What is what?"

"They are. . .I don't know your word." I knew Dad was sitting nearby and asked, "Dad, where do I find kissing in the Bible so I can translate?"

"Song of Solomon." This was from both Capac and my father. Capac suddenly lit up and turned to the passage in the Bible. "Here. Kiss me with kisses of the mouth. Is this what Solomon means to say?" He gestured to where Lydia and Jeremiah had been.

"Yes. . ." I was confused and checked the Bible. "Kiss is in English. What is your word for that?"

Capac laughed. "My people do not feel love from sharing their dinner. Better than wine? Heartholders may drink wine together, but not a mouth as a vessel. The thought makes me want to *lose* my dinner."

"Your people don't. . .kiss. . ." I tried another way. "Like the way I kiss Roy?" I kissed own hand, a peck as I would a child's head.

"Ahh. . ." he said in revelation. "You do this for affection? I have seen but did not understand."

"That's impossible. How can you not know what kissing is?" I spoke in English and laughed.

"Debs, different cultures do different things," Dad mumbled.

"Well, what do you do, if not kissing?" I was intrigued, and worried Dad would silence me. But I think he was intrigued too.

Capac spoke English for Dad's sake. "It depends on the kind of friend. And the kind of affection."

Dad stopped that immediately. I think he did not trust Capac to explain types of affection to me, given the clear cultural differences. For all Dad knew, Capac's people engaged in public intimacy, and as Capac mumbled to me,

"Your father protects you so very much. Very well."

I did get some of that question answered when Lydia came into the dining hall during one of our lessons, desperately requesting that I braid her hair to help stave off a hormone-induced hot flash. She sat on the ground in front of my chair, and Capac looked extremely uncomfortable as I started the braid.

"Everything alright?" Lydia was the one who noticed.

"I. . .you are braiding your sister's hair?" he asked me.

"Yes. I can do hers, but not my own. And she braids mine."

"Oh. . ." He stirred further. "This is normal for sisters?"

"To braid each other's hair? Yes. Very normal." Lydia laughed after I translated, then sighed when the hair moved from the back of her neck. "And very appreciated."

"Do you not braid hair at home?" I ask him.

"Yes. We learn to braid when we are young. For ropes and things. But only husbands braid hair." I took a moment to translate for Lydia, then Capac continued with. "It is done in private. A husband shows his affection in private, and all can see it in his wife's hair. A wife has many braids in her hair from his affection and a man has great honor from how beautiful the braids are."

Lydia giggled when she received the translation. "I *love* that. So what does a wife do to show affection?"

"This is also in private." Capac nodded to Lydia's vast abdomen. "But later shows for all to see. On a woman's body and on the faces of children."

I felt my cheeks go red before I could translate. When Capac laughed, Lydia needed no translation, because she put a hand at her belly, and he nodded. That put her in delighted hysterics. Braid complete, I helped my sister to her feet and she was off to, "Tell Jeremiah everyone can see my affection."

Never the tittering romantic my sister was, I remembered something odd. "So why didn't Sandani have braids in her hair when she came here pregnant with Roy? You said unmarried heartholders do not—"

"Debbie, that is not for innocent ears or light conversation. I want to respect your father's protection." He said something similar anytime I asked too much about his people. Though I burned with curiosity, I respected his wishes to remain silent.

In subsequent days, I abandoned the cloth at my waist, because Capac always seemed to be there if Roy would wander. I had a second set of eyes. That's really all I ever needed for Roy. But I think Capac saw Roy as his responsibility and me as a temporary nursemaid. It was I that was the second set of eyes. Regardless, Roy was well looked after, and I tried not to think about the loss I'd experience when Capac returned home. It was becoming clear that Roy had a greater purpose than growing up at this mission.

The final month, Capac slowly added a new motive. We were alone in the dining hall and Capac was reading the Sermon on the Mount. Slowly, and stumbling, but with a smile. He was reading the Bible.

" 'You are the light of the world. A city that is set on a hill cannot be hidden. Nor do they light a lamp and put it under a basket, but on a lampstand, and it gives light to all who are in the house. Let your light so shine before men, that they may see your good work and glorify your Father in Heaven.' "

I had been half listening, trying to deal with Roy's stubborn tantrum over not getting licorice after his nap. But when Roy finally quieted, the reading had stopped. Capac slipped in the proposition sideways.

"If only my people could learn about Jesus the way I did."

"Did they not? You said you taught them the accounts I told you. You've seen now that I taught them accurately. I'm sure you did too."

"They learned from me but did not believe me." He shrugged. "I got to learn from you."

I'm not all that observant. I missed a love affair that happened practically under my nose for years. It took me some time to understand.

A week later, Capac made a common request: "Tell me a Bible story." He was laying in the grass beneath my tree, Roy asleep on his chest.

"You can read them now," I told him, annoyed that he was keeping me from reading my Bible after our lesson.

"But I like how you tell them. Josiah. Tell me about Josiah."

"Josiah was a young king after the time of the judges."

"Judges like Deborah."

"Yes. Do you want to hear the story?"

He laughed. "Yes. Tell it."

"Josiah was a king faithful to God. He wanted to make repairs to the house of God and sent word to the priest Hilkiah to take account of the money so that they could pay those making the repairs. But while Hilkiah was counting money, he found a book. It was the book of the Law, which had not been read or kept during the time of evil kings that predated Josiah. Josiah tore his clothes because he was so grieved that the people had not kept the Law. He read it in their hearing and led his people to trust in God again. It's a beautiful story."

"A beautiful truth," he corrected.

"Yes."

"You missed the part about Josiah burning the idols and tearing down all the high places and perverted things. Josiah burned the priests on their pagan altar. This is in the Bible too."

"Sorry, I was not sure how far you wanted me to—"

"I am scared to defile the high places, Debbie. I am a coward."

Scarcely in modern times can a man relate so closely and literally to Josiah. Capac had been trying for years to remove the paganism from his village.

"You are not a coward."

"There is much you do not know. I want to tell you, but I am a coward."

Capac ended the conversation by succumbing to a nap with his beloved nephew. It reminded me of my father's midnight ramblings. *"We are running out of time."*

I took a walk that day as they slept. I so rarely did, but that day, the Spirit insisted.

Dad was sitting on the porch when I rounded the corner, looking out at the mission contemplatively as he always did when monitoring my lessons with Capac. He did not speak enough of the language to understand, but he always listened and "protected" as Capac always said. That day, he asked me a question as soon as I came within hearing distance.

"Do you trust him, Debs?"

"Dad, Capac is Roy's uncle. Why would I not trust him?" I stood before him to hear his newest complaint.

"I don't mean with Roy. I mean in general. Do you trust him?"

"With what, Dad? I don't understand."

"Um." Dad shrugged. "Your life, I guess."

"That seems like a bigger question than you just ask someone in passing."

Dad first paused, his eyebrows twisted in desperation before he said, "Then sit?"

I complied, stepping up onto the porch and completing the purpose of the two-seat bench Dad had built Mom probably the first year we came. I glanced over at the box he'd built for the third year of babies on. He'd sanded it smooth, but kept the wood raw. That made some blood stains of birth inevitable.

On sight of the box, I imagined Capac shushing the newborn as he walked with haste, pulling a handmade blanket around them tighter for warmth. Those rough hands protecting those children the way my father protects me. I imagined, though somehow we always missed it, when Capac placed babe, cord, and placenta into the box.

I imagined he probably told them they would be safe. Probably sang them a lullaby. Certainly didn't kiss them, but perhaps just one last tearful embrace.

"So, as I was asking," Dad spoke into the silence I had not yet filled with an answer, "Do you trust him with—"

"Yes." I looked out at the campus, though I think Dad was staring at me. "Of course."

"Of course?" Dad's voice quavered with laughter. Not of joy, but of disbelief.

I turned my head and smiled at Dad, then nodded to the baby box. "He trusted *us*. Only a trustworthy person trusts like that when lives are at stake. So yes. I trust him with mine. And with Roy's." I shrugged, that very concept weighing on my heart.

"You're so wise, Debbie. Stubborn, but wise. I can't always count on you to obey me to the letter like Andrew does, and that annoys the snot out of me."

Both of us hummed laughter. He continued.

"But I know I can count on you to follow God's lead. You'll do what's right, pretty much without fail. It was *right* for you to go find your sister in that pit when I told you to stay in the kitchen. It was *right* for you to raise Roy as your own. Maybe not acceptable or reasonable. But *right*. So, if you trust him, Debs, I know it's right."

"Why would it be an issue if I trust him?"

"It's not an issue, per se, but—"

I interrupted with, "I already know he's probably going to take Roy when he leaves. I'm trying to get my heart prepared for that. But like I said, I trust him. If that's what you were thinking, it's not an issue for me. Roy is mine, but he isn't *mine,* mine. Capac will take good care of him, and I know he has family there that will—"

Dad interrupted next. "That's what I figured too." He laughed once. Then twice. Then with a few tears, "But don't worry about that. I don't think Capac is going to take Roy or *anything* from you. I think you are going to be *given* something."

"Given what? I don't understand."

"Oh, probably the only thing I've ever wanted but God has repeatedly denied me."

"Um. I don't—"

"I know you don't see it, so I'll let God break it to you through Capac or however else. Just know that I felt this same call when I was just out of high school and met a twenty-two-year-old nurse who told me she wanted to be a missionary's wife. God barely warned me, but—"

"But you were married and expecting me by the end of that summer. I know the story, Dad. But this is definitely not that." I laughed. "He knew Great-Grandma and Great-Grandpa."

"So?" Dad was confused.

"So, he's closer to *your* age than to mine. It's not a 'heartholder' situation."

"No, I know. Mom says otherwise, but if I sensed that, I'd have run him off a while ago. No, I said it was *like* that. The call to missions, not the crazy summer with Mom. I raised my blond kids in a jungle over that call."

"Lydia and Andrew aren't blond," I corrected.

"Yeah, you had to be blond, didn't you? A city on a hill." He sighed. "Dark hair might have made things easier for you. Maybe."

"I love it here, Dad. I love these people and I love that God put us here to minister to them. I love teaching them and learning from them and serving them however I need to. Please don't think I resent you or something."

"No, that's Lydia. Debbie, you don't resent me. You *are* me; the version I was never brave enough to be. At seven, you were twice the man I'll ever be, so the joke is on me for not seeing this coming sooner."

"You're being weird, Dad," I teased, standing. "I'm going for a walk."

"Yeah," he said, like he was mourning something. "Yeah, I know."

NINE

Winter was ending, and I was waiting in the dining hall for Capac to conclude his nap with Roy and join me for a lesson. I knew it was coming, but I dreaded the day he'd tell me he had to get back to his people. From their slow, somber entrance, I knew that day had come.

"You have to go." I got to it before he even sat.

He smiled as he sat. "I have sent word ahead, and my people will expect me back. The moon is almost full."

Then I asked the question I dreaded more. "Will you take Roy home with you?"

He didn't want to come at it directly, I could see. "If I return with him, it will mean very much to my people. It will help me to defile high places."

"What high places, Capac? You have refused, for years now, to help me understand what evil thing you're fighting back at home." I sobbed. He was going to take my proverbial Samuel back home to the royal purpose God had for him. "You always say I'm too innocent, and maybe I am, but I wish you'd tell me how to pray."

"If you let me take him home, I will tell you. I promise. I will tell you everything."

"Do I have a choice?"

"Yes. It is not my hope, but if you want to raise him here, I will allow it. I trust you completely as I do my own sister."

"Sandani?"

"No. Mena. She has four sons at home and a good husband. Very many braids in her hair. She is a good mother. I brought her first baby to you the second winter. You named him Moses. The first winter was Genesis. She is the child of my oldest sister, Nur. She has no other children."

"Then why would she abandon—"

"I will only tell you if you agree to let me take Roy." He stood firm.

"How and when can you tell me *anything* if you leave?" I sobbed.

"Debbie. . ." he cooed.

"What?"

He was fighting against what he called cowardice. When he said it first point blank, I barely comprehended it.

"I will tell you on the journey. I do not *only* want to take Roy."

I stared blankly, wondering if I didn't understand. I don't merely translate language. I understand it in both tongues. Not one to the other, but each language as my only. Mistranslation is not common for me. Still, Capac whispered it in English to make it clear.

"I want you to come with me."

"My whole life is here," I said in English.

He changed back to his language. "Lydia says your whole life is Roy. And he will come with you."

"Will you take him if I do not go?"

He shook his head with fervor, almost angry I asked. "You are as Roy's mother. You will raise him, whether it is here or there."

"I help teach here."

"You will teach *there*. The things my people need to learn are taught well here. Here, you are a bright light among bright lights. You can hide beneath a basket—your tree—and no one knows. But my people are broken, Debbie. There, you could be a light in the *darkness*. What is your light for if not to put on a lampstand and light the way in a dark place?" Emotion always came easily to Capac. There was a different version of masculinity among his people. He was their king. Maybe their mightiest man, who nearly fought off five grown men once. And over the thought of his people's evil, he wept.

Mighty like a man of God who defiles pagan altars.

"Did you tell my father? He seemed to—"

"I did not. He is a good man. If he saw my village, he would see he is not so wise and powerful with his clothes and rules. But still, he is good. Will it anger him if you go?"

"I think he sees it coming. Still, they won't understand, Capac. If I go, they will think the worst of me. They will think I have decided to be a barbarian."

"If they think that, they do not know you, Debbie." He sighed. "I will go without you. But my people *need* you and Roy. God has made it clear that you will help me teach them in a way I cannot do alone."

"But will they accept me? You always say I am an outsider."

"I am an outsider here and still your people allow me to stay."

"We are at this mission to reach your people. Your people have been where they are for a thousand years, Capac. I might be seen as an invader. What do your people do to invaders?"

"Debbie, I want you to live among us and be our teacher. Perhaps they will accept you as one of us. I have never seen you fear anything. Do not fear this."

"Is there a chance they will reject me?"

"Yes."

"Is there a chance they will *kill* me, Capac?"

"They will only kill if you violate their laws."

"But it is a new culture to me. What if I violate their laws unwittingly?"

"Your questions do not matter, Debbie. You need only ask one question of yourself. If the answer is yes, you will need to trust that I will protect you with even my life as your father does. If it is no, stay here and look after Roy as before."

"That's not fair, Capac. What is the question?"

"Are they *worth* it? Are they worth rejection and death if that is what it comes to?"

"Of course!" I said without another thought, then added, "Capac, Jesus thought so. And if I am the vessel He wants to use to show them that, then they are worth anything that may happen. I have dedicated my life to serve their children, and I will do all I can to reach the rest of your people."

"That is what I thought you might say." He smiled, pleased.

"Are we going today?"

"Yes, if you are coming. The journey is far with a child. I sent word, and I must not miss the full moon."

"Okay." There was so much I didn't understand.

"We will go when you are ready. You can say goodbye."

"I will leave them a note. My family will guilt me into staying if I tell them I am going."

"You are going, then?"

"Yes. I do not want to hide my light anymore."

Capac told me it was a two-day journey to his village. Three with a young child. Jane was the only person I told, and I figured even that was a risk. She surprised me when she whispered,

"Finally."

"Finally someone gets to go?"

She shook her head. "Finally someone sees it had to be *you*."

"Why me? I don't understand. I'm just the one with 'a book or a baby or both.' " She had coined that term herself.

"Debbie, God Himself, when He could do anything to save the world, chose to make the Word *flesh*. A book. A baby. You got all you need, girl."

Jane assured me of her silence until I was safely away. She packed provisions for us while I raided the supply room in the chapel and the school for enough to teach a village about Christ, but a light enough load to carry for three days.

Capac waited under my tree and I returned with the supplies. He had changed into his kingly garments.

"I just need to get some clothes and personal items for me and Roy."

He laughed.

"Just a few things."

"My sister can make you clothes. We have all you will need."

I looked at his partially bare chest.

"Your face gets red when you are ashamed." He chuckled. "A woman's body is sacred to us. Women, especially unopened women, are covered. But you may bring your own garments if you choose. We cannot easily return."

I packed light and left Roy's royal blanket behind with his name and birthdate on a pin. I handed this to Jane. My last act was to write my father a note and place it on his desk as he conducted a staff meeting in the next building.

"Dad,

Jesus asked us to make disciples of all the nations, and I have been given a chance to go to a nation no one has reached. Know that I am safe and you needn't look for me. Should anyone care to wonder, Roy is with me.

All my love,
Debbie"

Before we breached the jungle's threshold, Capac nodded to my feet, adorned with hiking boots. "God gave feet as a protection and guide. They are our foundation and first defense. We do not cover them."

"Shoes protect feet, Capac. Must Roy have his feet cold and bare too?"

"Yes. Your feet will adapt. Leave the coverings here."

My load lightened as I removed my shoes and socks, then Roy's, then all socks and shoes from the backpack I carried. I left them in a pile at the edge of the jungle, removing any question as to where we went.

I departed with Capac and Roy in broad daylight without anyone's notice, the bright light dimming little. A couple hours into the journey, Capac told me he needed to relieve himself, and I asked him to take Roy along, who was likely in need of a potty break as well. I thought it was a better idea for him to learn to use the wild jungle from his uncle, not me.

When the two returned from their journey into the jungle, Capac was wide-eyed with horror as he handed me Roy.

"Is everything okay?"

"What did you do to him, Debbie?!"

"What do you mean?" I checked him over.

"His. . ." Then he used a word I'd never heard in his language. I also rarely said the word, if ever, in English. From Capac's gestures, I realized it was an anatomical term.

"Oh!" I also hadn't thought to mention it to his uncle. "Roy is circumcised."

"Why? The Bible says this is not needed to be saved. Men do this outside the Bible?"

"They do, in many cultures. We do not do it often at the mission because it invites unnecessary infection. But the Israelites did it to set themselves apart as God's chosen people. I had Jane circumcise him to set him apart. It was part of my covenant with God to raise him as my own. My parents did that with my brothers as an outward sign of dedicating them to God. So it was a symbol of his being raised in holiness, I suppose. We do not do it with any of the other babies you have brought us."

"Does it hurt him?" Capac was absolutely horrified and had begun walking again, while trying to sort it out in his heart.

"We gave him medicine so that he did not feel it. He was only a baby, and it only took a couple weeks to heal completely. He does not even remember that now and can still grow up and have a family."

Capac turned, walking backward, and shuddered humorously.

"Bad tradition."

I laughed at his sudden squeamishness. "I hope it does not offend you. You left him with me. I did what I thought was best."

"You did best."

Then he shuddered again at the custom and we continued our journey.

I followed Capac until sunset, when we reached one of the many shelters he had set up over the years. We built a fire just outside it and had some supper, then crawled into the low-lying shelter on opposite sides of a line of rocks. I gestured to them.

"So that you did not accidentally touch someone as you slept?"

He nodded, smiling at what he knew seemed a silly rule for his people to have to follow. Sleepy Roy, who insisted on walking most of the day, succumbed to sleep against Capac's chest. I was exhausted, and my feet ached. They were covered with tiny cuts and bruises and a mass of mud. The only relief was the ice pack that was the cold jungle air. Still, for the burning questions I had, I whispered.

"Capac, why do the babies get abandoned to strangers? You promised to tell me if I let Roy come."

He smirked. "You are a just and wise young woman. We have great regard for women, and believe them to be sacred until they are opened by a man. This is not quite the same in God's Word. Still, I see it in you."

"But what does that have to do with. . ."

"You are innocent and unbroken by evil because your father has protected you well. So you will not like my people when I tell you, though you will love them when you meet them. Still, I must corrupt you to tell you."

"Just tell me. I would rather know about the brokenness than be blind when I arrive."

After my insistence, he started right in. "My people have a holy ritual each year, just after winter. We call this ritual the 'Opening.' Not every man is born corrupt. Our holy men are thought to be of a sacred bloodline from the gods. Their children, male and female, are all holy when born to their wife. Their sons will be holy men when they grow older. The holy daughters cannot be defiled by man, but must not marry or touch a man unless he is the king or heir and he has chosen her. This is meant to carry on the royal line with the wisdom of the gods. But every other woman must take part in the Opening if she ever wishes to marry. Do you understand?"

"Yes, but. . .what's this ritual?"

"This ritual is for young women with a heartholder who has asked for marriage. They must first be opened by a holy man."

"What do you—" But I understood suddenly, with a hand to my mouth. To confirm: "You mean that your holy men are intimate with a young woman who is engaged. To make her holy?"

"Intimate" did not translate. He understood only with a correction. In a culture of bare feet, their term for sexual intimacy was closer to "walk with" than "be close with." Capac's people were community oriented, and he didn't understand *not* being close with someone. Obviously, he walked alongside his people, but the intimate type of walking was not the same term as in the literal sense. When I suggested the term "make love," Capac understood that better, but not in the case of the Opening.

"There is not love in the Opening. Only ritual lust. There is love when a woman can marry her heartholder after the next winter. They must wait a year, because—" He sobbed, signaling me for patience with his sudden emotion.

I continued for him, "If the holy men cause them to be pregnant—"

"Children—" He sobbed, but regained his composure. "Even more than women, we love children. But any child conceived during the Opening is sacred and must be sacrificed to our gods who gave the child only for that purpose. They are killed, at birth, in the temple or out in the jungle. But the jungle is the place of shame. The labor is hard, and the child must die on his own. We call this the 'Closing.' There *is* no greater evil, Debbie."

My gasped reaction turned quickly to tears and disbelief. "A woman cannot decide for herself if she wants to make the sacrifice?"

"The child does not belong to her. She is only a vessel for the sacrifice and can only choose *where* the sacrifice is made. That is *their* belief."

"And your belief?"

That, he quickly lobbed into the air as he stroked Roy's back. "No one should ever kill a child for any reason. The children were a part of no ritual and should participate in no evil against them."

Quickly, I connected the dots with memories I had manufactured from what I could see before me. Capac gently soothing Roy from stirring as he slept. Yes. He *must* have sung them lullabies.

"But you rescued them from sacrifice?"

Capac nodded. "I took the women days into the jungle at the last part of her pregnancy as is ritual. I built shelters for safety. They often gave birth right where you lay. For mothers who knew they would want time to mourn, this was an acceptable choice, even if shameful. Many of the women believe I placed the children where they could not hear their cries as the gods took them. But I delivered them all to your mission."

"Do the holy men know?"

"Very few know for sure. There are rumors only."

"That seems risky. What made you decide to do that?"

First, he laughed. "For the life of a child, Debbie? There is no risk too great to rescue a child."

"I agree, but your people barely knew us."

"We knew of your kindness," Capac said, and we both looked to the scar on his forearm. "Of the way you sacrificed what little you had to help a stranger."

"You didn't know we were there for that purpose?"

"My father knew. When we came to you, I believe he was testing that you were of the John and Debbie Davies we knew." He sighed that deep, pained sigh, then said, "Royal daughters must partake in the Opening, even with no heartholder. My sister Nur was pregnant at the same time she was learning the ways of a midwife from my aunt. She is just and wise like you, and we decided together that her child *must* be rescued. We shared a room. I watched my niece grow inside her, Debbie. Not growing for sacrifice. Growing for *breath*. Genesis looks just like Nur. Each year, I tried to come look at her to see her alive. When I brought her to you, God stirred in my heart. I convinced all the opened women to give birth in the jungle with me each winter. I was only an heir, but they listened. And I have seen them all alive at your mission."

"It has been a joy, Capac."

"It is the work of God, Debbie."

"Why did you not just stop the Opening as king? This would prevent the Closing."

"When my father died, I tried. But as punishment for trying, the holy men threatened to sacrifice the young children, as well. That was the year we lost Sandani and Roy was born. There was never such sadness or sacrifice as when they sent their children with me into the jungle. They still mourn them."

"That was probably heartbreaking for your people. But the children lived."

"They lived," he whispered with passion. "I would thank your family with my life, but I know their reward in Heaven is far greater. The children were better with you and Jesus than with us and our brokenness."

"I wish I could tell my father that you really are a hero."

"I am a coward," he whispered. "Once Sandani died in your home, they would not allow me to take young women into the jungle. They suspect that the children are alive and think I have upset the gods. They have sacrificed fifteen babies since Roy. So, I leave for the winter. I cannot bear it. But you make me stronger, Debbie. I will not be a coward this time. I will help God heal my people."

An old wondering occurred to me. "Do you leave your wife when you come to us for the winter? Are you not married to a holy man's daughter? You told me once you had a wife."

He sighed, turning onto his side, and settling Roy beside him. Then, he began an explanation that seemed to boil him to the point of searing anger.

"Holy daughters," he started, "Are born and trained for two purposes. First, they all work for the young heir's attention so that his heart is swayed for one of them forever. Then, once a royal wedding occurs, her purpose as queen is to distract the king the very best she can. With her beauty, her body, with royal sons and daughters and with many responsibilities and joys in the home."

One word confused me. "Distract?"

"Distract." Capac nodded. "This is an ancient conspiracy to sway the king's heart to continue the evil rituals. And so the queen does, in every generation, because she was taught this from birth. She holds the king's heart. From birth, an *heir* is taught and shown to give the queen all that she desires and more. The rituals break the king's heart in every generation. And in every generation, the queen persuades him to continue them. These teachings are nearly as sure as blood."

"I see. So you come into the jungle so your wife cannot distract and persuade you?" I teased.

He chuckled, then shook his head. "God knew very much better for me. This generation of holy men only had sons. Then my mother's sickness came early, with Sandani's birth. She died before I was a man. My father loved my mother very much, but he knew of the ancient conspiracy and hated the rituals. Once my mother died, he was free to teach us new teachings."

"Oh? What teachings?"

"My father allowed and encouraged my sisters to marry, but insisted that I do not. He taught me that the joys of a wife are many, but I must never marry. He said my sisters, free to hold a man's heart without swaying it, would make heirs to be king. But it was for me, a man without the poison of a holy daughter, to break the evil rituals." He concluded with, "The daughters of the holy sons are still children, and will become women to try to sway me. But they will always be children to me, and I will never have one of them as queen. God has made this possible, and I am grateful that I can serve Him without distraction."

"But what about children? You need an heir." I thought of the way Capac adored children, and cared for Roy with such tenderness and strength. My heart ached for him until he smiled.

"Roy will be accepted as my heir. An heir without distraction." Capac rubbed Roy's back, and the boy curled up closer to his chest for warmth, comfort, and safety. "He has been raised as royalty with holy hands. My people believe John Davies, your great-grandfather, was a holy man. My people choose to worship idols, but still they fear your God—*our* God. The only true God. So your people are protected. Some have even seen angels near your camp, protecting you."

I gasped the understanding, then confirmed as he nodded. "I see now." It had to be Roy, and I had to care for him. But I was sad. I knew I was losing him.

He added, "But I do not wish my heir to have no mother. My heart was sick when my mother died. Do not fear."

I sighed relief. "Okay."

"You have made me able to use their own laws to destroy them. Do you see that God has called you to help me rescue my people?"

"I do. I have seen that all my life, Capac." Then I added, "I am the same, Capac. I have seen my mother distracted by Dad and Lydia distracted by Jeremiah. But my friend Jane has great focus and wisdom. I am a mother to Roy, but I choose not to be distracted from serving God by wishing for marriage."

Capac appreciated that with a proud grunt, and, "Debbie Davies, fourth generation of John Davies, my little-teacher-outsider-friend who fears nothing and no one but God. You will do much for my people."

The next day was exhausting. Roy couldn't walk anymore, his feet sore and unlearned like mine. But Capac, with strength like the grip of a python, carried him on his back, even with the bag of books and pack of provisions across his body, his *matteh* his only support. I only carried the backpack of clothing, but the journey was exhausting for me.

I was overjoyed, then, when I saw that we were approaching the shelter for the night. This one was far different. It was more like a tent or a cabin than a low-lying safeguard from the elements. When Capac saw it, he sighed some nostalgic sigh.

"What is this place?"

"This is the place I was born, Debbie. My father wanted to share my mother with John Davies, but she did not want to be away from the comfort of their house. He built her this shelter, then brought her here sometimes to persuade her to make the rest of the journey. She spent the last of her pregnancy here as well." He looked to me for my interest, though he knew well that I loved a good story. He smiled and presented the moral of the tale. "The place an heir is born is very important. It tells something of his purpose. I used to come play here as a child, wondering what I was meant to do. Later, this place allowed me to rescue many women and children."

"And bring home your heir."

"Who was born at your mission, with great pain and sorrow. To be loved as your son." Capac nodded. "I am glad you chose to bring him home."

He lulled me to sleep that night with plans he thought through aloud. "Sandani's home is empty. I will have my people make it yours before you live there. These houses are only for the holy and royal. But Deborah Davies was very respected and you will be respected." He was always resolute about that. "I promise I will protect you as your father does, and I can do that well if your home is near."

"Right." I sighed, sleep arriving like a wave reaching the shore. I breathed a final, "Sorry," trusting my companion, his father's decades-old shelter, and our God to shield me and my child from the million dangers.

I cried the final morning as I brushed out my hair and attempted a sad French braid myself. Capac protested, asking me to brush out my hair.

"Why?" I asked as I complied.

"Remember? Women do not put braids in their hair. Only a husband can braid a woman's hair. This is law."

Convenient, I thought. I'd never braided my own hair and would never need to.

My heart suddenly got heavier, wondering who was going to braid my sister's hair. She would give birth without me. I was going to miss so much.

"I am sorry to take you from them." Capac, more perceptive than I thought people could be, lamented. "Your eyes tell me you long for your family."

"I am okay." I sniffled. "I can miss them *and* be wholeheartedly with your people. I can have both."

"Good." He hoisted the final bag onto his shoulder before saying with his whole heart, "Debbie, I can never thank you for what you have done for my people."

“I have done nothing yet.”

“God asked me to bring you here, and I trust Him. And I know you. I have faith that you will help me rescue them.”

TEN

We arrived near dusk, but I only saw jungle when Capac happily declared, "Almost home."

I could hear the roar of the river not too far away, and smell fires. But when I thought I'd encounter some horribly primitive people in war paint and savagery, we encountered something far different.

It looked like home. The structures, obviously generations old, were sound as if built by my father, and the children wore those same bright smiles when they greeted Capac, tackling him to the ground in laughter. It was the way he played with the children back home. Well, my old home.

What was different were the various looms of half-made lengths of fabric. Fish and root vegetables were cooking on open fires in the center of circled buildings. It was built for community and safety from the jungle but built *into* the various layers of the rainforest. Buildings were built into and around trees, and there was no clearing except at the mouth of a nearby cave. There were structures up in trees containing stores of food, and people were up twenty feet on ropes made of vines, passing things down to others.

Capac was only on the ground with the children for a moment. As adored as he was by children, he was equally as revered by the adults. Parents called their darlings away and Capac found his feet. We were there less than two minutes before I saw that he was truly set apart as king. The adults stood at a distance of at least six feet, a bubble forming around us as he moved further into the little village.

They were even out of range of his *matteh* should he choose to extend it. No one dared touch him, despite their smiles over his return. Many of them began hugging each other, however. They were clearly a people who touched, which deepened my understanding of how important it was that no one grazed him.

The women, as promised, wore full, sleeveless, knee-length robes wrapped around both shoulders and tied at the waist. The men were bare chested. Except, of course, for the four men who greeted Capac in robes with blue stripes along the hem like his red one. The holy men. Pharisees if I'd ever seen them. Shedders of innocent blood. All remaining children scattered when those men came near.

I was in the bubble with Capac, following him at about three feet, Roy in my arms. The holy men saw me and immediately began inquiring. They spoke the language about twice as fast as I'd ever heard it, and I could barely catch a word here and there. Capac, I learned, had always spoken slowly for me so that I could understand. That day, I learned how forbearing he had been with me when his words flew out faster than any others.

I held Roy closer. Capac's gestures and a few words here and there told me he was was explaining who Roy was. Finally, he called me to his side, still in that bubble, with all eyes and joys stayed on their king.

I felt naked. A hundred and fifty or so people were staring at me and my messy blond curls, scrub top and jeans. I didn't belong here. Why had I come?

Suddenly two women breached the bubble, and the people moved aside to let them through. They ran straight to Capac, forming a deeply felt group hug with tears. Capac sighed into that hug, and it occurred to me. How long since someone had touched him at all besides Roy? With my knowledge of the laws, I knew who these women must be.

I was overwhelmed and distracted when he first called my name, judging by the way they all giggled when he said it again.

"Debbie? Mena. My sister."

A woman perhaps older than Capac, came to me. They didn't shake hands in greeting—at least Mena didn't. She grabbed both my hands, squeezed them, then ran her lips along my forehead. She "kissed" Roy the same, strange way.

"Oh. . .Sandani. . ." she said, looking at Roy. I examined Mena's face. She did resemble both Sandani and Capac. High, prominent cheekbones and flawless skin. Mena's cheeks were fuller, though, and had a blush that didn't seem a temporary reaction. Her hair was a masterpiece of hundreds, maybe thousands of tiny braids about her head, relenting at her waist. One braid had a leather cord woven into it and was clearly the focal point.

Next I met Nur, the oldest sister. Taller, leaner, and with one streak of gray in her loose, bone-straight hair, Nur was strikingly beautiful, more than Mena or Sandani combined. More than any other woman there, in fact. I'd never seen such beauty except in models in catalogs and actresses in the few movies I'd seen. Her eyes exhibited that best, where beauty mingled with a brash sort of wisdom and grief and wit. They reminded me a little of Capac. But more, they reminded me of my adopted little sister Genesis.

There were no brothers to meet. That's why Capac was king. A patriarchy, I thought, except that it seemed that was just to keep the bloodlines straight. I remembered how Capac said women were deeply respected and considered to be sacred. The way they looked at Mena and Nur was nearly the same way they revered the king himself.

All these meetings happened quickly, and the sisters began chattering faster than I could comprehend and pawing at my freckles and frizz. I must have looked lost. Capac stopped them with a low grunt I'd heard him emit when Roy was misbehaving. Their response was as his; hands were at their sides, their mouths silenced at once.

"You must talk slower. She is very smart, and loves our words, but she is still learning. And her people do not touch so much. You are scaring her; be gentle." Capac turned to me as his sisters nodded, seemingly demonstrating the way he expected them to act.

"You will stay with Mena and help with children until I can prepare Sandani's house?"

"Yes." I nodded. "Where does Roy stay?"

"With me. King's house? Only the king and his family may enter," he was asking, not commanding as with his sisters.

"Um. . ." Roy had never slept without me.

"He is next to my house. It is close," Mena insisted.

"Okay. . ." I reluctantly agreed, hoping my three-year-old was as understanding.

"Royal child?" one of the holy men finally breached the bubble and asked.

"Holy," Capac confronted, not a coward at all. "A holy, precious child of God. And my sister's son. Raised as royalty with holy hands."

"This woman is holy?" one of them asked.

"Debbie is the fourth generation of John Davies—a man our laws have accepted as holy. Debbie's father is also a John Davies, and in their village he is holy man and king. A powerful man who rules with kindness," Capac implored.

There was some lightning-fast talking, and then Capac turned to me.

"They say that tomorrow they will discuss the terms of your acceptance among my people," he whispered, delighted. I sighed relief. They had not rejected or killed me yet, so I still had a chance to share the gospel.

They ate supper as a community, just like we did at home. Everyone looked to have contributed. Some had milked, others had gathered fruits, still others fished. Various cooks had brought it all together and prepared it for the meal, each with their own job. All contributions were valued and taken ownership of, but people did not live for the common goal. They would complete these community jobs and spend most of the day on recreation, building of their own homes, raising of children. I wasn't sure what kind of economic system it most closely echoed. It seemed like paradise if I didn't know the dark secrets.

Capac charged me with Roy as he ate far off with the holy men in some heated discussion. At some point Nur leaned over and whispered in my ear:

"Capac told us of your hair and skin and eyes, but he did not say you were *so* beautiful."

Lydia was the beautiful one. So honestly, no one had *ever* mentioned me being *any* level of beautiful. Even the concept of that was new to me, and it was practically nonsensical coming from Nur, the beauty.

When he was introduced after dinner, Mena's husband was almost familiar to me, but I did not have to seek long for the memory. Capac said, "Belen was gathering vines with us the day I injured my arm."

I knew the name Belen even better than his face. It was the only name they'd mentioned that day, and my parents said it often. *Belen and his people* was a common prayer request until we met Capac, their king. Belen chuckled at the memory, and I caught some of what he said. He was gathering vines for Mena to make clothes. He was wooing her at the time, though they would not marry until after her Opening and Closing. He was upset to give the vines away until he realized sheep were far better. Capac's father, the king at the time, had breached our camp for that very purpose. He liked Belen and wanted him to win Mena's heart so that she could make heirs, that's right. Mena is apparently now the most skilled maker of clothes, and the doting wife of the man who went to such great lengths to get her wool.

Capac sent me away to their home with them for the evening, but I watched him speak a command into Belen's face, "Belen, I have taken this young woman from the protection of her father, who is a man of the most high God. You will protect her with your life."

"Yes, my king."

After this, Capac took Belen's head and tapped his own forehead against it. He told the man he'd missed him, and the term he used to address him was a combination of *husband* and *brother*. It was clearly their term for brother-in-law, and that was their relationship. But it was closer. Deeper. Likely similar to why I did not usually call Jeremiah my brother-in-law. We grew up nearly as siblings, then he married my sister and solidified that he was a brother to me. I was closer to Jeremiah than I was to Andrew, and Daniel was too young to be much of a companion at the time. It occurred to me that husband-brother would be a clearer indication of that relationship. I liked that added intimacy.

As goes the language, so goes the culture. The two men were embracing far more deeply than my culture would allow for brothers of any kind. It made sense when Belen did not use that term husband-brother. He used "dearest friend."

When Mena sighed to hurry up the embrace, I realized this was a common progression of words. An argument of sorts. *King, husband-brother, dearest friend.* It also seemed common for Mena to end it the way she did, by whining out,

"Heartholder!" Which clearly trumped them all.

Capac grunted, lifting Roy to his hip. "Go. Let my sister distract you, Belen. The marriage path is thief of all hearts and reason!"

This, to tease his sister, who responded the way Lydia always does when Andrew teases her. But her squawking rant ended when Belen's hand met her shoulder. Belen smiled at his friend and put two young sons on one hip, to their laughter of delight.

"All my distractions are very beautiful, yes?" Belen then reached out and gently grasped a handful of Mena's braids, then brought them to his nose with sensuous eyes and a grunt of delight after the sniff.

Mena giggled, Nur bade us goodnight and walked to her own hut. Capac said,

"The most beautiful, Belen. Tend them well, and take care of Debbie."

"With my life, King."

Capac turned, walking away. "Husband-brother!"

"Dearest friend." Belen's laugh echoed, and I followed him and his family to the hut next to Capac's.

"Sleep well, little-teacher-outsider-friend." The last public words of the king in a place where his power was nearly absolute.

He disappeared behind the door of his hut, and my heart pounded as I entered the private dwelling of a royal daughter.

ELEVEN

After spending a night on a mat in a corner of Mena's house, sleeping soundly for sheer exhaustion, I spent the next morning trying to get acclimated. I learned to use a loom and spinning wheel, which had always interested me. Mena and I created a length of fabric that she deemed "too long but good practice." Too long for what, I did not understand. Nur visited for a time, and I enjoyed listening to the sisters' banter.

They rested in the heat of the day, just like at home. It was then that Capac approached his sister's house where I stayed, looking exhausted from a morning spent in a meeting at the temple cave. He greeted his weary nephews—Belen and Mena had no daughters—and had some small talk with his sister and husband-brother in the fast version of the language I didn't yet understand.

Then he looked to me at the spinning wheel and stated his business.

"Debbie, come."

I rose and walked alongside him, his *matteh* ever his companion.

"How are your feet?" he asked after a time.

"They hurt. Nur said she had a salve, but denied it to me."

"Your feet must learn. The salve will prevent the learning."

"Yes. She told me."

"Do you like my sisters? My people?" he asked.

"I love them, Capac." I smiled. "Just as you promised."

"Good. The holy men have decided terms but asked that I retrieve you before I hear them. They have promised that you will not be rejected or killed if you agree to them." He chuckled, half teasing, half relieved.

"I will do my best to honor whatever they ask, you know that."

"I know. You are courageous, Debbie." We continued to the temple.

There were four older holy men and six sons about Capac's age. That makes ten men that wore smug grins when we arrived just inside the temple. The cold stone beneath my feet defined the atmosphere well. One of the grinners had a dimple in his left cheek that reminded me of Roy, and also reminded me what we were up against. Evil. This man was clearly Roy's biological father.

Capac had been careful to follow every statute, despite his wish to change them. He was a Christian man among heathens, a light in the utter darkness, but he wanted to play by their rules where possible. The problem is, I was an anomaly. Never had an outsider been accepted into their people group. The only people among them who had seen anything but thick, straight, jet-black hair had met my great-grandparents at the mission. We both knew by those grins that they had twisted or invented some law to suit their purposes. We stood before them to learn what.

Their speech was deliberately too fast for me to understand, though I tried. They stopped at one point, laughing at me out of disrespect for Capac.

"They think you do not understand," Capac said in English, and they all began jeering him for using that language. He was the only man in the village who spoke it.

"They talk too fast," I managed. "I'll try harder, Capac. I want them to respect you."

I prayed for understanding. The Spirit gave me a word of warning, in no language but His. In the next beat, He supplied my need. I understood their decree plainly.

"We have decided that this outsider must make a choice," said the man who was likely Roy's father.

Choice was important in their culture. Spouses were chosen by each other for love. Work assignments were actually called "work choices," because they were chosen by the workers, though they usually passed them on for generations. Even punishments were selected from a few options. Free will was paramount, and there was complete freedom, except when there wasn't.

"What choice?" Capac asked the formality.

"If she wishes to be one of our people, she must be opened as our women are opened."

I was shocked, still horrified over learning of the Opening, but did not react.

"No! She is holy by our laws," Capac started.

"Yes, King. And she is an outsider by our laws. She cannot live among us as an outsider. This is also our law. To reconcile these, she cannot forsake the Opening, King."

"No holy daughter has ever taken part in an Opening. This is not our law."

Another spoke. "She will be opened according to our rituals. Or the fourth generation of John Davies will return to her people unharmed."

He nodded at the holy men, seemingly submitting to swine, then looked to me.

"Come, Debbie."

I followed him, and he held up a hand at my interrogations until we left the temple, crossed from the small clearing, walked through the common areas, then arrived in a secluded grove, where he stopped me so that we could speak face-to-face. We were alone, away from all ears, when the first part of his business included weeping.

"Capac?"

He put up a hand to silence me until he could compose himself. It only took a moment until he spoke again. In English, for enhanced privacy.

"I am sorry," he said. "The holy men are savages."

It was a word my father had once used to describe Capac. To hear him use it to describe any of his people astounded me. Finally, he looked up.

"What did you understand?"

"That to stay, I need to do the Opening ritual."

"Do you remember what this is?"

How could I have forgotten? I nodded.
"So you understand why you must return to your village?"
"What? No."
"That is the only choice, Debbie. I made you a promise. I did not remove you from the protection of your father to have you defiled by an evil holy man. This will never happen to you. You will return. I will send someone with you to protect you."

"No! Absolutely not. I will stay. I will do the ritual. And I will help you heal your people. They will never respect you if I do not." My voice rivaled the voices of the jungle, and I could feel the fire in my eyes that caused him to respond first with a step back, then with two steps forward. He challenged my space and risked touching me to make his point. His voice lowered to a growl, the intensity far more fervent than my yelling.

"You will *never*. Debbie, you are a woman of honor, and this broken part of my people is not yours to heal."

I kept my voice low and intense as well. "Capac, I love them. When I stepped into the jungle with you, I dedicated my life to serving them. I have served their children since *I* was a child. They are worth this to me, and I *will* do this."

"You will not," he gritted through teeth I knew to harbor no malice toward me.

"It is *not* your choice to make."

We were ten inches apart, stubborn black eyes staring into stubborn brown ones. Unyielding. The daylight was full and his every bead of sweat across his strong brow was clear to me, despite a hair that had fallen into my face.

Imagine, if you will, being that close to a "eureka" on an inventor's face when he makes his final breakthrough. Imagine the look on Peter's face when he stepped onto a raging sea and his foot balanced atop it. A leper's expression when he was suddenly healed. Impossible joy, that close, looks like a blend of terror and disbelief and the unfettered squeal of a child tossed in the air by his father.

His brow raised, and he stepped back six feet before he began full laughter.

I would assume my expression was no special anything except confusion. My friend and only steadiness in a crazy new place had lost his mind. He turned and walked. Pacing with joy. Then turned again and used his next words to prove how deeply unstable he'd become.

"They have decreed their own destruction."

"Um. . .how so?" Because it seemed they had decreed mine.

"Debbie, you are a holy daughter. By their own laws."

"Yes."

I assume it was my dumbfounded expression that made him realize he was now an inventor trying to explain this profoundly brilliant eureka to a child.

"Ah. . ." he began with a smile. "You want my people to respect me?"

"Yes. They fear the holy men too much."

He told it like a story. "Well, a man, to us, is the river. He is strong and wild and has hidden sickness in him. He can bring the jungle to life, but the dangers of the river are many. Alone, a man is dangerous. Even a king."

"Okay?"

"And a woman is fire. She has the strength to destroy all that a man has built. But she has the power to refine. And she is all that can warm the jungle night to sustain life and make it grow strong."

"Capac. . ."

"Alone, both are dangerous. No one respects what can bring death on its own. Together, they are *all* the strength of water. Because the fire heats and refines the river. Together, the dangers of the river and fire are *life*, just as a man and woman together can bring life from only passion after they marry."

I could not even form the correct question for why Capac was suddenly telling romantic fables of his people. I did, however, enjoy discovering that his people knew to sanitize water with heat. Being the furthest thing from a romantic, I nearly forgot what he was actually talking about.

"Marriage." Ah, yes. "Brings respect because a man and woman have contained their great power to use it for life. When a king is alone, he is seen as a dangerous force. Unrefined. But a king, when he has a woman. . .there is none who can disrespect this control and refining of his power. And because only a holy woman can refine a king, a queen is respected even more for the effort it takes." At this, he laughed once, which sounded self-deprecating.

I related this current conversation to a previous one, unsure why he'd bring it up with laughter in such a tense situation.

"But by 'refine' you mean control. Because you said a holy daughter is trained to sway the king's heart to continue the rituals. So, for you, marriage is not good."

I truly thought we were conversing. Just processing verbally. I was lost, confused, and taken off guard when he said, in a too-casual tone:

"*Most* holy daughters are taught these things. But not *you*, Debbie. You would *never* sway a man's heart to allow idolatry and murder."

"I'm not understanding." I was. But I let him continue.

"Debbie, you are a teacher, but first you are a powerful woman of God. Already a refined fire within yourself with His Holy Spirit. That is why I brought you here."

"So let me stay."

"I *will*." His voice lowered. Intensified. "And I can protect you. Perhaps even *better* than your father, which only God has made possible."

More verbal processing. Was he talking *to* me or just with me present? Still, I responded.

"You said that. You said because I would be close to your home, that—"

"Debbie. In. *In* my home," he corrected. "You will *not* be opened as a young woman is. If you trust me for this choice, you will be opened as a holy daughter is opened. And I can protect you."

"I thought a holy daughter was exempt, and that's why you thought they wouldn't make me. I thought she was unopened her whole life, which sounds just fine to me."

"But Debbie, one holy daughter in each generation is chosen by the king to be queen. Oh, Debbie. You could teach the people and earn their respect in a way that little-teacher-outsider-friend could not."

"I'm trying to follow."

"You would be *queen*. We have not had a queen in many years. The people revere the queen above even the holy men."

"Capac, I didn't come here to be *queen*. That's insane."

He laughed at that. "Debbie, I did not mean to ever *have* a queen. God refines us both, as we said. There will be no distraction. I will be a strong king, but respected. You will do as you came to do. Teach and love the people. But if you do these things from my house, I can protect you. Do you not see it is very wise?"

"I see it is very *crazy*." I laughed. "And dishonest. I cannot support that."

"Why crazy? And why dishonest?"

I rolled my eyes at what I first thought was annoyance. As when he would beg me to tell a story again or teach him for another hour. Capac would be exhausting. His brilliance and his energy.

"You think we can follow their decree and the laws without me having to do the Opening by you telling them that I am a holy daughter and you will marry me." I sighed. "But just days ago, you told me how fervently you wished to never get married. And I told you *I* was never getting married. So I will not lie for you. And I certainly will not live in your home under false pretenses to get around some law. You just said I am a woman of honor!"

His countenance sobered. Then he looked at me the way my father looks at me when his two decades more of life experience are about to trump my God-given wisdom with something profound and informative. My friend, who was certainly older, looked at me like I was a child, and said, gently,

"Debbie. You will wish to sit."

"I will stand," I insisted.

He crossed his arms with a sigh, then gritted his teeth at my stubbornness, giving no further warning before changing my life. "Debbie, this is not game or lie or pretense. Pretense will cost your life. You will not live in my home and *pretend* to be my wife and queen. You will need to *be* my wife and the queen."

"Oh. . ." I began, but he continued, again steeping into my space with intensity.

"And you escape *no* opening. Because of past queens who have lied, as I told you before, you will need to show evidence that you were opened by the king or you will be executed. A holy ritual completed by sunrise after a royal wedding. This act and the ceremony ties a queen *forever* to the king. This is true by our laws and by the laws of our God, Debbie. Marriage is no *plaything* to me."

Trying to process, but offended to be talked down to, I said, "Or to me. Marriage is not for you *or* for me and certainly not for *us*. I will not be *forced* to marry you because of some evil decree." I crossed my arms. "Did you know this could happen?"

"That I would be *forced* to braid your wildfire hair all my life? No. I did not know or wish it. It is a holy choice for the rest of your life and *my* life and a covenant with God. You are silly to think I would want this for you *or* for me." First, that offended me. Then, though unromantic, I gained all respect for my friend when he said, "But Debbie, all else is good. It will save your life. I can protect you. You will be in my home. In my care day and night. Under the protection of deep respect and deep laws. No one touches or speaks against the queen on pain of death. I can protect your honor."

At that, I began to pace in the small grove, trying to steady my breath, because we both knew "honor" would eventually be compromised.

"Debbie. . ." His tone became apologetic. He sighed, his head following me back and forth. "You are a woman of God in whom He has sown the seeds for a queen that can rescue my people. It will make an alliance between your people and mine. And I have prayed for a way to keep you from harm, Debbie. This is that way. There is much good."

I stopped my pacing and looked in his eyes again. "But at what cost for *us*, Capac?" I sniffled, trying to ward off a panic attack, which I'd never had to do in my life. "You just said we'll be tied together forever. By your laws and a covenant with God. That is a *great* cost when we both wished for celibacy."

"Are they worth this to you?" he whispered. "Worth the cost of being tied to me?"

"Of course," I whispered back, wondering if there was a length of wool that could tie the man down at all.

"And you trust me?"

I remembered what I told my father, and I think he did too. I wiped at a tear. "With my life."

He sighed. Relieved. "Then do not doubt. Choose this with me. God will do good things." This was his most intense request yet.

I sighed, close again to his eyes and sweat and desperation. "Do I have time to decide?"

His answer was quick. A bandaid ripped free. "We have weddings only at full moon. No other day will be within the laws."

"And when is the next—"

"Tonight," he said quickly, then worked to remind me, "Remember, I told you I needed to return by the full moon? We count all things by the moon. If you wait until the next full moon, it will be too late. The Opening is at New Moon. This chance for a marriage is only for this day. For this moment, Debbie. They will need your decision soon."

A transient idea of being married to someone called my parents to mind. The daytime cooperation and periodic bickering. The power, as Capac said, contained into what I had seen bring life to many and to the jungle itself. But the idea became less transient and far realer when he told me the timeline. At that, I crossed my arms and stepped back, as when someone walks in on someone changing. I was and had always been a private person, changing under my covers and showering at hours no one else was awake. Suddenly, I was going to have to bare all to a man who was and had always been my platonic, proper friend.

He sensed all that in my body language and his breath quavered. The nausea hit, but I was able to sit to combat it. Capac silenced so I could process.

Finally, I asked, "And the. . .the ritual?"

"To keep the bloodline pure, the king and queen must show blood and seed on a holy cloth by sunrise. The king presents this evidence to the holy men and they will decide if the queen is acceptable. Then the evidence is displayed as celebration for—"

First, I confirmed, "Seed?" He laughed once and I understood with an, "Oh! Gross! Displayed?!"

"It is tradition." He shrugged. "An honor for us."

I laughed then, trying to best him. "Well we kiss at the altar at weddings, so—"

"Oh!" He shuddered. "Gross. Very bad tradition. Will you need for me to—"

"No! I definitely don't need you to kiss me, Capac. Let's try to minimize the trauma?" I shuddered again.

"Yes, and—" He explained in his language, "There are ways I can honor you more. Let you be covered. I will do all I can." Then in English again, "Minimize trauma."

I laughed, trying to lighten things. "*Why* would they require this? Why would I need to be opened at all?"

That question hadn't occurred to him. Only the "what" and how to make it work. Considering the "why" caused him to think and sit with me, examining the smooth top of his *matteh*. A brilliant man, and a quick thinker, suddenly Capac's entire demeanor changed. His face resembled a triumphant smirk—a pure-hearted version of what the holy men displayed at the temple. Another eureka. At that point, he held out his staff to me and nodded. With a shrug, I took it. That caused astonishment to wait just behind that smirk.

"They fear you, Debbie. But they do not know you or your love for my people. They think you will shame me and run home this very moment. But they do not know that Little Deborah Davies fears nothing and no one but God. I believe that you are capable of far more than you think." I was trying to sort out exactly what he was saying. Not *what*, I suppose. But *why*. He seemed at odds with the staff being in my hand, and even glanced behind me once with an odd wave. I assumed he was seeing the way I'd exit.

"I do not plan to run, Capac. Why are you smiling?"

"Because they mean this for evil. They want to ridicule and disrespect me—distract me if they did see that I could choose you. But God means it all for good." He laughed once. I could see he was amazed by God's plan, but I never saw the big picture the way Capac always did. He led less than a thousand people, but his giftings could have made him effectively lead millions.

Yet he said the seeds of a queen were inside *me*. Seeds, not like evidence, but like those in our little orchard at the mission. Fruitful. I loved the way he used words sometimes. I admired words like math and science. For Capac they were art. He took the thing I analyzed and made it a thing of beauty in need of no analysis. Currently, my overwhelmed analysis turned to the way the woodgrain was barely visible on his *matteh* anymore from years of wear and dirt. Then my interests turned again, to Capac's laughter at my close examination of the *matteh*. He promptly explained,

"Do you know that I could have you executed for touching that?"

"What?!" I gasped, then handed it back with haste. "Capac, you must tell me these things! You never told me that, and I got it from outside for you years ago. When you were chained? You never told me."

"We were at your mission. My rule is not the law there." He shrugged. "But here, only royal hands can touch the *matteh*. The one who holds it rules the people."

"But—"

"But it is no mistake that you hold it without fear. God has shown me, Debbie. You were always meant to share it with me."

My silent tears quieted him for a time. Then he came near enough that our crossed knees nearly touched. He whispered:

"Debbie, I will be for you whatever it is you need. If you will be queen, you will have my deep respect. I will only touch you for this ritual and then never again unless we choose this later. If you will not be queen, I will do all I can to stop the Opening, though I cannot promise it. If you choose to leave, I will do all I can to teach the people."

"But Roy stays?"

"He is my heir. I proclaimed it today. This could only be undone by a son from my own seed." The evidence one again. This earned him a sickened groan, which earned me laughter, then an ever-so-gentle, "*If* a son should come from the one ritual."

He was already talking about children. Children came from private rituals, that's right. From even the suddenest, royalty-drivenest, life-or-deathest of intimacy. *Intimacy.* He'd never so much as brushed against my elbow. I felt dizzy, mostly because we both knew that marriage was not a ritual. It was a covenant. Though their laws may not, God would ask for more. He confirmed this fear by adding,

"If God wants marriage from us, He has sown seeds for many things that will need time to grow. For now? You would need to be prepared, so there is not very much time."

"Capac." I smiled. "Your people are worth this to me. Worth even marriage and all its rituals. And I know that you will protect me, and I will do all that will earn you respect. This choice has been made *for* us."

He nodded. "Then I will need to put a braid in your hair. The first braid is how we signify our choice to marry. Your hair is like wildfire. I have always wondered what it feels like."

I consented, not really understanding to what, and he scooted close, then reached up to touch my hair. He hesitated twice, withdrawing his hand. Finally after some silent self-encouragement, he gently lay his hand atop my head, his fingertips testing the texture of my hair before retreating to reposition himself. I knew there must have been deep gravity in that one gentle touch and tried not to consider that I was the first and last nonfamilial woman he'd ever touch.

In silence, he moved to my side and began braiding a little section at the top of my head where all would see. I pitied him to have to work with my frizzy, humidified curls. Wildfire, indeed. But his hands seemed not to care as he braided our unanticipated engagement into my hair.

Finally, and likely too late, I realized something. "I have touched other men."

"Debbie, you will need to have evidence of—"

"No not. . .not intimately. I have hugged my family and Jeremiah and Jackson. . ."

He sighed. "The proof of the pure royal line will be in your evidence, so do not worry over anything before today. After today, you must not touch other men besides your blood family and your husband."

I considered that, even mid-braid. Jackson gave such wonderful bear hugs, and Jeremiah was my husband-brother. With no guarantee that I would see them again, I allowed the concession with a nod.

I switched gears. "Is there anything special I need to wear or do for the wedding? I want to follow all customs. I know it is important that no one questions you."

"I will take you to my sisters and they will prepare you." He nodded to my scrub top and jeans. "Mena made you a dress. It is not a wedding dress, as I did not intend. . ." He trailed off with a little laugh of irony. "But I will put a royal garment on you and that will be enough. If that is sufficient for you."

"I don't have any idea what a wedding dress looks like to you, so whatever you have is sufficient." We both laughed at that, and he finished the braid, tying it off somehow with strands of my own hair.

"Not so bad," he said of my hair.

The next order of business, as Capac walked me back to the temple with my decision was this:

"As I speak, you must put your hand on the *matteh* with me. They will see that I have chosen you because of the touch, and they will know the extent of my trust."

When we got back, he planted the *matteh* in the ground, his hand atop it. He nodded, and I gently placed my hand on top of his, to the gasps of the holy men.

Immediately, he declared, "You have decreed that Debbie Davies, fourth generation of the holy man John Davies, must be opened to be one of our people. I, King Capac, have chosen Debbie Davies as my queen, and will submit to a *royal* Opening ritual this evening after our wedding."

At the urging of the Holy Spirit, I confirmed. They did not know I spoke the language, and so I let them hear it.

"I have chosen to marry the king and thus become one of your people, and their queen. As a holy daughter, will this ritual satisfy both the requirements of your laws *and* the unlawful requirement of your decree?"

Ten smug grins turned to dropped jaws. The men leaned in together and conferred a moment. Capac hummed laughter, proud of me, then placed his other hand on my hand. There, he squeezed encouragement and gratitude.

Roy's father spoke. "This royal Opening will satisfy our decree. Should this woman show evidence, she will be accepted as queen."

And there, my fears left me. He smiled. I smiled. And God confirmed to us both that even this sudden, insane thing we had to do was somehow going to be alright. We were in His will, which is the only place we ever need be.

TWELVE

Capac paraded me through the village, our hands on the *matteh*, and many reacted joyously to the braid in my hair. He dropped me off at Mena's house with simple instructions.

"Get Nur. Prepare Debbie for a wedding at sunset."

"A wedding?!" Mena reacted. "To who? To you?! You are never to marry!"

"I have chosen this holy daughter as queen, Mena. Do not argue." He claimed his authority. "Meet me here before dinner with my bride. Give her the dress you made."

"It is not a wedding dress!" Mena's eyes were wide.

"It will suffice," I told her. "Thank you, Mena."

"Mena, tell Nur," Capac quieted his voice and stepped closer to his sister. "The holy men have required an Opening, so prepare Debbie for ritual Opening. But the people will need to see a royal wedding."

"How can I do both?" Mena lamented.

"If someone can do this, you can do this," he complimented.

"I will try." Mena seemed to understand completely, however confused I was. She took to sounding like a mother and seemed frantic. "Go, brother! You give us not even one day to prepare her. Go to your kingly duties."

"Where is Belen?" Capac asked, backing away.

"He is in the garden and does not need your help. He took his path and we took ours. Let him be."

"Today, I am glad for his path, Mena." He nodded, and Mena seemed to soften. He said goodbye with, "Do as they say, Debbie. Trust them as you trust me." Then he was gone.

Mena banished her children and Roy from the house, leaving them in the capable hands of Belen, who was tending a sad garden of only greens. She called over to Nur's house with instructions to bring some water from the well. They took me into the room where I'd slept, divided only by a curtain from the main area as Nur put the water in the fireplace to boil. There, they began to remove my scrub top. I objected.

"We have a ritual to cleanse and prepare you for him. Water and herbs." Nur said it at half speed of her normal speech like I was stupid. I suppose I was. "You must undress. No man will see. You are still sacred."

As Nur explained, she tied back her hair with a strip of fabric. Neither woman seemed to question her brother's instructions, but I had questions.

"He said to prepare me for an Opening but that it must look like a wedding. Is there a difference?"

They looked to each other, then bickered at lightning speed for about thirty seconds before I understood a single word.

Mena finally slowed her speech and answered me. "A woman's only comfort when she must be opened is the dress for the Opening. It is short, and is not fully removed for the ritual. So he means for you to be covered. Our brother asks for this in respect for you because he must believe you are very sacred and honorable—"

Nur interrupted, her speech loud and bitter, "And because you are not his heartholder! On a wedding night it is all romance. The dress is long and for beauty. It is complicated so that it will take two people and the light to remove it. A woman is not covered with a heartholder. Capac wants *you* covered." Then her speech quickened and quieted for a few words, but I caught the familiar word "Capac."

"Love grows!" Mena insisted in response to whatever she'd just said.

"Our brother has no wish to love a wife. You are romantic, Mena." Nur, apparently their version of a feminist, shook her head.

Romantic didn't translate. Their term was more like "sappy" or "love-drunk" or even suggested a childlike stupidity regarding the ways of love, I would learn as time went on. It wasn't a compliment.

"Nur, you do not have a husband, so you do not get to say how love grows. Even as a child must *only* grow, so it is with love when it is sown," Mena said this with two outspread hands on a plump belly beneath her ample garment that had caused question before. But now it was clear, her point made. "You will not call me romantic soon. You will say I am right."

I considered then how hardened to emotion their holy men must be to perform these rituals year after year. It was under the cover of darkness and evil, but God saw all. I also balked at expectant Mena's understanding. Putting that braid in my hair had been downright painful for Capac. He did not want to be a husband. He was doing this for the people and to save my dignity. Honor, not romance.

Suddenly, Mena gasped and ran to a corner of her house where there was a haphazard pile of fabric. She returned, holding it up to me. She smiled at her sister who sighed.

"How much do you have?"

"Very much. I was teaching Debbie."

They were talking about the fabric. Probably, at least. Mena would spend all day creating fabric between caring for children. She showed me that she had to make quite a lot for it to wrap around a person and become a garment. This morning, she had added to yesterday's and said that this was far too long for a regular garment.

"To add to the other?" Nur asked, thinking.

"Yes. Long and beautiful for a queen bride." Mena shrugged.

His sisters gave me an embarrassing, fragrant sponge bath, my skin stretched and prickled into goosebumps, and burned in all the worst places, but I dare not tell them. The women bickered about this and that. It made me miss my sister for many reasons that day.

They rubbed my entire being in a dripping quantity of fragrant, tingling oil and lay a thin sheet over me as I sat in the area behind the curtain where I'd slept. They instructed me to keep my arms apart from my body and let the oil cleanse, and soften, and absorb.

There I sat in the awkward position on a mat, the breeze coming in through the high window in that wall.

They left me there in the quiet, and I listened to what else came in that window. I heard two men laughing.

"What of your vow?" This voice sounded like Belen.

"I cannot think of that now, Belen. I must do what is required." Capac. He was speaking with Belen in the garden.

Belen seemed angry. "We made a pact. I broke this pact for great *love*. A requirement is less than love."

"You are right. I know that I cannot now marry without your forgiveness." Capac sighed.

"My love for Mena was medicine after losing her child in the Closing. I broke my pact with you to be that medicine. You knew this, and still you ridiculed me."

"I was wrong," Capac boomed, then softened. "Belen, you know that I love your children and that I have accepted your marriage. My sister is cared for, and you have my gratitude. Forgive me, my husband-brother. And ridicule me if you must."

"I must." Belen laughed, suggesting that much of what they said was merely banter. The next statement was not. "She will distract you."

"She will teach. I will lead. Our marriage will not change that she came to be medicine for the people," Capac defended.

"You are a king, Capac. The best our people have ever known. But you are a man. You are a *river*. It is your nature. The same nature that will allow this Opening ritual will make her fire a distraction. You cannot have one truth but escape the other."

"I have asked that she be covered. Debbie and I have agreed this is only for the required ritual. Rivers and fires are for *love*, not ritual."

Belen laughed. "Capac, it is very clear you have never walked with a woman before." He laughed again, teasing.

"Of course not," Capac grumbled. "But this will not be a 'walk.' It will be ritual, which *you* have not done."

"My brother. My king." Belen sighed, and I heard what was likely a hand slapped onto a shoulder. "Debbie is your dear friend?"

"Yes." The exact translation of his next words was, "Very-very-dearest-dearest friend besides you." Capac declared as truth that which most would slide in as a mere compliment. Belen interrupted with,

"And she is beautiful, yes?"

Capac deflected with, "You have a wife, Belen."

"I do not see beauty in her with *my* eyes, Capac. I see it in *yours*," Belen whispered. "Each time you go to their village, you come back speaking of Debbie Davies with a bright morning in her hair and honey in her eyes. A man who speaks this way of a woman—"

"Be careful, Belen. I am still your king." That deep growl again.

"Cannot have a 'ritual' with her," Belen finished. "A good man who does this thing with a woman he cares for. . .it will never be ritual. And it will never be once."

"You are wrong. I have made her a promise."

"Unmake it." Belen then made a bold suggestion. No one spoke to the king this way. "You said one thing of this woman, but I see another. Perhaps you are distracted already. I pray that she will be what you hope."

"What do you mean?"

"You say she fears nothing but God. She is young, Capac. She is a fearful child. You will make this frail butterfly our queen?"

Capac's laughter began as a mumble and continued swelling until even Nur said from the other end of her house, "Why is our crazy brother laughing now?"

Finally, he managed, singing, "*The perfect butterfly with fire on its wings.*"

"*A beacon for the caterpillar's change,*" Belen finished the phrase, then sighed. "I see no fire in her. But I trust you always, my king."

"Thank you Belen. I pray you will see the fire soon."

The sisters retrieved me then and dressed me. First I was in their traditional garb that they all wore. Mena had made this garment specifically for me, and showed me how to put it on. Then, she wrapped that too-long length of fabric around my waist and tied and tucked and primped as a hairstylist might do. In the end, it was a long, flowing masterpiece resembling natural, bohemian dresses I'd seen in Lydia's catalogs.

"Very beautiful, Mena," The ever-abrasive Nur still knew to give credit where due.

"Yes. A queen bride's dress must not only 'suffice.' "

They sat me down by the fire in those two layers of clothing. I was finally warm, and it was good to be clean again. I hadn't showered in several days. But it wasn't good to be stared down by two women who resembled my husband-to-be without his beard.

Mena spoke again. "Love grows. Please do not worry. His heart is big. He hides it."

I nodded, smiling as I remembered the way he doted on Roy and all his other nephews and cried when he spoke of evil. "He does not hide it well."

"Debbie, *your* heart is big too. You are everything he always said you were. Kind and courageous with yellow hair," Mena confessed. "Nur did not believe him, and Belen does not believe him. I believe him. He was right all the time."

"Yes. Right all the time. And now he forces us to believe him about his Jesus. If Debbie is more than he says, Jesus must be too. Right all the time." Nur shook her head, grumbling, but smiling, as she disappeared behind a curtain.

Nur made me chew a bitter piece of bark that reminded me of aspirin for some reason, and had me spit it out only when the bitterness passed. Finally, Mena put a flower in my hair and an itchy floral bracelet on my wrist when it was time for supper. "You will love him your very best?"

They didn't have a mother anymore, so I knew that what Mena said was likely what a groom's mother would have said.

So, though I didn't love him, and thus wasn't sure how good my best was, I assured her, "My very best, Mena. I promise you."

Capac came to his sister's door to retrieve me for dinner. He stood with Belen, laughing about something I didn't catch, but his face changed dramatically when I stepped outside. It read fear to me, and I panicked.

"Capac, what is wrong?" I stepped closer to him, inside his confidence. But he stepped back as his face changed to a smile. He looked me over and his sisters teased him.

It occurred to me that I was not, in fact, a woman awkwardly prepped and fitted in foreign garb. What he saw was a bride on her wedding day. *His* bride.

"How does she look, brother?" Mena begged for a compliment.

"You have done well, Mena. She looks like one of us." Capac reached up and touched the braid in my hair, running a finger and thumb over it all the way past my shoulder, where my hair stopped. I couldn't read what he was thinking until he gave me the silly look he always gave me when teasing me. But he paired it with a whispered, "Except her hair is wild like fire."

I was sorry for that. I was sorry for so much that day.

"Brother, will you not tell her she is beautiful?" Mena, the wife of many winters, whined at the still-clinging-to-celibacy little brother.

Capac laughed once and looked into my eyes. "Do you need me to tell you that you are beautiful, Debbie? A woman who fears nothing already knows she is beautiful. A woman who is weak must have a man tell her."

"Brother! That is not true!" Mena protested.

But Capac had done far better than tell me I was beautiful, and he knew it.

Thirteen

After dinner, the ceremony was literally thirty seconds long. We stood before the people as Capac unbraided my hair, then re-braided it with a red cord tightly attached at my scalp and intertwined with the braid. As he did this, a holy man said a short blessing:

"He is the river. She is the fire. Together they are all the strength of water, and the gods are their peace."

That last part was blasphemy, of course. But as Capac braided, he whispered to me, "God. The One True Living God. He is our peace. Our marriage will have no gods before Him."

Up until that moment, I still kicked against the goads, unsettled over giving up *my* peace. *My* focus and *my* celibacy. I remembered Lydia not so many months before, curled up in the kitchen whining about "her" peace. Mom had laughed at the very idea, because personal peace is hard to come by when a woman chooses marriage. There is no "my." There is "our" peace. I knew that from being a mother. But even then, is that where peace is? In one's own body or another person's?

No. God was always my peace. He was my focus. No marriage, especially to a Christian man, was going to change that God alone provided all the peace I needed. When Capac smiled at me as he finished that braid, I smiled back. We were together in God's will. That would have to be enough peace.

The whole village cheered as Capac took an outer garment just like his and put it around my shoulders, declaring me his queen. It was softened by time, and I assumed it had been his mother's. This hadn't happened in a generation. One of the holy men handed Capac a white cloth, folded, woven with both blue and scarlet at the edges. Holy and royal. I knew it was for their proof. But to confirm, that man said,

"Blood and seed by sunrise or blood at sunrise. We will prepare the execution tree." The holy men looked smug, as Jackson when handing out a test to overconfident students he knows will fail it. This was a test. I had to pass it to save my life. Capac took the sheet under an arm, and my hand into his. He led me to his palace as the fear returned to my heart.

We walked in silence, our footsteps the only sound until we'd left their sight and the village conversation roared again. I heard Roy's voice.

"Ma!"

I turned with a start, but Capac squeezed my hand.

"He will be safe with Mena. I will return for him and he will sleep in our house." He smiled. "Your fear is too much."

"Capac, they are preparing the execution tree. What does that mean?"

"It means nothing." He was bitter, but still offered me a smile. "Except they do not know your strength."

We reached the door to his hut. He led me across one room, then into another room. Both were too dark to really know where I was. I think the second room had a door. Mena's hut didn't have doors.

"It is dark." I tried desperately for my eyes to adjust to the one candle he lit.

"Your eyes will learn." I heard a whoosh, and my eyes caught that white sheet spreading out on the ground on something. I blinked hard. It was a bed or a mat of some kind. As I adjusted to the dim, staring at the whiteness, suddenly Capac was at my side. I startled, putting a hand to my chest.

He looked at my hand with a smile. "Your heart is fast?"

"Yes," I whispered, trying to laugh it away.

This people had two words for "heart." The physical, beating one, and the one that can be held by another and protected. Maybe it did make me a little romantic, but I liked that, even having learned it from a blunder while he taught me the language three years before. I had told him that my mother had my father's physical heart, and he had laughed and gently corrected me.

"Is it fear?" he asked of my heartbeat as I was searching the darkness for where I knew his eyes to be. I could see the white of his garments and knew him to be my same height, so I looked straight ahead.

"Yes." I told the truth, but tried to keep focused. "You think I fear nothing. And I try to be brave, but sometimes I have fear."

He hummed endearingly and corrected me, "Your heart (physical) fears, but your heart (the love one) does not."

"Capac. . ."

"I have never seen you fear me. Why are you afraid?"

I corrected, "I do not fear *you*. I fear that they will not accept me and I will be killed."

"Debbie, only the ritual is required, and that is only with me. If you do not fear me—"

Some vulnerability crept into the room when I spoke aloud that I did not fear him. I did not attempt to stop my mouth, therefore, when it uttered my chief fear in a whisper, "Capac, it is a myth that all women bleed the first time they. . .the first time a man. . ." Still, the words were too vulnerable to say. Thankfully Capac understood.

He nodded first, then began a slow smile and moved his face even closer to mine. "We have medicine, Debbie. Nur spent much of the day preparing you. She made you chew the bark and bathe in herbs, yes?"

"Yes, but—"

"How are your feet?"

An odd question. But before answering, I wiggled my toes. Even odder than the question was the lack of desperate soreness in my feet. Capac read that in my eyes and hummed a laugh.

"The bark is for pain, but it also thins the blood. The bath of herbs and the oils soften the skin very much. Does your bracelet itch?"

"Yes."

Capac nodded, and removed said bracelet to ease the itching. "Then you will have evidence. Nur does this for all women who are to be opened, and the bracelet shows that preparation is complete. The holy men and king know to check the wrist for blush."

"Wait." I was confused. Offended. "So the evidence is just pretense?"

"This medicine does not work for a wife of many winters, Debbie. Only a woman whose body knows only peace." He breathed out slowly. "I never wished to steal away the peace of any woman, and certainly not yours, Debbie."

Because of the realization at our wedding, I whispered, "You will steal nothing, Capac. God is my peace."

Again, he hummed a laugh, perhaps realizing that on his own.

"Then there is nothing to fear. We should sit, Debbie." He removed his outer royal garment, then helped me out of mine like my father or any gentleman might do with a coat. I smiled at the irony of Dad having called him a savage once. He put the two garments on something nearby and I heard the light tap of him also stowing his *matteh* there. He returned to me then asked, "Can you sit in this dress? I want you to be covered, but I want you to sit in comfort."

"Oh, yes!" I began to untie the outer dress. "I am wearing two garments, as you requested. This one, I will need help with."

As he casually helped me unravel the beauty of my wedding gown, I asked, "If you are not holding the *matteh,* who is ruling the people? Couldn't someone break into this house and steal it and be ruler?"

"It is not the *matteh* that makes me king. It is the bloodline. But I can give someone charge of it sometimes if I cannot rule for a time. If a king is sick or must go away, he sometimes trusts the *matteh* to another. Anyone else who holds the *matteh* will be executed."

"But you always bring it with you to the mission."

"The only other person I could have trusted was also at the mission with me."

I smiled the flattery, then asked, "What about Belen?"

"What about him?" he asked, searching my eyes with his, which I could now see. He was like a teacher quizzing a student, yet again.

"I heard you talking to him today. No one else speaks to you the way that he does. There is something different about him," I mused as Capac wrapped that outer garment around his arms, then stowed it in something that looked to be a chest, at least in the dim light.

"Belen is a faithful friend, and very wise," he allowed, leading me to sit with him on the surface where he'd placed the sacred cloth. "He grows green food. His family has done so for many generations."

I nodded, but that was odd. Belen's garden was indeed filled with green food. It was something like kale, I think. But though it was part of the wedding feast, there was something off about it. It was wilted in a way that Jane would never allow in her garden. All other fruits and vegetables were plump and beautiful. Belen's greens were sad at best.

"He does not seem to. . .enjoy it."

Capac laughed. "Belen is a very bad gardener, is he not? He learned nothing from his father. I tell him he must tend it better, but he does not."

From what I had learned, Capac's people took pride in their work. They each had one job that they perfected throughout their lives, often for generations in a family. It was as the Levites in the wilderness, carrying one piece of the tabernacle so that all were perfectly cared for. How could a man be so negligent, when all he had to do was grow one vegetable all his life?

Capac nodded, finally getting to the punchline. "The growers of green food must stay among the houses of royalty, because that is where the green food is grown. Our families are buried beneath the next season's plot for growing."

"So Belen is actually tending graves?" I practically interrupted.

"No. Belen is tending the royal family, though most are not aware of this." Capac nodded to a small pot in the corner that had that same green food in it. "He is even permitted in this house. For the green food, of course." He smirked.

I gasped the understanding. "He is your guard."

"And the king's closest friend and adviser in every generation. But he must stay among the royal homes."

I gasped again and Capac laughed. He awaited some question, knowing well my insatiable curiosity.

"Does a royal daughter always marry a grower of green food?"

"Sometimes they are close relatives. . .you call them first cousins. But when they are not, there is often a union. It is not a law, but love grows where there is opportunity."

The knights married the princesses. *Lydia would love this.* Capac was still speaking.

"Belen wanted to rebel against the traditions because of what my father taught me. Because I made a vow to my father never to marry, Belen also made the same pact with me. We both wanted to destroy the rituals."

"But he fell in love with Mena," I finished the story.

"Yes. And my father encouraged it." Capac's people did not roll their eyes, but if they did, he would have then.

"And you believe that he is distracted by his wife and family." I recalled last night's conversation.

"Yes, his heart is for them."

"Is that not his job—to guard the royal family?"

Capac laughed, then livened the tone and volume of his voice. "Yes, and he is so good at his job that he continues to *grow* the royal family. Four royal sons so far."

And from somewhere near the front door, I heard, "Soon five." Then laughter from both men.

"Oh, yes. Soon five. Nur says daughter, but we do not believe her." Capac seemed to remember, and I remembered some of the reason for Mena's plumpness. When the two men concluded laughter, Capac called out, "My green food is well tonight, my dear friend. And you cannot be present for this ritual."

"Will Rune be near?" Belen said.

"Belen, I have a queen in my home now. I am well. Go see to my sisters."

The sigh was loud and reluctant, but Belen's voice mumbled, "Yes, my king," And the man went his way.

"Who is Rune?" I asked.

Capac hesitated. Fear? Confidentiality? I wasn't sure. Still, it was just a beat before he explained.

"We also have another guard, far humbler, far more loyal, and far more powerful. They call him the Tender of Footsteps. There is a family that is thought to be the lowest family. From this family comes the Tender of Footsteps with the uncleanest job. He follows after the king to conceal his footsteps so that no one can hunt the king. To do this well, he must cover his feet. That is why my people do not trust a man who covers his feet. This man is permitted to execute any who wish harm on me, even without my command. He is never far behind me wherever I go. Even to your mission. You did not notice?"

Capac thought so highly of me. My own family knew I could likely sit three feet from a jaguar and not notice its spots or its purring. I shook my head, embarrassed not to have noticed being followed when I was with Capac.

"He stays mostly hidden, do not worry that you did not see. Rune was at the grove when I put the braid in your hair. He drew his machete when you held my *matteh*. It is not permitted. I told you I could have you executed. Who did you think. . .?"

I gasped. "I thought it was hypothetical! I almost lost my life today?!"

"No. Rune quickly saw that you were accepting my proposal. He is the wisest man among us. Most discerning. Wiser even than the king."

"So he is your. . ." I had to switch languages, "accountability?"

"Ha! Yes." Capac noted a common term and explained that Tender of Footsteps means the same thing as accountability partner. Then said, "Otherwise, how would anyone know if I was to touch a woman or break other laws. My Tender always sees. When at your village, he is not my Tender and has no power there. He waits just inside the jungle."

I gasped. "That is why you refused to stay the night at our mission this past season?"

"He saw me get captured years ago and insisted that I stay with him in the jungle after dark, where he is permitted to protect me. He liked that he can see your tree from that place. He likes John Davies *very* much. Rune is the one who told me how well your father protects you. He calls him your Tender and says that I must work very hard to protect you the same."

"But we were alone with Roy when we traveled here," I tested.

"For a time, yes. Rune is a fast runner, and I sent him ahead to prepare the village for my arrival. He came back at night. You slept soundly," he seemed to tease.

"It was exhausting!" I reminded him in English. "It is odd I never knew this. I would assume you are close with him?"

Capac had trouble with that. "Belen is my dear friend, but will always agree in the end because he is under my command. Rune sees all, and tells me the truth even when it does not agree with my heart. I cannot call Rune my friend, because he has the power to execute even me. But he is very dear to me."

"If this man exists, he is very important. Not low at all. But terrifying." I got chills then, thinking that perhaps Capac was speaking of a guardian angel. This kind of tale was not uncommon. Apparently actual angels with swords protected my family and had since my great-grandparents arrived. Do not let that alarm you. Your filters are great. These people saw and experienced many things that a westernized Christian veils with modern medicine, technology, and many distractions.

Capac agreed that his Tender was terrifying. "Yes." Then he laughed. " 'If' he exists?" Capac kept his eyes on me, but turned his head a little, shouting to the wall, "Rune. Go and feast? My feet are covered now."

"King, my father says I must tend your footsteps for this ritual. Even blood and seed can deceive." It was a young man's voice.

Capac gave me a look as if to say, "*See?*" Then he argued with Rune through the wall. "*My* father told me *your* father waited near my Grower's house to give the queen privacy. You know that I honor my God and would not deceive you."

"Yes, my king." I heard his footsteps take him away.

"Is there ever *real* privacy?" I whispered in English.

"Sometimes. But know that Rune will sometimes see what is private for your people. And know that he also understands English." Capac laughed. Apologetic. Nervous for me. "Your heart will learn."

I nodded. I didn't like that at all.

"They know we are safe in the stronghold of our home, so we can have privacy here." He sighed. "It was a long day and I am happy to be at peace now with only you, Debbie. And God, of course."

Capac loved people, but they drained him of all he had. He needed time alone with God to recharge and give them more. Oddly, he never counted me as a person who drained him. We could sit contently under my tree for hours as Roy slept, reading separately or chit-chatting. Time together, apparently monitored by Rune, recharged us both.

I suppose Capac was always a part of my peace.

Fourteen

Our wedding night became my tree. We spent about half an hour cross-legged, knees nearly touching. We were chatting about rituals and romance as though we were seeing it all from a bird's perspective—commentators, not partakers, in the drama.

"Mena says that children are as flowers. There are never enough, and never too many. When I brought the older children to you, it was very much work to let my sister keep hers. Her whole life is to be a mother."

"And Belen is a good father," I noted, remembering both stern corrections and silly moments with any child near him. Roy already loved his uncle Belen dearly.

"When Mena gave up her child for the Closing, Belen said he wanted to give Mena a flower garden of children for her sick heart," Capac said through laughter.

My heart moved. "That's beautiful, Capac." Capac laughed. "You do not think that is romantic?"

"I *do* think that is romantic. Very silly." That was when I learned the connotation. "He wanted to walk with her."

I gasped. "That can't be true."

"It is true of all men, Debbie. Belen and the holy men and all. Men have little romance and must be *taught* to show affection by braiding hair. Otherwise he will neglect a wife's heart and care only for his pleasure," he declared. It seemed to disgust him, who had the perspective of celibacy, likely for decades. "Men are more like hunters than lovers. Surely your father told you this?"

"Perhaps." I'd been warned that some men were less honest than others and might be after only the physical things. Unfortunately, I'd been gifted with examples of honest men all my life. Even Jeremiah had treated my sister honorably as they navigated their error. I wanted to know how Capac could say that none of them ever acted with honor. "But tell me your heart."

"A man sees his prize and wants her with his eyes. Then he hunts her like an animal again and again. I have seen it happen many, many times. Belen will protect my sister all his life. And he will also keep hunting her and giving me nephews."

"And braiding her hair." I was not yet convinced.

"Of course. A husband learns to enjoy both. He does love her and want her heart. But it must be *learned*. His nature is to hunt."

Men like conquest. I accepted that. "And what are women like?"

"The animal. The hunted."

"Capac!"

"It is so!" he defended. "She cannot decide if she wants to run away or if she likes the way the hunter admires her beauty and strength. She likes to be hunted and she likes to make her husband believe he has hunted with skill. A wife sees affection in being hunted *and* in the braiding."

"Have you hunted? Animals, I mean. I notice your people only eat fresh fish or older sheep as meat."

"We hunt when an animal is a danger to us." He reached to the side and showed me a jaguar and sheepskin patchwork blanket. The underside was soft leather and sheepskin and the top boasted rough bits of wool alternating with gorgeous spotted fur I'd learned to fear.

"I see. You hunted that one?"

"I did." He laughed at himself. "I cried. She had cubs. But she had been killing our sheep for sport, so I had to kill her."

"Did you kill the cubs too?"

He shook his head with fervor. His heart was too big for that, of course. "We found another one and put the cubs with her. She took them in. The shepherds made this for me as a gift from both the sheep killed for sport and the jaguar. It is very warm and big enough to share. You will like it, I think."

"The hunter and the hunted, stitched together forever." I laughed, not realizing what I had said. But when we both related it, it caused a shift, a swift drop to Earth from the bird's eye, and invited the gravity into a bedroom we had just promised to share for the rest of our lives.

"It is not that for us. For this ritual. I want to respect you as much as I can, and we will not speak of it after this night. If you do not wish it, we will never do it again."

I nodded and looked down, nervous that we ever had to speak of *it* or cause *it* to occur. I moved my hair over my shoulder, careful not to disturb the one corded braid. Waiting for events to progress themselves, because I did not know how to propel them. But though he claimed otherwise, he proved that this was his to propel. He was the hunter, and he whispered,

"My heart is sick. I want the ritual behind us, Debbie. Will you trust me now for this?"

My heart began to be nearly audible again, but I nodded. "Yes."

"Close your eyes."

I did not comply at first. I stared, unflinching, into *his* eyes. He sighed through a smile. "Will you not let me protect even your eyes?"

I closed my eyes and realized he was standing. Very likely getting undressed enough for the utter awkwardness that was about to ensue.

His voice came close again and he whispered some request for me to lie on my back, which I did. From his warm breath, I knew he was lying next to me, likely with his head propped on his fist as I'd seen him do.

I was shaking, eyes still closed, when he whispered a low rumble beside my ear, "Will your father distrust me even more for this or is he a man who forgives?"

"Yes," I whispered, and Capac understood with a little hummed laugh at my ear. I opened my eyes, because he seemed too quiet.

He was shifting his weight so that he was over me, but not really touching me. He was on his hands and knees with me beneath him. In a quick glance, I realized he was still somewhat decent, and there wasn't much to shield my eyes from except maybe his hip where the smaller wrapped garment joined.

"Talk to me. Tell me about a wedding for your people." This was a distraction, of course, from what he was about to do. But I respected the need and complied, beginning with,

"Oh. A bride wears white. Her father takes her down the aisle and gives her away to her husband-to-be. . ."

I lay with my arms bent up as I told it like a story, a surrender gesture had I been standing, with my legs relaxed. All of me was relaxed, in fact. It was likely more ignorance than trust, but Capac glanced into my eyes before gently shifting his weight again. This time, he placed flexed feet between my relaxed ankles, his arms fully extended in a push-up position.

As he lowered the push-up and I rambled about wedding traditions, my mind went elsewhere, to the many years that Jeremiah and my brothers had used physical fitness to fill their boredom. Dad and Jackson would stand by correcting their form as they would have contests to see who could do the most pushups. The muscular Jeremiah always won, and I can't believe how many years I didn't realize Lydia was standing by not to tease our brothers, but to watch Jeremiah's muscles.

I realized it after the wedding when she made some whistled comment about his strength and he proceeded to stand and flex dramatically and go after her for a kiss or two with Dad protesting and Jackson and I rolling our eyes at the carnality of it all. A man doing pushups never did much for me. And this man, dipping still, taking a million years, I think, was having the opposite effect of sensual attraction, despite my general fondness for him. My heart started racing just before I knew I would feel his weight against me and knew what he would ask and do and cause. At that moment, I watched Capac as I prayed a prayer for God to give me peace and settle my heart to trust my friend. I stopped talking.

But just before his muscles would have relaxed at their destination for him to begin the ritual, my breath trembled before I held it in, my eyes snapped shut again, and my head turned just slightly. He was the closest he'd ever been to me. Close enough to feel and smell and nearly taste my fear.

And so that dip of that push-up never occurred. As my brothers after those contests, his arms shifted motives, and he lay again at my side, then tapped my hip. I'd obviously never felt it, but my body understood the nonverbal cue that I was to lay on my side to face him. He let out a frustrated sigh as we both propped our heads. As I expected, he mumbled something about him being a coward, and I mumbled a protest. Then he growled out:

"The Opening is meant to be a holy ritual, but the women are never the same near the holy man who opened them. It is defilement. Their hearts fear these men forever." The sorrowful little rant ended with a few deep breaths as I processed and he calmed. Then, in his usual gentle tone, he said, "Debbie. My dear friend. I could not bear for you to look at me with fear all your life because of this ritual. Belen was right. *I* am right."

"Right about what?" I asked in a whisper.

"*Every* man is a hunter."

"You woke up this morning a celibate," I teased. "How can you apply that to yourself?"

"I am a man, Debbie. A husband now." Seemingly without thinking, he reached out and ran his hand along my hair, then let his hand land gently on my hip with his sigh. His whole life, he avoided touching women. But in half a day of innocent touches, it had become a comfort for him. To remove a crumb from my chin at dinner. To grab my hand as we traveled from one place to another. Not a forced show of affection. A comfort for him to be permitted to touch a dear friend. That dawned on me as he was touching me in such an affectionate way outside the eyes of all.

"What does that mean?"

I watched him consider his words, and as he did, he moved his hand up and down at my waist the way he might do with sleepy Roy's back before putting him down for a nap. He began looking me over. Hair, face, neck. As his hand examined the same, I likely had questions in my eyes. I am unsure if he knew he was speaking when he answered those questions with,

"I know that you do not need to know that you are beautiful. But I am glad my queen is beautiful." He examined my eyes, hoping he had not offended or mortified me. Then he gave a self-deprecating laugh when he saw that I was unoffended.

A woman need not be in love or in the company of any particular person to be flattered when told she is beautiful. It is a reflex to relish it, likely part of our curse in Eden or the way to our fall. I was a deer, too admired to run, whether or not he was aware he was hunting.

I teased him. "A bright morning in my hair, and honey in my eyes?"

He laughed. "You heard."

"No one has ever called me beautiful until I got here. It is likely just because I am different." I rolled my eyes.

"No, it is because you are beautiful." He hummed laughter. "Even if your skin is almost the color of your garment. White like wool." He moved his free hand again and began running his fingertips along my upper arm. His touch relieved something in me; a balm I'd been long denied. I couldn't help but sigh.

He scooted in closer, using my waist as leverage to meet him halfway. He was right up against me. I breathed in a quick breath, gasping through my nose but trying not to let on.

"Shh. . .you are my wife," he whispered, "you are safe with me, Debbie."

But was I? I begged God to steady my heart.

He continued his soothing touch. Fingertips on upper arms, with the occasional reassuring squeeze. Though it was clearly awakening something, it became deliberately intimate when he whispered, "Do you like when I touch you?"

"Yes. Feels nice." I cleared my throat of the nervous rasp, humming a new sigh at the wonder of his hands on my too-sensitive skin.

"You know that I am hunting you?" It could have stirred us out of the peace. The comfort. But for some reason, likely because I knew it might continue, that question only deepened the relief.

"Yes. I know, " I admitted quietly. "But I know your heart is to protect me."

He laughed. Too loud, which I liked about him, then he said at nearly a normal volume, "Do not be romantic. My heart protects. My flesh hunts."

That vulnerability completely disarmed me. We knew the reluctant mission and the strategy, and yet his touch was peace. To give him the same peace and soothe any remaining honorable fears, I reached up and ran my thumb along his cheeks. His beard was coarser, and his skin far softer than I'd predicted.

He said, "Debbie. . ."

"Yes?" I whispered.

"Feels nice," he said, laughing the same way again. I knew he was undone and truly hunting when he moved my hand to his course chest hair and whispered, "here." And so I touched him there, barely able to fit my arm between us. His whole demeanor softened with another sigh and a much more intimate, "Oh, Debbie. I cannot decide if this is medicine or poison."

We found ourselves in a confusing place as we both laughed. Until that moment, we assumed we were headed for something akin to an invasive medical procedure that would save my life. However consensual and covenanted, it was to be just one awkward act that we'd sweep under the rug. So I think it startled us both when that first bit of closeness released all the right chemicals and hormones. We were suddenly a newlywed couple in candlelight, nervous, but not scared. Capac met my eyes with a smirk, and valiantly allowed the unspoken change in plans.

He grimaced. "Do you need for me to kiss you?"

I snorted a giggle at the inside joke. "No."

Before he'd reminded me, my cultural instinct had indeed told me that Capac might kiss me in a moment like this. But I then realized that it would be beyond his last instinct to do so. It would have been as disgusting to him as blood and seed evidence is to you.

We were silent for a precious few moments, considering everything. I liked to watch Capac think. I wondered if I'd ever thought deeply at all when he'd look away and ponder, raising up his strong, hairy arm to smooth back his hair. I would always surprise me when he regained focus back where I was and captured my eyes yet again.

And that night I wondered for the first time if maybe he was focusing all that depth on only thoughts of me. I wasn't worthy of that. But when it happened then, my heart started racing.

He smirked. I still wonder what all that looked like in my eyes. But I knew from his direct words that he was able to read them with accuracy. All I was thinking was that he was right. I didn't need to be beautiful. I just needed *him*.

"Walk with me?" he whispered. There is no such delicate phraseology in English that would make a proposition like that anything but jarring, even if welcome. In our language, it was different. So different, in fact, that it was clear what he was asking. An Opening was not the same as a walk anymore than an emergency appendectomy was the same as a therapeutic massage. He wasn't asking my permission to begin a ritual or make a covenant. He already had that permission. He was asking if we could forget all that and just take the obvious next steps in making each other feel good. Make love, despite the lack of the prerequisites. It seems unchaste now to think that my friend, never connected to any sensual thought until that moment, was asking for such a thing.

But unchaste as it was, I nodded. "With great joy."

We seemed to exist in a bubble then, like in the snow. In our bubble, there were no life-or-death rituals or threats. My father wasn't finding new reasons to hate Capac. There was just his gentleness and valor, like rescuing newborn babes against all tradition and reason.

He moved his head to my shoulder and took in the scent of my neck. I felt all his tension wash away. That one whiff transformed him. He brought his face close to mine again, taking in the scent of my skin. He smelled my hair and ears and neck, which he seemed to enjoy immensely, like it was intoxicating him. When he exhaled a tremored breath through an open mouth at my cheek, I caught his scent, and I was drunk too. I began to indulge in the same behavior, despite having never seen or heard of it. His scent and whatever else was happening raised my heart rate and awakened my whole being. I fought for the scientific explanation around the time those fingertips and that hand starting exploring and pulling me in. Suddenly he was the only human that needed to exist, and there was nothing he could do that I would not have allowed.

After only a few minutes of that, our obstacles were no longer a platonic friendship or an age gap or culture or anger over a required ritual. They were white wool, wrapped and tied far too many times around us. I was meant to be mostly covered out of respect. But suddenly our desires and pursuits demanded otherwise. Once we were freed from every length of fabric, the rest lasted only a few moments.

For a moment, there was only that yearning that the whole of history foolishly understates as "pleasure." I had never known a higher high from even the Epistles or a child's laughter. I was an enemy of purity and beauty, and I didn't even care that this was just an alliance or whether I had braids in my hair, or whether the sky was still intact. I think there was probably immense pain, there must have been, but I didn't care about that either. This man was giving me all I ever cared about, and I wanted to sustain those moments forever.

But the second it ended, the low was the lowest I'd known. It was lower than watching an attractive young man who had looked my way see Roy and look away. It was lower than my tears over all the babies these people had sacrificed. Lower than Job. Lower than Hades. And though I think Capac was trying to come back to himself and speak comfort to me, that low hit my gut. I pushed him off me, scrambled away from him, and heard his instruction just in time.

"The red one!"

I vomited my wedding feast into an earthen vessel apparently meant for such purposes. In a total of about five minutes, I had experienced the entire spectrum. I had seen the appeal and ease of lust. I had given in. I had rejected God if needed. And I had felt the hopeless shame of guilt. Capac, who apparently went through the same gambit, verbalized this.

"God, what have I done? Forgive me. Debbie, forgive me."

I was trembling from head to toe with spent adrenaline and the chill of the night. I shivered there only a moment before a seemingly disembodied remorseful sigh brought over a luxurious blanket made of lamb's wool and jaguar skin that covered all the nakedness that he had never intended to uncover. I looked up to see that Capac was dressing. He looked bewildered and stunned, expressionless as he gave simple instructions for which vessels contained purified water for drinking and washing, etc.

Then he had to escape. I didn't blame him. "I will take the holy men their evidence and return with Roy."

"Okay," I finally managed.

I knew he was outside when I heard Rune inquire in a low voice, "Debbie is sick? I heard—"

"Overwhelmed," my emotionally intelligent husband answered.

"And you, King? Are you well?"

"Very well. And very unwell. . ." Their low voices quieted, as did their footsteps.

To protect Capac's heart, I waited until the voices and footsteps were completely inaudible before I crumbled into tears. Though I washed, I longed for a bathhouse. A river, even. But I knew it wouldn't suffice. The wound was in my heart, and not the one that was picking up its pace again. I felt completely alone and out of place, especially when the village roared wild shouts of applause outside.

"Abba." I whispered between sobs, trying to stave off nausea. "Please keep me within Your will and give Capac's heart peace."

But there was no peace. Not anywhere. I had lost my focus. Everything. Sold it all for a few moments of pleasure. I finally understood Lydia, but not really. What sane, peace-seeking person chooses *this*?

To my relief, Capac was gone about an hour, likely falling victim to the scrutiny of the holy men and the scolding of his sisters. It was long enough for me to finish my healing tears and pull myself back together. Darkness had fallen outside, and the cold had set in. I decided to take the candle into the front room where we entered the house to look for the fireplace. I spotted another candle on a little platform and lit it. I saw a torch of some kind and took a chance, lighting it with a candle then using it to look at the rest of the room. Above my head, there was a wick with a burned end. Taking another chance, I touched the fire to it.

The wick burned only a moment before a whooshing sound caused a chandelier of some kind to illuminate and begin to warm the room. What I saw surprised me. I had lived a life of simplicity and so did his people. Here, there were silk pillows in every color. Fine blankets of fur and even some stone trinkets here and there. That was just the main room. It appeared that Roy had his own room off the main area, and it probably easily housed Capac and all three of his sisters as they grew up. The walls were wood and stone and a mud or pitch substance. The room I had just come from was fully enclosed—the private bed chamber of a king. The house was small, of course, if you're thinking of American standards. But it was far bigger than the house I grew up in on the mission campus.

I stepped back into the bedroom and found another wick. A similar, but smaller circular chandelier above my head illuminated the luxurious repetition of furs and pillows. Without knowing, and having simply obeyed God and trusted a friend, I'd just joined my life to the wealthiest man within likely hundreds of miles. "King" had been something I thought of only as a tribal leader. But I'd never seen such luxury or considered it to be that remarkable a title. Yet when I lifted a silver vessel as a mirror to be sure my tears were not visible, I wondered how he even acquired something silver this deep in the jungle.

When I discovered the small table full of jewelry, my heart stirred further. I examined the pieces, which reminded me of a catalog that was on my grandmother's table one summer we spent in Wyoming before Genesis had arrived. I couldn't believe that something that was simply pretty could have so many numbers in its price. But these jewels in my new bed chamber were elaborate pieces with weight and genuine gemstones that caught the light and scattered it clear. Rubies, diamonds, emeralds. They had age, but not tarnish. They were real. Vintage. I was having trouble putting a number on them given the size, the quality, and the age. And I'd looked at that catalog ten years before. These jewels were priceless. But I was confused.

I'd seen Capac in a white garment. In scrubs. In chains. In nothing at all. But never in jewels. Since no one but the royal family could enter here, the others likely didn't even know these jewels to exist, and he didn't flaunt them. My heart was doing something. My mouth, too.

"My word," I said in English.

"Ma's word." It was Roy's voice repeating me, having heard that expression a lot throughout his life.

Capac entered his bedroom in a smile, setting Roy on the ground to find some stone figurines he must have known to be his toys.

"You found the torches. Good. When I read about putting the light on the lampstand, I thought of these. This is what I wanted you to be for my people."

"Hmm," was all I managed in reply.

"An image of the perfect butterfly with fire on its wings." He smirked, hoping we had some memory we could crawl inside together like we had his bed.

But things were awkward, evidenced from my halfhearted giggle and my avoidance of his eyes. We both knew that. Still, he made the mistake of reaching out to me to touch my arm as he'd done to soothe my nerves an hour before.

Subtly, just barely perceptibly, my instinct caused me to draw back from that touch. I wasn't ready for him to touch me again. Not yet, and maybe not ever. But I hated the way he discovered that.

"Sorry," he said, but from his deep wince I knew I'd hurt him.

"Sorry," I replied, adding to the awkwardness.

He chuckled, which comforted me at least a little. "I will build a fire. Roy, bring your toys. Let's wait for Ma by the fire."

When I entered the front room again, it was already warm. Capac sat by the fire, and Roy sat in his lap playing with those stone toys.

"You have been confirmed as my queen and one of our people. The holy men had no dispute." He barely glanced up at me.

"None at all?"

"Should they?" Capac smirked to himself.

Hot embarrassment overtook my face at the very recent memory, but I redirected the conversation. "Were they frustrated that I get to live?"

Capac tried to conceal his smile for the sake of godliness. "Yes. And now they can never disrespect you without risking their *own* lives."

I smiled at his morbid pleasure.

"Come sit. I will not touch you," Capac offered, raising a hand in surrender, but seeing that I had softened. I complied with silence. "Did you like the jewelry? It belonged to my mother."

"Where did it come from?"

"Many, many generations ago. . . .a. . .um. . .a bird. In the sky. With people inside? Crashed to the ground."

"A plane crash?"

"Plane?"

"They make those trails in the sky. They carry people and cargo long distances."

"Yes. Plane. All inside were dead. The people buried them. The wood boxes inside contained these pillows and jewels and bright vessels. No one came for them for many months. The plane is still there. The people who found it gave these things to their king as gifts. The king gifts them to the queen as he chooses in each generation."

"That was a valuable gift. The size of some of those rubies. . ."

"Rubies. The Bible talks of rubies."

"Yes, the red ones. They are very valuable gemstones. Even in Bible times."

"For generations, the queen has decorated herself with these things. All I have is yours now. You may wear what you like. I do not need to gift them. That is only romance."

"That's a generous offer, Capac, but some of those jewels could fund my parents' mission for a year. I'm not just going to *wear* something like that."

"I thought you would say that." He chuckled. "Still, anything you ask is yours."

He didn't sound like himself. He sounded like a satisfied hunter, and I wondered if my friend Capac had a path back to me, despite my opening.

I was curious about a pressing matter, embarrassed to ask. "The vessels with water. No one is allowed inside, so how do we—"

"We place them outside in the morning," Capac explained. "Nur takes them away and our Taster brings new water. She tastes it before the Tender in the morning to show it is pure and safe. And she must often be as near to us as our Tender to serve us."

"Taster?"

"Yes. She boils our water and brings any food or medicine we cannot leave for. Jada is very wise. You will like her very much and she would give her life for the king and his family. Rune thinks *most* highly of her. He has put a braid in her hair for next winter."

"Love grows where there is opportunity," I mumbled. "I may have *all* I ask?"

"All."

I reached for the Book he'd set in a safe area of the house. "I would like to read."

He nodded, and Roy jumped up from Capac's lap and joined me on mine. He loved to read books, especially the Bible.

"Battle!" he requested.

"Okay. Joshua and Jericho?" I asked him.

"Jericho!"

As I read, Capac slipped me little glances I couldn't quite identify. Roy was oblivious to all of it, and I didn't mind. I was glad for the comfort of normalcy. Just me, my son, and my dear friend reading together, even if we were miles from my tree.

Fifteen

I awakened to a pleasant sensation. Capac was sitting next to me, playing with my hair. At some point, Roy must have come in and curled up next to me. He was asleep there as he was accustomed.

"There you are, my queen. Bright morning." I have always thought this an odd greeting; we live under a canopy, and unless one travels down to the river to see the sun shining like fire against the river, no morning is bright. Nevertheless, I would find myself speaking that hopeful, impossible saying thousands upon thousands of mornings.

"That feels nice, Capac. What are you doing?"

He smiled. "I am loving you."

"You do not love me." I snickered, trying to rise.

"I mean affection. Showing affection," he explained the difference in English, then switched back, as he often did. "It is easier when you stay still."

"What is easier?"

"Braiding your hair," he reminded me.

"Oh. That's right."

"It is my honor and privilege as your husband." He explained again the tradition. "It is important that the people see my affection. Is it okay that I am touching you? I had hoped you would remain asleep. I know you are not sure of my touch."

I was not unsure of his touch. I had experienced nothing more magnificent and life-changing than his touch. But last night we'd said it would only happen the once, so I certainly didn't mention loving it.

"It is okay." I wanted to be sure not to commit a cultural faux pas. "I want to give you every possible honor, Capac."

"Your affection for me already hangs at the temple. That is an honor for us."

He meant the sheet with the evidence that I hoped to avoid passing by.

"That does not seem like honor or affection. What else can I do?"

"In time, if God has allowed," he said, a smile in his voice, "it will grow in your womb and show on the face of a child."

"Oh. Yes. I remember." I tried not to be embarrassed. I tried to keep the mood a million pounds lighter than it had managed the previous night. "Is my hair difficult? Hopefully a child will not have my hair. I know you hate it."

"It is okay." He sighed twice, so I knew he was hesitating to say something. I gave him patience. Then he said, "Debbie, I do not hate your hair."

"You told me it is like a wildfire."

"*You* are a wildfire. You are just like your hair. I never want you to change your heart *or* your hair," he insisted, which I hope had nothing to do with what I was trying to forget.

"So, a person can look at a woman and see affection. But how can someone look at a man and know anything about him?"

"They have to look at his wife and children. This is why unmarried men are not as respected. As the Bible may describe, his family is his fruit."

"I will do my best to be that for you, Capac," I promised.

He tied off a final braid and I reached up to feel my hair. Despite my frizz and curls, he'd managed to put neat little braids across about a quarter of my head. I wondered if that would look odd, but as I sat up, he smiled, answering the question in my eyes.

"You look like a new wife."

Marriage in his world was constantly under pressure to be nurtured. A man had to always prove his love. The perfect words and lavish gifts were of little value here. Affection had to be shown with braids in a wife's hair, which proved time spent together without household duty or other physical distraction. A woman had the same obligation, if she viewed it as such. A woman loves to be pampered, and a man loves intimate pleasure. Maybe there was some variation, and every man needed to be attuned to his own wife, and a wife her husband. But their honor directly depended on the other's faithfulness, which had to be delivered in a tangible, service-filled form. Maybe somewhere the system could break, and certainly much of the culture was broken.

But their people didn't even have a word for divorce.

I stroked Roy's jet-black hair as he slept. "How did he sleep when I was not with you?"

Capac shrugged. "He slept well in his room. Sometimes a child only *needs* a mother because he *has* a mother."

That didn't make much sense to me, so I moved on. "What does a king do when he wakes up in the morning?"

"Breakfast. Just like yesterday. I asked Jada to bring it here when she came with the water moments before you awoke. We only eat outside, but we can be here. And then the holy men speak at the temple. The people go. I have many places I plan to go today to help my people."

"And what does a queen do?" I winced.

Before he answered, he considered that. He got some little smile on his face, and I assumed he was remembering his mother. How could I ever measure up to the woman who raised him?

"The queen does what she likes. She has complete protection and cannot be touched or disrespected without consequence. You may stay here and read, if you like. You are never asked to work with your hands or be among the people. Jada and any others will serve you however you wish."

I stopped his ludicrous suggestions. "I came to help you serve and teach your people, not to be served by them. I hope being the queen does not change my ability to serve them."

"No, you may do as you please." He smiled. "I am grateful for your devotion to my people."

"*Our* people," I whispered.

"Yes." He was utterly delighted. "God chose an excellent queen."

As his queen, I was permitted to follow Capac everywhere. I finally noticed Rune, a young man with covered feet, casually strolling along ten to twenty feet behind us. Capac was a servant, visiting the sick and helping with other work. He would climb trees and pick fruit and help men pull heavy fish to the shore. Then he would sit in his "office," which was a curtained room in the cave that was the temple, and tend to the line of people that formed outside, giving advice and making suggestions.

The people adored him. But he always made sure to capture my gaze and smile at me or make sure I was doing alright. I steered clear of men, knowing they could be killed for even grazing me. But I helped women with the washing or mending of clothes, the care of children, whatever was needed until Capac would call me to the next place.

"*Regi-mae.*" *My queen.* He'd say, then turn and walk away. I'd catch up with him, and follow him wherever he was going next.

That night, after we put Roy to bed and shooed away the guards, Capac asked, "Are you ready for sleep?"

Tired from the long day, I nodded, and he helped me to my feet. All was as the night before when we finally retired after reading. He shut the heavy door behind us. We removed our royal garments and lay down together. Capac asked if I was well. I nodded. And we fell asleep. Except for the reassuring squeeze he gave my shoulder, it was just like sharing a shelter in the jungle on our journey.

There was not a further contrast from that second night to the third one, when I wondered if I could address the lack of pajamas in the culture.

"Will you be offended if I sleep in my own nightgown that I brought from home?" I asked, bending to my knees near my backpack in the corner after we arrived in our bedroom. "I love this garment, but it is a little scratchy for sleeping."

By then he had removed all but the gathered loin portion of his own garments, which is how he'd slept the previous nights.

"Scratchy?" He asked of the word I had said in English. He took a seat on the mat that was our bed.

"Yes. Rough?" I tried, then ended up retrieving my blue floral nightgown from my backpack and walking on my knees the few feet to him to let him feel the cotton. "See? The nightgown is more comfortable."

He rose to his knees and only stopped when he was barely a foot away from me. There, he reached out and touched the fabric.

"Soft like skin," he said, never really having cared if I wore it. My eyes were on his hand as it touched the fabric, so it startled me when I looked up and his eyes met mine.

There is not a time Capac will avert his eyes when speaking with someone. I thought it was cultural until I saw the people did not look me in the eyes for the sake of reverence. And because he seemed to demand it of me, I did not look away. I didn't understand the cue. I had barely been married for two days. He tilted his head and made a common request when the silence grew pungent.

"Tell me your heart."

"Tell me *yours*. You are making me uncomfortable."

He laughed into that lack of personal space, then narrowed his eyes, twisting his thick eyebrows in confusion for the same duration as a blink. That was the moment I realized that though our marriage had begun with haste, the change was irreversible, like hurling oneself over a waterfall. He opened his mouth to tell me his heart, though I already knew from the flick of his eyebrow that his "heart" was going to instead be wit. "I wonder why you sleep in a garment soft like skin for comfort. Perhaps come to bed in *only* your skin, and I will do the same. Then we will both have comfort."

With my wide-eyed gasp, Capac received the rise he was seeking. He smiled before he did finally move his hand from that nightgown, but only to toss it aside and use his other hand to secure my waist.

He looked me over then whispered a sigh, though I was trying to avert my eyes. My heart. My understanding. What was happening?

Capac used his free hand to graze my cheek, then my upper arm—touches that were previously forbidden. Now I knew why.

He whispered, "See? Feels nice."

My heart was pounding. He had to have been able to hear it. Clinging to yesterday's innocence, I wondered if maybe this new closeness was his only aim. Such naivety. He came closer, and his nose met my neck.

"Capac?" I finally whispered.

"Debbie?" But he was pulling me against him and calling out all my most basic senses with his gentle touch.

"Why are we doing this?" I sounded dizzy when I said that, and he hummed appreciation that I was clearly melting into his advance. I think he also liked the connotation of that question. He already had permission.

Whispering his own dizzied tone, he let out a slow, "Shhh." Then, as if he had some other motive or I had some other wish, he said, "Walk with me." But it was a statement. I gathered I didn't have much room to refuse, not that I wanted to.

I don't know where he was in his heart after that walk, but I was deeply rooted in self-loathing and him-loathing as I began to drift to sleep curled against him regardless, his rough hand smoothing up and down my arm.

Royalty wasn't supposed to have rough hands. A king was a tool to be controlled. But Capac had clung to the top of that *matteh* with those hands until one became smooth and the other became rough. He was so refreshingly different. I had never felt safer or more afraid in my life. Never so protected or so needed. But was it wrong that it was from the physical pleasure I could give a man?

His eyes read remorse and he breathed in for speech, but I stopped him. "Don't."

He was relieved. Not because we didn't need to have a serious conversation and come to some serious understanding at some point. But because there weren't actually words just then. We both wanted exactly what happened, no one wanted to analyze it, and that was the point.

I awoke to him smoothing his hands over my hair and a river of regret flowing quietly from both of our spirits.

"Bright morning," he mumbled, not wanting to look into my eyes. He quickly sat up near my head and began braiding penance into my hair. No one spoke again, except to Roy when he woke up.

We went through the day with the people, glad that such a topic of conversation would be inappropriate. My regret remained, but the duties of the day seemed to lift his spirits, his need for penance fading and ultimately vanishing. I knew he was cured of it when he leaned into me at dinner and smelled my hair, adding a low hum to be sure I noticed. But after we read to Roy from Genesis then put him to bed, I refused to enter our bedroom with Capac. He stood in the doorway, and I stood on the other side of the frame.

I whispered, "we need to talk about what happened last night."

"What happened last night?" He was flirting again. I was not amused.

"You broke your promise." I crossed my arms. "I have never known you to do such a thing, and I am angry with you."

He whispered intensity, glancing his gaze across my body. "I have taken nothing that you did not give, Debbie."

"I know. But. . ." With this, I reluctantly followed him into our bedroom and let him close us in for privacy, though he had sent Belen and Rune away. "You promised the one ritual only."

"Was it only *ritual* for you?" He was patient for my answer, but looking vulnerable with crossed arms.

I didn't know the answer to that. Well, I did, I just didn't want to admit the answer to that. Still, he was giving me vulnerability, and I gave him the same respect. "No. It was not only ritual. You know that."

He was trying to meet me halfway, but I could tell he was hurt. "So I did not ask for you to repeat a ritual. I asked my wife to walk with me."

"What if I was not yet settled with all this?"

"Then you had freedom to refuse me." He laughed the hurt confusion, then made an accusation. Rather, he spoke aloud what we both knew. "But you did not *wish* to refuse me."

"It is not that simple, Capac. I am still sorting this out in my heart."

"I am the same." He was trying to comfort me, but he seemed far surer than that. "We have sorted out many things *together*. Why not this?"

"Because it is for pleasure, Capac. Yes, we both *wish* to, but does not mean we *should*. We are not heartholders."

"But I am your husband now. How many days and seasons should I wait?" He shrugged, apparently having stripped away much of his steadfast honor. No, *I* had stripped that away. I shut my eyes tight, remembering the way I learned how to unravel a Capacsi wool garment. How had I changed him so quickly?

I didn't speak. I didn't even know to whom I was speaking. He further removed me from my friend when he said,

"You are as passionate as you are courageous. That much, we sorted together."

My first instinct was to take that as an insult, and I looked down, stepping further away from him, my eyes still on the stone floor beneath us. The people had dirt floors, except in one house. This might as well have been marble or diamond. These stones were pulled from the river with great danger generations ago and installed with great care. I was in the palace of a king, standing in his bed chamber where he kept his rubies. And he was telling me, Debbie Davies, that I was passionate. Yet when he chuckled and I looked up to meet his eyes again, I was only looking at my dear friend, who was stepping into "my" personal space, those powerful arms crossed.

"Do not fear me. Tell me your heart." He was at ease to a depth I had never seen. I'd taken his intensity and left him as carefree mush in the past few days.

Still, I told my heart as directly as possible. It came out in English. "So. . .despite not being heartholders and also agreeing to only do it the first night, you want to continue to have sex?"

It was not a word I used often, and it had been an awkward conversation when we had reached points in the Bible that required the translation. Capacsi had a similar word, but not exact. The literal translation of "sex" into Capacsi was "right." Not quite as cold as a ritual, of course, but certainly not the gentle terms of walking together, making love or even sharing physical intimacy. I was essentially asking, *"Do you honestly wish to assert your conjugal rights?"*

Capac scoffed at the English and the way I used it. Yet he did not hesitate with his answer in Capacsi.

"Yes, Debbie. I wish to continue to have sex. Very much. Very many times. That is, in fact, my right as your husband." He laughed self-loathing and embarrassing truth, baring it all to me. "But walking with you? Making love with you? That is *comfort*. That is a joy." His correction disarmed me.

"Okay." I crossed my arms, mumbling my defeat.

"Okay? This does not seem okay for you."

"It makes sense, Capac. You're not wrong. I do wish we had discussed it, but—"

My heart forgot its purpose altogether as he interrupted me with a growled, "Is it not medicine? Are you not lost and found and remade when we walk together?"

I tried to conceal my smile. "Is that not unchaste?" *Unchaste* was in English, of course.

"So be 'unchaste' with me," he said with the same easy smile on his face that was weakening my knees. Half of me wanted to be in my nightgown for comfort. Half of me wanted to be warm beneath that blanket we shared. All of me wanted him. He wasn't even touching me. How was he awakening me?

"Unchaste is not good. It is sinful." I sighed at his translation confusion.

"Then we are not 'unchaste.' God has given us for marriage, and my flesh longs for yours, and I know that you are the same. Why must this medicine have so many words and complications? Let our flesh speak its own language?" As he whispered my demise, he ran his hand over the growing portion of braids he'd managed so far.

They were his affection, and everyone could see it. He wasn't asking for a public display. He was essentially asking for me to privately laugh at an inside joke. It was only between us, and it didn't matter why. I sighed, trembling, then heart pounding when his hands moved from my hair to my waist. I was bitter suddenly for the way two rational people could so easily break forever with one release of hormones under duress.

I shook my head, frustrated with myself and fully impressed with him. "You are a worthy hunter, my king."

He laughed and took the compliment. "And you are a very beautiful prize."

So it was settled. We didn't yet have any idea what we were awakening, but we would continue to awaken it. After that walk, we didn't speak. It had been a long day. I was his peace and he was mine.

We had an understanding—or at least an agreement that we *didn't* understand. So the next night, we sought that same peace, and there wasn't hesitation or conversation beforehand. But that walk took time—a quiet stroll instead of a passionate sprint. Time in the candlelight to reflect and share and explore and even laugh and ask questions and give gentle commentary that increased intimacy.

When that walk ended, something felt different in him. I felt the same: protected, cared for, appreciated. Repeating this act with him had grown on me, and that one was a comfort the way our conversations had always been. I was looking forward to a new normal. But after that time, he was the one to question things. His eyes read wide-eyed panic, and I was concerned.

"What's wrong?"

"This is for heartholders." And for the first time ever, he averted his eyes, despite their proximity to mine.

"Capac, I am your wife. We have talked about this. Medicine?" I flirted, confused by the swift change.

"You are no man's medicine. You are a *queen*." He was far beyond flirtation. "And my heir's mother, and John Davies's favored daughter. You are a righteous woman of God. Forgive me, Debbie. I was wrong. This is not who we are."

Capac carefully kept me covered, but rose, dressed, and walked out of our house. He was acting much more like the man I had known for years, but I had to fight against my urge to think I was suddenly disgusting to him. What had changed, yet again?

I hoped to find the answer in a muffled conversation outside the front door. I wrapped the blanket around me, then stood in my bedroom doorway listening.

"Are you going far, King?" Rune's voice.

"No, Rune. Go home. My feet are covered."

Rune's footsteps took him away from the front door, but only out of sight. I knew him well enough now to know he was still going to follow Capac anywhere.

"My king?" That was Belen.

"Go home to my sister, Grower." I focused my vision on a slit between my front door and the night, and saw Capac's white garment pass the door, back and forth.

"Capac, my dear friend." The pacing stopped, and Belen's voice was one of concern. "Tell me your heart."

"I did not mean for you and Rune to stay. I have not remembered to ask you to leave. I have been preoccupied."

"It is well. We know now to give you privacy and sat by my home. Rune was telling me about his heartholder. Young Jada, your Taster with the braid in her hair?" It was irrelevant.

"I know of Jada, Belen. Stop trying to distract me," the king commanded. But the hurting friend desperate for counsel said, "I am distracted enough."

"Ah," Belen said. He uttered no version of "I told you so." He instead clarified, "You have been enjoying your new marriage. Why does this upset you?"

Capac sighed slow and deep. "I have a calling from God. I cannot become distracted. I never wanted this."

"Still you have it," Belen whispered. "You have a wife. And so you *need* a wife."

"I do not need *all* that I have, Belen!" Capac boomed. "Some things are meant to make me stumble, and I will not be made to stumble. I have too much!" His voice got further away. He was walking off into the jungle night. His last, faraway command, "Go *home*, Belen," was met with a sigh.

"Do you require my service, Queen?" He said it quietly enough to suggest that he knew how very close I was.

"You know he will be angry if you are here when he returns," I offered.

He laughed. "Our king is a difficult man, yes?"

"Very difficult and very good," I added.

"The very best of men." Belen sighed. "And he was right about you, Debbie. Forgive me for being so wrong."

"That I am a fearful child? You were right, Belen."

"No," he said. "Forgive me. But I heard you crying the night of your wedding. I *did* think you were a fearful child until your crying became prayers and your prayers became strength and peace. You are very powerful, Queen. I know that God is with you."

"I am a distraction," I sighed, leaning on Belen's confidence. Missing the wise counsel of the friend I turned into a basket case.

"No. A respite, I think." He added, "You have settled him more in a few days than I have managed in a lifetime. I suppose you are a respite for me too." Such praise silenced me, and Belen offered the common goodbye. "Whisper night," was the literal term. But we all know the jungle never whispers.

Sixteen

We were still not heartholders, and for about a week, Capac avoided the thing that suggested otherwise. We grew closer in other areas, of course. We were one flesh; how could we not? We would carry out duties in the community all day and talk for hours in the evenings as we had in the months prior back at the mission. But in these new times, he also braided my hair as we spoke and laughed together. I appreciated his sense of humor, his kind, gentle way with his. . .our. . .people. I considered him my absolute best friend, which I told him, and he told me the same.

Roy began to notice the change in our relationship and asked if he could call Capac "Da." Capac smiled. He liked that. We were partners. Allies. Co-parents. It really was a wonderful growth of our relationship. But there remained a darkness, both ambiguous and corrupt, that lived dormant in our bedroom.

One night I dreamed of snow, but not the happy memory of my family before the jungle. It was cold and windy and dangerous. A blizzard. Did I remember blizzards? I was back at the mission, but no one was there. I called out for Lydia. For Dad. But no one answered. Each building was covered in snowdrifts and I could feel myself weakening from the cold. I found my tree to rest there. Die there. Then the whole world warmed as I leaned my back against it. It was spring and there were butterflies. Lydia was in the distance, waving to me. All was well when I awoke.

Then I was in the corrupt bed chamber, my nose cold and runny. And the tree was instead my husband's full embrace, his hands rubbing at my arms beneath the blanket to warm them. He spoke, likely hearing me startle awake.

"You were shivering. The heat from the fire warms Roy's room well, but not ours. I am sorry. I mean no disrespect."

"It is fine, Capac. Thank you." I told him my heart, as I did now without him needing to ask. "I was dreaming of my tree. And snow."

"Tell me snow again?"

He liked to make fun of me, because he didn't believe in snow. I had no proof; only memories. There weren't even pictures of snow back at the mission. So I walked into his trap, as always.

"Like cold rain, but it falls like feathers."

"Cold feathery rain." He snickered, deepening his embrace for greater warmth.

"Stop teasing! I remember!" I giggled along with his teasing.

"Your tree and the snow. What else was in your dream?" my dear friend wondered.

"Lydia." I sighed. I hated to tell him that. I did not want to appear to be so homesick that I could not attend to my duties as queen.

"Her child will come soon?" But he always encouraged me to talk about my family and miss them completely. He knew that was better for my heart.

"Yes. I was supposed to tell everyone the baby's gender when the baby was born. . .it's alright. I am here with you. My whole heart."

"I think girl."

"It will be a beautiful child no matter what. Lydia is so pretty."

"Her *sister* is beautiful, for certain," he said, smelling my shoulder from behind. I didn't know what to make of that, and I don't think he did either. We fell back asleep in silence.

The following night, I woke up around the same time, but it was because Capac was tossing and turning.

"Are you well, my king?" I asked him when I saw that he was staring at the ceiling in distressed thought.

"I cannot calm my thoughts. I think of this Opening to come, and my people and those evil holy men and so much that only God can control."

"What can I do?" I yawned.

He stayed his vision on the ceiling. "Men are not hunters, Debbie. I have never been so wrong. We are just sinners."

I had never known him to be restless. He usually slept soundly, knowing he could only do anything while well-rested and by the will of God. "What do you mean?"

"I never thirsted for this before. The taste of your fire haunts me." He grunted low.

Oh. That.

"Capac, all is well."

"It is not. I cannot sleep, Debbie. I need to rest for my duties, but my flesh will not quiet."

"So rest," I said, putting myself between his racing thoughts and his sight of the ceiling.

He sighed relief and wrapped his arms around me, too weak to refuse the advance. Our walk quieted him enough to sleep.

I usually awoke to my hair being braided. That next morning, I woke up alone.

I opened our bedroom door, and he was sitting against a wall reading our Bible. There was a high window in the wall opposite the fireplace that acted as a vent. And that morning, the sun must have been extra bright and situated just right through the canopy. A sunbeam came in, and Capac was using it as a reading light. His whole, handsome being in his royal garments and the Word of God were alight in that beam, even glowing. For a moment, I wished I'd brought a camera, because it was the most beautiful thing I'd ever seen. But no lens could have captured it as well as my heart, skipping and flopping over itself to record the memory. He looked up at me with a cheery smile.

"My queen! Bright morning. Did I wake you? Are you well?"

"I am well. What are you reading?" I asked, taking the invitation of his outstretched arm and cuddling up next to him.

"I remembered something and was trying to find it to memorize." This was a common behavior, but he was apparently shifting his attention, setting aside the Bible to hold me with both arms. Distracted. He sighed, a weight settling on his shoulders. I responded without his mentioning it.

"We need to discuss this, Capac."

"No, I need to apologize. I should have sought God in prayer and in His Word, not use your body for my comfort." The outpouring began.

" 'Use?' " I laughed bitterly at the word choice. The word in his language was more like 'wield' or 'utilize,' like one would do for a tool or a weapon. It was a cold word, and Capac did not often misspeak.

"Debbie, may I tell you my heart?"

"Always," I said, moving out of the fond embrace and sitting cross-legged in front of him. As he sometimes did even in front of the people, he scooted close and swung just one leg behind one of mine. Intimate, sure. But to them it was like him putting an arm around me.

"I do not think I can bear to be your husband if I am not permitted to walk with you. This previous night tells me this. I am not so strong as I thought, your beauty is a temptation for me, and your touch is medicine." I thought that was his full thought.

"You have permission. From God and from me. You know this. We can—"

"No. Because I do not think I can bear to be *king* and *continue* to walk with you. We are servants of God, sober-minded. It is medicine, yes. But also poison for us."

His pain and dilemma were so deep and impossible. I didn't know what to say. He sighed with nerves before he brought a clasped hand in front of me and opened it.

He was holding a necklace. It was not like most of the others. This one was delicate, and the pendant boasted one ruby about the size of my pinky fingernail inside a decorative setting. As he found the ends and advanced toward my neck, I protested.

"No, Capac. I told you I am not going to—" But as always, I sighed and let him complete the mission, then whisper into my ear and my heart his latest incredibly verbatim passage.

"'Who can find a virtuous wife? For her worth is far above rubies. The heart of her husband safely trusts her; So he will have no lack of gain. She does him good and not evil all the days of her life.'"

"Proverbs thirty-one," I whispered. I always wanted to be that woman. Today was the first I felt like her.

"You do good for me. I know that I can trust you not to sway my heart to evil. But *I* have done evil. You are riches and rubies that should never be used for only pleasure and comfort."

"Well what *do* you use those rubies for?" I laughed. He considered that, staying his eyes on mine. I continued. "Do you want me to sit on a table and be valuable with no purpose? You do not *use* me. We share it."

"Rubies are for the neck of a queen. Will you wear this for me? So that whether in my arms or with our people, I remember you are too valuable for me?" In some respects, it felt like he was a rich man wooing a harlot to continue her services. Maybe that's what it was. But in other respects, it meant something deeper I couldn't quite understand at the time.

He was never far from convincing me of anything, so I nodded. "I will wear it. Thank you for choosing one that is not so lavish."

"I know that I do not have your heart," he whispered. "You are a *ruby*. I am a thief if we continue to 'share' as we have. It does not fit who we are and the words I told your father when he asked the word for friend. If I partake in this, I am lying to him. But still I am tempted beyond what I am able, even though God promises a way to escape."

I sighed. "God will not protect us from being tempted, Capac. Marriage *is* His provision for these things. His escape. We are forsaking His commands for marriage if we abstain."

"I know." He laughed that same self-deprecating laugh. "You are the problem *and* the solution." He smiled, gently touching the new ornament on my neck, "I like marriage with you, Debbie. This suits us, yes?"

"Yes." It was nice to hear him say that. Then I shrugged. "So if marriage suits us, and walking together suits marriage, it is not stolen."

I watched him consider that. Deeply in thought, bearing the look of intensity I so liked watching. At some point, he glanced at the sun on my skin and concealed a smirk.

"What?"

"It is nothing." But he continued to smile to himself as he looked over my hair for any braids needing attention.

"It is something to you," I demanded.

"*You* are something to me. And your skin is white like wool. I see it well in this light."

"Is that funny still? There is a canopy. I cannot even get a tan here like at home. It will always be white." I worried that he would stop craving my skin, and that terrified me even more than it sickened me that I was thinking about it.

"It will always be beautiful too," he said, sensing that I was offended. "If your skin is white, then my skin is white. And if mine is brown, then yours is brown. We are the same. One flesh. That is why it is funny. Not *your* white skin. But mine."

He laughed again, only a hum as he leaned in and gave my neck a quick smell. A taste of his favorite medicine. He swept a single braid away from my forehead and peered into my eyes.

"I have distracted you. I did not want to cause chaos in your heart and distract you." I ached with my own impossible dilemma. Wanting our old relationship back yet enjoying being a wife.

"A river thinks he is strong until he must be joined with fire. We must grow before we sort it all out, Debbie. But you are not distracting me. You are refining me."

"Any fire is silly if she is not terrified of a river," I mumbled.

"Nothing will ever quench Debbie Davies, even if she is a wife. You fear nothing but God," he whispered into that bright morning. "I will respect your worth, Debbie. I want to have your heart, or your passion does not belong to me. I will try not to stumble."

"You will fail." I shrugged. "We are only made of flesh, Capac. A ruby would be stronger for you."

"But not so beautiful."

Our relationship wasn't conventional, to be certain. It was a crude combination of passion, service, and fellowship we had torn from each corner and braided at the seams. It was messy. Still, it was a marriage, and we intended to let it grow.

Seventeen

We never attended the daily teaching because we could not condone false teaching. The people knew that this rebellious king would attend breakfast and then depart very publicly, sometimes with an audible rebuke if anyone asked.

"Will you not stay? These same teachings are in your precious Book, my king," the holy man with the dimple like Roy's sneered.

"I have learned to read. Not one of your teachings is the same as the teachings of God's Holy Bible. And you would not know in any case. You cannot read." Capac took my hand and led me away.

The people were forced to stay for the teaching on threat of death, but the king and queen could do as they liked. Capac could have given them a quiet protest, but he wanted to obey the command to rebuke them in the presence of all. He wanted the people to doubt the holy men. He wanted their hearts.

We would take Roy back home and read to him from the Bible while the teaching occurred. That day, Capac had a meeting just after. When we heard the people stir and begin to go to their duties for the day, Capac set off. I was permitted to attend, but I gathered he would rather spare me. So I put Roy on my hip and walked out the door in the opposite direction.

There, I encountered a group of women not normally so close to my house. It was Nur, Mena, and three young women who immediately stopped talking and put their heads down, parting to allow me to pass through. It was still odd. In fact, it has been odd all my life since. Not long before that occurrence, I was the quiet, bookish daughter of the pastor who ran the mission. I was the practically invisible oddity with the little native tied to her waist with a cloth. I constantly had to shoulder my way through rooms with awkward *excuse me's*. I was the one who put her head down when I spoke. I was courageous, and believing that more and more. But I was always sorry for how different I was.

In short, no one had ever parted the way when I walked through, and it caused me to hesitate long enough that Mena spoke.

"Queen." She nodded her head, reminding me why I could guiltlessly walk through their midst.

I nodded back, walked through them, then continued on.

Capac found me about an hour later chopping fruit with the cooks and listening to their conversation. I had never spoken directly to one of the people because I was still learning to understand their quick speech. They thought nothing of my silence, and allowed me to do whatever I wished. Capac thought it was weird that I "wished" to chop fruit.

He arrived at my side that day and laughed dotingly, wiping my hands clean with a nearby cloth. *"Regi-mae."*

He took my hand in his, and that's when I felt the excess weight of his heart.

"My king?" I asked.

When we were away from enough ears, he began.

"I have just learned the names of the women to be opened at New Moon. There are three of them. Three sisters that were friends with Sandani. Jada, Lana, and Dera. They each have a braid in their hair."

"Jada our Taster?"

"Yes."

"They're *all* engaged," I confirmed, surprised.

"To three of our best young men. Rune, Hanan, and Ilian. Ilian has only just put a braid in young Dera's hair. He and Hanan tend the sheep."

"Rune?" I lowered my voice, looking behind us at our Tender.

Capac nodded. "The sisters waited until they could endure this evil together or not at all, and the three young men understood. They will wed together after next winter, no matter the pain until then. These six are men and women who question our ways, but do not speak it. They serve the people with their whole hearts. Rune serves *me* with even his reputation. This evil should never be done to them."

It occurred to me. "There were three young women outside our house with Nur and Mena."

"Nur and Mena prepare the young women for the ritual with herbs and oils. Not even marriage has as many days of ritual."

My hatred for all these rituals was growing even more quickly than my love for the people they imprisoned.

A few nights later, we sat with Capac's uncle and cousin at dinner. His uncle was one of the holy men; his cousin, one of the six holy sons. This uncle was Capac's mother's brother, and thus the chief holy man since he was related to the royal bloodline. Capac had told me that in order of rank, each holy man chose "his" young woman for the Opening. How my king sat near someone so disgusting, I did not know. He listened as his cousin spoke to his uncle.

"Have you chosen which one you will make holy, father?"

"Dera. The youngest." He did not hesitate.

"Why do you always choose the youngest?" His son was trying to learn.

"Her skin is always softest." That remark, followed by his cackle, followed by his son's appreciative laughter, ended my appetite for supper that evening. Both their wives were seated with us. The children of the next generation too.

"Her flesh is for her husband." My husband was valiant. So valiant. "Your flesh is for your wife, my aunt. That is God's way."

"Your God is false," his uncle growled, a bit of mango dribbling down his chin as he greedily bit it. It was tomorrow's mango if uncut. We had already exhausted the day's fruit, and still he indulged.

"My God is the One True Living God. He is good. And you are a disgusting sinner, my uncle. You are an evil man. But it is not too late for you. Jesus is Savior for all who ask. His blood can cover all this. Do not grieve His heart again by defiling another woman or murdering another child."

This conversation was commonplace. Capac witnessed to them daily and had done as much for years. Not just his uncle, but to all the holy men and their already corrupt holy sons. Once the son of a holy man was married, he took on many duties of the holy men. It was the holy sons that sacrificed the babies. The holy men sometimes hesitated to murder the children after watching their own flesh be born into the world. They could not complete what they believed the gods required. So their sons—Cains against innocent Abel—murdered their own half brothers and half sisters during the Closing ritual.

"Do not grieve my heart by refusing what the gods require."

"No Holy God would require this. No human is holy without Jesus's blood."

"You are a nuisance, young Capac. If you were not the king and my dead sister's son, I would crush your skull."

"But I am the king. And you cannot touch me. So I will be a nuisance if it will save your soul."

"I am only disappointed your outsider woman did not choose to be opened with the other women. Her skin is soft, no? The jewel helps you to admire it, yes? I would have chosen her if you did not choose to enjoy it yourself."

Capac growled, but kept the volume controlled for his nearby people. "This woman is my wife by a covenant with God, and she is your queen. It is disrespect for your tongue to speak of her flesh."

Rune, suddenly standing and drawing his blade completely, spoke over Capac with, "Tongue or life? You choose, King, how we may restore the queen's honor."

I thought for sure it was an empty threat, but I had never seen Rune take up arms. It was a sight, this valiant young man standing among the peace of the meal with a drawn machete.

"It was only a warning, Tender."

"It is unlawful to disrespect the queen. But at your word, I will allow opportunity for him to restore the queen to honor with only his tongue."

Capac's uncle laughed and tried to get the others laughing. The other three holy men and all six holy sons responded only with light chuckles, and previously overconfident eyes now looked to the ground. Capac's uncle rose and met Rune's eyes with great valor and stupidity, speaking first as though he was a child, then, with much deeper malice. "I will offer this child of John Davies no such honor. But for *you*, Tender? Perhaps not Dera. Perhaps I will make *Jada* holy in her opening."

Capac's reflexes were fast, and he stood, taking Rune's whole twitching bicep into his hand just as he almost swung that blade. The village was still gasping when Capac spoke close to Rune's face, which was near enough for me to hear. "He has earned only his tongue on this day. Not for the eyes of children this time? Please?"

"Yes, King."

To the holy men and all nearby, Capac said, "Uncle, I do not know why you have chosen this. Nur? He will need herbs."

Nur rose and ran to her hut as Capac's uncle began first a vicious rant, shouting it as Rune dragged the man away from the meal area. "This woman is no queen. She is an outsider good only for the pleasure of our lawless king. She will corrupt your seed inside her, Nephew. Her womb is an abomination. No! You will not silence me! I am a holy man. Descended from gods."

"You are an evil man, descended from evil men," Capac yelled, then stood, taking Roy on his hip. "Come, my queen."

I was too scared to speak, covering my mouth in horror as Capac removed me with as much haste as Rune removed the chief holy man. All were just as horrified. It was as though the tongues of all the village were being cut out when all that could be heard was the protesting, then the animalistic screams that turned to gurgled squawks and then sobs.

When we arrived home, Capac told me to go into our room. Thankfully, Roy had practically been asleep when we left with haste, so he could be put to bed in the adjacent room, innocent still. It was probably two minutes of standing with that gurgling scream still echoing in my thundering heart, hands still shutting my mouth, when Capac met me with an embrace. I do not think I took a full breath until he had his hands at my shoulders and growled justification into my eyes.

"He broke a law, Debbie. He has the lesser consequence. I have told you the laws. They must not dishonor you with any part of them. My uncle dishonored you greatly."

That was true, obviously. Those few words were already creeping inside me, perhaps the catalyst for the corrupt womb I now wondered if I had. But to cut out a man's tongue? No. Certainly, this did not really—

"King? What of the tongue?" That was Rune at the door. He meant the tongue. The actual man's tongue of an actual man, likely in his hand, dripping blood on my doorstep.

I did not know I was sobbing out a scream or maybe screaming out a sob until Capac silenced it with four gentle fingers at my lips and answered,

"Food for the fish at the river, Rune. Please let me calm my queen's heart?"

"Yes. Do not leave your home until I return."

When Rune left, I imagine I was still wide-eyed, but the room was fuzzy at the edges, and I worried I might pass out. But I knew better than to be some hysterical woman. I had heard better tales of strength and worth. *Debbie Davies fears nothing and no one but God*, I heard in my dear friend's voice despite his silent concern as he slowly removed his hand from my mouth. *They are worth this*, I heard in my heart, a promise I still meant with more than just a tongue. I called my breath into submission first with deep breathing, then with stillness that resonated to the gaze into my husband's eyes.

My companion and carer saw that I was coming back to myself and offered profound remorse in a whisper. "I wanted to protect you from all. Yet even as I protect your honor, I have not protected your heart."

Every wife I knew could give some sweet words about some mildly courageous gesture. But I was the only woman I knew whose husband had allowed his own uncle's tongue to be cut out because I had been disrespected. When I realized that, I pulled myself completely together. I shushed him and swiped away the tear that had escaped from my eye, and the one from his. I pulled him into an embrace and assured him, "You protect me well, my king."

He sighed deeply into that embrace and more tears fell. There was a laugh in his voice when he said, "They truly do not know your strength. Pray that I am strong as my queen and not a coward again. I cannot bear this evil anymore."

"You have never been a coward. Why do you always say that?" His heart broke there at that question.

"Rune protects me with his life and cannot even protect his heartholder from this. You *must* pray I can stop this Opening forever. And you *must* not hate me for what I must do. I would sooner die than know you hate me." He was distressed, grasping at his hair and letting tears to his eyes. He was practically sweating blood.

"My king, I will never hate you. But I will pray with you all night if you ask it." And so I did. Only exhaustion concluded our prayers.

It was the day of the Opening, and Capac insisted on spending the entire day in the corner of our front room on his knees in prayer. He emerged for no food or water and insisted that Roy and I leave him alone.

I went to see Mena, who was helping the three young women dress. She asked me about him.

"He will not come out," I told her in a whisper.

"He does this every time since he met God three winters ago." Mena sighed.

"Tell me your names." I requested of the girls, but their eyes sought the dust beneath their feet.

Mena's eyes shot to mine. "The queen does not speak to the people. Only to royalty or holy men. The people are beneath her."

It only took a beat for me to decide I had not made a cultural faux pas, but I had seen a flaw in the system.

"Mena, please go check on Roy for me?" I sent her and her archaic understanding away.

"Yes, my queen." And she left her house with apologetic understanding.

"Our people have not had a queen in many years, and I never met Mena's mother, so I cannot judge her. But *your* queen loves her people and believes no one is beneath her," I stated with eloquence not my own.

"We—" Jada began, but her sisters shushed her. Still, eyes to the ground, she continued. "We worry we will lose our tongues, Queen."

"For simply speaking to me? Never. Jada, you risk your tongue and life daily to honor me. You serve us so faithfully and I am grateful." They all seemed to relax, and I urged them still to converse. "I have been told that you two are Lana and Dera. Which of you is which?"

The three girls, likely in their late teens, looked up at me then, explaining that the two older ones were twins, Jada and Lana. Dera was their younger sister, and soon to be the choicest victim of the chief holy man.

"And you have braids in your hair."

They looked to my intricately and neatly braided hair with smiles of romance.

"Not so many braids as our queen," Jada said, scandal in her tone. "Nor rubies for our necks."

I had already been told by Mena that I had typical newlywed hair. Capac kept up with it meticulously, it was true. They giggled when I turned redder than my ruby and pawed at it. All appearances suggested romance, so it was often hard to know the truth—dutiful affection and frequent stumbling was all we had.

"Your ruby is very beautiful, " Lana told me. "But your cord is *more* beautiful. From the king's own garment."

"Thank you, Lana. He did not have time to prepare a cord, so yes. This was a thread from his garment." And thus they opened up.

"Ilian is already preparing my cord," Dera said of her love.

"Hanan wears my cord on his neck," Lana boasted. Capac had told me the young men did that often. He would display his love for his bride-to-be until he could remove the cord from around his neck and tie it into her hair at the wedding.

"Rune will take my cord from the sacred coverings for his feet," she said, flipping the 'r' of Rune with beauty and joy.

"Of course," I whispered. "Our Tender of Footsteps. The least in the kingdom, unless you ask the king."

The feet coverings were sherpa, and he walked with ease, essentially mopping away our footsteps. It was such an odd job, but he was truly looked down upon and also feared for his authority to maim or kill anyone who might harm the royal family. Jada was courageous, and a blessed woman, to agree to the marriage.

But quickly they all turned to sadness and Jada said, "You *are* above us, my queen. To be opened by a husband is a lofty joy we can never know."

They were three carefree virgins, joyfully anticipating their wedding day. But it had to wait for them to be defiled first. It had to wait, even, for the brutal murder of a child if a child was ordained. Anger and bitterness bubbled up and came out as a couple of tears.

Valiantly, because my husband would have it no other way, I spoke what I likely should not. "No one should open a woman but her husband. That is not God's way. I mourn for you. My king's heart dies for you."

Jada, more valiant than I, spoke endearment. "Our king is a good king. His heart is big. He mourns in the jungle all winter during the Closing, and Rune tends his footsteps, often running many miles to return for supplies. We know that he rescued the older children. He left with them in the night to save them alive from the threat of a new Closing. The king allowed this rumor to spread to comfort the hearts of the mothers and fathers. But Rune has told me more, Queen. Our king rescued *all* the children when the holy men let him take the women to the jungle. We have seen your Roy. I know, and now many believe he rescued them all. Our king and queen bear no fault in this ritual."

"Is it true our king was locked in chains when he rescued the older children and your Roy?" Dera asked, though her sisters shushed her.

"Yes. My father, John Davies, did that. He is a good man, but still does not know what our king was doing."

"Is it true my queen set him free?" Lana asked it low, with romance. Apparently, I was part of local legends. My marriage to their king surprised no one but us.

I looked to Jada, who shrugged. "Rune has seen much more than you know."

"I was not his queen. I was his friend, and I only did what was right."

"Was it not right for you to listen to your father? John Davies is your holy man and king," Jada asked.

"My father and I have the same Holy Man and King. And we do what is right according to His law. My father had to protect his people from what he thought was a threat. Our king is the same. He serves and worships only the Almighty God. His heart dies because this ritual is not right. It is against the laws of God. He has asked me to pray he has the courage to stop this sin against God and against you."

Their eyes were glistening. Alighting when they listened to me speak. Deborah Davies, the little-teacher-outsider-friend, likely would have been executed for the words I spoke. But the queen does, and says, what she likes. I sent those young women away with hope, if nothing else.

Eighteen

The holy men disgusted me more than ever. They had ritualistically cleansed themselves for this savagery, and their eyes were lusty as the three sisters were brought to the front of the temple. There were three weeping heads of long black hair with one small braid in each. Jada, Lana, Dera. Three young men stood by, trying to remain strong. They stood with strength, hand in hand in hand. Rune, with anguish in his eyes. Hanan, a cord around his neck. Ilian, not hiding his tears. Their love was about to be defiled when they were told she'd be made holy.

It occurred to me how honorable these young people were. These sisters waited to be victim to this ritual until they had all three been promised to a young man. They waited for a promise and did not allow any sister to endure this alone. That was the best they could do, standing there, arms around waists in solidarity against an impossible requirement.

The holy men ushered them in that way.

"They will be taken to a chamber that has been cleansed. When the third star is out, they will be taken, one at a time, into another chamber to be opened. They will hang their evidence on those posts." Capac gestured to posts outside the cave. Mine had hung there just weeks before.

"This is barbaric," I said with straight-toned bitterness.

"Yes." My king swallowed hard, embracing me securely at the waist as the women were taken inside. Outside, after they'd all been strong, the siblings, mothers, fathers, and fiancé's all fell to the ground in weeping.

"Your people are not barbaric. They are kind, good people. They need to learn the goodness of God."

"You spoke with them."

"I did not know I was not to speak to the people. You speak to them often, and—"

"The queen is a sacred, silent pillar of perfection who is to be decorated in public and make suggestions and children in private with the king. That is the tradition."

"You did not tell me—"

"You are a wildfire, and if I refuse to quench you, you will do great things for our people. Continue to speak to whomever you wish. Our tradition needs to be made new."

"I should be with these young women tonight. You protected me from what I would have gladly endured to serve them," I confessed.

"But because I protected you, you have made me brave enough to protect them," he assured.

It was a holy ritual, so the people were ordered by one of the sons of the holy men to clear the area of the temple and return to their homes, but Capac looked at him with anger, and we remained there until the first star appeared.

"Holy sons!" Capac called to the men at the veiled entrance, who turned to him.

"Will you, for another time, allow your fathers to commit this evil against the Holy God?"

They'd heard it before. Capac's own cousin responded.

"Will you stop a holy ritual and profane our gods?"

"Your gods are made of wood," my king growled, causing me to have to beg my heart to still. He spoke again, "I will give you every chance, holy sons, as I did for your fathers. You must turn from this wickedness and worship the One True Living God. He sent His Son to spill His blood to die for even this. Will you trust Him? It is not too late."

They laughed at him, and Capac checked the sky. Still one star. Capac walked me to our home and stopped at the door. He handed me his *matteh* and took up something else that had been leaning against the outside of the house. I couldn't quite see what it was and didn't remember it being there.

"Where are you going?"

He answered only with grave instructions. "If I fail, let no one bear this *matteh* but you, my queen."

I heard a male voice behind me. "Capac."

"Belen, I am your king, and you will not address me so informally when you are on duty," Capac growled.

"Will you force me to remain here at my post?" Belen boomed. "Let me come with you. You will need me."

"Grower of Green food, remain outside my home and protect my family. I will bear this alone."

"Yes, my king." Belen sobbed.

"Bear what, Capac?" I worried, trying to catch sight of what was in his hand through the darkness.

Belen seemed to be obeying, against his better judgment. Rune, however, came into Capac's view and stood beside Belen in the position of a warrior only temporarily at ease.

"Tender, you will stay away from me. Do not—"

"King, you know that there is no command of yours that is greater than my call to protect you," Rune said with valor that caused my courageous Capac to shrink back. It seemed like a known creed when he said, "I will not obey you. I will defend you."

"Then do not follow me, Tender. Walk beside me," Capac conceded.

I implored him in English. "Capac, do I not deserve to know what is happening?"

He sighed, and I read the remorse, the command in his eyes. He softened the command with, "I must go quickly, my queen. Put Roy to bed. Be sure he is asleep when I return."

I didn't question him further.

A strange fear crept inside me and I complied. I tried to listen against the silence in our candlelit home and the million voices of the jungle outside. For an hour, then two, I wondered what was happening, as did the entire village. These poor people, sending their daughters to be destroyed. Capac finally opened the door and ran inside.

He was a rush of adrenaline. Breathing heavily and wide-eyed, he stood before me. What I saw didn't surprise me, oddly, but the reality of it was shocking nonetheless. He was covered, practically head to toe, in blood.

"Capac!" I rose to my feet. "Wha—?"

"Debbie, help me to wash."

I couldn't believe he'd ask, but assessed the situation immediately.

"We'll need the river."

I stepped outside.

"Grower of Green!" I called. Belen startled me, having been standing just to my right.

"Queen?"

"Tend the plant inside. I do not want to leave Roy alone," I whispered.

In the firelight from my window, I saw Belen's eyes widen. "I have never been inside."

"Belen, your purpose is for this night," I whispered as Capac stepped out, sobbing and pacing.

"Tender! I know you are near."

As expected, Rune appeared from behind the partition that is set between two trees in front of our door. I was startled to see that he was in a fresh set of clothing. Even his feet coverings were clean. His eyes read peace. Satisfaction. An unsettling contrast to the mess my husband was, though I knew the gruesome task was shared.

"Will you obey me? I do not think I know the rules. . ."

"I will serve and defend you, my queen. What is your need?"

"No one can see where I am taking him," I told Rune. "These steps will be difficult. But after you cover them return here."

"Go into the temple when you return. Take all who will follow," Capac was somehow lucid enough to command. "Queen, the river."

We walked the quarter mile down the hill as we often had, leaving Roy in capable hands. We passed a massive bonfire on the way that I assumed was some ritual to go along with the Opening.

It smelled like cooking meat sickened by singed hair. There was so much I didn't know about the culture.

"Do not look at the fire," he instructed. I obeyed.

The riverbank was dark and the moon was new. I feared all the beasts of the water as I stood in the cold shallow, undressed my husband, and repeatedly washed him with the buckets we left there for laundry. I used the herb mixture we prepared for holy garments, washing down his whole trembling being until the metallic scent of blood began to wane.

Up at the temple, I heard a scream that chilled me and broke his silence.

"I did not take their wives or the holy sons' children. I am no better than them if I slaughter the innocent." Ramblings of a madman.

It was what I suspected. "You killed the holy men."

"And their sons. Yes. I murdered them with a machete. It was quick for the first two. The others fought me, but I am stronger, and Rune defended me. I burned their bodies with their gods on the altar. They are too sinful for our honorable burial. Ten. Ten men. I murdered them, Debbie."

"You didn't murder them," I whispered, not even my lips believing it. "You executed them for their crimes." But as I said it, I believed it. "For their murder and rape. Their idolatry and blasphemy. This is justice, Capac. I understand."

"I am their king. They are my people. I had to rescue my people." He sobbed, trembling uncontrollably. "They begged me to stop. I grew up with those men. They respected my father. My uncle, my own cousin. . ." He rambled on. "I hesitated. Rune did not."

"Where are the young women for the Opening?"

"We killed the sons, then snuck the girls out the other entrance. We waited for the holy men to come into the chamber for Dera and I asked them one last time. . ." He sobbed.

"You gave them every chance to turn from evil," I encouraged.

"And the girls are untouched. Unopened. They are free to marry and be wives. Free like my wife. If you had been there, I would have saved you. You were right. You could have chosen that and been safe. Instead, you chose to marry *this*." He was completely beside himself.

"Shh, had I been there, my king, who would have been here to wash you?" I took him into my arms. He was washed of blood and stripped of royal garments. He wore nothing and probably felt nothing. But his adrenaline was still pumping. So much adrenaline, and I saw it coming before he did.

He reached out and untied my garment. "I need you to settle me. Will you?"

"Of course," I whispered, but I heard the familiar gentle pant of a runner arrive.

"Leave us, Rune. I am protected," Capac growled, continuing his pursuit unscathed.

"Yes, my king." Rune often had to simply shake his head at the king's choices then walk a short distance away and turn his back or hide himself behind a tree. He had to keep watch, I understand.

I still was not used to such things having an audience.

Capac was a killer and likely would have understood if I never let him touch me again. But I knew better. I had what he needed and didn't withhold it. He had the power and the history to destroy me, and I trusted him not to. That's what love is. We didn't have that. But I suppose that's what marriage is too.

When it was over, he caught his breath and senses and we both cried for a little while, naked on the riverbank, mourning his choice and the reason he had to make it. After a time, we dressed in our royal garments, stained and dyed with blood, and made our way back up the hill to the village.

"Will they hate me?" He asked his co-leader. "Will my people hate me?"

"I do not think they have a reason. Did you go against any system of judgment or trial?" I worked to advise him.

"By our laws, the king is the tender of the holy men. No king has been able to do this because his mind has been poisoned by the holy men, but it was always the duty of the king." He sighed. "I must appoint judges that are not also the holy men. I will ask you to teach them from the Bible. You will be our holy woman."

"No. I will be our Bible teacher," I corrected. "But let's not make plans today, King."

"Yes." He sighed. "Debbie, I do not know if I want them to love me or hate me. They *should* love me. And they *should* hate me."

I did not respond to that. We were approaching the temple then. It was dawn, and the people were drawing buckets of water from the well, washing the blood out of the temple.

"*Resgatei!*" That was the first opinion when they saw their king. That cry came first from Rune, but they all began chanting it, and someone else brought out the remaining families of the holy men.

The first generation was four older women, their wives. The next generation was six young wives. The next, a total of ten children. The youngest child was about a year old, and the oldest was a young teen girl. They were quiet, in varying states of shock in their robes with a blue stripe.

"What should we do with them, King?" Rune asked.

Capac raised his voice so that they all could hear. "You should mourn with them. They were just relieved of their fathers, sons, and husbands. You will treat them as any widow or orphan among us. Anyone who values life will understand that they should live, but that their fathers had to answer for their crimes. Give them new garments and burn these. The way of holy men is now changed forever. Tomorrow, my bride—your queen—will begin to teach you about the One True Living God that our holy men would hear nothing of. I have removed the idols from our temple and burned them with the bodies of the men that desecrated my people. A god who can be burned on a fire is not big enough to fear. You will fear these idols no more."

The man could give a powerful speech and earn the praise of his people with ease. He could carry out judgment in one breath and mercy in the next. He was a rescuer and a king. But with me, he was simply a man. When we arrived at home, I embraced my dearest friend as he fought sleep with bitter tears.

"You have done righteously."

And after he finally succumbed to the fall of adrenaline, I prayed over him.

"Lord, give him peaceful sleep." I stroked his thick black hair. "Please don't punish him for this. Lord, use this terrible thing for Your glory, and keep my husband's heart stayed on You." I whispered over him, wondering also if by supporting his actions I was Jezebel, an evil queen. Is that how they would see me?

After a time, I heard a gentle voice at the door to request my presence. Our people do not knock, as we do not all have doors. It was Mena and Nur.

"Did he sleep last night? I know Belen stayed to look after Roy." Mena said.

I put a hand to my lips to quiet her. "He needed to be washed at the river. We were there until morning. But he is sleeping now."

"You look tired," Nur commented in a whisper, remorsefully.

"I also have not slept." I sighed. "Did you know he was going to do this?" I asked them, blinking wearily.

"Kings have wanted to do the same for generations. Our father prepared him for this," Mena explained.

"He did?"

Nur spoke next, but only after an endearing laugh. "He was never to marry. If a king killed his wife's father, he would lose her heart forever. But I am glad God made a way for him to marry. You, Queen Debbie, you made him able to do this. And you will heal him. Capac is a kind, gentle man. He has done a great thing, but it will be a ghost for a man like him. A man needs a woman to help him with his ghosts."

"He has God. But I will do all I can." I sniffled, exhausted. Wincing a little when I heard the patter of little Roy's feet. I didn't know how I'd care for him that day. He came to the door next to my legs.

"Roy!" Mena exclaimed in a whisper. "Come to my house and play with your cousins!" Then she looked me over. I was in the soft nightgown I brought from home. "Give me the garments he wore when you came back from the river today. His and yours. I will burn them and bring new ones tomorrow." The woman could make clothes from scratch in extraordinarily short amounts of time.

"But those are the ones that were blessed generations ago," I objected. "And blessed by God. Capac's God. I prayed over them."

"They are no longer blessed. He does not need those ghosts. We will burn the garments and you pray over *him*."

I nodded, then retrieved the bloody garments, his practically dyed red, and mine stained from helping him wash his harsh justice into the river. Mena had Roy in her arms, so I handed the garments to my sister-in-law with the same eyes as Genesis—Nur, the unmarried woman. I didn't know whether to tell her about her child.

"Thank you, Mena. Nur. You are a blessing. I will rest a little and come get Roy."

Nur smiled sensually. "You will rest and comfort our brother. Sons come from times like this. Roy will be safe with us."

We slept until dinner, arose, and ate with our community. Normally people would do whatever they could to sit near Capac. That day, we sat alone. Before, they loved and revered him, and that didn't go away. From then on, they also feared him.

NINETEEN

For generations, the people gathered at the temple in the morning to hear from the holy men. The "gods" required it. Still in shock, and not knowing what else to do, they did the same the next morning. Capac stood before them.

"This gathering is no longer required. The gods you believed to require it were easily burned in a fire. You are still invited to stay and listen, and I hope you will. For generations, you have heard corruption the holy men claimed was in this Book, which they knew to be God's Holy Word. I will not ask you to trust me for the truth. I only ask that you trust this Book. You will find that it is true, giving us a history of God's people from the beginning, and when they could not meet His requirements, you will learn what He did to redeem us all. Queen?"

Armed with only my great-grandmother's translation of the Bible, I sat among them at the mouth of the cave.

"In the beginning, God created the heavens and the earth. . ."

I read for about ninety minutes each day, and often heard the villagers discussing, in wonder, what they'd heard—as you might discuss a new novel or movie. I read some from the Old Testament and some from the New each day. History and Jesus. I would then sit just outside our home with Roy, and people began to approach me. They would ask me questions about the Bible, since they were now encouraged to speak to me. If Capac was with me, he would always "command" me to answer then stand watch with Rune as I did.

Rune was required to be on alert all hours, but when we were near our home and Belen was there, Rune relaxed some. Often as I was speaking with someone, Jada would take it as an opportunity to seek the attention of Rune. We always allowed him the break. Jada would approach, Rune would smile, and Capac would nod, allowing the young couple to walk off together for a time.

A few days after the Cleansing as I answered an hour-long question about Genesis and our origins, Rune and Jada had not yet returned. Capac did not like having a constant guard, but it was indeed constant enough that his absence was unsettling. So as our questioners went off to other pursuits, Capac scanned the village with his eyes.

Then, though the reason escaped me, Capac sighed and mumbled some version of "not again." And he walked off confidently in some direction that would have earned me getting lost. I followed at his command. We approached a grove of trees that I did recognize as something Capac told me to avoid. Outside of it, Capac said. "*Aqui yo*, Rune."

That's when what I now knew was giggles, not some new creature, stopped. When the two emerged, Jada was clearly frazzled. She walked away, but not before hearing and returning our people's version of "I love you, goodbye." Far deeper and surer than in English, the correct translation is something like, "Hold it steady" and one only utters such a thing to the person who knowingly holds their heart. When married, I often heard, "Keep your cord tight" because that was all a wife was permitted to keep tight at the base of her hair in the case of an absent, or deceased, husband.

After his smile over hearing "Hold it steady" returned from his love, Rune looked annoyed. No, angrily rebellious. Rune's behavior, though fiercely loyal, often bordered on flippant disrespect. Rune leaned on a tree at the entrance of the grove and crossed his arms, then shrugged at Capac's scowl.

"She is yet unopened, King. I honor Jada. You know this."

"Rune, if I touched a woman at *all*, you would have executed her. The way you touch Jada leaves many questions about many things."

"Those things are not for you to question." Rune shrugged again. "I say she is unopened. You accuse me of lies, King?"

My mouth began to correct Rune, but Capac put up a hand and sighed. The hand was not directed to me, but to Rune's machete, always at his side. Was he expected to harm me for uttering barely a syllable of rebuke? Rune laughed.

"King, I know all and see all you do. I have great love and regard for our queen, whom I have watched since she fetched milk for Nur's baby. I will defend her even more than you, who are distracted by that which you protect. Still, you must teach her who I am. I know you have not."

Capac nodded, then turned to me for a private conversation, right in front of ever-present Rune.

"Debbie, Rune does not *only* answer to me. And only to me if it is right." I was confused, and I'm sure my eyes read it, so he continued in English, to Rune's frustration. "He tends my steps. Not only my steps, but my words and actions. He weighs them against the truth. Against what is right. Rune has the right to harm *any* royalty without consequence, and I can speak to none of his actions unless he asks me to."

"By what standard?" I demanded. "Doesn't that make *him* the king, not just an accountability partner? I do not believe *Rune* would harm you, but what is stopping a Tender from overthrowing you at any moment because he is cruel or evil?"

Capac sighed again. "Many bloodlines have a gift, Queen. I dream dreams and lead with love and warmth. It is my gift. The Tender of Footsteps *is* cruel and cold. Never warm or 'tender' at all. Most fear him, and it takes a valiant woman to love him and continue the line. But he is never evil. He is bound to the truth alone."

"I don't understand."

He went further. "As Paul says in Romans, what is right and wrong is known in us from birth. He has God's truth in him, Debbie. It is his gift. Rune is taught to protect the king unless the king does wrong. He is a *perfect* judge of character and intentions. He is why I know that it was right to rescue the women and babies. Rune was there with me and protected them with me even as a younger man.

He will *always* harm a man who seeks to harm me or my family. You have seen this. And he will *never* harm a man who does not. He is missing the part of him that feels sad for it, Debbie. He killed the holy men with me and felt nothing. Only justice."

"So he's like. . ." I glanced at Rune, who likely understood what we were saying, "My parents said there is a psychological disorder—like a sickness in your mind—that makes men like this."

Capac nodded. "Rune does not follow most traditions. Only truth. I see that in many ways this could be a sickness. But for us it is medicine."

I switched languages and turned to Rune. "But why. . .you are not appropriate with Jada. Is this truth and justice?"

"Jada is honored by the standard within me. She is unopened." Rune shrugged.

"But a Tender honors *only* this standard," Capac revealed. "There are affections he and Jada do not withhold as others do, and it makes the seasons before marriage very long. I have tried many times to convince Jada to marry him, but she did not wish it. She wanted to wait to be opened with her sisters."

"*I* wished it." Rune laughed. "I am not without great *love*, King, even if it is not the same as yours. I do for Jada whatever she wishes or does not wish."

"Distracted by that which you must protect," Capac teased.

"Yes, my king. And we will complete our affections *after* our wedding moon. Jada is worth these remaining seasons."

I was glad for the explanation, though I now feared Rune even more. He assured me constantly that he had no standard against me or Capac, and so we need not fear. He couldn't lie, so that should have assured me. Still, when a dazed looking man ran toward me with a skull-sized rock the next day as I read the Bible, Rune took off the man's head without so much as changing his facial expression. He then nodded for me to continue as stunned villagers took the man's body away and his wife screamed in horror.

I was still so naive, but learning the harshness of the world daily. My father had indeed protected me from all that could corrupt me. But in just weeks, I had learned that my dearest friend who respected me was also capable of unbearable lust and even taking lives. I learned that death of everyone I knew waited at the door and did not tend to knock. My loyal guard was also my executioner if needed. Nothing was sacred and no one was safe. The jungle, with human evil added among the million voices, was dangerous.

I was so alone and far from home. I did not know whether the suffering was building or releasing, and supposed that my whole life was probably a combination of both, with little room to heal. A horrific nightmare, Roy's head falling aside just as that man's had, awoke me in screams and then desperate sobs and tears that night.

Capac's arms wrapped around me, though he was not much stronger or any level of a worthy comforter. Nothing he could offer—pure water, good conversation, sex, rubies—would suffice to heal me. He knew I would have rather my daddy wrap me up in his arms. No. I needed Jesus to wrap me up. Capac always hated that he could never protect me well enough. But that night, he said—sang—the perfect thing.

"The perfect butterfly with fire on her wings. A beacon for the caterpillar's change. The wings will burn the trees, but if the caterpillar knows, he'll be caught up in the wings and fly away."

My sobs began to wane, and I said, "Again?"

He sang it again. And again. Until the tears subsided, or at least shied back for the next nightmare. When my heart steadied, the Holy Spirit whispered to me what I spoke aloud to Capac,

"They are worth this to Him." Then, "so they are worth this to me."

Capac's ghosts started to appear not long after that night. Sometimes he would stay in bed instead of coming with me to read. I recognized this as depression, which I'd seen my brother Andrew suffer from. I tried to love him through it and offer hope whenever he was willing to receive it. I couldn't be angry, as I knew the weight of killing men is something a man can carry for life. But I sometimes wondered if the weight he made me carry in those times was even heavier.

"Take my *matteh*," he would mumble, rolling over for sorrowful sleep after tending to my braids.

I had the weight of all these people, when I had barely been their queen a few weeks.

A second time, a person charged at me. I saw in this woman's eyes the wild rage of someone possessed, and I rose to meet her.

But again, Rune's machete did its worst before I could get fully to my feet.

My lips let out a roaring, screeching "NO!" Then I turned to the bloodied Rune over the woman's separated head and body. "Stop KILLING them!"

"You hold the *matteh*, Queen. I will protect you, no matter your heart." His breath was only quickened from exertion, not the adrenaline of death.

Though I knew I was risking my life, I approached the young man, screaming in his face. "You are right, Rune! I hold the *matteh*, and this woman was one of my people! I loved her. You are not to kill my people."

"She tried to kill you. You will love an enemy?"

"Yes! With even my life if I must. Jesus taught me to love my enemies."

"And they killed Jesus, yes?" Rune smiled, doing battle with me.

"No. He laid down His life to save their souls. Rune, I cannot save that woman's soul. I am not Jesus, but I have His words. These words are *life*. Let me read them. If someone comes at me again, you let me handle it."

He laughed, glancing back at the men taking the woman's body away. "You will die. Who will read your words of life if you are dead?"

"My king can read. I taught him." I shook my head. "But I am not concerned, Rune. God sent me here to read these words. You and the king made a way for me to do it. I trust now that God will let them be heard."

Two days later, another day Capac did not want to face the people, it happened again. A man twice my size ran at me, and I stood. My heart pounded, awakening my fear as I scrambled to my feet and put a hand out for Rune to hold back his judgment. The machete was drawn, but he allowed my wish.

"You!" I screamed at whoever was inhabiting the man, "are no longer welcome here. Leave this man alone!"

It was in English, but that entity understood with something other than language. The man responded to me in some raspy, grotesque sort of English that made nearby children scream in horror and run off.

"You! The Holy One is with you!"

"I have brought Him to this people. They will no longer worship *you*," I screamed. "Get out of him, in the name of Jesus, the Holy One of God, by His Spirit."

There was no horrific cry. No ceremony. The man simply slumped onto the ground, unconscious. Rune was stunned. He said nothing. He just stood before me wide-eyed with all the others who were present, then nodded for me to continue my reading.

Anytime Capac was absent, this occurred. It was like they knew his authority, but did not recognize mine. Capac eventually got word, and did his best to be present, however soul-weary. One day when Capac was present, two people ran toward us from inside the cave, and we did not have time to react. Rune had them both dead on the ground before Capac had even swept me behind his back for protection.

That night, I voiced the concern as we lay on our backs watching the lamp whisper its last light. "If Rune keeps killing them—"

"It is his duty."

"He reacts too quickly. Can nothing soften him?"

Capac sighed, trying to be present, though I knew he was heeding his ghosts at that moment. He took my hand in his and pressed it against his face, using the last light now to capture my eyes and try his best to smile. "Only a river can soften a fire."

TWENTY

One day, after the reading, I saw a young woman sitting among the children and watching them play. I knew her to be Alda, the oldest of the children of the holy sons.

"Hello, Alda. Bright morning."

"Queen." Her eyes shot to the ground, and her breathing increased. She did not like that I was speaking with her, but likely only because she had been taught to hate and fear me. So I persisted.

"Do you like children?"

She nodded to the ground. In our village, it was like asking if she liked breathing. It wasn't even a question.

"So do I. Do you know the song about the butterfly? I heard some of them singing it earlier."

Again, she nodded to the ground.

"My sister loves butterflies. She used to chase them, even into the jungle. I thought she might outgrow her love for butterflies, but she loves them the same. She is married now and very soon she will be a mother." I concealed my continued anguish over missing the birth of my niece or nephew, then continued, "still she loves butterflies."

But what I had tried to hide was the thing Alda needed to see. Finally, she spoke.

"Do you miss your family?"

"Yes. Very much." I took a chance. A wild leap of faith and asked, "Do you miss your father?"

"Sometimes yes." She began to open up. "When I see a child with her father, I miss him and I am angry with the king for taking him." She hiccupped, regretting having said it.

"Thank you for sharing your heart. Do not stop."

She nodded, trusting me. "But sometimes, when I see a father with his child I remember that my father loved me but murdered so many other children. And I remember that he could be very harsh. I do not miss him those times. And I *love* our king for taking him." She sighed. "But—"

"Most times it is both." I understood completely.

"Yes."

"Both is good, Alda."

Alda had been Capac's one chance at following the traditions of his people. He could have waited for her to "flower" and then married her. She seemed to be a young teenager at the very oldest, so Capac was decades older than her. Many men would have looked at her soft skin and silky, waist-length hair and eagerly awaited her to come of age in a year or two. Not Capac. He craved maturity and intellectual stimulation and a chance to rescue his people. For Alda, Capac's choice meant she could never marry—until recent changes. I noted them.

"Do you plan to marry and have children of your own?"

"I do not know. My plans have never been my own."

"Well, if not, there are plenty of children here to love. Come, help me sing the butterfly song with them. I know it mostly in the wrong language."

Capac approached me while we were singing that song with the children. We finished and Alda, still part child, ran off to play with them. Capac spoke.

"I think I will make a decree today." He smiled. "I am going to give someone good news." Then he set off. "*Regi-mae.*"

I followed, as always. I checked again for Roy in the group of playing children, and Capac took me to a place I'd never been. It took me time to work out with the way everything was part of the jungle, but the layout of the village was not random. All was planned. Our house and his sisters' houses were on one side of the camp.

They were in their own row with nothing behind them, and partitioned off. Set apart. The rest of the people built theirs in rows of trees along two other sides. The temple and holy homes were the fourth edge.

Among the homes were larger bunk-type houses. But these were for "grown-up" teens not yet ready for marriage. There were a few for young men and for young women. The smaller homes, little mud huts, were dotted back in rows for generations. When an elder died, a younger member of their family would take over that home when they married. No one was ever without a home or hands to help them build one. I adored this people.

That morning, Capac grasped me by the hand and walked me among the people's homes. He was looking for someone, but seemed to have known generally where to find them. When he reached the end of his knowledge, he turned back.

"Which way, Rune?"

"My king?"

"To your home. Which way? Lead me."

"Yes, my king."

Rune led us to the to one of the houses of young men. When we arrived, five other young people were outside it. They were, of course, the three sisters, and with Rune, their three fiancés. They looked to be all preparing to head to their duties for that day, except Jada, who panicked.

"Was your water not enough?"

The rest of them stood at attention when they saw the king walking their way.

"It is always enough, Jada. Very pure," I told her.

"King. Queen," they all said, bowing their heads a little.

These women now had special fear of Capac. He was their rescuer and they had spread the word of their blood-covered king sneaking them out of the temple before killing the eldest generation of holy men. He was their hero, but I gathered that the image of him bloodied had not left their minds any more quickly than it was exiting mine.

"It is a beautiful day." Capac smiled at them, and they agreed, not meeting his eyes.

Rune spoke up. "How can we serve our king?"

"I have a very special request for all of you. Is this the house where you live?"

"The boys live here. We live a few rows over," Jada offered.

"We are building other houses to be ready after next winter," Hanan explained.

"After your weddings, yes?" Capac confirmed.

They agreed in nods and coy smiles.

"I did not mean myself for marriage, but I have found that I enjoy having a wife very much. Her goodness heals me. It is not fair that I was engaged and married in only one day, and all of you *intend* marriage but must wait a year. Since we have no more Openings, we do not need to wait a year for a wedding. The full moon is in three days. How much work is left on your houses?"

"King. . ." Ilian was the only among them to manage as much.

"I will be clearer. What would it take—materials and manpower—to have your three houses ready for three new marriages in three days?" Capac looked among them with authoritative, demanding eyes.

"We are close," Hanan managed. "We have all come together to help. We have one house left of the three because Ilian only put a braid in Dera's hair recently. It must be built from the ground up. Three days may not be enough."

"How many men will you need?"

"Dozens." Ilian chuckled. "And we have our duties with the sheep. And Rune with you, my king."

Capac put his hand on that young man's shoulder, looking directly into his eyes, "My son, *you* are the duty. Our broken people owe this to the six of you. For the next three days, I will move our manpower to help this house be built. The daughters of the Cleansing will all be married at the full moon. We will not have your weddings next winter. We will celebrate your first *children* next winter. Your love, undefiled by adultery, will help us all heal."

They were all in shock. Capac turned to the young women. "My sister and her women will make three beautiful dresses. Do you still intend to honor the braids in your hair?"

They all agreed fervently, beginning to hug and rejoice.

"Go build your house. Forsake that duty for nothing but food and the reading at the temple, if you choose to listen."

"Yes, King."

Capac again took my hand and began to walk away, then turned to Rune.

"Build the house."

"King? Your steps."

"Who is a people who cannot even follow their king?"

"You know that I do not only follow for your steps, King. There are whispers over what we did. Your queen has been attacked many times. You need me near."

"I have my Grower."

"But you do not stay at home."

"Rune, you will be a husband in three days. You will have other important matters for which you cannot cover your feet. I expect your absence for a time," Capac teased the young man, then turned, brought him into an embrace, and said, "I am doing this for *you*. God has made me see the treasure of life, but He has often used my wife to show me. You *have* a heartholder, and so you *need* a heartholder. I want you to marry her and let her tame the river in you."

For the only time ever, before or after, I watched Rune's face twist into tears. "My king, I am a Tender of Footsteps. There are things inside me that cannot be tamed. I deserve no God. I deserve no wife."

Rune was clearly the little brother he never had, and Capac took him in, whispering to him. "And yet God will give you a wife in three days, Rune. A strong woman who can make the river pure for the mouth of royalty."

"You need a Tender," Rune sobbed.

"God will protect me," Capac implored.

Rune sighed. "I will send my father, but he is old, you know this. Please do not wander much, King."

"Send him today. Then work on this house. I do not wish to see you in my steps for a moon cycle, do you understand? You have a winter child to entrust." Capac smiled, and I was trying to translate that final word. It did not make sense contextually.

Rune tried not to smile. "Yes, King." And we turned again.

"You just ordered them to get married and make babies?" I noted as we departed.

"I did." He looked to me. "I could not have them waiting when my wife lives in my house. You were right. I did not see this. I do not see many things in these times. Only darkness."

"God is in control, Capac. He will have mercy and fill the gaps for you. And you have a queen to help you for these times," I encouraged. But I was still confused. "King, what did you mean my entrust? Entrust a child?"

He chuckled. "Entrusted. With a child? The way that Mena is for Belen and your sister for her husband."

"Pregnant?" I said in English.

He waved his hand, pushing that word away from that meaning. Wrong connotation, apparently. "That is *what* she is, not *why*."

I wanted to prod further, but he was deeply in thought. I decided to accept that "entrusted" was the substitute term for "expecting" and moved on. I watched him think, then listened when he decided to do it aloud. "The fruit is enough for three days, do you think? I can take some of the fruit pickers and ask them to help build the house."

"Jesus will thrive here, my king." I noted, "They may wonder why Jesus had to teach people to love one another. They understand that."

"They do. Murder and adultery are not common now that the holy men are gone. But they were idolators."

"They *were*. I will do my best to teach them how to worship Jesus."

He nodded, then made a wild subject shift, back to a moment before. "We have been married almost a moon cycle."

"Yes, I suppose we have."

I thought nothing of the random mention until he elaborated.

"The cycle of the moon is the cycle of a woman." He stopped and turned to me.

"Yes, it is generally the same length of time. A month or so." I could tell from his tone he was trying to ask me something, but I knew I was too dense to know what.

He laughed, trying to help me understand. "It is time enough to know if I have entrusted you. With a child."

I probably turned red. Not because of what he was casually mentioning, but because it occurred to me that our periodic stumbling might become public. The same act that comforted us could start a child. I knew that, of course. But this was like my mother reading me storybooks about blueberries when I'd never tasted a blueberry. We visited the States once and my grandma made us a blueberry pie. It didn't taste anything like I thought it would.

My hand mindlessly floated to my lower abdomen. A moon cycle before, my womb was the cold cavern of a self-appointed spinster. It couldn't possibly be anything else. No angels had erupted in song. Shouldn't I know if I had an additional living soul inside me?

Capac must have seen fear or wonder or something of both in my eyes when they met his. He sighed, placing a hand on my fully braided hair. Then he whispered, "When a man walks with his wife, he does this knowing—hoping—that his seed will fall in such a way that he entrusts her with a child. That is why a man must only walk with a woman he trusts to grow his seed."

Oddly, I thought of my dad again, asking me if I trusted Capac, and of course I did. But Dad quickly faded from my mind when my heart leaped at something I had never considered. Capac trusted *me*. Enough to lead his people. Enough to hope that I would grow his child inside me. Entrusted. I understood, or thought I did.

He finally said, "And so our walks are joy, but only a half joy. Children are the other half of the joy."

I liked that. It was okay if I didn't feel something new and spectacular. Not when I was just waiting for the other half of the joy.

"How will I even know?" I requested of his eyes, feeling naive. "If you have 'entrusted' me."

"Your moon cycle will change and you will begin to feel different." He shrugged. My husband was practically a midwife. It was usually the job of a royal daughter. Nur was the expert. But Capac had attended dozens of births with her and Rune in the jungle. He would have to begin convincing the women to give birth in the jungle early in the pregnancy. He knew pregnancy well.

"Everything is different!" I whispered back. "Your food is different. The clothes, the smells, my daily activities. This moon cycle I have had my life threatened, I have seen men killed, I have become a wife, and I have helped you wash blood into the river. I have not felt so many emotions or introduced my body to more things in all my life than I have this moon cycle. Nothing has been the same since I left home. Different is my normal."

"Hmm." He responded with only that, then a look of intrigue and a little laugh. "Smells?"

"Yes. Especially the fish the past few days. They almost smell rotten to me."

He chuckled. "After the full moon, you will wake unwell. Then it will be time to go see Nur."

"Why?"

But he walked away chuckling, then reached out his hand. "Come, Queen. We need to set the pickers to work on the house."

Twenty-One

"Rune. You are the river. Jada, you are the fire. Together, you are all the strength of water, and God is your peace."

Capac repeated the same to two more couples as three nervous men braided carefully crafted cords into gorgeous black hair. Afterward, he prayed over the couples, then sent them off together while the rest of us feasted.

My fondness for my husband grew as I watched him perform that ceremony, and over the extra fruit that always came with wedding feasts, Capac caught me staring at him with contentment.

"Are you well, my queen?" He murmured in confidence, just having been laughing at a joke told by Rune's father.

"Very well, my king." I shrugged.

He smirked. "You have passion in your eyes."

"Does that mean I am not well?" I flirted.

"It means you have a need. You know that all I have is yours."

I sighed. "I have no need but you and my God."

"Then perhaps we should go to our house so that you can seek us both," he mumbled.

But Nur, seated on his other side, stopped that line of thinking. "Not now, brother. You will wish you to stay."

That was difficult grammatically. It meant that Capac would wish that he had stayed if he were to leave. As I was sorting it out, Capac was protesting.

"I am a husband of barely a moon cycle, Nur. We must tend to our affections."

Nur shook her head. "You have tended enough for now. Look at the color in her face."

"Her face is red when she is ashamed. Her people do not speak so much of affections." Which I'd told him.

Nur laughed a devious laugh. "The color is not for shame. Her affections are seen."

I didn't understand that for another week, but we'll get there.

"Seen, but never complete." Capac was still not dissuaded.

"Stay. You will wish it," Nur insisted. "Your romance will not wane until then."

Capac grumbled.

"It is well. We have all our days for stumbling. We will stay to celebrate new marriages," I allowed, and that calmed him.

We were glad we stayed. About three minutes later, just thirty minutes or so after the couples had departed, I saw Rune at the far side of the trees, where the houses were. I was puzzled. I was told newlyweds disappeared for days or weeks after a wedding. It was not customary to see one so soon.

He did something even more unprecedented, approaching the feast, and then the king. He stopped in front of us, a bundled white cloth hanging from his strong right hand.

"Rune, you have other obligations and joys, why are you here?" Capac asked with warmth.

"King. My rescuer. May I address your people?" he asked, some mix of passion and nerves and bewilderment in his eyes.

"To his honor, I hope?" I interjected. A devoted wife and queen, and not so afraid of this joyous version of Rune.

"*All* is to his honor for me, Queen." Rune smirked.

Capac nodded and arose again, holding up a hand to silence the feast.

"Rune wishes to speak." Then he nodded to the young man.

Rune lifted his voice to be heard, and was apparently not a bad orator.

"Our king is a rescuer. I have heard many of you whisper of the old ways. I have taken the lives of men willing to attack our queen over the old ways. But the old ways were to our shame. Our king rescued my wife's flesh from evil. From shame. With his new ways." The crowd was silent, and all could hear the whoosh of Rune unfurling the cloth in his hand. It was not all white of course. Tell-tale evidence had been placed there very recently. "Jada is my wife. And her flesh is only for her husband. Let no one say she has not been rescued."

Rune relished it, not when the crowd gasped as he hung the cloth on the requisite pole, but when Capac shed a tear at the gesture, taking the young man's face into his hands, I heard the gentle words spoken only for Rune.

"God has blessed us, Rune. Know that it was Him who rescued you. Go now and treasure your wife."

Rune exited, leaving Capac stunned. But Rune passed Ilian, who was approaching. He stopped first at the pole, displaying a sheet of evidence. Then he approached the still hushed crowd.

"You built me a house to share with my wife. My joy is for all of you to share. Dera was to be the first defiled. But she has been rescued, and I have cared for her. Her flesh is only for her husband." Then he turned to his king with a fist at his chest. "*Resgatei.*"

Capac sobbed then, gave the youngest of the men a similar word of truth and love, and Ilian returned to his new home and new wife.

It was half an hour more when Hanan, known for his long, intellectual discussions with Lana, arrived. I recalled a long conversation with my husband on our wedding night, passions far from our mind. I imagined these two had engaged in the same.

"There he is," the girls' father teased, and Hanan replied with a bright smile when he would normally scowl at those who teased his meticulous ways.

"This night is for joy. You cannot take it." Hanan then looked to Capac, who was sobbing when he nodded permission for the boy to continue. "An opening should be for joy and love, not fear and sorrow. At the new moon, my Lana was meant for fear and sorrow.

But she was rescued. Tonight she has been opened with joy and love. Her flesh. My wife's flesh. Is for her husband."

Hanan unfurled the cloth that had been at his side, then hung it with the others on the pole. Completely disgusting. Completely beautiful. Capac caught him into a bear hug and whispered in his ear.

The girls' father had risen when Rune left, also hugging each of them with gratitude. His daughters had been loved, not defiled. His joy was complete. My king's healing began. He needed that night. He needed to know some good came out of it.

Later, in the privacy of our bedroom, after secret affections, Capac spoke to me.

"I did the same."

"Same what?" I asked.

"Kings before me have quietly presented their evidence to the holy men. I spoke to the people and presented it openly. I told them that a woman's flesh is only for her husband. I told them I would rescue them so they could honor God. I did not tell you to not make you feel shame for the evidence. I know it made you feel shame. But it was honor. And that is why they did this tonight. It was to honor marriage and to honor me."

"My king. . ." I was even more dizzied by him after our walk.

He was distressed. "I am praying that soon it will be to honor God. I am not their rescuer. I wish for them to know Him."

"But you are God's instrument. His *matteh*. With you in His will, He can rescue and rule your people," I encouraged.

"His *matteh*," Capac whispered. "Yes. Together. We are His *matteh*."

I nodded. Smiled. He said one last thing before departing to his dreams:

"Passion in your eyes. Color in your cheeks. You are the most beautiful queen, Debbie."

A week later, after increasingly rotten-smelling fish that everyone told me was fresh, I awoke too sick to rise and read to the people.

"Capac?" I said in the grogginess of morning.

"Yes?" He was barely awake.

"I feel unwell."

He turned to me with a smile. "Go see Nur."

"Will she tease me? She always teases."

"Yes," he admitted with a laugh.

"Can you read today? And take Roy?"

"I am a bad reader!" he worried. "But I will try. You rest and then go see Nur."

Nur took one look at me and laughed, leading me into her home and behind a cloth. "Undress."

"Okay." I was nervous, but complied. She had seen me in as little before.

Nur poked and prodded me, and I wasn't even sure everything she was looking for before she finally concluded:

"My brother has entrusted you with his seed. He will be a father." This was almost said in bewilderment, and that made sense. Capac had never intended to do anything of the sort. Then she looked me over as I dressed. "So white. Does your skin burn?"

"Yes, but thankfully there is a canopy here." I smiled, thinking of white skin. "Capac says my skin is white like wool."

"Mena was right. Love grows." I did not have the heart or the time to tell her otherwise, because she followed up with, "Winter child. Debbie, you will have a *son*." That last word whispered out in astonishment. Gratitude. But I read it as fear.

"Is all well with him?" I worried.

"*Very* well. Your sickness tells me so." She nodded with the rare insight into her methods. Then a little laugh. "*My* brother. A *father*."

When we emerged, Capac was waiting on the other side of the curtain with Roy.

"A son?" He asked his sister to confirm what he'd overheard.

"Yes. An heir from your own seed," she promised.

Capac literally jumped in the air for joy, then embraced me.

"Thank you, Nur," he declared.

Capac told Roy about the new baby as fact, showing him my belly where the baby was being carried. Apparently, Nur was to be trusted.

That night I lay restless as Capac was working to calm his spirit to sleep.

"What is wrong, my queen?"

I promptly unloaded. "Your culture is beautiful, Capac. I believe that Christ will thrive here among them. But you cannot live for Christ and believe superstitions. Nur told me this baby is going to be a boy. No one could know that this early. The science of that makes no sense."

"Nur has her ways. She has never been wrong. This is her gift."

"But that isn't science. It is superstition."

"Debbie, your medicine is great. But our medicine is old. Just as oral tradition dies with the written word, so old medicine is called superstition when new medicine comes. Writing and new medicine are only good until they make us forget what we know is true."

"But—"

"Did you not tell me that the people in your 'United State' trust science and not God?"

"Yes, but some things—"

"You said the mysteries of the Bible sometimes become the things men prove with science. And yet your science calls your Bible superstition."

He wasn't wrong. I let him continue.

"I do not know Nur's ways, but she is not superstitious. She believes what she sees, which is why it took so long for her to trust in Jesus. I think Nur's old medicine is science and she just keeps her secrets. I believe circumcision is the same."

"I suppose it is. There are legitimate medical arguments for both circumcision and for avoiding it. Dad did not have your orphans circumcised because he believed it was not his choice to make with such a risk. I had Roy circumcised to set him apart. It was an outward sign of an inward distinction."

"I want my son to be circumcised. This heir I have entrusted to you."

That surprised me more than the day he started speaking in perfect English behind the bars of that hut.

"You said it was a 'bad tradition' when you saw Roy was circumcised."

"Everything is different now," he whispered, taking my stomach under the warmth of his hand. "My son will be set apart as royalty, and servant of the highest King. And we will declare it in his flesh."

I tried not to remain restless as Capac fell asleep. But the outcome of my visit with Nur was not what had rattled me. It was just two words.

"Love grows."

I was sleeping next to a man I preferred over all others. I was carrying his child. Our marriage was strong. Strong enough that it did not rattle me to calm him when he'd wake up swinging at the air and then commanding me to wash him in the river when all was well in our home. We were *strong* together. But I honestly didn't know if he loved me. It didn't matter. That's what I told myself. I could grow a child, I could grow marriage and now, I could grow a love for God's Word in a whole people group. Love need not enter my thoughts. That was nothing but romance.

Twenty-Two

Two months later, after I completed another reading that included circumcision, though it was Paul telling the gentiles they need *not* be circumcised, my husband finally snapped. I attribute his choices in those seasons to the "ghost" that was his taking ten lives with a machete. He was looking for penance and renewal. So after that reading while I was sleeping away some morning sickness, my king decided he was "set apart as royalty" and circumcised himself. He used the knife from his *matteh* and didn't sanitize it.

I had been outside just a few minutes when he did it. I was livid as he got the bleeding under control. Then as he moaned in pain for days, I became concerned. The area had become infected, and I went to Nur.

"I remember you had leaves for—"

"For my stupid brother? He could die or ruin chances for more children," she ranted, echoing my same feelings on the matter.

"I know. That is why I need something for the infection. I need your medicine."

"My medicine cannot help him." She sighed, fretting in sadness. "As a child, he was healthy. But after your people gave him medicine it poisoned him for my medicine."

It would be the ramblings of a witch doctor if not for my scientific knowledge of a person's body becoming more susceptible to bacteria due to overuse of antibiotics. That one unnecessary dose of penicillin when he was a teen was apparently enough to ruin him for natural remedies. I didn't like it, but I knew Nur was telling the truth.

I needed to call up an old debt to save my king.

I spent the next hour trying to find the fastest runner—make that deep jungle marathoner—who also knew where the mission was. Thankfully, such a man existed among the people. I finally got someone to say,

"You mean other than Rune?"

Frustrated, all I did was turn around.

The newlywed Rune was known for running long distances to keep up with Capac and replenish supplies throughout winters they were away. He had run between the mission and our village more times than he could count, and knew the way with ease. I sent him with a letter and a promise that we would make no footsteps until he returned. Capac was bedbound. In the letter, I left out most details, but asked for penicillin and hoped that it wasn't too much trouble. I gave them a promise I was safe and asked them to feed and house my faithful runner for the night.

Rune set out in the morning and returned in the evening the next day with the penicillin and an EpiPen should the recipient prove allergic. Either they didn't hate me, or they at least still cared for these people. The note Dad sent suggested it was both.

"Debs,

We are overjoyed to hear you are safe. It seems you were right to trust your friend with your life. Please do not hesitate to ask or just come home should you need anything else, big or small. This favor isn't nearly big enough to cover our debt to you. We will welcome you and any of your people at any time. Mom is sending a kiss for you and Roy.

All our love,
Dad"

I wept over the letter, laughed over Capac having been only my friend just months before, then administered the medicine. Capac was back to his bull-headed self and attempting to cause me to stumble within the week.

It was only days after Capac healed that I awoke in the night to the sound of a new creature I had never heard. When my ears came to themselves, I realized it was actually the sound of a woman singing a word, starting lower at the first syllable and lifting the second up an octave. The word was *Bobo*—our word for "baby."

Capac laughed, then nearly deafened me when he responded by doing the same. He arose and pulled me outside, where we heard hundreds of weary voices singing out "*Bo-bo*" in various rhythms and lengths of syllables, but all the pitches were the same the first voice demonstrated. Capac tapped me, and gestured to his own upturned chin. He wanted me to sing too. I managed to get out just one syllable, because all at once, there was silence. Before I could ask questions, Capac placed a gentle hand at my mouth to quiet me. His face shone pure delight.

That is when Nur emerged, not from her own home two houses away, but from Mena's beside ours.

From there, she released a loud whooping sound that raised in pitch right at the end. Beside me, Capac echoed the same along with those other voices everywhere. Nur repeated the sound. Then we all did the same. Nur did it just one more time, and we repeated it. After the third call-and-answer whoop, Nur then started the "*Bobo*" chant again and all voices cheered in response.

Capac looked over at Nur, who was practically emitting light. I had never seen her so happy. He laughed aloud, but it was a laugh of disbelief. Nur simply nodded, then gestured for us to follow her back into Mena's house.

"We will get Roy and come soon," Capac said to her. Nur nodded and disappeared into Mena's home.

I tried to sort out what was happening, though I did have some idea. "Mena's baby?"

Capac nodded enthusiasm before he remembered he should probably explain. "Nur calls us to listen. Then one cry is daughter. Two is son. Three is *royal* daughter. Four is royal son. Five is heir."

"And this was. . ." I wasn't sure which sounds to count.

"Three. Royal daughter." Capac laughed again like the maniac he had become. "Debbie, Mena has a *daughter*. Nur told us so before, but we thought she was joking."

"I thought God only gave them sons," I said.

"Because of Mena's fear of the Opening, yes. She begged for this and God allowed only sons. But the Opening is no more, and God has blessed us all. Come, let us get Roy to meet his new cousin." Capac jumped in the air. "Ha! A girl!"

From the shouts of the people despite it being the middle of the night; from their utter euphoria and the way Capac sobbed when he held his niece against his chest as Belen danced and laughed around the room with his four young sons, I knew. I had been told that these people loved babies and cherished the birth of each one. But I had never seen such celebration. They were kindling the fires and forsaking sleep to sing of butterflies. Yet it was from their joy I realized the evil that the Closing must have invited. I couldn't imagine the wailing. The agony.

But, oddly, I think it was from that evil that they knew how to have such joy. How can the summit of joy reach so high without the equal and opposite counterpart that is the ocean trench of sorrow? And is there even a place for temperate peace between the two? If so, how, when the way we rebel against lamenting is with the sound of singing?

I wailed in the night for the sorrow of losing so much and nightmares of seeing so much death. And I wailed in the night, too, for the delight of new life. In those times, peace seems an absurd goal that God alone is capable of. No one asks for mere peace when bliss is an option. Perhaps, then, we should not be so quick to reach for peace when sorrow wants a melody too. Suddenly I understood the "erratic" actions of my husband, who knew how to experience all parts of the spectrum more profoundly than anyone present.

Unfortunately, that spectrum darkened and deepened completely into sorrow. Sorrow, for a man, can look like anger. While Capac did not have it in him to abuse me or Roy in any form, more than once I heard him get harsh with Belen and even go head-to-head with Rune once he returned to our service.

One morning, I woke up from a deep sleep to Jada's horrified scream. I ran outside to find that Capac and Rune were in a brutal fistfight. Over what, I never quite knew, and they all refused to tell me. But ultimately, the marginally stronger Rune had his king on the ground, cheek in the mud, Rune's knee between my husband's shoulder blades.

Rune lowered his face to the level of Capac's when it was clear he was no longer fighting. And he said, "I will *not* obey you. I will *protect* you, my king."

Only then did I notice a man lying still beside Jada. I gasped.

Rune explained, "he frightened my wife. Took your water from her and poisoned it. He denied it."

"He denied it and you killed him?" Emotions were high, so I said it with intensity. Perhaps Jada had not softened him at all.

"No. Today he was your Taster," Rune said. "I will take Jada to get more water. Keep *him* inside." He stood, then wiped his mouth of blood Capac had drawn and led Jada away.

That night, I whispered my suspicion to him across the darkness of our bed. "Did you try to drink the water?"

"Do not ask me," he growled.

"Capac, did you try to *hurt* yourself?"

"I protected Jada," he said.

"Jada has training, King. What would kill you would only make her sick. Why would you—?"

"Rune has entrusted her with a child. The child has no training. I could not allow—"

"But it is not your duty, King. You have other duties that require you to be alive and well. Why would you be so reckless?" I whispered then with fervor.

He began to weep then with open sobs and allowed me to hold him as he wept. "I deserve no son. I deserve no queen. I have taken lives. Precious lives in the image of God."

"Still, you have a son. And you have me. I am growing an heir for you, Capac, my dearest friend. Will you stay with me? Will you raise this child with me? I will stay for you. Please stay for me?"

Capac made no other rash attempts at peace. His angry outbursts were rare, and mild enough for immediate apology when they happened. He was healing. Still, he was capable of fervent apathy toward his duty as king. He held the *matteh*, but not really. He answered no questions at the cave, despite the people's renewed need to understand this new way of life. He left me to speak to them. To read to them. And Rune to defend me.

The people's spiritual leader after the death of their holy men was a powerful man of God. But he was a broken one. Their *resgatei* was absent. Walking into the jungle and spending days there. Skipping meals. Often refusing conversation when he came home, but asking me to walk with him when we were alone. I did. My braids were secure, and an heir grew until all could see him at my belly and rejoice. But my heart hurt for my king.

I knew he was trying. He was praying. He knew his failings. He told me I was helping God to sustain him, and so I continued to pour into him. But increasingly so, I had no one but God to sustain me. I was exhausted in every way. Trying to be strong for a people still hardened to the new ways.

When I was around six months pregnant with a probable little boy, fighting his active mornings as I read the Bible to the people, Ilian and his wife Dera approached me. They were always eager to listen, and the first to arrive at the temple each morning.

Evidence of their affection shone in hundreds of beautiful braids and on the young woman's abdomen, nearly as prominently as mine as they approached.

"Queen?" Ilian began.

I hated that Capac wouldn't allow them to call me Debbie. "Do you have a question?"

"Many." He snickered. "I want to be saved by Jesus. But I worry, because I am a coward."

"A coward?" I smiled, trying to conceal the leap of joy in my heart and my son's. "How so?"

Dera spoke for him with a giggle. "He does not want to be circumcised."

"I have read to you that you need not be circumcised," I reminded him.

"But Roy is circumcised. Your holy son. And the king became sick from being circumcised," Ilian rebutted.

Children of Roy's age rarely wore clothing. It was cleaner, less work, and they potty trained practically without assistance. It was genius, and no one considered their innocent nudity to be a problem. Everyone could see, however, that Roy looked different. And it was widely known what Capac had done to himself.

"The king asks that only royal sons be circumcised. You need not do it in your flesh."

The young man sighed relief, then said exactly what I planned to next. "But I will circumcise my heart. I will change my heart from sin to love Jesus. Me and my wife. Tell us how to be saved by Him."

"If you confess your sins and declare that Jesus is Lord, then you are saved already."

"Lord?"

"Yes. That Jesus is God, was born to a virgin in human flesh, lived a sinless life, died on the cross, then rose again on the third day. This makes Him Lord, but we must believe in Him."

"A virgin." Dera looked remorseful. "Was Mary opened by a holy man?"

"No. Jesus was not conceived by any man. He was conceived of the Holy Spirit."

Oddly, or maybe not, that science confused them.

"It was a miracle of God. Never before had it happened, and never again. No man is holy but Jesus. He had to be born of a virgin."

"But marriage is holy," Ilian fretted.

"Marriage allows us to walk with our spouse without sin or shame," I explained, then smiled at Dera's belly. "Your baby is a gift from God. Does Nur say boy or girl?"

"Daughter." The young man beamed. "By God's grace."

I looked at Dera's long, silky black braids and soft skin, all Ilian's. "A beauty."

Ilian laughed nervously in agreement when his wife smiled coyly, slowly batting her long eyelashes.

After that, I prayed with them both to accept Christ.

The following day, Rune and Jada came to me. But Rune was a different man. Our chief warrior if we had an army. God had something similar for him, but first Rune had some questions.

"For a thousand years our holy men lied and now you say this Book is truth."

"Yes."

"But how can I know this is not some new lie?" Rune demanded. I was glad to finally know his heart.

"Rune, you are speaking with our queen," Jada told him.

I looked between them, confused, wondering if Jada did not know Rune's power. He answered the question in my eyes.

"I have sinned against you and Capac, Queen. Truth and justice are perfect in me, but not kindness or respect."

"But those are not required," I reminded him.

He interrupted with, "I require these things of others for you. I must also be what I expect of others. You have read this in your book. Judge not, lest ye be judged."

"Well, yes, but—"

His tone was still harsh. "This is God's standard. The same that lives in me. It changes for no one. For no Tender. It is difficult for me, but there is no excuse to break the standard." He softened before continuing. "So I am sorry, my queen. Every word you have spoken from this Book is truth, and the standard within me knows it. Still, I struggle. How was the truth buried in the dirt like death? How can the holy men lie and I did not know? Tell me which is true, please."

"I was a lover of God's Word all my life before I became your queen. You will not offend me if you ask questions from your heart," I assured him. "May I read to you from the Book?"

"But if it is not true, then—"

"Then nothing matters, Rune. Nothing at all. Please, let me read you a passage to begin to answer your question."

"Yes. Read it," Jada answered for her doubting, fuming husband.

"Okay," I flipped through the Bible, then came to the passage.

" 'He is despised and rejected by men, A Man of sorrows and acquainted with grief. And we hid, as it were, our faces from Him; He was despised, and we did not esteem Him. Surely He has borne our griefs And carried our sorrows; Yet we esteemed Him stricken, Smitten by God, and afflicted. But He was wounded for our transgressions, He was bruised for our iniquities; The chastisement for our peace was upon Him, And by His stripes we are healed. All we like sheep have gone astray; We have turned, every one, to his own way; And the LORD has laid on Him the iniquity of us all.' "

"Rune, who is this about?"

"The Man Jesus, who my king and queen say died for the sins of the world," Rune answered with sarcasm.

"Are you certain?" I asked.

Jada nodded fervently. Rune nodded with doubt.

"But this was written many hundreds of years before His birth by the prophet Isaiah. It is in the Old Testament. How can this be about Jesus, who is in the New Testament?" I taught.

Rune tilted his head. Then he and Jada shrugged.

"Jesus Himself read from this scroll during His ministry on Earth. The way that God would redeem His people was long foretold. Many things are foretold. Thus far, God has brought them all to be."

"Is there anything that has not yet been brought to be?" Jada, enamored, asked it.

"The end of days is yet to come. Christ will return. Because He has kept His promises, we know we can trust Him to return for His people, and to judge the world. He is, I would say, our Tender. That is all in this Book as well," I explained, watching Rune's face.

When he did not respond, but considered my words, I said more.

"I know this Book is true because It has proven Itself to be true. Your holy men promised many things that did not come to be. The Bible promises nothing that God will not fulfill, and that much has been proven." I leaned in closer. "And God requires nothing, Rune. No rituals or sacrifices. Not since Jesus. But He desires your heart. If you give Him your heart, nothing you have done matters. If you do not, nothing you ever do will matter."

"God required my king to take the lives of evil man. And I have taken many lives," Rune reminded.

"But God has our king's heart. He will ask us to obey Him the way a father does, but only if He has our heart." I nodded to Jada's stomach. Another child of the Cleansing. "What does Nur say? Boy or girl?"

"Son." Rune nodded, his mind elsewhere.

"Does not my queen have the king's heart?" Jada asked, glancing at the ruby around my neck.

What a question. I trod lightly, wondering if *anyone* had his heart anymore.

"God is first in his heart and in mine," I explained.

The next day, because Rune needed a sleepless night to consider it, I prayed with them both to accept Christ. The day after, it was Lana and Hanan, who arrived with the other two newlywed, newly redeemed couples. Hanan was one of the few among them who kept count of the years, and even knew himself to be about twenty-two years old. This was only inexact because he was not sure which of his first years he learned to count. He asked me why, if God is a God of order, the gospel accounts do not line up perfectly. For that answer, I looked to the three young sisters.

"Ladies, if it is not too offensive, please describe what happened the night of the Cleansing."

Jada began. "We were taken to the first room, and right away we turned and our king—"

"It was not right away. It was much time. It felt like so long," Dera offered.

Lana, rubbing at the third child of the Cleansing, shook her head. "It was only a moment, Dera. But he had his *matteh* and—"

"*I* had the *matteh* that night," I corrected.

"Oh." Lana winced. "But he had the machete."

Dera again. "Yes, and he took us through the front entrance and I saw one of the—"

"You saw nothing, Dera. We went through the side entrance with Rune that we did not know to be there," Jada corrected.

"I *saw*. Your face was the other way. But I will never forget the sight of a man without his head, Jada," Dera insisted.

I put up a hand to stop them, hoping Capac had not heard. Then I looked to Hanan. "Was that a precise account, Hanan?"

They all chuckled. Hanan nodded. "Jesus chose men, and not perfect ones, to follow Him and tell His story."

"And would you have believed a precise account from these three?" I asked.

"No. It was many months ago and they were very scared. I would not expect them to be precise." Hanan laughed. "Pray with us as you prayed with them, Queen? Help us to accept Jesus."

"With great joy."

Twenty-Three

The three "rescued" couples often led the charge in matters of faith. The people, who had been lax in attending the no-longer-required reading, began to come again. Daily, they began to surrender to Christ. When I was not present myself, I learned that a member of those three couples was. I would often turn when stopped with a Bible question to see that Rune was answering another. Hanan and Ilian began to join him in his walks behind me. He was no longer lowly. He was a trusted apprentice of the Bible teacher, and so were they. These three men began to ask me to repeat stories so that they could retell them. *With precision*, Hanan would add.

In the final month of my pregnancy, all three couples, having discussed it beforehand, came to me at once after the reading. We had just finished Matthew again, and the Great Commission in Matthew 28.

"Go therefore and make disciples of all the nations, baptizing them in the name of the Father and of the Son and of the Holy Spirit, teaching them to observe all things that I have commanded you. . ."

I knew these bright-eyed young newlywed believers. I saw the question coming.

"Must we be baptized?" Rune asked.

"Not for Salvation, but Christ commands it. The symbol of going into the water and coming out new is a public profession that God is renewing your heart."

They all muttered among themselves and then their spokesperson Rune asked it.

"We wish to be baptized."

"Usually a pastor or church elder or a parent at the very least does that. My father is a pastor and baptized me," I explained.

"Your father is a good, kind man. Perhaps he could baptize us." Rune had spent a night at the mission to retrieve medicine, and had likely experienced their fervent hospitality. Certainly, he knew it from afar.

"I will speak with the king and ask him what we should do."

They agreed, and I had to search for an hour, but found Capac in the inner chamber of the temple. I sat on the cold stone floor in the darkness. It was a welcome relief from the heat, but it was not peaceful. He spoke first.

"You grow more beautiful each day, my queen."

"Your son grows bigger and kicks me constantly. That does not make me beautiful," I corrected him, glad he was at least in a cordial mood.

"Then perhaps I was not speaking of my son, but of my wife," he said, the flattery meeting my face with warmth.

Capac, who had been sitting against a stone wall, scooted forward and hooked his leg around me. Physical affection was always welcome, and I relished it.

"What do you require, my queen?" he whispered.

I nodded. "You need elders, Capac. Advisers. Lawmakers. A group of men and women you trust to create a new system. Right now the people are sheep without a shepherd. The holy men are dead, and you are absent. They have only my reading, and they are lawless otherwise."

"You have said this before, and I am here considering that very request. I am trying to be what is needed, Debbie, but I am broken. I am a coward," he whispered.

For the first time, I sinned by thinking he might be right about the coward thing. But in the next beat, I repented and looked into his eyes. "It does not matter if you think you are a coward, Capac. Your people need their king."

He sighed. Then he rattled off a list of names. Definitive names.

"First, my queen. And Rune. Jada. Both of their fathers, who are wise. Hanan and Ilian."

"Not Lana and Dera?"

"No, they will be needed for the sheep. But I welcome them to tell me their hearts."

"Are there any others?"

"Belen, of course. There is also a fruit cutter and her husband, a fisherman. Nur. Another that I cannot name to you. And Alda."

"Alda is a child." I laughed. "She might defy you. Sometimes she hates you, King."

"Good. God is wise to have chosen her. These came to me in a dream. Kings dream. I have told you this. The dreams are of God." He sighed. "Not *all* dreams. Some dreams are a ghost."

"Those are good choices. The ones I know of, at least."

"They meet the qualifications in the Bible, and they can represent *all* of my people with concerns I cannot see," he said. "But you did not come to me to speak of elders."

"No, because what I came to ask is a very large request."

"I will capture the moon for you like a fish, my queen."

"We now have a Cleansing day. The first new moon after winter. May I choose what that day celebrates now?"

Suddenly, he was wary. "Tell me your heart for that day."

"Rune, Hanan, and Ilian. God's chosen elders. They have asked to be baptized along with their wives. I think we should do it that day. Cleanse them, like you cleansed this temple. But with water as Jesus commanded."

He was wary of that, because he knew that was not such a large request.

"And who will baptize them?"

"I thought perhaps it could be my father. It would be after our son is born, and the other three children."

"And you could see your family?" He placed his hands on my belly.

"Yes, I could see my family." I sighed. My husband had learned to braid my troublesome, wispy curls into elaborate curves and beauty. But I still missed my little sister, now a mother.

"I will need to pray about this, Debbie. Your father will be angry that we left. Angry that I took you as wife and entrusted you with a child. Angry that I took lives. . .how can I ever face him again?"

I nodded. "I understand. But for the joy of baptizing new believers, he will forgive us. He says we are welcome to come to them at any time."

"I told you I will consider this, my queen. Give me time to consider."

A few days later, Capac called these names together. Most of them, at least. There was still the one he had not yet named to me, and Jada had some family obligations. After that meeting where they all joyfully agreed to represent their corners of the village to help us rebuild, we exited the temple to find a flashback-inducing sight. Jada, Lana, and Dera were standing outside in tears, awaiting an audience with their king. The three sisters were holding one another, and their husbands, who had been with us, all came out in a panic.

"What is this?" I asked, because Capac, who was also likely reliving a terrible night, was stunned at the sight.

"My queen, we are not worthy. But still, we come to ask." Jada sobbed.

"Anything you ask will be yours." Capac, coming out of his stunned silence, said this from behind me. It was something he'd say to me. But these young women were something like sisters or daughters to both of us, and he stopped at very little to care for them when he was up to caring at all.

"Our grandmother's sickness is ending." Jada spoke again.

I was working at the translation still, I thought. If her sickness was ending, why were they crying?

"The wrath of the gods?" Capac asked with immense compassion. What did he mean? There were no gods before the One True God. They all knew that.

The girls nodded, sobbing. They were so close in their embrace that their three innocent unborn children were likely dancing together at the rhythm of sobs and sorrowful hearts. I was like them. I thought they should be dancing. But they were mourning.

"Then her sickness will end." Capac sighed, releasing a tear. "So what is it you ask?"

Dera spoke this time. "King. Queen. Will you come to her? Will you tell her what you can about our God?"

"You know much about our God," Capac reasoned.

"But she will not hear us. She has invented her own god." Jada's bitterness flowed out in the next few sobs.

Capac nodded. "Let me speak with my queen."

Capac took my hand, then led me about ten feet away.

"I don't understand," I whispered in English, which is what I did in those days where the culture evaded me.

He spoke into my ear in English. He told me that there was an illness among them. It took the old and young alike, but it was not contagious. It came on swiftly and lasted only a few days up to about two weeks. Sandani's had astonished him when it lasted a season. But it eventually killed whoever got it, without fail. They called it the wrath of the gods, but Capac knew it was just some kind of incurable illness that took people in their time. His people died of little else.

"But they said it was ending." I noted my confusion.

"There is one way this sickness ends, Debbie." He sighed. "It is okay. We accept this death. Life is suffering, and it ends one way. If we are in Christ, we need not fear that end."

I sighed, "But they fear for her salvation."

"Yes. Will you go to her?"

"Is it customary?"

"I have rarely gone into the homes of my people. It is not customary at all." He laughed. "And this time I cannot go. A woman whose sickness is ending needs her hand held. For that I must send you."

That's right. He couldn't touch her. And I think he had other motives. But I obeyed, following the three sisters to their grandmother's home. They led me to the door, but did not enter. I didn't know the reason, but I understood this mission was my own. They told me her name, Cunei, and stepped back.

I entered the modest hut alone, and there was a frail old woman coughing in the corner under a blanket. I knew her face from the girls' wedding and from her steady hands chopping fruit. The people aged differently than you know. She was not an old woman to my eyes. She looked about Mom's age, but math told me she was closer to Jane's age. They lived under a full canopy, and sunlight was never direct. Others were older. Why was she dying so young?

She coughed, then in a raspy voice, she whispered, "He said you would come."

"Who told you I would come?" I smiled, crouching down and taking her frigid hand in mine.

"I do not know His name. Only that He has many. My husband told me he met Him when his sickness came. He died trusting this God. And when I sleep He comes to me."

She had hours. Moments, maybe. Her lungs sounded like a wet rattle and her face was as pale as mine. I didn't have time to turn her from a false god. Still, I prayed in my heart for God to make a way for her to know Him.

"Have you heard my teachings at the temple?"

"Oh yes." She smiled, then slipped back into delusion. "He told me you speak of Him."

"Cunei, the God of the Bible has many names. Which did He tell you?" I was terrified to play into her delusion with precious few moments, but the Spirit urged me to.

She spoke slowly, in a rasp. But I had no purpose in life but her, and patiently listened. "I asked Him His name. I told Him I am not worthy of a god to be in my dream. I am a fruit cutter and no queen. And He said that today my queen would hold my hand as my sickness ended. And that she would tell me His name."

It wasn't possible. Of course, it wasn't. But my father had told me stories my whole life of missionaries who had arrived at unreached people to find they had been reached in dreams and visions by the Spirit of God Himself. Sandani had been fed by El Roi Himself. So I didn't even hesitate, though the tears flowed freely. "Cunei, He does have many names. But today, I will tell you that His name is Jesus of Nazareth, and He is the Christ. You were visited by a Man whose footsteps I am unworthy to cover. I am a queen, but He is the King of kings. And He came to Earth to take away our sins and be raised again so that fruit cutters and lowly queens could live forever with Him."

"I have heard you say His name," she said with all her feeble passion. "This name is in your Bible."

"And it is the most beautiful, is it not?" I sobbed. "Is He beautiful, Cunei? Was He perfect?"

"He was just a Man, my queen." She laughed, "He was God, of course. Just as He said. But He was also Man."

"And that is why He is beautiful to me," I whispered.

"He told me I must tell you," she whispered. "You will know. But He asked me to tell you."

"What did He say?" My whole purpose rested and awakened at what this woman would say.

"He says He is coming quickly," she whispered, her eyes not opening so easily or quickly anymore after each blink. "And you are running out of time. This sickness will end soon."

The conversation ended there. I held her hand as she fell asleep. And then, as had been promised, I was holding her hand and felt her sickness end. I cried there a moment, in mourning and astonishment. I never told them what she'd said. I never even told Capac. But when I emerged from the hut, there was something I could tell them.

"Her sickness has ended," I whispered, and the family erupted in sobs. But I looked to the three young wives and clarified, my eyes ablaze, "No. Do not mourn. Her God is Jesus. Her *sickness* has *ended*."

TWENTY-FOUR

Our son refused to come at home, after a day and a half of labor. My insides started to swell, and the baby tried to turn and come breach. Nur, present only for this allowed intrusion, approached Capac with sorrow.

"Brother, this child may not live. Our queen. . .this is as our mother with Sandani."

"Nur, I cannot lose either of them. Please."

"This only happens when the place is wrong. Is there anywhere else, Capac?"

"Nur, this is our bed chamber," he insisted. "Our marriage began and grew here."

"Why does that matter?" I blubbered between contractions.

Nur clicked her tongue, then elaborated. "A man cannot grow a child alone. And so he puts a seed into his heartholder's womb with great love and joy. The child grows safely in his mother until he is ready to breathe and meet his father. Then, he gives his mother pain so that she knows she must return to the place he was entrusted to his mother. He must be born in that place and onto his father's knees so that he knows whose he is and where he came from. The place, and his father's love and joy will make him be born with ease and with strength." I now know this is the way we explain the facts of life to a small child. That is what I still was in their ways, despite actively birthing one. I immediately knew the flaw.

"Oh no. Capac!" I sobbed. "Am I going to die giving you a child because his seed is from stumbling, not great love?" I panicked first, then when a new contraction came, I cried out in agony, sweating despite the cool weather.

"Shhh, Debbie. God does not punish a child for such things." Capac said, dabbing at that sweat with a cloth and indeed staying before me on his knees, ready to both comfort me and accept his heir when he came.

I caught a glimpse of a cold, harsh glare on Nur's face, directed at Capac. A question. A reprimand. All so plain and loud in her eyes that Capac responded verbally. "That is not a matter for today, Nur. My wife is not well."

"Then there is another place," she insisted.

It occurred to me that I was the one being punished, not our son. Between contractions, I tossed around the idea in my head that they could simply cut him out. This is what was done with Sandani. My life and all the jewels and the moon itself were barely a down payment for the life of Capac's heir.

Nur prodded further. "Our God makes no mistake where He begins a child, Capac. It matters more than you know. This child is an *heir* and he must be born where God intends so that you will know his heart."

"There is no other place!" Capac shouted with anger, which I had not heard him do in months. It seemed like superstition, but I wondered if maybe it was old medicine. Still, I did not understand how it applied. This was our only escape for affections, with few wild exceptions.

Suddenly Belen was in the room. "My king."

"Belen, you have not been invited." Capac had recognized his previous shout, and tried to keep his voice down.

"Rune has a message. He says, 'The night of the Cleansing.' "

We both gasped, then said in unison, "The river."

Capac lifted me immediately and carried me a quarter mile down a hill to the river, Nur barely able to stay on his heels, and Roy happily bouncing along on hers with Rune. When we arrived, the sound of the river soothed me and our son within me. I remembered stripping down my mortified husband and washing off the blood in near pitch darkness. Instead of remembering it as trauma, though, we were thanking God.

The break between contractions was just enough that we shared a few tears that cleansed and renewed. Yes. Of course he began here.

I knew there was still danger, and Capac took our time there to cry out to God.

"Father, I know that I killed many men, but please do not punish my wife or my son for these sins. If there is a life to be paid today, let it be mine. But if you let me live, Lord, I will serve you and my people with my whole heart all my days. Father, let this child come and ease the suffering of my wife. Lord, do not take joy from me. I did all for you. I do all for you. Let me at last have joy." He sobbed. I contracted. Pushed. Cried out in agony.

And our son was born directly onto his father's knees. An heir, his first breath claimed beside the mighty river. He was strong and healthy. Perfect. I accepted their medicine, and Capac wailed gratitude at God's blessing.

When Nur arrived, she let out that now familiar ear-piercing chant and then whooping. A quarter mile away, a hundred voices answered with the same. This repeated four more times. The last was followed by a far less organized, but monstrous cheer greater than any I had heard before.

"Five is heir," Capac told me over the cries of our son. "I was crying too loudly to hear the last time we heard five."

I would have laughed if not for the pain and exhaustion. Capac was moments old, a generation before, when he himself inspired five cries from a shelter a half-day's walk into the jungle.

I saw then that Capac was breathing heavily from carrying a full-term pregnant woman a quarter mile with haste. He sat against the tree beside us, catching his breath.

"Josiah," he decreed.

"His name?"

"Yes. Josiah. Fathers choose names. It is tradition."

"That is a beautiful name, my king. But why Josiah? This is not a traditional name for our people."

"I found a Book. You taught me to read of Josiah, who also found a Book. And this was the beginning of my sorrows." Capac chuckled.

"And your joy." I smiled.

"And my joy."

We all napped there by the river until sunset, when Nur, who had gone to tend to other duties, returned for us.

"We should return," Nur suggested then.

"I will try to walk." I conveyed to by husband.

"You will carry Josiah. I will walk," he insisted.

There was a group of people at the village when we arrived, again cheering us to the door of our home. They were dancing and kindling fires over once-in-a-generation joy.

A month later, there was a week straight of such celebration surrounding the full moon. One daughter and two sons. The children of the Cleansing.

For another month or so, we met daily with these new representatives God had chosen. My life got busier then, because Capac required me as one of these advisers to help him solidify and simplify the laws with the elders. I nursed Josiah and looked after Roy during serious legal meetings. The equivalent of a session of Congress in the States, where all professions, schools of thought, ages, and genders could be equally represented.

We relished Nur's sharp tongue over injustice and Alda's insight about the residual whispers of new holy men. Rune and Belen fought for security, Ilian for simplicity. Jada, nursing her own son, was practical, reasoning alongside our fruit cutter and fisherman to streamline and improve ancient processes that made no sense.

We had two elders, who, when they spoke, the rest of us silenced. Even Capac knew that the wisdom of many generations could illuminate the many troubles of the present. Capac had repented early on, apologizing for being absent and allowing things to get out of hand. We all forgave him, each having experienced our own turmoil.

In the end, we came up with just a dozen common-sense commands that worked together but did not restrict the people too much. The rest was tradition, but one of the laws was for tradition to never go against the Word of God.

Each day as we got things established and Capac heard the concerns of the people through their representatives, Capac would always ask Jada of her well-being, particularly her ability for strenuous physical activity. I thought it odd, but Rune seemed to understand the purpose. One day, Rune was candid after everyone but he, Jada, and Capac had exited the temple.

"King, my wife is well. She comes to the river each day for your water with our son tied to her, and had the strength still to protect herself from your enemies and attend your meetings. My Jada is strong. She could run many distances if asked." Rune chuckled. "And our son is not even a season old and still we have started our affections again. She is well."

Jada shook her head at that with a smile. Rune could give far too much information sometimes. But he was not wrong. Jada was standing and swaying her son side to side, braids flowing gently. We were the same. Our duties had called us to regain our strength quickly postpartum.

But I still didn't know why Capac was asking.

Finally he nodded, smiled at Jada, then turned his attention to me.

"Debbie," he started, but that was a name he rarely said in public. Then he corrected with, "My queen. I have considered. And my heart and my God have told me to take you to your family. You need their love. I need your father's wisdom and counsel. John Davies is a good man who forgives, and my people have formed a marriage alliance with his. I need to reconcile with him, and I will ask him to baptize me. And Rune and Jada have also agreed to come with us and be baptized. Our sons and their son will come. The others will uphold the new laws while we are away, and we will baptize them when we return. But we will all be refreshed by your family for a season."

My response was not words. It was a sob, then many tears of gratitude. How I longed to see my family and for my husband to receive exactly what he just said. It had been my chief prayer in my own heart, even through the legislative process. How could he know that?

As I calmed under the gentle embrace of my husband, we heard a voice at the entrance to that chamber. A treasured teenager with loose hair and maturity far beyond her years.

"My king? Queen?"

"Yes, Alda?" I asked.

Capac elaborated. "You know you may always speak. You are an honorable lawmaker appointed by God."

She nodded, then stepped forth into the chamber. "I have a request."

I looked to her feet, sliding gingerly across the stone. I always thought it an odd contrast, the beauty of these women against the wide, calloused, general unkemptness of their feet. No shoe would ever fit the shape, and any covering would insult the sheer practicality. Still, there were parts of me that never bent to the culture.

"What do you ask? I will do all I can for you," Capac said. It was the gentle way I remember him speaking to Sandani, his baby sister.

"I have heard that you will go visit our queen's village." She breathed heavily, thinking the request large. "My mother, my siblings. The families of the holy men have rejected me because I have served you and chosen to serve our good God and not their idols. Each day they ridicule and reject me."

Jada nodded and elaborated. "Alda has been staying in the house I used to share with my sisters. We have cared for her, Queen. She did not want you to know."

"Alda. . ." My heart was broken. How had we not known this would happen?

Capac was three steps ahead, as usual. "And you wish to come with us for a season and be refreshed by John Davies and the family of our queen?"

"Yes. It is a big request." Tears gathered in her eyes, and her voice quavered.

"It is no trouble at all. You will bless us with your presence just as you have blessed us with your service. Alda, no request is too big for all you have sacrificed for your people."

She nodded, her gratitude echoing my own. "I will be of use. I will help with your children and with any needs at your mission, Queen, for I know the work is very much."

"You need not serve, Alda. You can just go and be refreshed," I encouraged.

"Queen, my life is my own. I can *choose* in what way I will serve. I choose to serve you. And your people. And your God. That is refreshment for me." She nodded. We all silenced at her grace and strength. Before she left, she said, "Please tell me how I can help prepare for the journey."

When Capac knew he could trust his appointed judges to manage things to his standards, we began the journey. Actually, revise that. Rune's father was Capac's eldest adviser. He charged the village to *God's* standards due to that gifting.

The journey that had taken Capac, Roy and me three days the year prior took about a week. I led the way, and Capac took up the rear. In the evenings, I explained to Alda that she would see some familiar looking children. She admired the king even more when she learned how true the rumors were. He was always a rescuer.

Twenty-Five

The night before the journey, Capac sat cross-legged, and I lay with my head propped on his knee as he braided my hair, with Josiah at my breast beside me. I thought of my mother, Jane, Lydia. I was a mother now twice, and missed them fervently. I longed to hear their coos. Their delight. Their disbelief, even. I still do not understand how he does this, but it was like Capac heard those thoughts.

"You are eager for the journey? To see your family?"

"Yes, but I am content here, Capac. How could I not be?" That was true.

"But still, your heart is troubled enough that we should go." That was true too. "You carry the weight of a queen, but without the roots of her people. It is a very heavy weight."

And so I asked. "You have been royalty all your life. A king for many years. How did you bear this weight when it got too heavy?"

"I was a coward." He sighed. "I am doing what I have always done. I would leave my people for a season every year to camp outside your mission. To hear John Davies teach his people the Bible. And to watch a beautiful young woman study her Bible and her books."

"You would come spy on me?" I teased.

"Debbie Davies, you have ministered to me for many years. When the weight was heavy, I watched the way you carried yours, and God would bring my heart to peace." He sighed again. "You have blessed me with this same peace as my wife. And I have failed to minister to you in the same way. I have protected your body and your honor, but I have failed to protect your heart."

Josiah had fallen asleep, and I sat up to meet my husband's eyes. My first instinct was to offer him encouragement. To tell him it was alright. But that would have been a lie. The odd realization is that it changed nothing to know he was right. That in his sorrow he had forsaken his duties as king. His ministry as a husband. I understood. I prayed my deepest prayers over him and poured all I had into him, caring for the people, but not nearly so much as I was concerned over my dearest friend.

In fact, looking into his eyes that night, I realized something even more terrifying. If the whole village had burned to the ground, my mission would have stayed the same. Because these people, however fervently I loved them, were never the mission at all. Capac. My husband, who was never supposed to be my husband, had been the mission all along.

With a sob, I made the confession. "You are not the failure, my king. My dear friend. God sent me here to be your wife above all other things. I know that now. And I have failed to *love* you." I sighed into the tears. "The people were worth everything to me. But you, Capac. You are the one who was worth all this to me. And to God. *Oh,* how I have failed."

He scooted in close, both Josiah and I wrapped up in his leg. He reached out and pawed at the ruby around my neck, smiled, then pulled my forehead into his, then laughed and said,

"You are my favorite one to fail with."

I remembered that night as I sat, weeping, on a mossy log ten feet from the pit where I'd climbed to retrieve my sister a lifetime before. I was alone for now, keeping a good lead to give me time to explain our presence before the others arrived. I could hear the children playing, and smell Jane's recipe for vegetable soup on the wind. It was late morning, and I was so, so very close to home. But was it still home?

Josiah stirred. He preferred the constant movement of my walking all day. I moved aside the sling that pressed him against me to check on him. I adjusted the wool hat over his full head of blond curls. He was the image of God in His purest, most perfect form. I knew I wasn't worthy of a child of my own, and yet he stared back at me with his father's onyx eyes. I was terrified of the notion that my family might not find him quite as perfect. Josiah moved a fist to his mouth, and I sighed.

"If I feed you now, I will lose my lead. Can you wait just a few more moments?" I was weary. My heart itself was a burden.

I rose onto my filthy, not-yet calloused bare feet. I looked behind me, and barely caught a distant glimpse of Jada, Rune, and Alda, also sitting for a rest. Capac was likely a mile or two behind me with Roy. As planned, I was alone to deliver so much news.

"God, please don't let them be too angry with me." I sighed. My feet took me further and Josiah settled with the movement.

When I reached the clearing, something odd was at the edge. It was my hiking boots, weathered now, growing into the grass, and Roy's little shoes, set up together like a memorial. There was a stone plaque beside them, containing two chiseled words and a reference: "*Go therefore. . .*" *Matthew 28:19*. It looked almost like they might be proud of me.

I looked up to see if I could find a person. The first adult face I saw was Jeremiah, who carried the familiar raggedness of a new father. But it was Lydia who spotted *me* first, a baby wrapped around her on a sling, just like me.

First, I heard her say, "No. It's a person. A woman. Look. Is that—?"

Then Jeremiah laughed as Lydia screeched out in joy and ran to me.

"Debbie?" When she arrived, she pawed at my probably peculiar hair and clothes before even realizing what I carried in my own sling.

"Lydia."

"Oh my goodness, look at you. You are gorgeous! I have never seen you so beautiful. I didn't recognize you," she schmoozed, then yelled behind her. "Mom! Dad! Debbie is home!"

Lydia glanced at my sling with a smile and a loving little eye roll. And only then did it occur to me that it may not even faze them for me to be carrying a baby. Often throughout my life they would tease me. *"That girl always has a book or a baby or both."*

God was protecting me. I was safe for now in their pigeonhole, adjusting Josiah's cap to cover all the blond.

Lydia turned to show me her own treasure. She was a brown little angel barely young enough to still fit in a wrap. She smiled brightly, and I fell quickly in love with my niece.

"This is Deborah. We call her Baby D. I'm glad I learned to manage all your curls all my life, because look. She got these from Jeremiah, of course." Lydia smoothed her hand over soft black spirals. The perfect mix of her parents. Lydia's blue eyes and flirtatious smile. Jeremiah's nose and eyelashes. Her skin just between theirs.

"Oh, Lydia. She is absolutely beautiful." I had to work to find the language.

"You have an accent! Wow. That's so cool!" Lydia laughed.

"Really? I don't hear it."

"Well you wouldn't, silly."

I shook my head and continued. "Why did you name her after me? I wasn't dead or lost. When I sent Rune for the medicine, I assumed you all understood I was safe." I was touched, yet defensive.

"We were thinking of naming her Deborah before you even left. You were a blessing to us like you don't even know." She shrugged and then confronted me, though I could see the sting had faded. "But you didn't say goodbye. That *hurt* like you don't even know."

"I left a note."

"For Dad."

"And I sent a letter."

"For *Dad*. For penicillin."

"I couldn't say goodbye. You would have easily talked me into staying. And I needed to go. God needed me there."

"That's what Dad said." Lydia sighed, gesturing to the little shoe memorial. "As you can see."

"I've missed you every day. I kept having nightmares around the time Debbie was probably born. I'm so sorry that I missed it." My whole heart was in those words, and I had to swipe at a tear.

She took me into an embrace, the best she could with two babies between us, and all was forgiven. When she drew back, she finally acknowledged my sling.

"So you took in another baby?" She smiled, wiping away her own tears.

"In a manner of speaking." And that's all I offered.

But when Lydia reached in and touched his head, the hat moved slightly and revealed a few blond curls. Only half paying attention, she commented,

"Oh! I've never seen one of them with blond hair. Do some of them have different features?"

"No, they all have straight black hair besides me and Josiah here," I answered.

"So—" Then she looked at me, wide-eyed, drama in her open mouth. "You have. . .braids. . .in your hair. Doesn't that mean—?"

But Dad was approaching, and I begged her for silence with pleading eyes and a gentle "Shhh." The Lydia of a year before had never been discreet or prudent. But this shorter-haired, slightly fuller-figured Lydia was someone else. I had pulled her from pits and softened our father's rebuke as needed. For the first time, she knew she owed me this. But in true Lydia style, she winked.

"Hi, Dad. I hope it's not too much trouble that I—"

But my words were swallowed up in his warm embrace when my hand shielded my son's head. Then, when he stepped back, he noted.

"Wow, listen to that accent."

"It's great, isn't it?" Lydia giggled.

"I rarely speak English. I am barely remembering the words." I laughed. Dad winced at the baby he just noticed.

"Sorry, I didn't see." Then he laughed to himself. "Always a book or a baby still, huh?"

"Yes, though we only have one Book." I nodded the laugh and oddly, he didn't even ask for an explanation yet.

"So first, are you well, Debbie?" he asked, "I worried with the penicillin and then you not asking for any more that—"

"We have our own medicine that is very effective," I explained. "But it does not work for someone who has used modern medicine before."

"What were you infected with?"

"It wasn't for me, Dad," I answered. He didn't inquire.

Instead, he lit up completely, bursting and placing his hands on my white wool covered shoulders.

"Okay, *now* tell me *everything*. You are the first person to get to them in four generations of trying. Tell me everything about them and tell me what God is doing."

I snorted laughter at his zeal. "God is doing wonders, Dad. And we hope to stay long enough for me to tell you as much as I can. But I'm here because I am calling up that debt. You said I could come back for anything, big or small?" I confirmed.

"Anything, Debs. This mission exists for these people." He smiled. "I assume this is big?"

"Very. I am not alone. I'm just here first to give you a little notice. They will all arrive soon. But Dad, I need you to baptize four new believers who have been eagerly awaiting it. And I need you to teach the Bible as well. And we need. . .just some respite. A chance to heal. We need your wisdom and counsel for a season, if that will not be too much trouble." I nodded. "We have left other believers behind to care for the village, and we will baptize them when we return."

"We'd be honored, Debbie. That's incredible. So you have friends with you?" He looked to the baby I carried. "And are you bringing more children, or. . .?"

I nodded, my heart forgetting what his mind didn't yet know. "We have three children with us. Two babies and Roy."

"Lydia, go tell Jane. We'll have to get the nursery things out again." Dad gave the instruction with a bit of sadness in his voice.

"No!" I stopped the motive. "No, they are *with* us, Dad. And they will stay with us. Two of the believers are a couple, and they have their baby, and they would love to have you pray over him and dedicate him. Then there is a young woman with us as well. But my people will never bring children to you again. God has healed that part of us."

"Oh. Alright." But Dad had a good math brain. "That's three to baptize. You said four."

I cleared my throat. "If you are not too angry with him, Capac, our king, would also like for you to baptize him. And minister to him specifically as one leader to another. He will arrive last, and he has Roy with him."

Lydia had a good math brain as well, but those weren't the dots she connected. She released a gasp, glancing at Josiah when Dad was looking away in thought. Dad looked to me again, confused at Lydia and my matching tucked lips of secrecy. But he was used to such things having raised a set of sisters.

"Angry? No. Debs, he protected you enough that you could minister to the people. I can't imagine that was an easy thing to do."

Lydia snorted laughter. Dad sighed, confessing. "I struggled for a while with the fact that he kidnapped my firstborn child."

"Well, I certainly was not kidnapped. I went with him willingly because he promised that he would protect me the way that *you* do, Dad. He's quite obsessed with the idea and has been since before we left. So when he arrives, please do us both a favor and tell him he's doing fine? He's concerned."

"Clearly you've been protected. Why would he be concerned?" He chuckled once.

"Dad, you literally put him in chains once. You didn't trust him with me for me to teach him. And then I went with him, so I know that I am not wrong to think that angered you."

This triggered something, I saw in both Lydia and Dad. Dad's eyes started to tear up like I'd brought up the death of an old friend. Lydia sighed, remorseful, as if she was comforting him. Then she looked to our daddy and said, "I think she deserves to know."

I looked frantically between them. "What happened?"

Dad cleared his throat, but his voice held onto remnants of some deep pain. "Like I said, I struggled. I was angry for months. Your shoes sat here as a memorial because I gave you up for dead.

I hated Capac and I thought you were naive to have befriended him."

"You called her ridiculous. Reckless. . ." Lydia mumbled.

"I said a lot of very stupid things," Dad admitted. "Then one day a young man runs out of the jungle with a letter for me and it's from you. Needing medicine. And God brought me to my knees. He reminded me that the purpose of this mission is to reach these people. I had this idea in my head of how that should be done and meanwhile I was annoyed that my daughter was making a *disciple*. And that's the command!" Dad laughed through tears. Got animated.

Dad took his hands and squeezed both of my shoulders, gritting his passion through his teeth. "I. Am. *So*. Proud of you. For obeying God and following Jesus. . .and Capac. . .into that jungle. He took you right to them! And you made more disciples."

"And *they* are making disciples," I nodded. Sniffled at my own tears. "You will see Rune again, too. It is him who is bringing his wife and child."

"Oh, that is. . . I'm so proud. We made this stone and sat here and did some reteaching. I encourage everyone to come here and pray for you every day. You are *bathed* in prayer, Debbie. I hope you felt it. Now we are jealous and feel silly because we had this whole master plan, and all you did was the simplest thing. You made a friend."

"Capac is my very dearest friend, Dad." I sighed and began my own confession. "But the way he had to protect me. . .you may still be unhappy."

Dad, the now middle-aged missionary and grandfather, sighed compassion and crossed his arms. "I know. It's been difficult. I can see it in your eyes."

"Every day has been difficult. Some days far more than others," I sighed, trauma returning wet to my eyes for a moment. "But God has been faithful every day too."

Mom arrived then, changing the entire dynamic of the situation. She was in blubbering tears, taking her oldest baby into her arms.

And when she felt him between us then saw him, she took *my* baby right out of the sling and held him against her.

"Who is *this*, Debbie?" She said through wailing sobs. Barely in the next beat, Mom frantically looked around my feet, "Oh no. Where is your Roy?! Debbie, I'm so sorry if I ever treated him as less than your son. Your first note made it clear how wrong I'd been. Please forgive me."

"It's alright, Mom. He's in the back, likely being spoiled and carried all day. That happened yesterday and Roy barely slept. We had to tie him to us to make sure he didn't wander off as we slept. Like when he was little?"

"I remember you doing that. I didn't help you enough. You shouldn't have had to do that." I'd left everyone in ruins apparently.

"It's okay, Mom," I encouraged her. "I know it was hard for you when I took him in. And you *did* help me. He remembers you always singing with him and Daniel running with him and Andrew—wait, where is everyone else?"

Mom answered, "Jane is doing her soup today, so she's helping in the kitchen. Daniel, last I saw, was on mile nine. He does a half marathon each day, and a whole one every month. You know teen boys. Helps him clear his head and gives him goals to chase. I'm sure he'll be rounding the corner soon."

"And Andrew?"

"Well, that's why Daniel started running, I think. You left, and now Andrew is in Wyoming with Grandma and Grandpa. After you left, he begged me to graduate him as soon as possible and then headed back to the States. You know his heart has never been in this mission. He's starting college soon."

"Oh." I already missed my brother's shotgun and gangly arms, but tried to be supportive. "He has to do God's will for him, Mom. Is he happier there?"

"Much." Mom nodded. "I think there's a girl. . ."

"Oh! How wonderful!"

Mom nodded, then lit up again when Josiah stirred in her arms. "Sorry, I didn't even let you answer. Who is this baby? I should have known you'd take in at *least* one more of them."

"Yes." I smiled. *They are worth this. Capac is worth this.* I said to myself. Then, "But him I acquired *far* differently than I did Roy. This is Josiah. He is the heir to carry the *matteh* after his father is gone. The king entrusted him to me."

"Capac's son?" Dad laughed, delighted. "He has you carrying his children now?" Dad was, for a moment, interested in only the baby in Mom's arms. Lydia snorted laughter, to which he responded, "What? What did I say?"

"Um." I sighed. "Yes, actually. I carry him everywhere. On this journey, and even in my womb for three seasons." I removed Josiah's cap. "I think when I sent the note for the medicine, I was in my second season of pregnancy. I didn't think an urgent letter was the right time to tell you."

Dad laughed aloud once. "No."

"Oh my word! John, look at all these curls."

I watched Dad intently, and he was watching me. I adjusted my backpack, unsure what to do with my arms without Josiah. So there I hung with empty arms and a wandering mind at the mercy of my father.

Dad breathed in once, and then silenced himself with a hum against his fist, rethinking his words. Then he breathed in again and quickly said, "So when you said I might not be happy with his methods for protecting you. . ."

"Dad—" I began, but he was not ready to listen.

"Are we mistranslating what 'protect' means, because I figured he would have worked hard to protect you *from* things of this nature. Not *cause* them."

"Dad, I told you he is very worried that you'll be angry with him. Or hate him. For this very thing."

"But not *too* worried, though." Dad shrugged, the muscles in his lips erratic as he withheld anger. He gestured to Josiah, "Because obviously. . ."

I raised my voice. No, elevated it. To the way a queen might speak. "No. You misread what is obvious. Capac has had to make some very difficult decisions this past year. He could not always do exactly the thing you'd most approve of. He opted instead to do what was *right*." My command of English came back as I protected my husband, despite my mother's confusion.

"Whoa." Dad put up his hands in defense. "Okay. Wow. That was *fiery*, Debs. Who even are you?"

"Still your daughter, I hope." I sighed, trembling with spent emotion.

"I've just never heard you defend someone like that." I looked into his eyes. Pain. Fear. Mercy. Love. He was proud of me still.

"He has defended me with *far* more." I sobbed, unsure where it came from.

"No, I. . .I believe you." Dad sighed, then spread his hands. "But put yourself in my shoes—"

I laughed once, from the same mysterious place as the sob. "I don't wear shoes anymore."

"You know what I mean. I thought Capac had a wife back home and you'd been toying with the idea of celibacy. Did I read that incorrectly?"

"No. Well, yes. Capac did not have a wife. I learned that on the way there, when he and I had some good conversations about the virtues of celibacy. He made that choice decades ago and commended me for considering the same. Less distractions for a king. More focus and time for serving God. Made sense for him. Made sense for me."

The three present members of my family looked at me, wide-eyed, as one does before correcting a child who has spoken an embarrassing mispronunciation of a word.

"Okay, you know what I *mean* by celibacy, right?" Dad said.

"I do." I sighed, reaching out and touching Josiah's exposed foot to be sure it wasn't too cold. "Clearly, God had other plans. It is a long story that is painful to tell. Must I tell it now?"

"Of course not." Mom shot a look at Dad, then said, "Josiah is a pretty name, Debbie."

"Well, it is our tradition for fathers to pick a name that is kept secret until birth. It usually tells some story about the seasons leading to his beginning," I explained. "His father chose well."

Mom stopped her mom-swaying to think.

"He found a Book. And you read together." Dad shook his head. "Not the most riveting origin story. . ."

"Dad, this is so Debbie." Lydia was swiping at tears of joy, her voice nasal and stuffy in the effort. "'A book or a baby or both?'"

Dad guffawed, though bitterly. "Never did I think that a book could *lead* to a baby. I trusted him *way* too much."

"You never trusted him at all, Dad," I reminded him. "But I likely trusted him enough for both of us."

"Well I can *see* that." Dad wasn't happy. I was crushed.

Lydia spoke up, though she mumbled embarrassment. "Dad. You forgave Jeremiah, right? Can we just skip to that with Capac? Look how gorgeous she is. He's clearly taking care of her."

"Yeah, I'm gathering that as well," Dad mumbled back.

Mom smiled at Dad, then allowed a quick and intriguing, "Told you." Then she started her swaying again. She released Josiah's head for a quick moment. He was now awake, looking around, and held his head true. She bounced him, checking his weight. She seemed confused. "He's how old?"

"Um. . ."

But Daniel literally ran into what he had no clue was a tense situation, just like Mom had. Winded from running and sweating through a tank top and shorts, he was confused by the gathering. Then he saw me, and that bright-eyed little boy came to life in the young man before me. He gathered me into a sweaty embrace.

"Debbie, oh my gosh! When did you get here?" His voice was shockingly an octave lower than I remembered, and he drew back from the embrace and looked me over. "So, are you royalty? I'm confused. You're dressed like royalty."

I was glad my brother hadn't judged or danced around circumstances. "Hello, Daniel. You got tall."

"You got an accent." He smiled brighter.

"I'm sorry. I still don't hear it." I laughed.

"Royalty?" Mom was puzzled.

"I noticed the same thing." Dad nodded, and began sharing an analysis I didn't know he was making. "The clothes. That's what Capac always shows up wearing. With the red stripe?"

Daniel added, "Yeah, he told me one time the red stripe is royalty, and that blue is for priests or something. She's wearing that same vest cloak thing he wears. With the red. See? And that's weird because. . ."

Dad mumbled, nodding and proud of his son's observations. "Because he has always said they consider us to be *holy*, not royal. So you should be in blue, right?"

"No one wears blue anymore," I corrected, then nodded. "But you have a good memory. Only the king and his family wear red."

"Ew!" Lydia said, and this was the rebellious kind of speech I remembered. "No, Dad has a *terrible* memory, Debbie. I'm looking at your hair, because Capac told me the cultural significance like forever ago, and Dad's over here accusing Capac of *God* knows what. It's gross, Dad."

"Ha!" Dad was offended. "Gross?" Then his eyes widened again, and he gasped. "I'm an idiot. Debs. Forgive me. They are monogamous, and he is ritualistically pure. If he didn't have a wife, Capac has never touched a woman before."

"We couldn't even *graze* him," Lydia rolled her eyes at Dad then winked at me. "It appears he's been 'grazed' now, and Debbie is still alive, so. . ."

Jeremiah arrived then. I had glanced over once to see him rounding up the children and taking them inside, likely to Jackson. He arrived with arms open wide for a brotherly hug, but I took a step back and outstretched my arms.

"Okay, you and Jackson *will* be angry." I sighed. "But you can't touch me."

"What?! Why? We're family!" Jeremiah's arms fell devastated to his sides.

"Not *blood* family. And you are male. There can be absolutely no question the purity of the royal bloodline. A question is a death sentence. So don't touch me."

I lifted my hand and turned my head to show them my cord. "This braid is the first time Capac touched a woman and the last time I have touched a man besides him. It didn't have the cord in it until—"

"He married you," Dad said, barely above a mumble.

Daniel, obviously much more grown than I remembered, gasped like the teenage boy he was, covering his mouth and laughing.

"You married Capac?" He asked excitedly, severing all remaining tension with his innocence. This was news to both he and Jeremiah. "And you have a *baby*? Is this your baby?"

"Uh. . ." Dad winced as if to pity and protect. I don't know why he didn't think it was that simple. Maybe it wasn't even that simple to me. But the Holy Spirit urged me to set things right with him.

"Yes. My people call me '*Regi*.' Queen. Most do not even recognize me as 'Debbie.' Only Capac calls me that, and only in private. Queen is a very serious title with serious responsibilities and privileges. The bloodline goes back a thousand years. Now there is curly blond hair in the bloodline." I gestured to my son.

Daniel was the first to point to the jewel around my neck. "Whoa! Is that real?! Where did you get that?"

"It was a gift from—"

"Someone who was either apologizing for something *real* stupid or wanted something *real* bad," Jeremiah said, and Lydia punched his arm, trying to silence him. "Ow!"

I shrugged. "Might have been both, actually. Another long story." I laughed and Lydia gasped, her smile desperately needing to know more.

"Not to be rude, but that guy didn't waste much time before making you royalty and continuing his bloodline," Jeremiah noted. "Should I be worried?" He looked to my brother and father. "Are we worried? Do we kill him?"

"I plan to hear all these long stories before I decide, Jeremiah," Dad said.

"Maybe we just lock him up again," Daniel teased.

"Guys, stop," Mom demanded. Josiah began to stir and fuss in my mother's arms, rooting around at his fists. "John, perhaps our daughter would like to sit somewhere after her long journey and feed her son?"

"Her son. The heir," Dad repeated. "Yes. Of course."

"Wait." This was Daniel, who put up a hand before gazing behind me into the jungle. His eyes were wide, and he took two steps back. I feared a jungle danger until he said, "Who. . .what. . .is *that?*"

The "what" didn't make sense to me. All that had happened is Alda appeared beside me, then bowed her head a little as she greeted me.

"*Regi.*"

I switched languages, and my family looked on in wonder. "Alda, where are Rune and Jada? You were to stay with them for safety."

"I saw you with your family. The way was safe and clear. They are slow with the baby. I hope that is okay?"

"All is well, Alda." I turned to my family, and said, "Everyone, this is Alda. This is the young woman we brought. She is very special and very important to us. She speaks exactly zero English, but wants to learn."

At this point, I pointed to each family member, and she nodded a bow to each of them as one might for a celebrity. The last introduction was Daniel. When she saw him, she did not bow. She took a step backward and said, in our language, "Impossible."

She was paralyzed there, staring down my baby brother, born in the jungle. And I looked to him to realize what he meant by "what is that?" It's like he was having trouble convincing his eyes that she was human. Perhaps because of cultural differences, but probably not.

Alda was a holy daughter from a long line of women practically genetically designed for their beauty. With soft black hair down to her knees and a gentle glow of her brow from the sweat, there was no standard of beauty in any culture the young woman would not meet.

The stare-down was awkward, and with obvious purpose. Lydia was beginning to smile gossip into her face until I spoke. "What is impossible, Alda?"

"I dreamed this man. A man with our queen's hair and eyes the color of the sky. . .can eyes be the color of the sky? I did not believe this part of my dream."

"My people have blue eyes sometimes," I explained as she stared and stepped closer to him. "Alda, this is my brother. His name is—"

"Daniel." Alda finished that sentence with a whisper. Impossibly.

Daniel startled. "I didn't hear you say my name, Debbie. Did you tell her my name?"

"No. She. . ." I cleared my throat. "You should know that our people have spiritual experiences sometimes that might be new to you. Daniel, Alda says she dreamed you."

"What was in the dream?" Daniel asked immediately, looking to me to help translate, but stepping in closer to Alda.

"He wants to know what was in your dream."

At that, Alda shook her head, stepping back. Then her head went down in a bow and she went silent.

"I can accept that." Daniel laughed once. Then tried to breathe himself to calm, the way Capac will sometimes do before telling me I'm beautiful. Everyone besides him recognized that kind of breath.

Dad spoke firmly. "Four more miles?"

Daniel looked at his left wrist. Four rubber bands. Nine on the other. Daniel, still far wiser than his age should have allowed, nodded and spoke his own predicament. "Yeah. Good advice." And he ran off, to all our stifled giggles.

Twenty-Six

We left Alda with Lydia and Jeremiah to accept everyone as they arrived. As soon as I was seated in Dad's office on the "couch"—a collection of pillows and cushions on the floor, much like my own home—Dad began his interrogation. The babe at my breast under a cover seemed a sensitive place to begin, but Dad began there nonetheless.

"Debs, your Josiah can't be three months old," he said it with quiet.

"Yes, about a season. We don't really count the days there and I lost track. I don't know his birthday, as silly as that seems. But he was born about a season ago," I over-explained.

Mom sighed, biting her lip with concern. Then, "And he was full term, and. . ."

"Yes. Three seasons."

"Debs, how long after leaving here before you were expecting him? Or was it. . .before?"

"Dad!"

"How long, Debbie? I'm having trouble with the math on this one. And with what happened between all those heartfelt conversations about celibacy and making a baby."

I sighed and started in. When I began talking, they sat back and listened with their whole hearts.

"There were rituals that his people used to do for thousands of years. Jesus was walking the earth, and Capac's people were. . ." I gasped for air and fortitude and finally, "Sacrificing newborn babies to their gods. Babies that had been conceived in another ritual that was a lot like when you told us about the first rights? It used to be that our women were not permitted for their own husband-to-be their first intimate experience.”

Mom was stuck. “Child sacrifice? You can’t be serious.”

“Not anymore, Mom. God healed that part of them.”

I took a moment to explain both the former Opening and Closing rituals but realized I hadn’t answered their question when Dad interrupted with,

“Wait. . .Josiah was conceived by a ritual!? I thought he was Capac’s.”

“He is. Sorry. I was getting there. Capac is the king. When we arrived there, the holy men decided that I needed to be opened. The only exception to the rituals was the daughters of the holy men, so we didn’t think they would require that. Dad, they consider you to be a holy man because all the people fear God and His power. I’m your daughter, so that made me a holy daughter.”

“I remember that you could wash the royal garments because of that,” Mom said.

“Right. The royal bloodline had to be pure, so the king would marry the daughter of a holy man and open her himself. And Capac was not quiet about his celibacy, so they assumed he wouldn’t be willing to, but. . .”

“He married you,” Dad said for the second time.

“Yes,” I confirmed. “To save me from the other Opening.”

“And did this opening himself?” Mom asked.

“Yes,” I confessed my frustration. “So, within hours of talking about celibacy, we were married and sitting in our bedroom laughing at the irony.”

“And then creating a kid.” Dad couldn’t get over it.

“No, actually.” I rolled my eyes, running my ruby along its chain, which Dad analyzed.

“So he happened later?”

“Yeah, a couple weeks.” I sighed. Going back there in my mind hurt and brought up so many memories that trickled into the present and reminded me I am a sinner.

"Ah." Dad looked at Mom, who rolled her eyes. "I wish I'd been allowed to have the 'sleeping dragon' talk with you girls. Lydia didn't give me time, and figured it out on her own, and you essentially eloped."

"Sleeping dragon?" I was genuinely confused.

"The Bible says, 'Do not stir up nor awaken love until it pleases.' I say we have a sleeping dragon in us. Celibates are really cool, and I think you could have done it. Probably both of you, to be honest. You see the sleeping dragon. It's there. And you just. . .leave it alone. Most other people, especially couples in love, will sort of tiptoe around it—try not to wake it. But the temptation to wake that dragon is just unbelievable." Dad was speaking the metaphor, the euphemism in a way that made me a bit uncomfortable when Mom giggled. But I didn't get annoyed.

"The dragon is sex?"

"Debbie a year ago wouldn't have gotten that so fast. I am both impressed and mortified." He laughed. Dad went on in a somewhat goofy, always pastory cadence. "I gather you figured out the problem with waking the dragon. Even if you do everything right and you're married to someone you at least *trust* and the guy has never even touched a woman until that day, there's a problem. I'm sure you both figured, yeah, we'll do this thing we have to do and then lull the thing back to sleep."

I sighed. Whispered, "But it doesn't go back to sleep." Mom giggled again, then I asked, "So wait, this is normal? Because he *promised* me when we were being forced into this marriage that we would do it once until we figured things out in our hearts."

Dad threw his head back. "And how long did it take him to 'figure things out in his heart'?"

"Like forty-eight hours, Dad. *Less.* He *transformed* on me. He was a totally different person."

Dad glanced at my ruby. "You took a minute."

"Yes and no." I sighed. "We both *wanted* to. I don't want you thinking I was an unwilling victim. But while my ideal solution was to take time to figure out *why* we wanted to, his solution was to just do what we wanted to do." Then I recanted. "Sometimes. He went back and forth. At first. Then we came to a really weird understanding when he gave me this. And he had memorized that part of Proverbs 31.”

“He wanted you to stop giving him grief and let him love you?”

“Ha!” That confused me. Dad was right about everything until that point. How had he missed that one? “Love? No.”

“He gave you a ruby. As a gift for his wife. Doesn’t seem common.” Dad seemed confused.

“Yes.”

“And broke his vow of chastity to save your honor.” Dad nodded approval. “That’s romantic, Debbie. Sorry to say.”

“Dad, no.” I laughed. “We aren’t. . .it’s not like that. We are dear friends—just like before—who were forced into a physical relationship that became a stumbling block.”

Dad laughed loud and strong, and through whimpers of tears of laughter, said, “You *would* think intimacy is a distraction from better things. Oh, Debs, you never disappoint.”

“It is!” I laughed so as not to make him uncomfortable. But then I shrugged. “We *like* being married. It makes serving the people together much easier. But we feel like impostors.”

“How so?” Dad asked.

“People marry for love, Dad. And their people always say ‘Love grows.’ Love can *only* grow. But while we’ve grown our marriage and honored God, love. . .that may be a story for another time. Or maybe not, and that’s fine too.”

Mom and Dad just stared at me. First with pity, then Mom concealed a smile and Dad allowed a smirk. He changed the subject.

“You mentioned to Daniel that no one wore blue anymore. You talk about the holy men in past tense. Waiting for the other shoe to drop on that one.”

I knew that concealing and couching and coating the words in sugar would never make them less shocking, so I began the tale again straight away.

“On the night of the Opening I would have been a part of if not for our wedding, Capac and Rune took machetes into the temple. They executed ten evil men that night and rescued three innocent young women. Jada, Rune's wife now, was one of them. Her sisters were the other two."

Mom gasped yet again. Dad shook his head.

"Is that hyperbole, or. . .?"

"I washed the blood off him myself." I nodded. "He was completely beside himself. I tried to comfort him, but. . .that just got us Josiah."

Their silence begged for me to either recant or continue.

"Debs. . ." Dad was swatting at tears. "A man's heart does not easily return from something like that. He really killed them?"

"And burned their bodies and robes in the same fire where he destroyed their idols." I nodded. "His heart is very tender. He is a leader, but not a warrior. He still suffers from nightmares and even behaves erratically sometimes. It has been so difficult that. . .he needs you, Dad. This broke him."

"Does he hurt you? Are you and your boys safe?"

"He is *more* gentle with us now, I'd say. He knows what he's capable of, and refuses to go near that boundary. But he did try to drink poison water once. Also, he chose to circumcise himself with an unsanitized knife."

Dad's face went white and stoic, and he barely uttered,
"Uh. . .why. . .?"

"Something about setting himself apart. Kept saying 'with power is pain.' I don't know. He was vague. And far too impulsive. Sanitizing the knife would have taken thirty seconds."

"The penicillin," Mom mumbled.

"Yes. He's healed now. . .physically."

"So this all explains the aging in your eyes," Dad said. "Are you okay? Is he okay? This marriage has definitely been tried by fire."

"Yes. And this all happened just two weeks after I arrived. It's been a long time now, and we have the joy of a new child, but yes. It was very difficult."

"We can certainly sympathize. If you recall, Mom and I were married within weeks of meeting, so. . ." A familiar spat began on cue.

"Three months."

"Marla. Vegas counts."

"No, it doesn't, John."

"Debbie happened between Vegas and the wedding, so it better count."

"The wedding was before God. Made it *holy* matrimony."

"Vegas made it legal."

I ended the quick little friendly argument with a laugh and, "You would be *disturbed* by the the way we do weddings." I didn't let them inquire before, "Can I have your word that you will not give Capac any grief over all this? He needs to be ministered to, not judged." I realized then my voice was cracking and shaking from tears I did not know were behind these statements.

"You have my word," Dad promised.

Mom handed me a handkerchief and Dad used his own before saying, "Debs, you know the only thing I refuse to accept about all this?"

"What?"

"You thinking you're not madly in love with this man."

"Dad, you're a romantic." I laughed. "Of course you think I'm in love with him. He's my dearest friend. You know this. Of course I'm defending him. Just like I did years ago when he left me with a newborn baby at seventeen."

At that, Mom giggled. Dad rolled his eyes, conceding something.

"Debs," Dad whispered. "You loved him *then*. You've never heard Mom say that?"

"Mom! I told you it was tradition and ritual."

"Debbie, I didn't come to the jungle with a 'dear friend' because of tradition and ritual. Only wild, crazed, romantic *love* takes a woman into the jungle with a man."

"How can you—"

Mom started in, "He wails for days, despite knowing his sister was out there. You walk in and he's speaking English and coming alive. Years later, he finds a book and who does he run to? Debbie. My sweet Debbie. This man has loved *you* for years. That precious friendship you two shared was so much more than you thought it was. And we know it was innocent and you may not have had conventional 'crazed romance' symptoms, because both of you are . . .well. . .unconventional. The man wasn't even permitted to touch you, and Dad didn't mind that. But tell me. How difficult was it really to wake up that dragon?"

But I could not process such information after all that had happened over the many years, especially the most recent one. After one flash of the desperate passion of our first candlelit night together, I silenced her invasive inquiries with a sob and a whispered, "Mom, please. I can't. . ."

"Marla," Dad said. And that was it. He simply said, "I'm just glad he had you. And I'm glad he protected you. I won't give him grief."

That's when the knock came to the door. Then it opened.

Roy ran in first, wearing the new clothes I had Mena make for him before we left. He jumped atop my father's lap, "Apa!" He began speaking to him a mile a minute.

"Roy." I stopped him, smiling. "English."

"Yeck! English." Capac entered with a grumble and a teasing smile, stopping just inside the doorway.

Lydia peeked in. "The others all arrived safely and Jane is feeding them lunch. Come over whenever you're ready. But I figured I should bring these guys to you." She winked. "Daniel wants to know what happens if he touches Alda."

"He absolutely better *not*." Dad laughed.

"Kidding. But wow! Did you see those sparks fly?!"

"Thanks, Lydia. That's all for now," Dad said, shaking his head in laughter.

"Uh huh." And then she was gone.

"Ama!" Roy said, running and jumping onto my mother's lap next. He touched Josiah's feet, exposed from under the nursing wrap. "Ama, my brother! Jojo!"

"I know, he's precious. And you are so big, Roy!" Mom was in tears at the sight of him.

But most of my attention was focused near the door. Dad stood up from behind his desk. "Hello, Capac."

I had forgotten Capac was so much shorter than my father. He looked up to him.

"Hello, Pastor John Davies." Capac was so smug and sure of himself, but so lighthearted and loving. He pulled my father into a mighty embrace, then lit up, "Did you see I gave you a new grandson?!"

"The shock of my life. But yes. He's beautiful, Capac."

"For that part, I can take no credit. My son is beautiful like his mother." Capac swooned, then plopped in front of my crossed legs and swung a leg around me as always. Dad about fell over. Capac gently turned my face side to side and ran his fingers across my arms, checking my health. Then he cradled my neck and joined our foreheads, asking in a low mumble, "Are you well?"

"I am okay." I smiled.

Dad was watching intently but smiling as Capac peeked under my nursing cover. It was innocent, of course. We both chuckled a little when the baby looked up at his daddy and smiled.

"Yes, Da is here!" Capac said in a lighter, higher pitched voice. "I came just to see you!"

As often occurred, I lost Jo for nursing at that point.

"Why do you do that?" I accused.

"He can eat later. Da is here now," he declared, carefully pulling him out from under the wrap, turning aside to sit next to me, and putting him on his knee to bounce out a burp.

"Josiah is a good name, Capac," Mom commented once Roy took a breath from talking.

"Yes," Capac acknowledged.

"You say, 'Thank you.' She knows you named him," I corrected in mixed tongue.

"Oh, thank you, Marla." He looked to my mother and pawed at all Josiah's blond curls, and then touched my hair. "Yellow like Debbie."

"I see." Mom nodded.

Capac then set his eyes on my father, watching him converse with Roy in some English-Capacsi hybrid. Roy had returned to 'Apa,' energy abounding. Capac corrected Roy's English a couple of times so that Dad could understand him.

"Da English?!" Roy asked.

"Yes, I know English, Roy," he told him in English. "You cannot have any more secrets with Ma now, huh?"

"Roy calls you Da," Mom noted. "Aren't you his uncle?"

"I married the woman who is as his mother and I became as his father. We are *as* mother and father to him, so we *are* Da and Ma to him. There is no difference," Capac said.

Roy was energetically bouncing on Dad's lap and I sighed the realization.

"You carried him, didn't you? He should be tired by now." I smiled, mumbling to Capac. "You spoil him."

"He kept wandering off. It was safer to carry him," Capac defended. He smirked, touching my hair. "I will need to find time for you. It is clear you are lacking my attention."

"It is not bad, but I think we can find time soon."

"Your language is so beautiful. I can't believe how quickly you speak it, Debbie. You sound like it is your first language," Mom commented.

I got my linguistics gift from Dad's side. He had learned some of the language, and had apparently understood.

"Give Roy to Daniel and he'll wear him out for you. That kid has way too much energy, and Jane usually has him run the preschoolers to get their wiggles out."

"Oh, that will be good. He talks about Daniel sometimes," I replied, then turned to Capac. "Alda told me she dreamed Daniel."

"Daniel is the young brother? Yellow hair?"

"Yes. My youngest."

Capac nodded, "You trust him with Roy?"

Mom giggled. "Daniel's an old soul, Capac. He was born here in the jungle and I don't think he'd ever do well in the States. He loves your people just like Debbie does."

"Yeah, he's a good kid. Very trustworthy," I promised.

"Good. I thought so." Capac was satisfied, though it was not like him to ask me about someone's character.

"Why do you ask?" I wondered.

He suddenly shifted my whole world when he confessed, quickly, in our language, "I have dreamed Daniel too." Then allowed Dad to change the subject before I could react.

"Do you have some issue with Debbie's hair, Capac?"

Capac chuckled, offended. But he did not answer directly. "Yes, it is like wildfire."

My face warmed. I was terrified over a possible confrontation. "Dad, our men braid their wives' hair as a show of how much attention he has given her. The trip has not allowed for attention like that. My hair is normally pretty much perfect, even though my curls make that difficult."

"I see."

"Let's go get some lunch and then go see Uncle Daniel, Roy." Mom felt the tension mounting between Capac and Dad, and took Roy to the dining hall, leaving with, "I can't believe how big you are!"

After the silence took over the space, Capac spoke first. "Are you angry?"

"No, I don't tend to be an angry person." But Dad sighed.

"Whatever it is you tend to be, I ask you to not be angry with Debbie. She has done no wrong. I did my best to protect Debbie from wrong." He spoke gently, Josiah beginning to drift off to sleep in his arms.

"I heard, Capac. Debbie told us a few stories." Dad examined my husband. Searching for something eyes can't see. I could see his dilemma. He was looking for how a man with a touch gentle enough to lull a baby to sleep, and words smooth enough to lure his level-headed daughter into the jungle could also have taken the lives of ten men. He couldn't find that in him—not with his eyes. "Shortly before you two left last year, I remember hearing you talk about Josiah. I don't understand your language completely, but from what I understand, you wanted Debbie to help you tear down high places."

"Yes." Capac nodded, sadly.

"Did she know then that the idols were men?"

"No. She was my wife before she completely understood that. And I did not intend for her to bear that burden with me the way she did," Capac began, then let his eyes drift from the rise and fall of his son's chest to the river of my father's eyes. "Tell me, John. Tell me a way I could have told your Debbie what awaited us and not lose her love for the people. If there is a way, and I was at fault for not telling her, please charge me with that fault."

"Capac, I am not your judge," Dad softly encouraged, "I only ask that you look after my daughter's heart in the aftermath. She assures me she looks after yours, in whatever way this marriage functions."

Capac looked to me and smiled. "I do my best." He broke down into tears as he sometimes did when remembering. "Do you forgive me?" Capac said after calming his tears.

"What, for stealing my firstborn child away into the jungle?" Dad chuckled, calming his own tears.

"I do not apologize for this," Capac admitted. "She is better, and the people are better. . .and I am better with her there. Here, she was ignored. There, she is queen. I offer no apology for giving God a chance to use her light."

"Nor should you, I suppose," Dad conceded.

"I offer apology because your people ask for a father's permission and Debbie has told me a father gives a daughter away at the wedding. If I knew Debbie would be accepted as wife and queen and that God wished this marriage for us, perhaps I could have made a way for this tradition even many winters ago."

That was news to me for the reason my father then mentioned.

"I understand why this marriage had to occur, but I would have taken issue with a marriage of convenience or survival then. I'd have *insisted* on crazed romance if you asked." Dad laughed, but I could see it was a test.

Capac shrugged. "Love grows."

I pondered that in my heart, never having heard my husband use the term, but still concurred. "We could have raised Roy together. I certainly could have used your help."

"And we may have many more children by now," he reasoned.

Dad burst the bubble. "She's a bit younger than you, Capac. 'Many winters ago' she was a kid. Seventeen when you left her with Roy."

Capac looked at me for cultural understanding. "Is seventeen not an age to marry? You were flowered as a woman at both times."

"Capac, there's more to being a woman that just being. . . 'flowered.'" Dad chuckled, though a little embarrassed.

Capac knew that, of course, but truly didn't understand the difference with me. "Well, Debbie has *never* had the heart of a child. Only her flesh."

Dad laughed. "I've said the same thing her whole life. She skipped childhood. At seven, I remember telling her she was a better man than me."

Capac liked that irony, and said, "I am thankful God sent Debbie the *woman* with me. Not the child and not the man."

"Yeah, a man wouldn't have accepted the ruby." Dad stared Capac down. Capac swallowed hard and Dad tilted his head. Capac gave a half smile. Dad gave a full one. I was still trying to sort out the body language when Dad said in a quiet voice, "When did you give that to her?"

"Just days after our wedding moon."

"Like a week after I got there," I clarified the measure of time Capac would not know, but their eyes were stayed on each other, locked in some understanding I couldn't read. They were not listening to me.

"And that was a year ago. Last winter?" Dad asked him.

Capac answered in a hum and nod.

"Ha!" Dad sighed as if remorseful. "First of all, happy anniversary. Second, you are an extremely patient man. A year? *That* is longsuffering."

"Dad!" I didn't understand. But it felt insulting.

Capac laughed loud, like he was flattered, then shrugged and said, "Debbie makes even longsuffering a joy."

Dad glanced and nodded his head at Josiah, then said, "Clearly." The two men laughed again at the joke I apparently missed, then Dad said the last thing I expected. "Thank you, Capac.

I've been praying all her life that someone could show her how much of a light she is and how precious and beautiful she is. Forgive me for not seeing how much of yourself you'd be willing to give to protect her. I don't care what it took. I'm honored that you are my son-in-law."

It was only the last word Capac did not understand, and he looked to me. "Husband-son," I translated, though my voice was faltering from tears. "He is glad you are family."

Capac was relieved. He sighed with passion, then began schmoozing. "I want to tell you that your daughter sits at the front of the temple and reads to my people from the Bible. She answers their questions and prays with them, all with my son at her breast. She is the best queen, and the best mother, and the best woman I have ever known. I want to be sure you are very proud."

"I am. Very proud," Dad noted. "Now, Capac. Tell me how I can pray for you and your people."

Twenty-Seven

That evening, I was helping Lydia and Jane clean up after dinner. Mom was leaning against the counter checking on the supplies for the next day's menu. All the men were off putting children to bed or helping guests get settled. Us ladies were having a colorful conversation. They wanted to know about my people, including bathing practices, cooking techniques, clothing styles, and communication. They had met Rune and asked why he carried a machete, and I told them who he was. I told them who Alda was and Lydia gossiped about the way Daniel tried to communicate with her hours before.

Eventually it morphed into an interrogation by Lydia, who had to know absolutely everything about everything about my new-to-her intimate relationship. She was simply appalled that I had never been kissed, despite having given birth to a man's child. They also learned about the ritual that occurred on my wedding night and it was like medicine to share even my worst with them. As she rinsed her final plate, and I dried it and stacked it on the others, I caught my sister staring at my braids, and I heard my mother whisper something to Jane, but couldn't make it out. Each woman dried her hands and turned to lean against a counter in the industrial kitchen in the jungle, and I was the last to join them. They were all smiling at me.

"What?" I worried, smoothing down my braids the best I could. They were in need of attention.

Jane answered first. "We're proud of you." She cleared her throat, the tears having choked up her last words.

"You're such an incredible young woman." Mom sniffled and Jane handed her a tissue. "Or just woman, I suppose."

"And you're *gorgeous*," Lydia added to both the unsettlingly flattering commentary, and to the chorus of weeping women. "I can't get over that."

"I just have braids in my hair. I've certainly grown from seeing things, but I am still me," I tried to ensure them.

"How are you doing with all this, Debs? I know it hasn't been easy," Mom asked. "While you're here, you can talk to us if you need to."

"There is nothing to say. They were worth everything that wasn't easy. I would do it all again." I shrugged.

"Blood evidence and vomit and all?" Mom, Lydia senior, teased, having just heard about that part.

"All of it." I rethought. "Except I'd have liked to do it in shoes. I miss socks even more."

"He really won't let you wear them?" Jane worried over some kind of domestic abuse.

I laughed once. "Honestly, shoes disable a person. Capac, who isn't even a climber, can climb thirty feet up a tree in less than a minute just because his feet are trained to help him. Their feet have a completely different shape and function."

"I've seen. It's so weird." Lydia crinkled her nose. "So many of their ways are just odd."

"But I'm not there to change who they are. I just want them to know Jesus. I'd give up far more than warm, comfy feet for them."

"Even love?" Lydia batted her eyes.

"Not fair, Lydia."

"Also not *true*. I can't believe you actually think you don't love him." I should have known she'd hear that on the wind.

"What we have works very well," I whined. "Can we leave this be?"

"*Does* it work?" Lydia asked. "At dinner, I heard you say you *love* Josiah and Roy, and you *love* your people, and you *love* all of us. But then when someone mentions something about you loving your husband you give some cop-out like 'we have a strong marriage.' Well how do you have a strong marriage without loving your spouse?"

"Lydia, stop," Jane tried.

"He loves *you*. Dad says Capac is 100 percent aware that he's in love with you, and that he's just being patient for you to be on the same page. They were talking about it right in front of you, and you have no idea what you're doing to him. So maybe it's him I should be worried about. Your miserable, unloved husband," she ranted.

"He's not miserable. We take care of each other. We respect each other, support each other, and we are *happy* together."

"Debbie, that's *love*. That's what we're telling you," Lydia stretched out her hands with passion.

In hindsight, it was clear of course. But that day was the first someone had said it to me like that, and it kept happening. Then again, maybe it wasn't the first time. I thought of a look between Nur and Capac when I was giving birth, scared the delivery would be dangerous because Josiah was not conceived with love. Maybe he was, and Capac knew that. Maybe love wasn't some extra thing we were refusing to do. Maybe love was what we already had. Still, I fought.

"Lydia, everything we do is for the love of our people. But you all seem to want us to turn into goo-goo-eyed romantics, focused only on each other." I rolled my eyes.

"I'm sure you *do* when you're alone." Lydia winked and the others giggled. Even I laughed a little.

"That's enough, Lydi." Mom smiled, then looked at me. "Debbie, you have so much of your dad in you, you know that? You can't even imagine how proud he is. For months, he's been saying, 'She did it.' These people are all he has ever cared about."

"And *you*, Marla," Jane corrected.

"Well, no, actually. Dad almost wasn't *anyone's* dad. He was completely stubborn and oblivious to all but being a living sacrifice for these people. You are *so* much like him, Debbie."

"Why does that feel like an insult?" I asked. "I'm not even sure that's true. Dad has always loved you. And he seemed disappointed that I'm not melting all over my husband, which is weird, to say the least."

"It's hard to see your child make the same mistake as you." Mom shrugged. Smirked. "And yes, he always loved me. Since the day we met. He just didn't always *accept* that."

"Nonsense. John would be lost without you. At the very least, the man would starve." Jane, Mom's dearest friend, both encouraged her and teased Dad.

Mom patted Jane's hand endearingly. Then she sighed. "Trust me, I know."

"What do you mean he didn't always accept that? You met and married him in two weeks," Lydia reminded her.

"Three months," Mom giggled her common correction, then sighed herself to sincerity. "Lydia, those two weeks were almost my *entire* acquaintance with Dad. Beginning to end. At the time, it felt like God inserted the perfect match into my life only to tease me and then take him away forever. Those two weeks were excruciating for me."

"Why? I don't understand," I asked.

"Because I loved him, Debbie. All the ways that you claim you don't love Capac and all the goo-goo-eyed frivolity and all the rest. And he knew that. But he tried to be a martyr and ignore it and ignore the same feelings in him."

"Why would a person do that?" Lydia was hyper interested suddenly, and I wasn't sure why.

Besides that day under my tree, Dad had only told the story in fragments, so Mom indulged us all, and told us the story of how they met and got married. The way Dad likes to tell it, my parents were married and pregnant within weeks of meeting. I was born in my grandparents' basement to a nineteen-year-old construction worker and a twenty-three-year-old nurse. But that's only if you tell some of the story. The fragments. The scandals. I know I was born to heroes who enabled me to serve God in ways that made even them blush.

At some point while Mom was telling the story, Capac had slipped right in among us, Josiah in arms. Remembering the rules, the other women avoided making physical contact with him, but otherwise did not mind his presence. Capac liked that Mom didn't even break her storytelling as he nodded to a chair, then helped me get settled nursing Josiah. He sat in the chair across from me and listened to the rest of the story. In the end, she reiterated,

"You're just like him, Debs. Somehow you're both keenly steady and willing to rush into whatever God has for you. If it somehow serves the people, of course. Other things tend to fall by the wayside." Mom was cryptic, likely because Capac was present.

Capac mumbled another conclusion in our language, "Debbie Davies fears nothing but God."

He said it often to tell me I was courageous. But this time, the tone seemed different. Maybe I was oblivious, but how can one even know that. How can I know what I do not know?

I was searching his face for the answer, and his eyes were steadily burning into mine, as always. But they were displaying a language I could not read. I was glad for Lydia's giggle.

"What did he say to you?"

But I couldn't answer that. Not really. So I began looking around Capac's feet. I inquired in our language.

"Where is Roy?"

Josiah had nursed on both sides by then, and was looking adorably milk-drunk. We both cooed at it when Capac took him from me and lay him gently over his shoulder. Our son looked so tiny in his arms. So protected.

"Roy is with your father and brother; asleep. Now that Josiah is filled, I will take him there too."

"To their home?"

"Yes. I asked him to keep them for a time. Until Josiah awakens for your breast again."

"Why? I was almost done here if you needed—"

But his face begged me to listen, not speak.

"We spoke of finding some time together." He glanced up at my head, then back into my eyes. "For your hair."

"Oh. Yes. Thank you," I nodded.

"How much do they understand?" He asked of Jane, Mom, and Lydia. And though they were all listening, no one gathered what Capac was saying.

"I think they understand some. If you want to speak to them, you should speak English." I grimaced, knowing his hatred for English.

He chuckled and took my hand with the one not steadying our son. He ran it along his lips, and drank in my scent with a sigh. My heart chose a slow, steady increase, and tested my passion. I fought to remain steady.

"I only wish to speak to *you*," he cooed. The three women were silent as he whispered. "Are you very tired?"

"I am okay. Why?"

"What is he saying?" Lydia whispered to Mom.

Mom elbowed Lydia, I think. But I was distracted by eyelids that didn't want to stay open and the scent of his skin as he touched my face with the back of his hand. I tried to focus.

He smiled, then asked our darkly-humored twist on a legitimate question. "Will you stumble with me tonight?"

"You know how clumsy I am." His favorite answer to my favorite question.

"Good. I found some candles and a blanket, and I built a fire. It is the place where you removed my chains. They do not use that place anymore, and your father said we could sleep there while we are here. But take all the time here you need while I put Josiah to bed. Your family heals you."

"I will not be long," I promised, but I added a warning in a frantic whisper. "We are twenty miles from home. We would have to travel for a birth if we started a child here. We should not do this often."

He shook his head, standing up and using a normal speaking volume, but still in a different language. "There is no risk for that with Josiah at your breast. Old medicine."

"Medicine!" Mom giggled. "I know *that* word."

That was in English, of course, and the three women giggled. Capac reached out and smoothed his hand over my corded braid and said, "You stay and talk. I will wait for you."

"Okay." It was barely a whisper. His touch and his scent had taken all my strength and voice away. He so easily got to me in those days. Not much has changed, of course. But that night, I hated him for all of it.

I watched him walk out the kitchen door, handsome even in scrubs, and listened as his calloused bare feet took him into the darkness. I cleared my throat and looked to my family. As I rose and rejoined them at the kitchen counter, all three women laughed at me.

"What?"

"Wow!" Lydia proclaimed. "I don't even need a translator to know what he just asked for."

"Stop!" I tapped my sister's tennis shoe with one of my bare feet, essentially kicking her.

"Debbie," Lydia whispered with intensity. "That was *highly* romantic. Tell me you didn't just reject the poor man."

"No! That isn't done. Not with our people or with us. We do not refuse affection."

Lydia looked intrigued. "But he asked you."

"Well, it's also important that I *choose* him, Lydia. Begrudging affection isn't affection at all."

"So you're a tease, then." Lydia, matured but still spiteful when she wanted, changed her tone. "Your people call their lover a 'heartholder' whereas you call Capac your 'dearest friend.' It's teasing. Any idiot can see the guy is in love with you."

I clenched my teeth, deeply insulted. I couldn't even speak.

"Lydia, learn when to stop!" Mom tried, but Lydia was already rolling down the long hill to my destruction.

"You're doing the same thing to him that Dad did to Mom, only it's been like a year, not two weeks. Jeremiah would be heartbroken if I walked around for a year telling people I didn't really love him while caring for his child that we made together."

"You need to stay out of my marriage, Lydia!" I finally commanded.

"Girls, that's enough." Jane was often the great de-escalator when it came to arguments between us sisters. "Debbie, when Capac was here, I was thinking how it might be nice for you to have some alone time with him. We have an overabundance of goat milk and bottles that aren't being used. So, if you needed a sitter for the night, you know I am always willing to cuddle with a baby. Have you ever really had alone time with him without a thousand other duties? Lydia, maybe instead of judging your sister's marriage, we give them time to grow whatever it is?"

I sighed, trying to will away the anger. "Jane, that would be wonderful. Thank you."

"Go to him. We're all finished here. I'll look after Josiah," Jane encouraged.

"And I'll take Roy." Mom smiled.

"Jane's right." And suddenly mature Lydia surfaced again. "I shouldn't judge. You have a lot of pressure on you. I'm sorry. I'll help look after the boys."

She looked like she was considering something in her heart, shaking her head with quiet stubbornness and looking to the concrete floor Dad poured in sections from bags when we were kids.

There was silence until Mom spoke. "I bet you're an excellent queen. From the way those women admire you. Jada and Alda? I know it isn't just a respect for the position. They look up to you."

"I look up to *them*. They have already been a wonderful influence in our village. And though they are no substitute for my own, they are like sisters to me," I said.

Lydia looked like she might be wiping a tear as she turned to the fridge and took out some goat milk. She seemed unwilling to converse at that point.

Mom whispered, "But you are also a wife, Debbie. Never lose that among the other responsibilities. Go to your husband. We'll look after your boys."

The door to the time-out hut creaked, and I found Capac inside with firelight, as I expected.

"You came quickly. I only just took Josiah." He smiled, rising and meeting me. But he began to fret at the tears in my eyes. "My queen. . ."

I shook my head, then welcomed his warm embrace.

"Debbie. . ." He tried again, "Tell me your heart."

I shook my head. "I would rather not speak right now."

He accepted that, then accepted my affection. After that, we were both wired from the eventful day, too tired to sleep. This happened often. So I lay my head on his lap and he began tending to his affections in my hair. He was respecting my silence, so he likely expected my next words even less than I did.

"Capac, are you in love with me?"

"Debbie. . ." He sighed. "Please never ask me that."

I sat up, mid-braid, and faced him, wrapping up in the blanket that was my only garment at the time.

"I wish to know. I am not a romantic. I will not be hurt if you do not love me." I looked across at his eyes and laughed once, tucking the half braid behind my ear. "So just be honest. That is all I ask."

"Debbie, I *know* that you are not romantic." He smiled. "My answer *will* hurt you."

"Even still, tell me," I whispered.

With that, Capac reached out and adjusted my necklace. The realization washed over me. Floored me. And he said, "You carry my heart with you always, my queen."

"No! Don't you dare." I sobbed.

"It changes nothing to know that I *love* you," he whispered, not honoring my wishes.

"It changes everything." I sniffled, sobbing.

"Why?" He laughed. "Did you think my heart was made of stone and that I would never love the woman who shares my whole life with me? Love *grows*. That is all it knows to do."

He wrapped one leg around behind me and sighed at the tears in my eyes.

"Loving you has been my greatest joy."

I sighed. "But I am heartbroken that I did not *know*."

"But I told you." He chuckled. "I told you a wife is like rubies and a man's heart safely trusts her. I tell you often. You choose not to hear."

"Is that what you were saying to me? Is that why you memorized that passage?" I gasped.

He just chuckled into an embrace, laying us on our sides. "I heard Lydia say that I am miserable and that I am in pain without your heart, but I am not. You are everything I need you to be. Do not let your heart be troubled."

"Can I ask a very stupid question?"

"You never ask stupid questions. But ask."

"Do you think that I love you?"

He laughed. "That is for you to know, Debbie."

"Well how did *you* know? When did you 'fall in love' as they say?"

"I did not fall." He smiled. "I learned. I discovered. It was there already. Days after our wedding, I learned." He laughed at himself. "And when I learned, I swore not to touch you and prayed for it to not be so. I felt I had betrayed you. But I was a fool to think I could unlearn it."

"I remember." I realized then what went through his heart that night he panicked. "But what do you mean by learned?"

"I learned that the way I admired your beauty and your love for the people and your smile and your mind; the way I longed to see you for seasons and years when we were apart and watched you from far away to heal my heart. The way I trusted you so well. . .it was *all* love. I have only *ever* loved you."

"But if it was there, how could you not know?" I snorted laughter, teasing him.

"Love must be chosen, Debbie. The seeds were there, growing and blooming already, but I did not see because I did not choose to see. I was asleep to it."

"Technically we chose it when we said wedding vows, Capac. I chose you, and you chose me."

"We chose *marriage*, and that is harder in many ways. But I think the ways marriage is hard were already grown in us. Sacrifice, commitment, communication, and respect. These parts of marriage were nothing for us to grow." He sighed and explained another way when he saw I did not follow. "Marriage is the cloth we use when we tie ourselves to Roy. We are tied together for a common goal. But over time, Debbie, this tie will be a burden. Love is the choice to surrender to it—to be glad for the way we are tied together and wish for nothing else."

"You are not a burden to me, Capac. Not yet, for certain," I promised, my voice low. Was I hurting him?

"And I am grateful." He hummed a laugh when he was finally required to confess in words, "I think love was asleep in me until we walked together and it could not be ritual. What else can wake a man's love but his heartholder's touch?"

"And then I threw up!" I groaned, then laughed, thinking of dragons.

"I did not care. I was dizzy with romance even the first time, though I did not know what it was," he admitted. "That night by the river when I needed comfort, it was not your body that gave it. It was your *love*. Josiah began with great love, and even Nur was confused that you did not know. So yes."

"Yes?" I laughed.

"I *know* that you love me. I think it was growing and blooming outside your notice. I think more was hiding under that basket than just your light for God. I long for you to choose love and see it, but as your father said, I am patient for it."

I rolled my eyes. "I am not 'dizzy with romance.' I thought we were like-minded in that."

"Nothing needs to change." He shrugged. "But if you are willing, we *can* choose love and let it grow."

My heart bent for him. He wanted romance. He wanted to be dizzy-eyed lovers instead of just affectionate members of a marital partnership. When my whole heart changed and wanted that too, just to give him everything he desired, I realized the obvious.

In just a blink of my eyes, my heart echoed snapshots to my memory. My husband and king carrying me to the river then calling out five times for his heir to be celebrated. The same man sitting in the one beam of light reading about rubies. The same man, my friend, protecting and laughing and learning and just *being*. Finally, I recalled the "savage" looking out from between the bars when I was just seventeen and he was fully a man. *You understand*, he had said. Language, he meant. Or maybe not.

"You loved him then," Mom had said. And as mothers often prove of themselves, she was right.

I came back to myself and responded to him.

"Why a cloth and not a chain?" I hummed. "I think I would have very happily been chained to you here in this room if I had seen my love then."

He gave a look of disgust. "I was filthy and very distressed that day."

"I fell in *love* that day."

"You brought me my *matteh*. You were so very kind and beautiful. But when you defied your father and removed my chains, I saw your fire. That is when I loved you."

"Forgive me for not knowing?"

"If you will forgive *me*! I saw my *queen* that day, and was too silly to recognize her. All along, your father had this 'crazed romance' he wanted for us, and we did not know!" He laughed aloud, a lampstand of joy, probably loud enough for people in other buildings to hear. Then he pulled me close to him and whispered so that my heart heard it best, "Do you know the best part of love for us?"

"What?"

"We need never *stumble* again."

Twenty-Eight

When I emerged from the old time-out hut the next morning, Lydia was pacing outside.

"Hey," I said like a question, seeking my baby with haste. My pained breasts told me I'd missed more than one feeding.

Lydia was on my heels. "Debbie, I was up half the night, and I've been dying to talk to you."

"Okay, what's wrong?"

Jane emerged from the nursery with my Jojo then rushed back inside to tend to other children. I cooed at my son, then promptly found a spot against a building and sat down to feed him.

"I'm jealous. Debbie only nursed for like six weeks." She tried to build a bridge between us. We'd never shared motherhood before.

"Well, we don't even have bottles at the village." I laughed. "Did Jojo take the bottle last night?"

"Yeah, he took it just fine. I—" Lydia made a confession. "I looked after him myself. He's a good baby."

"You didn't have to do that, Lydia." I sighed. "Jane said she would. You have your own to look after."

"I was awake anyway. Jane is getting older. I let her sleep." Lydia shrugged. "Debbie, listen to me. I was wrong, okay?"

"About?" I was straining to remember the conversation.

"For judging your marriage. I know there are cultural differences, and that things started in a terrible way for you two, and I am being an idiot for thinking that you'll just—" She was animated and overflowing, but I interrupted her.

"He told me he's in love with me. He said he didn't always know it, but he's *always* loved me."

"What?" That was weak and wide-eyed.

"And apparently I'm also in love with him." I scratched at my newly tight and neat braids. "We know the moment it happened."

Lydia laughed. "You're serious?"

I nodded.

She whispered, seeking gossip. "What was the moment?"

"Um. . .you remember when Dad locked him up?"

"And you went to talk to him? And then he just started speaking English randomly?" Lydia giggled. "Of *course* I remember that."

"Well we connected, Lydia. I understood him even *before* he spoke English."

"But that's what you do. That's your gifting."

"Yeah, but it was more than that. I knew that if I fought for him, I'd be fighting for his people. But what I didn't realize is that even if I'd just been fighting for *him*, that would have been worth everything."

"So you were like." Lydia lowered her voice. "Attracted to him?"

That was something I'd never considered in such words, but when I did then, it was with a laugh. "Oddly, that was never even in question. There was always physical attraction, we just didn't see it that way. I know that probably doesn't make any sense, and I feel like a fool."

"Well, you shouldn't. It makes perfect sense. Your romance was built on a foundation so solid you didn't need all the frivolity." Lydia smiled at a fond memory. "Like when Capac was teaching you about the different words for friend and he used the same word for my marriage and Mom and Dad's marriage."

"Heartholders. I don't follow."

"Well Jeremiah and I were like this crazy bright flame. Like when you add a log to a fire. Stupid in love, honeymoon phase. *Way* too hot. A fire like that needs to calm down before it's actually useful." She laughed at that. "You can't serve God like that. You can't parent like that. You can't actually learn to be married and care for one another. You just. . .burn. Nothing else matters and no one is safe."

"I guess we had maybe a week like that after we got married, but still didn't recognize it as love."

"That was just waking up the dragon Dad talks about. I doubt you were ever as stupid hot as me and Jeremiah. I was seventeen and we weren't even engaged! What were we thinking? Debbie, you would *never*. You and him are like Mom and Dad who are the useful fire. No one is scared of it popping, and you can roast marshmallows and sit around for hours. Your love radiates out and warms people and does so much good."

I couldn't disagree with that, despite it being basically just flattery. I was beginning to see the good our love could do for others, and how deeply God had laid that plan in us. Lydia continued.

"It's like you two started with embers. Also pretty useless for most things, but then you grew together to be the useful fire. You never had that big crazy fire. So it honestly makes sense it you didn't notice it."

"That doesn't even make sense, though." I didn't like that. I wanted Capac to have a fire if he wanted one. "I've proven that I'm perfectly capable of being passionately in love with a man. I don't understand why it didn't happen that way."

"I do." Lydia shrugged. "You chased Jesus, even to the point of thinking you'd be celibate. You weren't constantly looking for some romance to be your peace. *God* is your peace. You didn't have to figure out marriage, because you were both just obeying God, and it just fit."

"You make it sound boring. I do *love* him, Lydia. Even if I didn't say it that way before."

"Boring?" She snickered again. "Debbie, no. I'm jealous! You know how hard it's been having to come around to the fact that I will never have peace in just Jeremiah? Marriage is a disappointment if you expect them to be everything for you. But when you find peace in Christ, marriage is amazing. We are *just* starting to figure that out. You did it exactly right, and I'm jealous."

"Well, you shouldn't be!" I laughed. "We've felt like impostors for a year."

"Nonsense. The reason I wanted to apologize is because you love him, Debbie. You didn't need to say those exact words for it to be true, and that's what you were telling me. You love him. He knows that. That's what matters. Not some words that people say when they are just trying to convince themselves they are still on fire."

She was right. I burped Josiah before switching him to the other breast, letting the silence swell then settle between us. Lydia broke it.

"However, I am going to give you a gift soon. And your 'king.' I want you both to know how goo-goo-eyed romantic you are. Even a small fire burns steady." And that sounded more like Lydia. "You'll thank me."

"I'm not sure I will. This is all quite new for me," I assured her, ironically while nursing the son of the man I didn't know I loved yesterday.

"You'll like it. Trust me."

Jada approached, her own babe asleep in her arms. I welcomed the interruption.

"*Regi?*"

I switched languages and learned that my father was requesting our presence in the chapel.

Dad, who likely stayed up all night to construct it, told us his plan for teaching us the Bible. I translated as he explained that he'd try to get through much of it in a season. Capac and I would be translating a lot.

We had arrived on a Monday (apparently) and there was not room in the schedule for all of us to make the trek to the river for the baptisms until Sunday. We didn't realize the weight of our usual royal duties until we went a week without them. Dad spent that week making sure everyone knew exactly what baptism entailed. Capac and I would translate for that half hour each day, but spent much of that week relishing the hospitality and freedom that was available childcare and a lack of responsibility and the lack of a

Tender of Footsteps always on our heels. Rune had been instructed, and himself perceived, that we were perfectly safe at the mission. Josiah began sleeping through the night because of the intermittent goat milk he'd been getting, which gave us even more time for rest and to explore what it meant to be in love. That first week was like a vacation. A honeymoon, even.

Sunday morning, in place of their usual chapel service, we marched the entire mission down to the river. My father gave a message there and baptized Rune, Jada, and Alda. But first, Dad baptized their king. Capac was never so beautiful as he was when he came up from that water.

When the others set off back toward the mission, Capac handed Josiah to Jane, who was in attendance, and put Roy's hand in my mother's. That was normal, and no one minded helping us to rest. Capac took my hand and kept me near the river.

"Capac." Lydia said it, and then when Capac shook his head at her, she winked dramatically.

"Okay, whatever that was, he doesn't understand winking," I told her.

"I understand." He hipped his hands. "My sister-in-law" (that was pained and in English) "explained some customs to me when you were translating two days ago."

Capac and I translated in shifts, so he would have had some free time. I panicked immediately when she first giggled, then ran to catch up with the others. What did Lydia say to him?

When the group left our sight, Capac took me into his arms and leaned his forehead into mine. "Your father's teaching will begin tomorrow. We will not have as much time together."

"We will have as much time as we have at home." I shrugged.

"I know." He sighed. "But I just wanted to have this one more moment."

Capac then, without warning, did something strange that always disgusted him, and planted his lips on mine. My heart thrilled. Lydia was right. I didn't know I was a romantic until the first time my husband and the father of my children kissed me on the mouth. He saw my smile and kissed me again, opening his mouth and letting his passion cross forbidden cultural lines and personal hang-ups. My eyes felt swimmy when he looked into them and whispered the most romantic possible thing, "Your kisses are better than wine.'"

I snorted laughter, then asked, "Why did you do that?"

"Lydia said what you know as romance means kissing too. I asked if you wanted me to kiss you and you said no. I should have known you were not truthful."

"You think kissing is gross. I have never had a problem respecting that."

"But your heart is fast," he whispered, his hand moving to the part of me that was tattling. "I like to make your heart fast." And by moving my hand to his chest, he made his own rapid beat of confession. Then he kissed me again, relishing it. "I think we can make kissing part of our romance now."

We arrived at the mission as the others were beginning to settle back in for the afternoon. Roy ran to us, and the three of us sought Josiah. We found him in the clinic, where Jane and Mom were chit-chatting. Jane had a bottle in Josiah's mouth.

Capac gasped when he saw that. He did not offend Jane by ripping his son from her arms, but the bottle is what offended. He took it, wide-eyed, and set it across the room in distress.

"It's goat milk, my king. We fed it to all the babies. They grow well on it," I explained. "That is what they give him when they have him. It is even helping him sleep. I thought you knew that."

He put his hands over his face, then shook his head. He was distraught.

"Oh no," I said in English "Did I break another law accidentally?"

Mom and Jane both winced.

"No!" he reassured us all in English. But then he tilted his head with a little smile. "Just break medicine."

"Okay, what medicine did I break?"

He grunted at a smile and sighed. He was cheery despite being distressed, like a man in love having just received his first kiss.

Lydia arrived then, baby Debbie in arms. Upon examining our faces, she said, "What's wrong?"

"I don't know yet. He doesn't like that I gave Josiah goat milk." I switched languages. "Is he defiled now?"

"No, he is not defiled." He looked to Jane. "How much goat milk?"

"Not much. He's still getting everything he needs from Debbie's milk, Capac. Don't you worry." Jane spoke it so eloquently. "Maybe one or two feedings a day?"

He sighed defeat and thankfully spoke Capacsi. "Debbie, that much goat milk will make me a father again."

I gasped. "Is that Nur's medicine?"

He nodded solemnly, then got animated and spoke English. He placed a hand on my chest and looked around, scolding the other women. "Only Debbie feeds him. Too late, but we can try from now."

I was getting frustrated. "You are making no—"

Jane sighed. "Oh, Debbie, I should have had you pump. What was I thinking?"

"Pump? Why? He's saying something about being a father again." I spoke to him in English. "Nur said if Josiah is at my breast, we will not have another child until he is older. I don't understand."

"But you have to breastfeed *exclusively*, Debbie," Lydia said. "Every feeding. If you miss one, you pump. Everybody knows that. It keeps your supply good too."

It was normal for me to not catch what everyone already knew. I was awkward in any culture.

"Oh. Well, I only missed a few feedings." I shrugged. "I won't do it again." I rolled my eyes at their concern. "I'll be fine. My body isn't ready for another pregnancy yet so I won't get pregnant, right?"

Every woman in the room cackled. Capac shook his head at me and explained the medicine.

"Debbie, you *told* your body you are ready for a new baby. Your body thinks the baby is old enough to have our food and miss breast feedings." He said that in English. Then mumbled in Capacsi, "And then our love grew."

"But only this week. It was more than normal, but not by a lot."

Capac laughed. "It takes only *one* time for God to start a child, Debbie. We have offered *many* chances and will continue to. This medicine is not to be fixed. Your moon cycle will return. You will see."

"Well, who did you think was feeding him when we were 'growing our love'?" I scolded him.

"I did not think! I was distracted!" he allowed in English with a smile. There was so much romance in his eyes as he looked me over that I think he had every woman's heart fluttering. But, never awkward in any culture, he knew when the tension was rising. He backed out of the hut with a pointed demand at all my companions. "No more goat milk."

"Wow," Lydia said when he was gone. She tapped my arm and whispered, "Did he kiss you?"

Mom and Jane's eyes told me they were wondering the same.

"I can't believe you told him I didn't think he was 'romantic' if he didn't kiss me. That's not true. You can start a whole child without ever kissing, and we have."

"But you liked it, though."

"I like most things he does. I'm blinded by romance, Lydia. Which is why I need you to tell me all the things I'm doing wrong, so I don't make more stupid mistakes. I'm not even sure how I survived a pregnancy without you three," I pleaded, and my mother snorted a burst of laughter with her dear friend Jane.

TWENTY-NINE

"Queen!" Alda said as I walked outside with Josiah. "I have a request!"

At first, I read it as alarm or warning, until I saw something new adorning Alda's face.

A smile.

She reminded me of a younger Lydia, then. Bright-eyed. Happy to be alive.

Capac walked past chuckling. "Anything, Alda. Why do you insist on being so formal?" He nodded at me and kissed a cheek as he walked away.

"What is your request?"

"Teach me numbers. For counting. In English." She seemed adamant, and in a hurry. "Please?"

"All of them, Alda? When do you need to know?"

"I only have a few moments until I need the first numbers. Come quickly!" She gestured and walked to sit in what seemed a random spot near the edge of the clearing.

"Okay, um. . .One. Is first."

"One," she said. "One."

"Good. How many do you—" But before I could finish, she was shouting that number out with a smile.

Just then, Daniel jogged past us on the path he had trodden first in the clearing, then through the forest where there was less jungle cover. He was startled first, then his face lit up. His appreciative laughter faded only as he ran past and around the bend.

"You're counting his laps?"

"Yes." Then, in very pained, accented, terrible English, Alda said, "Track one mile. Half marathon thirteen point one mile. Marathon twenty-six point two."

I laughed aloud. "Alda, that's wonderful! Daniel is teaching you?"

"Yes!" In English again. Then, in our language. "Daniel is running his whole marathon today. He likes to run too far to trick his brain. Twenty-six laps. One-half lap. The last lap, I will go across to the end to help him finish."

"Wow. How long will that take?"

"Daniel is happy, because last week he ran his whole marathon in less than five hours." She rose, then led me to a tree, where a stopwatch was hanging on a nail. "He tells me the numbers are here, but the numbers are hard to learn. I only wish to learn the numbers until twenty-six today. Will you teach me?"

"Will you tell me your dream? About Daniel?"

Alda's countenance darkened. "The king says I must not tell you my dream. It is the same as his dream, he told me yesterday before we were to be baptized. The king says he loves the queen, and that he does not keep secrets from you. But he says that the time is not right to tell you this dream."

I trusted that. I hated it, but I trusted it too. So I sighed, rolled my eyes, and said, "Two. Two is next."

"One. Two," Alda repeated. "Two." That one was hard, as our people do not often have such a hard "t" sound. It was more like "do" which is the way Capac says it. Alda smiled, having seen my smile. "This is how your king says this word?"

"Yes. The accent is the same," I explained.

"The love in your eyes for him is very beautiful, Queen."

I nodded, then tread lightly at my next question. "And you are going to sit out here for five hours to count Daniel's miles?"

Alda allowed a coy smile, then reminded me that she was not simply a young girl with a crush. "Your people are good and kind, and they support Daniel learning to run. But there is no one who has taken the time to count his miles. Everyone is too busy. *I* am not too busy."

"Will you not attend my father's teachings?"

Alda shook her head with cautious defiance. "I will learn God's Word from my queen at my village."

"He is not just reading God's Word. My father means to be an encouragement for us. Medicine."

"It is no medicine for me to learn holy things from a man who is called holy. The Spirit inside me is Holy, and no different than the Spirit in him."

"I understand, Alda, but—"

"Queen, it is medicine for me to have this freedom to count these miles for my friend. And it is medicine for him to know his miles are counted. Between the miles, I can serve in other ways. I can learn in other ways. My heart cannot learn from a holy man in this way." She sighed. "Will you allow me this medicine? And to deny the other?"

I smiled, approving deeply. Feeling for her deeply. "Your own life, Alda. Your own walk with God. I will allow this with great joy."

I put Roy in Alda's care that day. Every day but Sunday, actually. Daniel rested on Sundays. It amazed me how clever Roy was. He had just learned all his numbers to one hundred in two languages. Each day, no matter what distance Daniel was running, Roy and Alda could be heard all over camp shouting out the next number as Daniel ran by. Roy even chased him until he got to the trees sometimes, and the giggles filled the air.

Lord. Teach me to take time to count the miles.

After a week of translating as my father discipled Rune and Jada, I noticed a void in the dining hall at lunch time. While my night owl husband rested, I translated in the mornings when Dad would teach values and morals of the faith. Capac would translate the afternoon session when Dad would teach strictly books of the Bible in massive chunks the way I had taught Capac. Between sessions, we all ate lunch together.

That morning, however, Capac had stopped by when Dad was teaching the moral side. At lunch, Capac and Dad were missing.

"Has anyone seen Capac?" I wondered.

"He's in Dad's office with him," Mom told me in a yawn.

Jeremiah, baby Debbie atop his lap, grimaced.

"What's wrong?" I asked.

Jackson explained, "sounded a little heated."

"It's about the class I think." Jeremiah's classroom was nearest Dad's office.

"Oh. Ah, ah, Roy!" I changed languages. "You eat that crust. We waste nothing."

Jackson chuckled. "That is *not* how I remember that language sounding."

"I was barely proficient before. I got to the village and it was a few days before I understood anyone. I didn't realize Capac had been dumbing it down for me. Now I speak it closer to correct, but it is still clumsy and with an accent."

"And your English has an accent now too," Jackson noted.

"I know!" I laughed. "I can't win."

Josiah stirred, and I looked down into my sling, shushing him.

"He's cute," Jackson said. "Am I allowed to hold him sometime?"

"Of course! It's just *me* you can't touch, Jackson," I reiterated the rule, having broken his heart when we'd arrived and I had to refuse his bear hug.

"And what happens if I do, again? Like what if you hand him to me to hold and I accidentally graze you?" he joked.

I glanced at Rune, who gave a slight smile. He was always listening.

"Um. Don't."

The room silenced when we heard the booming voice from near the office.

"*No!*"

I winced and looked at my mom. "Should I go intervene?"

"Debbie, no. Capac will be fine." Mom stopped me.

"Mom, I'm not worried about Capac."

"Dad knows how to converse with a young man, Debbie."

"A young man? He's probably not too much younger than Dad, Mom."

"Debbie likes older men," Lydia teased, then sipped her water with casual drama.

I rolled my eyes. "I like *Capac*. My husband?"

"Whose age you don't know?" Jeremiah didn't like that.

"We don't count years." I retained my focus. "Mom, he's not just some young man. He's a king? Capac has spent the past few months in meetings with elders convincing them of the laws we need to modify. He knows how to get his way, especially when it is God's way. He will quote chapter and verse all day long."

"And Dad won't?" Mom was offended.

"Dad *will*. That's the problem. How heated do we let this get?"

"It's not appropriate for you to interrupt a meeting between two men." Mom tried to be discreet.

I stood then, smiling. "You know what Capac calls me sometimes?"

"What?"

"Queen Esther." I looked to Roy. "You stay with Ama and eat that crust."

I took my babe in my sling, uncomfortable with the scrub top sliding and bunching up at random, and heard the argument when I was still thirty feet from the door. I couldn't make out words. I arrived with a knock, but didn't wait for a response before entering. They were red in the face, and Capac's scrub top was clenched in his hand, not on his body.

"What's going on here?" I asked. "We can hear you yelling."

"Deborah, this isn't your business." Dad, of course. I was Deborah when I'd done something wrong.

"John, Debbie is my queen. She may go wherever I go, and my business is hers," Capac commanded.

"I understand that, Capac, but—"

"Dad, a king is good, but he sometimes needs his other half. A man is a river, a woman is fire. Together they are strong, and separate they can be, um. . ." I looked at my shirtless husband. "Why are you not wearing your shirt, my king?"

"I had so much pain to stop holy men with laws that are not in the Bible." His English got a little clumsy when he was emotional.

"What laws? Dad, what has he been saying?"

"That he won't wear our clothes anymore suddenly." Dad shrugged quickly and gestured violently to my husband before planting himself in his chair.

I started inquiring in our language. "Tell me why—"

"No! Not fair. English," Dad insisted.

"Okay, Capac, tell me why you won't wear their clothes."

"And *you* will not!" Capac started to try to remove the baby from around me and undress me.

Thankfully, Dad and I both protested and Capac stopped.

"I ask him to teach the Bible, not America. They will learn Jesus, the prophets, the Psalms, not the best way to wear clothes. I have read all the Bible and the Bible does *not* have these garments," Capac boomed, throwing the scrub top on the ground.

"Capac. Calm down, my king," I said in our language, and he softened when he saw my eyes. "Sit?" He complied, taking to the couch in the office, where I joined him. "How did this start?"

"Capac heard me teaching Rune and Jada about modesty today," Dad said.

I winced.

"You were there, Debbie. What did I say wrong? You translated everything."

"Well. . ." I winced again. "No, I didn't, actually. I modified what you said because what you said would have been a cultural nightmare to explain. I was glad Alda wasn't there. It might have been traumatic if she understood any of it."

"How often have you misrepresented me, Debbie? You asked me to help you, and that's all I'm trying to do." Dad was hurt.

"Just today. And I know you have taught the Bible well, Dad. Right, Capac?"

"Yes. Just like my queen," Capac conceded.

"Right. So, a woman's body is sacred for us. It would have been confusing to hear that a woman whose body is uncovered is a source of sexual temptation. Nudity is different for us than for you. Our only fabric is wool, so we only cover nursing babies for warmth, not modesty. As it gets warmer, you should expect Jada to nurse uncovered," I explained. "Children under about five wear nothing. Men never wear shirts. It's just very different for us, Dad."

"So you're saying a man can never be tempted by an undressed woman?"

"Of course he can! He can also be tempted by a *fully* dressed woman." I laughed. "Adultery and sexual immorality happen because of sin, not wardrobe choices. But with us, it's rare. We value family bloodlines and do not like to cross them. And before marriage, couples rarely *touch*. They like the new ceremony, and that takes complete abstinence to accomplish."

"What about your husband standing in my office half naked? Is that decent?" Dad laughed.

"Do the muscles intimidate you, Dad?" I teased my dad and complimented my king. "By our standards, he isn't naked. But he usually does wear more than other men."

"I will wear my royal garments," Capac said. "And you will teach only the Bible. And teach Jada to teach the Bible. Not just Rune. I have heard you say only Rune may teach."

"Men should be teachers, Capac. That *is* in the Bible," Dad said. "I know Debbie has been teaching, but that is because she was the only option."

"Debbie was God's choice, not only option." Capac commanded the room. "God sent a woman to be our queen and my partner. A man, the holy men would have killed. He put in *Debbie's* heart the stories of the Bible and great love for me and my people. God intended for me to entrust this *woman* to carry and raise my heir. Do you think a *man* would suffice for this? No! Not 'only option.' God's *ideal*. All the rest is *your* interpretation."

I worked to de-escalate again. "Dad, I love the Bible. Jada loves the Word of God. Teach them both like you taught me. And then they can both teach back home too." I shrugged. "I agree with my king. The moral things have to stop. They do not translate. You might confuse them if you teach anything other than what the Bible says plainly."

"Okay." Dad shrugged. "Thank you. That was far more diplomatic."

"And we will wear *our* clothes," I added, backing up my man. "To remind you that even though you are my family, my people are not you."

"Fine. Whatever you say." Dad conceded. "I should have known I'd end up with a son-in-law more stubborn than you Debs. How did you manage this?"

"God made this match, Dad." I shrugged and moved on. "So, I wonder if perhaps we should have Old Testament in the morning and New in the afternoon?"

"To get through it faster, or—" Dad was worried we'd leave early.

"No, you could slow down and go more in depth." I shrugged.

"I think I'd like that." Dad nodded, looking to me and realizing I had more pull than he thought.

Mom helped me wash our garments each week. We only changed into scrubs for washing day. The children and all the mission staff suddenly stood taller and were more reverent when any of us would walk within their presence. Rune, Jada, and Alda moved from the schoolhouse to the chapel where they slept on blankets on the dirt floor to feel more comfortable than on a bed. Capac and I slept in the old time-out hut with our boys like we had been. We respected the customs and ate when they ate. But we did not become them, or in my case, revert back to being them.

We were halfway through our intended season there, and Mom and I were chatting and doing laundry with Josiah wrapped around me. He was getting big for the sling, but still I kept him close and nursed him exclusively after the week-long misstep. But one morning I was mid-sentence and hanging a garment when my instincts felt the dizzy spell and promptly removed Josiah from the sling.

"Mom?"

"Yeah, Sweetie?"

I handed her my son, and don't even remember hitting the ground.

I woke up in the clinic to a cool rag on my head and Jane and Mom's worried faces around me.

"Sorry," I said, then sat up. "I probably did not drink enough water."

"No, stay, or you will sleep again." Capac, apparently present, instructed then approached me, checking me over.

"Josiah?"

"He's fine, you handed him to me. I couldn't even catch you." Mom worried.

"I have to feed him. He can't have goat milk." I was so woozy.

"No. Too late." Capac laughed. "Your face tells me."

"My face?"

"The color in your cheeks. A woman who faints should be pale, and you are especially pale normally. But your cheeks have color. I have entrusted you with a new child."

"No," I whined, not ready for another pregnancy just yet.

"We can't understand you," Mom said. We hadn't been speaking English. I didn't even think in English anymore.

I sighed. "Capac thinks I'm pregnant because my cheeks are red."

"It's a hot day." Jane laughed.

Mom shrugged. "She *is* glowing, Jane. Do you want to take a test, Debbie? I think I have a few."

I chuckled at the irony. "I've never in my *life* taken a pregnancy test."

"How did you find out last time?" Jane was intrigued by our ways.

I teased Jane, feigning primitive ignorance. "I didn't find out. My stomach started growing, and then I had a bunch of pain one day, and a person came out. I didn't even know how he got there."

Capac was laughing.

"Oh stop." Jane clicked her tongue.

"I hope you get to meet Nur someday. She'd get a kick out of *your* version of medicine."

THIRTY

A few days later, I found myself visiting the bathhouse instead of attending breakfast, and a voice startled me when I walked out.

"Alda." It was Daniel. "Over here."

That's when I saw Alda looking around, then following that voice to the shade of the chapel building. I positioned myself to see them sit on the grass together.

"Daniel," she said. Nodded.

"I really hate that I can't say more to you," Daniel whispered to her, though she likely did not understand. "I love that you count my miles, and being near you is just. . .it is so nice to have a friend. I just wish we could talk."

In our language, Alda said something similar. "I want to know what you say. But I love for you to say it."

They needed a translator, but something told me to keep my distance. Something was budding there that I did not understand, or didn't want to.

Suddenly, Daniel gasped. "Do you know the butterfly song? Debbie, sorry, your queen says you know it in your language."

She sighed, shaking her head, not understanding.

So Daniel started singing. "*The perfect butterfly with fire on her wings. . .*"

Alda gasped. She sang the next line in her own tongue. They finished the song together in two languages, then spent the next hour learning the song in the language they did not know.

When it hit me that it was not music that started to draw them together, I understood what God was doing. They *needed* the language barrier. I thought of the way we often draw near to God when it is hardest to see him. The language barrier was a reason to lean in—to work hard to understand. Their common ground was the Bible and that song. To find each other, they would be forced to seek God.

She counted his miles, and he taught her the Bible. Alda could be herself with Daniel, without the weight of being a holy man's daughter, a traitor, a societal anomaly caught in a horrific transition. Daniel could be Daniel, but not just the pastor's son who ran around the mission and in and out of the forest all the time. Their interactions were wholesome, but I know how quickly things can change.

Once, when I was monitoring them from fifty feet away, Capac came and sat with me. He asked exactly what I thought he might. "Is that the way we looked when we did not know we were in love?"

"Do not even say that, King. They are so young. . ." I said.

"I ask because this is the way your father would watch us. The way you are watching them." He laughed at me.

I rolled my eyes. Perhaps I was a lot more like my father than I wanted to admit. "It will break their hearts when we have to go back home. Who will count his miles?"

"Daniel will be well."

"I hope he doesn't just forget her or something."

"I longed for you always," Capac admitted in a whisper. "You were a beacon for my heart. I loved you so very greatly." Then he nodded to Daniel. "A man's love grows powerful even when his heartholder does not know she is his heartholder. Even when they are apart. Time is nothing. Miles are nothing. Love is everything."

It was coming time for us to go home again, but we had a problem. My morning sickness kept me mostly bedridden. I was making it to about one translating session a week as Dad taught the Bible. Capac had taken over completely.

I was in a nearly empty dining hall with my parents and husband. Capac sat beside me rubbing my back while we brainstormed the journey home.

"Just take it slow, Debs. Take enough food for three weeks and do a mile a day," Dad suggested.

"That's a lot of food, John!" Mom said. "Who would carry that?"

"Stupid goat milk," I mumbled, laying my head on the table.

"Debs, goat milk didn't do this to you. Sorry to say." Dad raised an eyebrow at my husband, who could be disturbingly sincere when the need arose.

"Are you embarrassed that your daughter's affections are seen?" Capac said it with a straight face to my father.

"I'm irritated that you two were not more cautious. There is a time to refrain from embracing." Dad could also be sincere.

"John, our love and marriage were growing. Caution is sin in those times." Capac tried to be lighthearted.

"Well now your family is growing. Congrats." This time Dad was *not* sincere.

"Thank you. A child is always welcome to me. Is it not the same for you? Why is your heart different for your own grandchild?"

"Capac, I didn't say—"

"Okay, you two. That isn't helping," Mom whined. "Debs, just stay here. We have plenty to support you."

"I will not leave my queen. She and the children are my. . ." Capac sighed, unable to find words.

"Responsibility?" Dad offered.

"And my joy."

The hormones and despair set me to tears then. "And your distraction. We let ourselves get distracted, and I promised I'd try not to. . ." But I took to sobbing enough that I didn't hear Capac's shush or his sigh, but I know he probably did both. He turned and tapped me to have me do the same, scooting in and placing one leg behind me. But Dad didn't protest at the intimacy. He listened, understanding what he could.

Capac placed his hand at my stomach and demanded I look at him. His eyes did not waver as he said in our language, "Debbie, you and our children are not a distraction from the work. You are *part* of the work. You are my first responsibility and joy, and the Bible makes this clear. I am no man of God at all if I do not choose and serve my family."

"But the *people* are your responsibility," I reminded him.

"And it is you and our children that made me care for them with more love and passion than I have in my whole life. You taught me just what I was rescuing. That is no distraction, my little-teacher-queen-heartholder."

I shivered a laugh through the tears at his endearment. But I could see he was distraught, clinging to me even as he comforted me in the embrace.

"I am safe here," I whispered what I knew must be the answer. "Leave me and the boys and go care for the people. Come back when it is time for the baby to be born onto your knees."

"And what if I am delayed or the child comes early? No. I will not leave my family behind."

"What are you saying? Can we speak English, please?" Mom begged. When I had calmed, they could see we were talking logistics again.

I repeated to them what I had said.

"Onto his knees? I don't understand," Mom said.

"Labors go better and babies are healthier if they are born in the place they were conceived. A man entrusts the baby to his wife when they walk together, she carries the baby, and then the baby is born back onto his knees. It's not just tradition. It's important."

"Sounds like superstition to me," Dad noted.

"I thought so too until me and Josiah almost died during childbirth. Then we went to where he was apparently conceived and he was born within minutes."

"It could have just been a hard labor," Dad suggested

"Maybe, but our bodies remember things we don't."

Mom tilted her head. Dad looked confused.

"You're not honestly thinking this is valid, Marla. You had flawless labors here in our clinic."

Mom cleared her throat and quizzed him. "John, before we had staff, where would you and I run off to to be alone together?"

"The building that is now the clin—" Dad finished that word with a fist over his own mouth and a throat clear.

I giggled at him. "Exactly. I have to give birth here, and Capac needs to be here."

"Take everyone home, Capac. Make sure everything is in order there. Then come back for Debbie around the time this baby is due. She will be safe here," Dad begged.

"And my sons?"

I smirked that Roy was always included.

"It will be easier for you to make the journey without them," Mom implored. "We will take care of them."

"It will all be as it was before you came. I am not alone. I have a wife and children. I cannot be as I was," Capac resisted.

"You'll come back for us, Capac. You are not as you were." Our language again.

He brought his face close, then kissed my cheek. "But my heart will not be with the people. It will be here with my queen."

"It better be," I flirted.

I was grateful the day they set off for home, that Capac had been introduced to kissing. Goodbye didn't seem complete without that kiss, one for the heads of each of his two boys. And another for his unborn child.

"I will return before your final season, after I am sure the elders can manage without me again," he promised, then crouched down to Roy.

"You keep Ma safe while I am away."

"Keep Ma safe!" Roy puffed out his chest and declared his obedience.

"I love you so very much, my son," he told him. Because he hadn't stopped telling him since he'd met him.

"I love you, Da," Roy promised back.

Daniel was nearby, having just said his goodbyes. His face was red as he fought tears.

"You will help Roy? To look after Debbie?" Capac requested.

"Of course." Daniel nodded with fervor. "I'll help keep them safe for you." Daniel glanced at Alda.

Capac spoke low. "Alda will be safe. I will tell Rune to protect her as royalty."

Rune nodded, having understood.

Finally, Capac touched my hair, sobbing, "Keep your cord tight for me?"

"I will."

"And hold it steady?" he whispered, touching the ruby around my neck.

I nodded. "Hold it steady."

With a final kiss, I watched them all walk off into the jungle, following their king.

I slept alone in the time-out hut with my boys. The nights were colder without our warm, muscular, big-hearted protector, but I held them close the best I could.

The worst part was my hair. My braids eventually fell out with no one to put them back in. And since no one but my husband was permitted to re-braid the cord into my hair, it was merely tied there in a knot, hanging loosely. Other women at our village looked the same. Older women. Widows. I was the wife of a king, but I had the hair of a widow.

I began to feel better as I entered my second season of pregnancy, but my parents shut down any notion of me trying to make that journey.

"He'll be back," Mom would promise.

I knew everything was fine, but something in me screamed that it was not. The confirmation started with a single cough. Daniel was chasing Roy around the mission one day, and Roy stopped suddenly on the path. He coughed, just once. But I was his mother, and my heart knew something was wrong.

The cough continued over the next week. First dry, then wet. Then for hours until he bruised ribs and became pale and weak and bedbound. No one else was sick, but we kept him from everyone else as a precaution. Antibiotics failed. Nebulizers failed. We gave him everything our modest clinic had, and still the cough worsened. I had no other choice.

"I need Capac. And I need Nur," I told my parents outside the clinic.

"Debs," Mom gave me the grim of perfect bedside manner. "I don't know if he has the time it would take, even if Nur did have something that could help him. But you have said their medicine doesn't work once they've had ours."

"But isn't it worth a try?" I blubbered. "Please tell me he's worth trying anything to save. At the very least, Capac needs to know."

"We'll try anything, Debbie. You know that," Mom assured me.

"How will we get word to them? Capac isn't due back for two months." Dad said it.

"I can—" But my hands went to my now protruding belly.

"Debbie, you can't." Lydia, along with Jeremiah and Daniel had been standing nearby listening.

"I'll do it," Daniel said, feeling like his chasing had somehow turned into this awful sickness. "How far is it?"

"About twenty miles, but that isn't exact." Dad supplied knowledge from his maps that I had helped him create. "And it's rugged, Daniel. Dangerous. The path you cleared is much safer than what you would see out there."

"I would still be there in less than a day." Daniel calculated.

"You don't know the way." I sobbed. "It's hidden. You can't even see it until you're there. What if you get lost?"

"Draw me a map." He shrugged. "Debbie, I'm not letting something happen to Roy. I'm going."

"Do you want me with him, John?" Jeremiah asked our father. He used to run laps around the mission when he was a teenager. It was a good time sink for angst.

"You'll slow me down, Jeremiah. No offense. You haven't run in years," Daniel said. "I'll go, and I'll bring him back, Debbie. I can do this."

Dad put his hand on Daniel's shoulder and gave him a steely gaze.

"Tell me this isn't an excuse to see Alda?"

The surprise in Daniel's eyes convinced me eternally that he was an even better man than my father. "No, I. . .I hadn't even considered that. Dad, Capac told me to look out for Debbie and the boys. God gave me the exact gifting and training that I need to do this, so that's all this is."

Roy suffered tremendously for the next three days in the time-out hut. The clinic was useless. I was helpless. All I could do was keep his fever down with cold water and hot tears as I lay next to him and his cough. No one else would dare. We knew my great-grandparents had succumbed to some quick respiratory illness and didn't know the origin or the way it was acquired. Sandani had died the same way. I knew what this was, and I alone was willing to hold him as he suffered through it. Mom thought it was the extra antibodies from the pregnancy that kept me from getting sick. I wasn't even permitted to see my other son, who was fully on goat milk in the care of Lydia.

On the third day in the evening, I was sobbing as Roy slept. I didn't hear the creak of what was once a cell door in the time-out hut. I only felt the rough warm hand gently join my arm. I opened my eyes and saw my beloved king, huffing and puffing and sweating as if he'd been running for hours.

Leaving Roy at my side, I transferred my embrace to my husband, and there emptied the rest of my sobs. He cringed at the state of my hair paired with the bump at my belly. My affections shone, and his did not.

"My queen, you have suffered enough," he whispered. "Go care for Josiah."

"Did Nur come?"

"She will be here soon." He nodded. "But Debbie. . .she does not think she can help him."

"But he's not getting any better. I don't know if he'll get better without—"

"You speak English." He seemed disappointed. "I should never have left you. This is my responsibility. Go."

"I'm not leaving him. I will wait for him to get better."

"Debbie, he will *not* get better. You know the way this sickness ends. You have done what I asked and more. You raised him alone when you were barely a woman and loved him and treasured his life. This burden is mine."

Something was missing from his presence and I looked around a moment before realizing it. "King, where is your *matteh*?"

"I will discuss that later."

"Did you leave it with someone? You did not even leave it with Belen when you came for the winter. Who did you trust to—"

"Debbie. Not now. Go."

I didn't understand why then, but I was put out of my temporary home with an heir in my arms and a spare in my womb. Capac lay with Roy day and night. Reading and encouraging and weeping. Because even if God would take his beloved nephew that he raised as his own, he dare not let him lose the battle alone. Nur tried, but she told me she'd never won the battle against this illness. But he was just a child. I didn't understand.

Roy was the bridge. He was the healing between his world and mine. He was the answer to the brutality of his biological father. He was redemption. A holy child. Just four and a half years old. He was learning to read and write and count the miles in two languages. A mass of potential for God to transform and use for His purposes. He was my son whom I raised as royalty with holy hands, against the wishes of my family and the reason of my mind because it was right. I did *right*.

But God took him anyway.

One morning, as I ran from my parents' house to check through the window of the time-out hut, Capac was emerging from it. I froze when he turned his solemn face to me. And I knew.

"No. Capac, no." I fell to my knees, pregnant as I was.

They whooped and hollered when a child was born. I often wondered what they did when a child was lost, but realized that day that the song orchestrated itself. I wailed there on the ground so loudly that I lacked no arms to embrace me, even when I pushed them away. I was held and nurtured against my will, but I was grateful for it.

English doesn't have a word for it. A widow has lost her husband. An orphan has lost her parents. But English has no label for a bereaved mother. Capacsi does, having lost so many children to rituals throughout their existence. The English equivalent, though it does not fully translate, is "closed." An Opening invites seed to grow in a womb. The Closing ritual was one of child sacrifice, if that helps to understand the poor translation. I was closed, though I'd never opened to grow Roy in my womb. It was the same to them and the same to me.

THIRTY-ONE

I mourned him a month with little other occupation, as was custom. I didn't speak to Capac the entire time, save when we stood together and buried Roy. We burned the pillows he'd slept on and everything in that room, even though with Capac's enduring health, we knew Roy had succumbed to something that wasn't contagious. I think Capac needed to burn it. That's how he mourned him. He was closed too.

We began our marriage succumbing to a private ritual against our wishes. We mourned the same, only the ritual wasn't the same. Capac would spend hours and hours braiding and re-braiding my hair. It had never looked so perfect. We had never been more broken. Besides visits to the bathhouse and gracious food deliveries, we saw no one else but Josiah, whose innocence began to heal us.

After the customary moon cycle of mourning, we emerged hand in hand and walked to the clinic. My family was talking in a huddle, and stopped upon seeing us.

Nur smiled immediately. "Oh. A girl." She said it in English, which she had learned some of as a child and had likely been forced to use for the past month.

I didn't understand at first until Capac placed a hand on my stomach. He looked at me. "Girl. A little wildfire like my queen."

I smiled all I could for the lingering heartache. I looked around and noticed a void.

"Where is Daniel? I wanted to thank him."

"He hasn't told you?" Lydia asked, wide-eyed. "You've been in there an entire month and he didn't mention anything?"

"The moon cycle is for grief. I told you. No other business," Nur sassed, and Lydia cowered. I was sad to have missed them getting to know Nur but was glad to finally see the result. Nur reached out and touched my hair. "You grieved well."

"Yes." I looked to Capac. "Please tell me what you have not told me."

"Daniel sits in the temple where we make the laws. My guards and elders are with him. Many more of the people were beginning to fight the new ways," Capac explained. "He holds the *matteh*, Debbie. Daniel is, and has always been, the final elder who had not yet joined us."

"Your dream. *Alda's* dream," I said, astonished.

"The dreams were different, but yes. He held the *matteh* in both."

"So you left my brother behind? He doesn't speak any of our language!" I began to be concerned. "And he's *fifteen*, Capac. You left the power of the entire village with a young boy."

"He is holy to them, just like you. He was my only chance to come back for Roy. You trust him. That is enough for me." Capac looked around at my family, and they got the clue. They all left us there, except Nur.

"But it was Roy that made them rebel," Nur revealed. "Roy was more than a holy man. He was more than a royal son. He was both. The holy families were waiting for him to come of age."

"Why? And that doesn't matter now. He's gone."

"Roy began to die the day of the Cleansing. But know that for you, my queen, I tried to catch the moon as a fish."

"What do you mean?" He had softened me just a little.

"Two generations. I was permitted to preserve the third and all the women for my cowardice and soft heart. God is gracious. He wanted to cleanse us of two full generations of them. He was clear, my queen, that it meant Roy too."

"You were going to kill him?"

Capac shook his head. "God forbade me to kill an innocent child. I loved him. I love him still. But God told me He still had to take him. The people would have made him a holy man and started the old ways again. There had already been whispers when I arrived home without you. Our family would have met the end of a machete in ten winters when Roy was a young man. I saw it in a dream. Roy, an evil holy man. And my queen and children slaughtered with me."

"When did you have this dream?"

"Many times. The first was the night you became queen. The last was just before Daniel arrived to tell me Roy was sick. When Daniel came, I knew it was time for both him and Roy."

"Why did you not tell me?"

"Would you have believed me?"

"They have been whispering about the 'days of the holy men' since before you came here. Have you not heard it?" Nur asked.

"I have. My life was threatened many times. They longed for people to teach them holy things. Who is teaching them now? We came here and left them without a shepherd."

"Jesus is our shepherd. But why do you think I left Hanan and Ilian behind? They have done well to teach the people." Capac smiled. "And Rune and Jada have surpassed them all in knowledge and wisdom because of your father's teachings."

"Will you go back? You were not meant to come yet."

"Debbie, I returned to find that many of my people were turning against me. My people, whom I rescued. Your people will never be my people, but mine are not either. *You* are my people. And I will be where you are. I will never be apart from you again."

I nodded. I liked that. "What about Daniel? He's probably so lost."

"We will return as soon as this child comes. We have Nur with us to make a safe journey with the child. Daniel has Rune and the others. They will protect him. He has his dear friend Alda to care for him. He is not lost or alone. But he is needed there."

We stayed in the time-out hut together with Josiah, and they prepared it like a birthing suite for us. When the time came, I labored most of the night, but we let everyone sleep for a while. When the time neared for the baby to come, Nur ran to get Jane, Lydia and my mother upon my request. My father also stood in the doorway just as Capac got on his knees in front of me.

At which point, for the first time in a very long time, Capac kissed me, if only on the hand. It caused him a sigh. I started crying.

"Stop, I have to focus," I said in our language, laughing until a contraction hit.

He shushed me. And with the final contraction, I let him know. "It's time."

And again, our child was born onto his knees. He laughed out loud after my scream of labor and the baby's cry. After the laugh, I warned my family.

"Cover your ears."

But they, of course, didn't understand until after Nur began announcing the birth of a "Bo-bo." Nur, in the enclosed area, but with open windows, let out three whoops, and received three replies from Capac, babe still in arms, also in the enclosed space.

"Okay, what was that about?" Lydia wondered.

Capac explained in English amid sobs, "Royal daughter."

Capac handed me the baby to nurse and lay down with me after getting me all cleaned up. My mother covered us with a blanket for modesty. Lydia tended to Josiah, whose presence seemed odd to her.

"Why does your culture have midwives?" Jane felt useless, though enamored at the way Capac had helped me with the placenta and cord cutting and everything.

"He attended deliveries for most of the children at this mission, Jane. Husbands don't always know as much as him," I complimented. I blinked slowly, speaking into Capac's eyes. "Tell me her name, my king."

"Esther," he whispered. "The queen who always interrupts, and always does right."

I nodded. Lydia was blubbering at the beauty. "What did he say?"

"Her name is Esther," Capac said in English, delighted to be moving sweaty blond stray hairs from my face. He looked down at his daughter and switched languages again. "Black hair."

"Why does that surprise you?"

"I am not surprised, just happy," he explained. "God let her look like me. I'm unworthy of all this."

"Esther?" Dad said, entering timidly.

"Esther." Capac raised onto an elbow to better see my father from my side.

"Out of curiosity, what is the last name?"

Embarrassingly, I'd never considered that.

"Last name?" Capac didn't understand either.

I explained the best I could. "We have two names. Three, actually. The first name and middle name are given by the parents. I'm Deborah, first name. Then Joy is my middle name. The last is the family name. Do you have a family name?"

Capac tried to understand. "Like Davies?"

"Yeah. So. . .a woman traditionally takes her husband's name and that is everyone's last name to signify the family they came from," I explained to him. "So I'm not Davies. I'm whatever you are."

He laughed at the strangeness and I looked to my family to bridge another gap. "We just say like, so-and-so's son. With us, they call us King and Queen. It isn't really a question who our children are. They don't even have a written language and last names are for legal documents."

"Okay." Mom had trouble with that one. Her grandchildren didn't have a legal last name.

"Primitive and barbaric," Capac said with straight tone, eliciting a laugh from all of them.

"Ow! Stop," I scolded him. "Laughing hurts."

But they all witnessed when Capac lay his hand on my head and asked, in English, "You have *Joy* in your name? You have never told me."

"Oh. I never thought about it. Sorry. At home, we don't have middle names, so. . ."

"My queen has joy in her very name," he said again, but announcing it to the others. "It is no wonder you have given me so much."

Dad let out a "Ha!" Then walked away with a, "Not romantic, huh?"

"Why don't you two get some rest?" Mom said after a giggle. "Do you need anything from us?"

"I stay to help," Nur insisted. "You go sleep."

When Esther was three days old, I felt well enough to walk outside. It was not long after sunrise and a group of girls was walking from the schoolhouse to the bathhouse behind their typical line-leader—Genesis. When I saw Nur standing outside the hut, I carried my tiny princess and leaned against the wall with Nur. As I expected, Nur's eyes were on the line of girls as they neared. She stood, staring at them. I realized then that she'd been there a month and likely knew their routine by then. She had emerged just to watch them.

"Bright morning, Nur."

Tears were in her eyes, and she looked to me, not having seen my approach. She immediately began swiping at those tears. I knew then that she knew.

"Did someone introduce you to her?"

Nur shook her head. "She is the oldest, and I knew her but a moment at birth, but I know her face."

"She was the first. She was raised as my sister for many winters until she felt led to serve the others and live with them," I explained. "Her spirit is very much like yours, Nur. She forsakes what is comfortable for what she knows she must do."

Nur sighed in pain and wonder. "She is very beautiful."

"Like her mother."

She nodded, then explained, "we try to heal in different ways from the Opening and the Closing. Mena will have children until her last moon because it distracts her heart from the one she lost. She loves a man by choice because she was forced to open to a man she did not love. But I *cannot* love other children. And I *will* not love a man. Neither of us is healed, and there were never any gods to appease with those rituals." Nur was perpetually broken, but also resilient. "It was my brother that taught me the way the true God is. It was him, who saved her. And then it was her, who saves them."

Nur nodded at Genny, who saw her standing there and gave her a friendly wave. There was nothing else I needed to say. She was standing fifteen feet from her only child, which may as well have been across the planet or a dimension away. They both had work to do. It was right for them each to do it, but there was a gaping hole in the very place that sought the work. It was times like that, walking back inside and watching Nur and Genesis smile at one another, that made me desperately long for Heaven, where the only work is fellowship with God.

We remained there at the mission a half-moon cycle. We were planning a Cleansing at our village for after the winter, and wanted to be home. I had been away almost four seasons when I had intended to do one. The morning we were setting out, my family cried.

"I live twenty miles away, Mom. It's not the whole world." I laughed. "And don't worry, I'm sending Daniel back. At least for a time. It will be his choice."

"Tell them to visit," Capac said to me.

"You can't tell them? You're so stubborn."

"It will mean more from you."

I sighed. "The twenty miles go both ways. Our people are good people. You could visit."

"Could we?" Mom turned to Dad.

"We'll discuss it," he said.

"It's not as though we can write a lot of letters. Come for Christmas. We'll prepare for you."

"Christmas?" Capac asked, then remembered. "With the gifts. For the birth of Christ."

"She assimilates with natives, but still teaches them Christmas," Dad teased.

"I'll have to work out which moon phase to explain it to them. They don't do calendars."

"Christmas in Capacsi," Lydia remarked, and Capac was amused.

"Besides Belen, yours was the first name we learned, so the language and village are named after you," I explained.

"Deborah Capacsi," he said to himself. "Josiah Capacsi, Esther Capacsi. Family name."

"Capac Capacsi isn't as good." I laughed. "But you're the king, so I think it will be acceptable."

"Roy was a Davies, though," Dad reminded me of the headstone they'd placed near the chapel.

"I wasn't married then, so that's fine, Dad," I told him. "Thank you for helping us to heal."

It took us a week to get home. An excruciating week.

"You're both so patient with me," I told Capac on the third stop in an hour on the fourth day. Patience is learned, of course. They had done this journey with grieving, postpartum women many times.

"I will wait for you always, my queen." He adjusted Josiah on his shoulders. Esther was attached to his front in a sling. My heart still searched for Roy at every stop, and I often panicked when I didn't see him. It was a high of anxiety that plunged to depression over and over. Still, I could not train my eyes not to watch for him bounding after butterflies and my ears not to listen for him singing the same song for hours on end.

"It is okay. You will not be well if we go fast." Even Nur was patient. A good chunk of her heart was behind us, speaking English and saving hearts from pain.

Thirty-Two

I slept an entire day away upon our return, barely waving to my pathetic-bearded, long-haired teenage brother over at Sandani's old house where he was staying. Capac returned, *matteh* in hand, with some dinner for me in the evening. We ate it outside the front door, of course, and he told me about the wonderful Bible teaching that was occurring again. But there was distress in his voice. He was buttering me up with small talk.

"Tell me your heart?"

"Daniel was good. He is homesick, but he ruled well in our place. He is young, Debbie. You will forgive him?"

"Why would I forgive him for ruling well?" I laughed.

"For all else," he implored.

"Okay?" I laughed.

"I will let him speak with you in the morning when you are better rested." Then Capac dropped the matter.

Josiah barely remembered our house, but he played with the stone toys Roy used to enjoy, and it comforted me. The following morning, I decided to pay my brother a visit to find out what I was forgiving him for. I took Esther in her sling and yawned my way there at sunrise.

We didn't knock, because not everyone had wooden doors. So, as tradition dictated, I called out, "*Aquiyo*" or "I am here." Then, realizing my brother was not one of us, I knocked anyway.

First, he laughed as if he'd been hearing a joke inside that house. Then, he said, "*Aquiyo*." Which is the proper response. That meant I could enter. So I pushed the door open, and his face turned from a bright, delightful smile to one of complete horror.

"Hey, what's wrong?" I asked in English.

"Uh. . ." Then as he said, "Nothing," he also reached back and more securely shut the curtain that led to the back of the house—his bedroom.

But for that millisecond, my eyes caught exactly what he was trying to conceal. It was a woman dressing. Her bare back was turned, and she was just beginning to tie her garment around her body. A cascade of black hair was being moved aside to complete the task. Is this what I had to forgive?

My wide eyes met Daniel's horror. "Daniel, are you *kidding* me? Tell me that isn't Alda."

"Debbie—"

"They call me *Regi*," I corrected. He was not going to try to charm me like my wild-haired blue-eyed little brother had always done with our mother.

"Okay, *Regi*." He rolled his eyes. "Maybe let's talk outside?"

I barely took those few steps back into the morning, and I know the shock had not left my face. Daniel seemed to hobble outside, like someone walking on a foot that had fallen asleep and had yet to awaken.

"Why are you limping?" I asked first, then remembered the priority. "Nevermind. I'll give you thirty seconds to explain."

"The limping, or. . .?" Daniel smiled.

"The woman in your house!"

"You left me here for six months, Debbie."

"And?"

"That was just Alda, Debbie. Of *course* it's Alda. Why on Earth would it be anyone else?" He laughed.

"I didn't mean it would be someone else, Daniel. I just don't know why she is sleeping in your house. And. . .walking together, I assume? Having. . .you know. . .intimacy?" I whispered, despite barely anyone speaking English, even if they were awake.

"Debbie." First, he crossed his arms, embarrassed. Then tilted his head. Acting more like Daniel when he answered honestly, humbly. "I mean, yeah. You're right to assume that. I won't tell you it's not what it looks like, because it is."

My heart shattered. I closed my eyes and there was a little boy there. Sweet Daniel with the charm and wisdom and justice and warmth. How could he go the way of Lydia? "Daniel, my people don't do this. Fornication is quite rare here. The rituals are no more, but they still have a wedding tradition that—"

Daniel laughed at that. He uncrossed then re-crossed his arms, the concept completely strange to him. I took a moment to read his eyes. He was the happiest I'd ever seen him. His eyes were warm and soothed, not wild and angsty like they were when I arrived at the mission with Josiah. Or terrified like when Alda walked out of the jungle that day. Nor were they filled with impossible longing like when I watched him count the miles alone. It was the same change I saw in Capac's eyes the night he realized we were in love. I suddenly knew the journey Daniel had been on before he even had to say it. Still,

"Alda has a cord in her hair." He laughed at himself. "And Rune laughed at me because I didn't know how to braid hair and her first braid was pathetic. So, Ilian had to teach me the day of the wedding. I still haven't managed to get it all braided at once, but I'm always working on it. Like, why did *my* wife have to have the longest hair of anyone?"

His heart and smile were wide open, and I dare not ridicule him. So I let him continue.

"Debbie, I would never have been inappropriate with her. If *that's* what it looked like, then it's not that." He snickered. "I only walk with her because it's. . .I mean, we're married. Married people do that, right?" He teased, gesturing to my daughter. "Esther, I hear? That's a pretty name."

I was floored. Too floored to speak. Why was my baby brother telling me he was married? He must have seen the bewilderment in my eyes, and kept explaining. But the subject seemed to change.

"I broke it. My ankle. I stepped in a hole about two miles before I got here, and I knew how close I was, so my pace was fast. And after I broke it, I just had to keep running. I was in agony by the time

I got here. Nur says I broke a bone in my leg and a couple in my foot. She set it, but the healing process was painful. At one point, she had to split me open to relieve pressure."

I looked as Daniel showed me a couple of scars on his right leg and bare foot. Then he explained, "it's healed now, I just walk with a limp most times." He cleared his throat, stating a fact that was no doubt painful. "I'll never run again."

"Daniel. . .I'm so sorry."

He smiled. Nodded. "It served its purpose. I'm at peace with that." He changed the subject back. "We were going to wait to get married until after you got back, but we didn't know how long you'd be, and it was becoming clear that waiting wasn't the best course of action."

Finally, I spoke. "It might have been, Daniel. Any fool could see you two were in love, but rushing into marriage? We would have liked to be involved."

"The people were rising up, Debbie. It wasn't pretty. When we taught the Bible, one of us would teach and the elders and guards would all have to stand against the people that kept trying to literally murder whoever was teaching." I saw tears in his eyes. "They would scream horrible things, and some of them were possessed. Rune is the only one lawfully allowed to execute them, so most of them lived. But this place was a nightmare when I got here, and I was injured badly. The last thing Capac wanted to do was leave."

"Wow." I was in disbelief. "I can't believe he left."

"Exactly. They needed Capac, not me. But sometimes, God asks you to do the last thing you want to do, I guess. For months, I sat at the entrance of that cave all day with that *matteh* thing in my hand. Capac told me only to leave if I was eating or sleeping, and I didn't want to mess up all the work you've done, so I listened." He chuckled. "Also, I wasn't capable of much else with the ankle situation."

"Thank you, Daniel."

He didn't feel ready to accept gratitude yet. He continued with haste. He was well beyond his thirty seconds, but still he tried to honor my need to understand. "Alda took care of me. Changed dressings, brought the medicine Nur would give her for me. She helped me grieve running. She finally started learning English with some help from Rune, and we could have real conversations after a while. First thing she wanted to learn to say to me was, 'We will find new miles to count.' "

I laughed once against the tears. "She's something, isn't she?"

"Understatement," Daniel admitted through his own tears. "We had tried talking a lot back at the mission, but I had no, like, context for what she was saying then. We converse pretty easily now."

He smirked there. "After a few weeks of that, people started talking about Alda spending so much time with me and taking care of me. And whispers went out about how she and I were close. And then the people started calming down and the Bible teachings started to be peaceful again. I didn't understand what was happening until the rumors got back to me."

"Rumors?"

"Alda told Jada her dream. Jada told her sisters. And it spread like wildfire." Daniel cleared his throat. "Alda dreamed of me by name. We knew that."

"That you were holding the *matteh*."

"Yes. And she dreamed me putting a cord in her hair."

I gasped.

"When it finally got back to me and they explained it to me, she came to me and told me the rest. She told me God had said this cord in her hair would heal the people. She hadn't told anyone that, but we could see that even unmarried, there had been a change. It was Rune that convinced me to marry her as soon as possible."

"Why would you need to marry her now? Why not wait?" I still didn't connect that.

"It was a big deal, Debbie. Because when her father and grandfather and all of them were alive, she was supposed to stay single her whole life because Capac married you. It wasn't fair. The elders got together and decided that if I married her on a full moon that was not set aside for any ritual or anything, that they would see just how free Alda was under the new laws. Free to love on her own terms. God's match. Not some ancient mandate. Rune was right.

People who thought Capac's ways weren't as good as the old ways suddenly started to see that maybe it could be good to change some things." He quickly followed up, "but we still did the evidence though. Apparently, that was an important *new* law thing."

"Oh no. That was probably awful for you. I'm so sorry." I grimaced.

"Honestly, I didn't mind it." He shrugged, then explained, "Back home nobody ever trusts me with anything. It's always, 'Everyone else go do the meaningful stuff and Daniel, do your chores.' But that night, my best friend trusted me with *everything*, and the elders did too. To them, I was a man, you know? Not a kid. And after that evidence, everyone else thought like they did. They recognize me as an elder now, which is cool."

"You're fifteen," I noted.

"Yeah, Alda's just barely of age to get married too." Daniel smirked. "But they kept telling me it was the right age. Hanan says Dera is about seventeen. So that means she was sixteen when she got married to Ilian. Most people don't count the winters, but Hanan likes to keep track of that stuff. And Lydia was seventeen."

"You're *fifteen*," I reiterated.

"Yeah, and I get to share a house with the girl I love and consequently help heal a society that was broken. I'm really having trouble seeing the downside to this." Again he smirked, and Alda emerged from the house I now understood was also hers.

She gasped a little when she saw me, putting her eyes to the ground, "*Regi*."

"Hi, Alda. I hear you are a married woman now," I said in our language.

"No." Daniel smiled like a proud teacher. "Speak English, Debbie. Just like, not too fast."

"English?"

"Yes! Daniel is teaching me!" Her eyes were alight.

"And why am I teaching you, Alda?"

"To go to live at the home of my husband," she responded, very slowly.

"Wow! That's excellent, Alda. Your English is lovely."

"Thank you." She bowed a little.

"Look at my eyes, Alda. And speak your heart. I have told you this before." I spoke softly and slowly.

As she lifted her eyes, she looked beside me to see that Capac had arrived at the conversation. "*Rei.*" She bowed again, then lifted her eyes with a smile. "*Resgatei.*"

That word brought an immediate hiccup to Capac's throat, and as he pounded his chest with one thankful fist, a tear came to his eyes.

It seemed like a strong reaction, even for him. Daniel articulated. "The people respected his position as king and so they all still called him *Rei*, even when he wasn't here and things got squirrely. But the ones who respect *this* king, Capac, for all he's done, call him *Resgatei.*"

"Rescuer," I translated with a whisper. It was more than that, I saw when Alda nodded again to Capac. He'd rescued Alda from far more than anyone else. After the moment, I turned to my husband, the king, "Uh, Daniel says he's taking Alda back home to the mission?"

"Yes. The holder of the *matteh* made that decree in our absence. They will split their time. Mission and village," he said, then smiled at Daniel, speaking English. "See, I told you she would not be too angry. My queen is romantic."

"Am not." I rolled my eyes, offended.

"She carries a new princess at her breast and says she is not romantic." Capac laughed loudly and walked away, tending to kingly duties that had been in less capable hands for a time. First, of course, he planted a kiss on my cheek. Then he was off.

"She is beautiful." Alda looked to my daughter.

"Thank you." I nodded.

Daniel sighed. "I heard about Roy yesterday. Debbie, I am *so* sorry he didn't make it. I ran the fastest marathon in my life to get here. So I did all I could, I just—"

"Daniel, you did well. Thank you so much for all you did. Capac made it and got to be with him."

"I know, but. . .I *loved* that kid." His voice faltered.

"Thank you for loving him. I guess that's all we can ever do, right? Just love them every second. Time is *always* limited."

"Yeah, I guess so." Daniel sighed.

Alda was closer to me, looking into the sling at the baby, and I noticed the delightful hint of blush in her cheeks.

I gasped, then looked to Daniel.

"What?" he asked.

"How long ago did you get married?"

"Like a month. . .a moon cycle. Whatever."

"And you plan to go back home?"

"Yeah, probably in the next few days."

"You know she has to give birth *here*, right?"

That drew Alda's eyes to mine, first with disbelief, then with fear. Then with delight.

"Only if we conceive here, and we're trying to get home fast to prevent that. We're splitting the time. So I guess we'll see what—"

Alda, who learned to love from one of *my* people, was suddenly planting excited kisses on my little brother's lips. They were teenagers in love, which seems like a nightmarish time to allow love free rein. But when Nur confirmed it later, my scared-of-spiders baby brother was rejoicing over that teen pregnancy. That wasn't anything like what he was taught. He was acting like one of my people. Maybe he was both. Or maybe he was just a married man and he wouldn't have seemed old enough for that even at forty.

It had been two years since the original Cleansing, and about half the village walked the river en masse. There, Capac and I baptized Dera, Ilian, Hanan, and Lana. They had waited faithfully and kept the heart of the people stayed on the Lord all this time. There was a great celebration that day, and Rune spoke to the people about the baptism of Jesus.

With that public display, a peace washed over the village. I have other gifts, so I did not see. But the rumors came quickly that sometimes angels were seen at the outskirts of our village. We were cleansed. Sanctified. Protected.

Two weeks after Daniel headed home, I was tending to my children in a meeting of the elders. We were composing a song. We wanted to be able to teach our new laws to the people so that they could all recite them verbatim and know that they echoed God's Word.

The whole time, and for months before, God worked in my soul, calling out a new song I had never sung for this people. As we were finishing up and Capac dismissed everyone, I told him what was on my heart.

"My king, I have a request." I brought it up in English.

"English? You know I dislike English, Debbie. But you know I will catch the moon for you—" He spoke his language.

"As a fish. I know, my heartholder," I told him, scooting in closer to him and letting my thumb touch the softness of his beard.

"Your *heartholder*?" He hummed at that word we now spoke openly and as often as possible, eyes drooping with the comfort of my touch. "This request is big?"

"Yes." English.

"Tell me your big request." Also in English, to show me his surrender.

"I don't like that you do not like English," I told him, and then a fire lit inside my soul that vented fully, but in Capacsi. "We talked once about how oral tradition keeps the mind sharp but allows for corruption. Wisdom and knowledge of things like other languages should not just be for the king. They should be passed to the people. I understand if you do not wish for them to speak English, but I think they should all read and write so that Scripture is not just what their royalty and elders say it is. Practices like that lead to lack of accountability and widespread ignorance and rebellion against God that includes child sacrifice."

"Our culture does not read and write. We will lose ourselves. We have songs."

"You can keep your culture and traditions and songs. But what if those songs get changed over time to suit the preferences of new people? What is written cannot be changed as easily. It is like the Bible that sat here unread for a generation. Your laws are good laws, and you can keep them *longer* if your history is written down instead of passed down and distorted like a thousand-year game of telephone."

"What is telephone?" Capac asked.

"Nevermind." I giggled openly, speaking English. "We're even. I mess up and give our baby goat milk, sure. But you don't even know what a telephone is. We're even."

That annoyed him, but his heart was elsewhere. "We do teachings every morning. We will lose telling stories for generations if we write them down to read at home."

"Capac." I sighed. "In my home country, we have buildings with more books than you even know to exist. We have technology that allows us to put those books into a device that can fit in the palm of your hand. That same device can allow you to hear the voice of someone thousands of miles away with no delay at all. We have stories too. We have stories and music that people record into a device, like the pictures you've seen at the mission, but they move and talk. But Capac, people still come for miles to sit together and listen to music. Children still love to be told stories and sing songs around campfires. Your culture won't die. I promise you. In fact, most people in my culture would consider yours to be paradise. There is so much we miss about this kind of life. I found everything I need here. Don't let the good you've done get lost in memories. Let me teach them to read and write."

"Okay." He allowed it. "Your home country seems like a paradise."

"It is not. Child sacrifice is prolific there too."

"You don't miss your country at all?"

"I left when I was three and have only visited a dozen or so times since then," I considered. "I do miss snow."

"Cold rain, right?"

"Yes, frozen and light like feathers or wool. We would play in the snow then go inside and get warm by a fire and drink hot drinks. There was no greater comfort than warming up after the snow."

He appreciated that. "*You* comfort me. I have darkness in me, like you say and like your father says. I have the Lord who works inside me. But you are a gift from Him, and you help me feel peace. Also, the children help. Any time I am forced to be tender, I remember how easy it is to be hard and cruel if I do not work for peace."

"My dad used to say something like that. He said that I was a better man than him, even though I was a girl. He told me later that he meant I make *him* a better man. He says his children are responsible for much of who he is," I said.

He smoothed his big rough hand tenderly over his daughter's tiny foot as she nursed, and said, "You are the best of your father. And these children are the best of me." Tears filled his eyes. "I do not deserve to see the best of me. But still I see it. And so I need it."

I whispered, "Then let's have a whole flower garden of them."

He chuckled at what he knew to be only romance, and said, "And we will teach them all to read the Word of God."

Thirty-Three

Four days before Christmas, it was serendipitous that a cooler day had begged us to take our language lessons outside instead of in the temple cave. My eyes were the first to see the familiar strangers arrive.

I didn't run and greet my family immediately, because watching them arrive was too beautiful.

"Wow," Dad whispered. But in looking around at the village and turning several times in quiet wonder, the rest was expressed only in tears. It was Dad's dream to find these people. Even though they'd already been reached for Christ, it was still his dream. My people were his life's work, and it shone on his tear-streaked face as he breached our borders.

In years before, I would have feared for them arriving like that. But now, the only person authorized to harm them was instead chuckling beside me as he stood guard.

"Do you see, Queen?" Rune asked it quietly, relishing their wonder himself.

"I see. Our lesson is done for the day," I told the young people of about seven to ten. I kept the lessons short and exciting, so they always expressed disappointment when they ended. Then the children happily ran off to help their parents. I approached my family, and Mom had joined Dad in a sobbing embrace.

Jeremiah and Lydia were arriving behind them. Baby Debbie was in Jeremiah's arms, and Lydia was visibly pregnant. As I approached, Nur beat me to them, passing by quickly with fervent words of correction. She was gone, leaving them wondering what they did wrong.

"Um. . ." I cleared my throat, and my first words were, "She said, 'never trust a man who covers his feet.' "

Quickly, they complied with the barely spoken instruction, removing their shoes and socks and stashing them in a pile outside the village. My father had changed so very much. It was not like him to relinquish his garb so easily. When they returned barefoot, I began my true greeting.

"You came," I said, hugging my family except Jeremiah.

Jeremiah rolled his eyes. "So I can *never* hug you again? We're family."

"But not blood." I shrugged. "Capac left it in the laws because he didn't feel it went against God's laws. Rune could literally slit your throat for hugging me. I don't think he *would*. But the law must be enforced or it means nothing."

"Has this *happened?*" Jeremiah asked, his voice high.

"I do not think you wish to know that." I smirked. "Merry Christmas, by the way. Is this everyone?"

Mom rolled her eyes after wiping the tears. The drama flowed freely from her lips, "Well, *Daniel* couldn't make it because his *wife* is recovering from a couple of awful months of morning sickness."

"Yeah, suddenly you showing up with a baby was no longer the shock of our lives." Lydia laughed.

"Is Alda okay? She seemed fine when they left," I fretted.

"She's feeling better now, but she was so sick when they arrived that Daniel was carrying her. We think the journey was just a bit much for a girl her age in that, uh, situation," Mom said. "Jane forbade her to come back until the baby comes."

"Daniel was gone six months," Dad finally said. "I knew there were feelings there. He and I had talked about it, and I did expect him to spend some time with her here. But how and why did he and Alda come back *married?*"

I shrugged. "Their marriage is a very good thing for us."

"But is it good for *them*?" Mom worried. "You know we love Alda. That isn't in question. They are just *so* young."

"I suppose if you treat love like it is a distraction from more important things, disillusionment will follow quickly," I explained, because I knew this conversation would come up. "But if you live your life knowing love is the *point*, you realize you have far fewer burdens in your life. And far more blessings."

"Yes. Children are blessings. They are also a huge responsibility, Debs. That kind of love, designed for adults, also carries adult consequences. Daniel is *not* an adult. That's what we're saying."

"A consequence? God is a just God, I will give you that. Many things in life are direct consequences for our actions. Rewards for good, and punishment for bad," I began, and Dad was listening. "But life, especially *new* life, is the most valuable possible thing. Why would he give the most valuable possible thing as a punishment? The Bible teaches that children are a reward, not a punishment. If that is the case, what it takes to get them is the very best thing."

"Love is the very best thing," Lydia said, rubbing her belly.

"Exactly." I nodded. "And you are wrong about them, Dad. Have you ever held the power of a whole people group, preaching the Word with a painfully broken ankle while getting regularly attacked by demon-possessed people?"

Dad sighed, smiling. "I suppose not."

"Daniel was born for this. To face the lions. That's how you named him. Alda was born to a man who *was* a lion but she chose Jesus. I cannot *wait* to meet the living person God has molded using their love."

"Well it's disturbing," Jeremiah added. "Daniel melts all over that girl every time she talks and they spend *way* too much time locked in their hut together. It's disgusting."

"And I'm carrying *your* baby. Again. Is that disgusting?" Lydia caused Jeremiah to stir and his eyes to get nervous.

"Weren't you listening? That baby is my reward for loving you," he mumbled, and the rest of us snickered.

I reached out and touched Lydia's stomach. "How was the trip?"

"Well, I'm trying not to complain, because you've done this three times, all without shoes. Once with a baby strapped to you, and another time three weeks postpartum. But it hasn't been fun. We'll say that much," she explained.

"You did great," Jeremiah corrected and complimented.

Dad was looking around and sighing again. In paradise.

"It's beautiful, huh?" I asked him.

"You have no idea." Dad chuckled. "By the way, thanks for doing all the work for me so I can just come enjoy it."

I giggled. "How long are you here? I have plenty you could do."

Capac, one of his children on each arm, saw my family and leaped for joy. "Family!" he allowed in English. Then he let out one yelp from his throat that silenced the village and set them to attention from their jobs. He introduced my family and told the people to treat them as royalty. With kindness and generosity and respect. He spoke it proudly and charismatically, as always, setting my heart ablaze.

"What is he saying?" Jeremiah looked worried.

"He's saying we're going to cook you and eat you for supper," I whispered sardonically, then winked at Jeremiah.

For weeks after I first arrived, people would whisper as I walked by. My skin and hair were like nothing they'd ever seen. That day, Jeremiah was subjected to the same. His dark skin and bald head were a new experience. Baby Debbie, though, fit right in with the others her age.

"Where are we staying?" Mom asked after a time.

"Sandani's house, which now belongs to Daniel and Alda. But we spend most of the time at the temple. Come see." I told Capac where I was going, then walked them the fifty yards to the cave. "We mainly use it for when I teach them, but the caverns inside aren't used often." When we arrived inside, I gestured to one room. "That's Capac's, um. . .office?" The word barely translated. "He prays and meets with people for disputes there."

"Like a judge in the OT," Dad noted. "Like Deborah."

"Deborah sat under a tree, and no, the irony of that is not lost on me. But that's what a king does here. We're doing all we can to teach the people the Bible so that they can better rule themselves with the help of the Holy Spirit." We arrived at the other chambers. "These rooms. . ." I hesitated. "Used to be for pagan rituals. Capac originally considered closing up this whole temple but wanted to make sure we always had a reminder. You can easily repeat what you don't remember."

"Is this where he—" Dad started.

I cleared my throat. "Yes. I considered having you sleep here, but then I remembered Sandani's place was unoccupied."

"Oh good. We get to stay were our brother lived with his child bride." Lydia rolled her eyes.

"First of all, he and Alda are not considered children here. Second, I sleep in the room where most kings are born. Not Capac. But his father. And his father. And so on. Don't complain."

"Born and made, right?" Lydia teased.

"That's the custom. Capac's a bit of a rebel, though. I've yet to give birth at our house."

"Oh." Dad feigned dramatic relief, "Thank you for that information."

"You're welcome, Dad." I giggled. "So, do you need to rest before dinner or would you like me to show you around some more?"

Mom and Dad expressed a desire to continue the tour at the same moment Lydia and Jeremiah requested a rest.

I called to Capac, who conducted the tour while I took Lydia and all their things to Sandani's house. We passed by Nur's just as she was emerging. They greeted one another.

"Oh! A boy!" Nur then said.

"Really?" Lydia was ecstatic.

Nur nodded fervently, then departed, allowing me to take the young family for a rest. When I got them settled, Lydia remembered something.

"Oh, Mom has something for Nur. A letter or something."

I caught up with my parents, husband, and children as Capac was sampling some of the fruit for the evening meal. A king, grazing in the kitchen without consequence.

I scolded him as the fruit cutters laughed. Then I took Esther from him and addressed my mom.

"Lydia said you have a letter or something for Nur?"

"Yes! I kept it close." Mom reached into her jean pocket and handed me a bundle of folded up notebook paper. "It's from Genny. She had been asking when the lady by the time-out hut would be back. Sweet of her, right?"

"Did you read it?"

"No."

"But, did you tell her, though?"

"Tell who what?"

"Tell Genny. Who Nur is."

"Yeah, I told her she is your sister-in-law and that she lives here with you. She was there to try to help—" The still-grieving grandmother couldn't complete that sentence, and I was grateful.

"All that is true, but—"

"Debbie. What is the benefit of them knowing?" Capac warned.

"Because Nur knows. And Genesis is a smart girl, and she's barely a girl at all anymore." I shrugged.

"I'm confused, Debs," Dad said.

"Well, Nur is Genny's mother. I already knew that because Nur's baby was the first Capac brought to us. Nur figured it out when she was there."

"Did Nur say anything to her?" Mom asked after a gasp.

"No, she saw that Genny is really important at the mission and didn't want to shake things up for her."

Mom looked to Dad. "Could Genny know, do you think?"

Dad shrugged. "Can Nur read?"

I laughed. "No. I'm teaching everyone to read, but Nur is refusing to learn. She's stuck in her ways. I'll read it to her and translate it for her. And if she gives permission, I'll let you know what's in it."

Other than the few tears when she watched Genesis walking the girls to the bathhouse, I'd never seen Nur cry. But the letter, which I had to read and translate at the same time, had her in buckets of sobs.

"Miss Nur,

Hello. I hope you are doing well. I never got a chance to tell you this story, so I am sending this letter.

When I was little, I was very sad because my mother abandoned me and we didn't know why. A mean doctor lady told me that I wasn't supposed to be sad. So when I was sad, she would put me in the time-out hut in chains. Miss Marla, who is the closest thing I have to a mom, let me be sad, and she taught me to be thankful. And Jesus helps me be thankful, so now I am not so sad. But since then, I have hated to even look at the time-out hut. It makes me remember being sad and being punished for being sad. I have to pass it a few times a day when I take the girls to the bathhouse and I hate it.

When you came to stay with us at the mission, you made me stop hating the time-out hut. Every time I walked by, you were there smiling at me. So now I see the hut and I don't remember the bad times. I only remember you. I miss you Nur. I hope someday you can come see me again. I am thankful for you.

With love,
Genesis Davies"

"Did you tell her?" Nur blubbered.

"No. But I think her heart knows."

Christmas signaled a modest gift exchange in the morning, and the same daily routine as always. It was a full moon, so my family witnessed a wedding after the evening meal. I translated for my family as Hanan performed the ceremony.

"He is the river. She is the fire. Together, they are all the strength of water, and God is their peace."

The young man braided a cord into the young woman's hair, and we cheered. Hanan handed them a sheet and they retreated to the area of the houses.

"That was a wedding?" Lydia seemed disappointed.

"I thought it was beautiful." Mom was sincere. "I love that about the river and the fire. You've told us that, but I didn't know it was part of the wedding tradition."

Capac caught my eye, then ran his fingers down my corded braid in my hair, which earned us a few smiles.

Lydia continued to express disappointment. "So, Christmas isn't much of a thing. You do this same community meal every night. And weddings are the same, and you do them every month. And birthdays aren't a thing. And anniversaries?"

I shrugged. Capac still wooing me with only his eyes.

"So do you celebrate *anything*?"

I broke the gaze with my husband to address my sister. "What do you mean?"

"There's no break in the days. No holidays or festivals or celebrations."

"We have the Cleansing." Capac shrugged. "Now we celebrate that we are clean and holy in Christ."

"And that's beautiful, but—"

"Lydia, most of these people die of the same mysterious illness that killed Roy and Sandani and both of Capac's parents and Great-Grandma and Grandpa too. It is the only thing I've seen take anyone, besides justice, but it comes on suddenly."

"So?" Lydia demanded.

"So no, we don't wait and celebrate periodically. We celebrate *everything*. We feast together daily, and we remember the joy of our own marriages when another occurs. We celebrate the lives of all our children when a baby is born. We are constantly celebrating."

Dad's brow scrunched in confusion.

"What's wrong, Dad?"

"Well, your wedding was different. It was forced. You said joy."

"Our wedding was not our choice," Capac supplied, and I translated for him. "Joy is our choice."

Dad nodded. "Of course, but—"

"Do you not see joy in my wife and children? Do you not see my love for them?" Capac asked, more for understanding than anything.

"Capac, I do. You know that," Dad clarified. "But it was different here then, wasn't it?"

"Very much is different," Capac said in our language, apparently not in an English mood as he smoothed my braid again. "You do not have to tell them that. But you have made me a happy man, my queen."

"God made you a happy man."

"And you chose to obey Him."

"My joy is full, my king. Thank you for choosing me."

"What are you saying?" Lydia asked desperately of the romance in our eyes.

Dad, who understood enough, smiled. "I think that's how they celebrate anniversaries here."

Jeremiah rolled his eyes and mumbled, "We just ignore *other* calendars and go camping together and end up with another kid."

Lydia punched him, and I looked to see she was blushing.

"Where did you go camping?" I asked.

She shrugged. "Close to the river."

"Make sure you give birth there?" I suggested.

"Not happening." My stubborn sister rolled her eyes.

"Then you will have a difficult labor," I promised, then remembered. "So are Daniel and Alda coming back in a few months for the baby?"

"Yes! Alda is very adamant about that." Mom nodded. "Dad and I are planning to bring them when she gets close. So, plan for us to come in about five or six months."

THIRTY-FOUR

Four months later, I wasn't surprised when Daniel stumbled out of the jungle and grabbed me in haste like I hadn't been away from him for the better part of a year.

"The baby is coming soon. She can't walk anymore," he said, out of breath.

"How far away?"

"Not far. The grove right over here."

I knew I didn't have time to summon Nur, and merely signaled Capac, running off into the jungle with my own predicament at my abdomen. It was only about a hundred yards in that I found my mother comforting a distraught Alda who was screaming for Daniel.

When he arrived, he had to calm himself. A then sixteen-year-old boy, about to become a father. It was breathtaking, the beauty of it.

"It's okay. I'm here. I have Debbie. She'll know what to do."

"What's the matter?" I asked my mother, kneeling at Alda's side.

"Hi, sweetheart," she greeted, wanting to inquire about the bump on my belly, but forced to wait. "Alda can't move any more. We didn't expect the labor to come on so quickly. She's still about a month out. I'll be happy to have your hands."

"Do you have any cloth or towels or anything?" I sighed, realizing that wasn't in English, then repeated it as such.

"In the bag that we left back with Dad aways. We had to carry her this far."

I smiled, and carefully removed my royal outer garment, which became the bedding on which Daniel's daughter was born. I thought he'd be a tad squeamish for it to be onto his knees, but he kept to tradition. I smiled at the joyful new mother, then called out for attention then let out one loud whoop, to which the villagers responded with joy.

Daniel looked up at me once Alda was nursing.

"Debbie, she was in serious trouble. The labor was awful until we got close. She wouldn't progress at all. But. . ."

"Then when we were in sight of the village, she just dilated the rest of the way and baby was engaged and ready to go," Mom finished. "There might be something to this custom of yours. I like this one where I meet two grandchildren in one day." She nodded to my belly.

"Christmas present." I touched my belly with a smile. "Due after winter. Nur says boy."

"How wonderful! I bet your other two are getting big."

"They are. Esther is taking a few steps at a time, and Josiah is talking up a storm." I nodded, and tried not to think about what *Roy* would or should be doing.

Then I looked to Daniel with, "What's her name?"

"Ruth," he responded.

Alda looked at him with weeping joy, as was the usual response when a husband announced his child's name. Daniel explained by quoting Scripture, " 'Your people shall be my people, And your God, my God.' When I asked to put a braid in Alda's hair, that's how she responded."

Dad came along eventually, looking like a pack mule. By that time, Capac had come from the village and took his burden. Dad gladly carried Alda to her royal house where she could rest. She was too weary to carry the baby, so Daniel's hands were occupied. Ruth had his whole heart from her first moment.

Once we got them settled, my parents looked to Capac and me the way a criminal does before a confession.

"Is something wrong?" he asked in English.

Dad replied, "Yeah, we have a bit of a problem. We waited to come speak with you until Alda was ready to come have the baby. But it would be best if we talked soon."

I worried, seeing that family members hadn't made the journey. "Is everyone okay? Where is Lydia?"

"Everyone is fine, Debbie," Mom encouraged as we headed to Capac's office. "Lydia has had a difficult recovery. We had to perform a cesarean with no spinal block. The baby is a healthy little boy they named David. They just weren't up for the trip this time."

We all sat on cushions in his office and Capac nodded at Dad. "What is this problem, John?"

"With Daniel not being able to run anymore, he and Alda weren't spending time counting miles and getting to know one another. So Alda decided to serve with the children. She would gather them up in their rooms at night and tell them stories in your language, and it really added something we didn't have before."

"So what's the problem?" I wondered.

"None of us adults that work with the children speak your language. Alda and Daniel converse in English. Not even he knew what she was saying. We had no idea she was telling them the oral history of your people, which wasn't a bad thing. But what shook things up—irreparably—was when she told them where they came from. She told them that most of their parents were still alive and missing them today."

"That is the truth," Capac responded.

Dad confirmed, "Yes. A truth that has caused a complete breakdown of our entire mission. The children who barely spoke Capacsi are suddenly learning it perfectly. Alda encouraged it. She taught them. She started telling Genesis that she is a princess."

"Nur has no other children and no husband," I explained. "Genny is royalty here."

"No children." Mom couldn't fathom it, or the pain of losing a child that was once hers. I'd known that pain. I knew the pain of my people.

"We were broken. Many women did not marry after losing a child to either the Closing ritual or to your mission. They were *broken*, Marla," Capac emoted.

It occurred to me. "Many of those children are Alda's family. Aunts and uncles, I guess it would be. What a wonderful opportunity to—"

"To destroy everything we've worked for?" Dad mumbled.

"To *fulfill* everything we've worked for," I corrected. "Dad, what if Alda's actions aren't a problem? What if she's the solution?"

"What fulfillment is there to missions, Debbie?" Dad was devastated and distraught.

"To make disciples of all the nations." I smiled. "To reach the unreached for Christ until the day of His return."

"That's what we do here," he pleaded.

"No, Dad. That's what we *did* here. This people group is *reached*. Rune and a few others have already started planning to travel to other villages within a two-hundred-mile radius. Our commission as disciples is to make other disciples and send them out to continue to do the work."

"But what about the children and their education and understanding of what is proper and—" Mom argued.

"That wasn't the calling, Mom. The calling is for them to know Christ, not change their culture unless it goes against Him. And not create a closed system that only feeds itself. By doing what we've done the past twenty years and what Great-Grandma and Grandpa did for forty years, we've helped to heal this people group. I'm here to stay. My husband and family are here. But Mom and Dad, you have a gift. Go heal *another* people group."

"And the children? We can't exactly just abandon four dozen children."

"Bring them back," their king decreed. "I entrusted them to you, and can never in this life be thankful enough. But it is now safe for them to return to their land. Reborn onto the knees of their people."

"Capac, we can't just bring them back." Dad chuckled. "How will we know whose children they are? What if some don't have parents anymore?"

"We all take care of one another here," I reminded my father. "Also, Jane and I saved their blankets they came in with the date they came. The women here make those blankets with specific family patterns and they would recognize them. It's like a signature. A woman is not going to forget the blanket she wrapped her baby in before she was forced to give them up. I remember everything about everything surrounding the time God took Roy. They'll know the blankets. And they'll know their own children. You would do us so much good if we had the children back."

"My Deborah, the queen judge," Capac endeared. He thought a moment. Ready to make a thorough decision. My mom started to speak, but I shushed her.

"He's thinking," I murmured my defense.

"Daniel?" Capac asked. "Will he be Capacsi?"

"I suppose they'll have to decide that," Mom allowed.

Capac nodded, making his decree. "Debbie, we will travel to the mission and retrieve the blankets and bring them back for our people to identify and prepare the village for the children. John and Marla, you will prepare the children of my people to be returned home. We will come again to retrieve them when my new son is old enough to travel. Daniel is welcome to stay or Alda is free to leave. They may make the choice by winter."

"Am I free to negotiate?" Dad laughed.

"Dad, they're his people."

"I know. But Capac, we *love* these children." My father finally said the thing that resonated with my Capac.

"Genny," Mom whimpered. Missing her child already.

"Genesis will do what you've always taught her to, Mom. She'll bring joy where it is needed. And she'll no longer be an abandoned child, but a rescued one."

Thirty-Five

The mission would become a staging area for missionaries from our village to reach other villages in the area. Some of them were violent and our missionaries never returned. Much dust was wiped off feet as they were thrown out of others. It was worth it, though, for the ones who listened.

With each village reached, we had a sense that we were running out of time. Still, the women who had "lost" their children to our mission had time to spend with them in the end. The joy upon their return was unrivaled by any yelp of childbirth before it or moonlit wedding after. They were home. We commemorated the day for the remaining years, and my parents always tried to return for it.

We were running out of time, but my parents moved across the world and reached others, taking five unclaimed children with them and returning for the Return each spring. Jane, Jackson, Lydia, Jeremiah and their children moved to an inner city in the States, reaching youth for Christ. Jackson married a young woman and a new family was starting. We were running out of time, but new life was ever welcome.

Daniel stayed, returning with the children and learning our ways, our language, from his young wife. His babies ran around naked with the others. Daniel and Alda freed one another. Alda worried each time Daniel went out to reach the surrounding villages. He returned each time, mourning those who didn't. But still he went out. We were running out of time.

After the Return, Nur and Genny spent a solid season just chatting about Jesus and books and butterflies. In the coming seasons, Nur watched a loving, godly man deliver her grandchildren onto his knees and she dwelled with them all and helped them grow.

As for me and my Capac? He is brown and I am not. He is the river. I am the fire. Together, we are all the strength of water, and God alone is our peace. Our children grew. Josiah fell in love with Dera and Ilian's little Grace, and their full moon came. Our heir produced one of his own. He would have been a good king, and she a gracious queen.

Instead of that loss of my heartholder and the coronation of our son, we ran out of time. The day it happened Capac emerged from our house and laughed when he landed outdoors.

"What is this in the air?"

It was winter—a cold one. Yet when I emerged to assist in his questioning, I barely recognized the phenomenon with my wrinkled eyes and jungle-weathered skin. My tongue barely remembered the word, which had to be in English.

"Snow."

"A frozen, feathery rain." He repeated my description from all the years.

Our seven children ran around catching the wet flakes on their noses and tongues, despite their age. Our grandson blinked at flakes on his eyelashes and nose and his mother giggled dotingly.

It was snowing in the jungle. I had always wanted my people to see the snow, and we were running out of time. It snowed. And time ran out.

It was snowing and then we were feasting at a great wedding moon with Christ. We feasted with my parents, my brothers, their wives, and everyone else lost to distance and death. We have always been feasting. He was coming. He came for us. Now there is no hourglass to empty. There is no urgency. There is nothing but this.

He is the River. He is the Light. He is our peace. And our sickness has gone.

ACKNOWLEDGMENTS

In previous works, it has been an honor to write about all the great people in my life who directly or indirectly brought that work into being.

Now? Well. The circle is quite small. The difference is so stark that there is now a disclaimer in all of my previous books.

I would like to formally recognize:

My Deliverer. In reality, LORD, this one is completely Yours. They all are, of course, but this one is special. I'm in awe that You saw fit to give me this years before I needed it. You guided me through this work, teaching me so much along the way. You have already used this book for Your glory, and I pray it reaches many more. But come quickly? This place hurts.

RJ. My heartholder, brainstorm partner, proofreader, business partner, and greatest support in all things all the time. The guy who chose me when it cost him everything and everyone. There are no words, Berdind, for how deeply I owe this work to you.

Caleb, Levi, and Chloe. Previously, you have helped me by being a joyful "distraction" and reminding me what is important. This time, my babies, you gave me that and so much more. Chloe, your talent; Levi, your wit; and Caleb, your writing camaraderie. All of you helped keep our home functioning when your parents were barely making it. I so appreciate you. I'm in awe at who God grew you to be despite many trials.

To the people God sent. Most notably: Daddy, Momma, Meghan, and Jessie. We are all in different places, we don't always agree, and each of you contributed differently. But only the living write books, and I'm alive because you chased me all the way into my darkness and dragged me all the way back home. Those first seasons of grief, change, and deliverance were hard for all of us. Even still, you continued to show up for me when I couldn't even breathe. I am forever grateful and forever in your debt.

Missionaries. All of you. Past, present, and future. Near and far. Some of you I know. Others, I can't wait to meet at that feast. This book was initially inspired by the diary and faith journey of a missionary as she put her life in danger repeatedly, so I couldn't finish this book without giving you a nod.

Dan Hooker and Robert Beech of Rocky Mountain Calvary Chapel, Inc. in Colorado Springs. I started writing this story years ago, but it was way too dark for me then, so I set it aside several times. Your words and actions in Fall 2024 generously provided the trauma that allowed me and this story to finally understand one another. So, I am recognizing you here by name to finally obey a command as one of many witnesses (1 Timothy 5:20). God is faithful. He meant it for good, and I forgive you.

About the Author

Rebekah Tyne McKamie *is a Christian author and book editor with multiple published works. She holds a Master of Arts in Composition (& Rhetoric) and a Master of Arts in Professional Writing. Mrs. McKamie is a wife of many winters and is currently concluding her journey of homeschooling her three children through graduation. She relocated to the beautiful Pacific Northwest to heal near many waters.*

Instagram: @rebekahspelledlikethebible

TikTok: @rebekahtyneauthor

Facebook: facebook.com/rebekahtyne

Website: rebekahtynemckamie.com

Book Editing Services: repriseeditorial.com